Intuition

THE PREMONITION SERIES
VOLUME 2

AMY A. BARTOL

Also By Amy A. Bartol
Inescapable: The Premonition Series Volume 1

ISBN: 1466266732
ISBN-13: 9781466266735
LCCN: 2011917393
CreateSpace, North Charleston, SC

For Aprille, my sister, and her anxiety over running out of pages to read before I could write more

And to Buns, Brownie, and Weitz, who I love like true sisters

Contents

Evie

CHAPTER 1

New Year's Eve

"Okay, sweetie, it's time to get up now," Buns says in a brisk manner, as she breezes into my room at noon. She heads immediately to the windows to open the curtains and thereby dispels the cave-like atmosphere. Light bursts into the room, causing me to squint at her and cover my eyes against the glare.

"Buns, what are you doing here?" I ask her groggily, shielding my eyes with my arm. I love my room in Reed's Crestwood house, but the windows let in a lot of light. "Aren't you supposed to be at Russell's house until next week?" I ask in confusion as I grip my pillow and pull myself up to a sitting position.

"Aren't you amped to see me, Evie?" Buns counters with her hands on her hips as she assesses me. I'm sure I look really bad because I haven't brushed my hair today so I probably have major bedhead.

"Of course I'm glad to see you, I missed you. How was your holiday down south?" I ask, thinking about how warm and beautiful Buns had described Russell's family to me on the phone. She and Brownie had gone to Russell's house in North Carolina for the winter break, as protection, so that he could see his family. Brownie had posed as Russell's girlfriend, while Buns masqueraded as Brownie's sister. They had no trouble pulling it off either because they both have an elfin, tree nymph look about them that seems familial. That, coupled with the fact that they both have fair hair and blue eyes, lends credence to their charade. At any rate, I'm sure that Russell's family hasn't suspected that they're really angels, since I didn't even know that until I saw their butterfly wings.

"It was a lot of fun, very endearing–I was having an amazing time. Scarlett, Russell's sister, is just like us. She's ready to stir up some trouble at a moments notice," Buns says, eyeing me shrewdly.

"Is Russell back, too?" I ask her, sitting up straighter in bed and rubbing my eyes.

"Russell is still at home with his family. Brownie stayed with him. They're fine. They'll be back in a few days, just before classes start. I came back early because Reed called me," she says with a disapproving look.

"He did? Well, you should've stayed with Russell. He needs you. What if something happens?" I ask, feeling uncomfortable with the fact that Russell is still several states away with only Brownie for protection; even though Brownie is strong and vicious in a fight, it still worries me because fallen angels are even more vicious.

"Nothing will happen. They're fine. You, on the other hand, are not. Reed said you aren't getting out of bed. He's worried," her reply is stern as she looks at me like I let her down.

"I get out of bed." I say with a frown, trying to remember when I was last up. It was yesterday I think...or maybe not. "I'm just tired," I finish defensively.

"No, you're doing that self-helpless thing again like you did before when Reed wouldn't talk to you. I don't think I can live through another one, so you're getting up now," Buns says, pulling me out of bed without effort because she is really freaking strong. "I don't want to hear another word about this until you've showered and gotten dressed. The clock is ticking, let's go," she says in a militant way.

"FINE!" I retort, and storm toward the bathroom feeling harassed. After I take a shower and get dressed, I rejoin Buns. She is sitting on my bed waiting for me.

"We're getting you out of the house today. What do you want to do?" Buns asks as she gets off the bed and moves towards where I stand by my closet door.

"We're allowed to leave the house?" I ask her in shock because I haven't been out for most of winter break.

Buns frowns, "You are now and I'm gonna lose it if they have a problem with it. No wonder you're so depressed, sitting here with nothing to do but dwell on everything that has happened. Those Power angels can't figure that out?" she asks rhetorically. "They're going to have to compromise their need to have every angle covered, and keep in mind that you're part human, too. You need to be out doing stuff. You're a teenager!" she says, as if that would explain everything.

I've been on virtual house arrest since waking up from my injuries a few weeks ago. Just thinking of what happened then sends shivers down my spine and I have to lean up against the wall by my closet door. I can hardly think about the massacre at the 7-Eleven without feeling a wave of panic hit me. Being FUBARed by my ex-friend, Alfred, has taken a serious toll on me.

"What are we going to do?" I ask her, feeling like I can crawl into bed and go back to sleep.

"Let's start out with a run, and then we'll plan what we're gonna do tomorrow night." Buns says with girlish excitement.

"What's tomorrow night?" I ask her in confusion because I don't even know what day it is.

"Evie, tomorrow's New Year's Eve. You didn't know that?" she asks me with a worried look.

I shake my head. "Things have been a little out of focus for me since you left—kind of abstract. Reed and Zee have been great. I feel really bad that I let them down," I reply.

"You didn't let them down. They just don't know what you need. It's just like when you didn't know you were an angel. You had Reed menacing you and you were evolving abilities you couldn't possibly comprehend—you needed a distraction, so Brownie and I tried to provide that whenever we could, so you wouldn't dwell on it," she says, smiling at me.

"I'm still floored that you knew all along what was going on and I had no clue that you and Brownie were Reapers. You could've let me in on it," I say.

"Sweetie, we couldn't tell you, and since we are really good at fooling humans, you just never guessed," she says, shrugging. "I doubt you would've taken it well if we just announced to you that we were angels of death. That's kind of a dark freak flag to be flying as far as most humans are concerned. Even though we knew you're both human and angel, we kind of reasoned that you weren't really aware of that."

"Why did you decide to help me out?" I ask, since I don't understand just why they have been so good to me.

"Like we said before, Evie, you're a kindred spirit. You have a bit of a wild side in you, just like Brownie and me. Not all angels are like that, at least, the divine kind of angels," she says, handing me my running shoes from the closet. "And, we thought it was kind of lame that you had to go through your evolution into angel here on Earth with all of the dangers clawing at you, while every other angel we know of has gotten to evolve in Paradise, safely tucked away with no care or fear to mar the event."

"Oh, that sounds nice…I didn't know I was getting completely gypped," I reply with sarcasm, wondering what it would've been like to feel completely safe while all of this is happening.

"Evie, I hate to be the one to tell you this, but if you had been a Seraph in Heaven when you evolved, you would've been completely pampered," she says with a sheepish smile. "You would've been the darling of the Seraphim, I'm sure."

I give Buns a skeptical look. I doubt that any of them would ever think I'm darling because of the fact that I'm not full-blooded Seraphim angel, but a mixture of Seraphim and human. "Pampering is for wimps," I say, trying to make light of it all.

"Exactly!" Buns replies happily. "So, we'll just go tell the boys that we're going for a run, and then we'll plan New Year's. We'll probably have to stay somewhere around here because I doubt Reed will let us go to London or Paris for it. He'll probably have a problem with New York, too. Maybe I can convince him to let us go to Chicago. That would be epic," she says, beginning to get excited about getting out of Crestwood.

"Good luck with that. I couldn't convince him to let me out past the courtyard," I reply, giving her a pessimistic smile. Reed has been extremely sweet, but unbending when it comes to what he considers dangerous and risky.

"Well, this conversation will have 'awkward' written all over it then, because I plan on getting my way," she says with heat in her voice.

But as it turns out, Reed is very accommodating when it comes to Buns's requests. He just retrieves his shoes and coat when he hears we plan to go running and follows us out of the house without a word. I am surprised until I realize that he must really be worried about me.

Running out to Lake Arden, I feel like I can breathe for the first time in days. It's cold because it's the beginning of winter but that doesn't bother me like it would've before I started evolving. I am starting to acquire the armor-like angel skin that protects me from things like cold and extreme heat. The transformation has been seamless, happening a little bit each day. Reed said it would take several more months to complete the transformation.

It's strange, this new skin; it is smoother than human skin and lacks normal imperfections. It is also a shade paler than my human skin was, but it has a luminosity to it that is very hard to discern, even with highly sensitive eyesight like mine. I marvel at it, because it's tougher, more resilient, than the skin I had before.

After we run around the lake, Buns pauses on the trail that leads back to Reed's house. "Sweetie, I'm going to head back and see Zee. I've missed him," she says, smiling, as she looks from me to Reed. "I want to start planning for New Year's, too. You should stay…get some more exercise."

"Okay," I reply, watching Reed. She nods her head, and then she is gone in a fraction of a second, leaving behind only her light footprints in the snow.

"Do you want to walk this time?" Reed asks, falling in step beside me on the path.

"Sure," I reply, trying to concentrate on the scenery around me, so that I won't stare at his profile. The beautiful angles of his face make me want to reach my hand out and touch him.

Reed puts his gloved hand in mine, tucking my arm securely in his. We walk for a while, not talking. The butterflies that pull me toward him are ever-present, but it's more reassuring than sensual at the moment. I turn my face toward the lake, feeling the breeze coming off of it. Smoky breath rises from us, mixing together above our heads like lovers entwined.

Finally, I break the silence. "I'm sorry, Reed," I say in a strained tone that disturbs the quiet hush of the snow-blanketed trees.

Reed looks surprised when he turns toward me, his green eyes searching my face. "For what?" he asks.

"For not being able to deal with this better," I say with regret. He squeezes my arm tighter as we walk closer together.

"Evie, you have nothing to be sorry for," he says quietly. "I'm the one who should apologize. I've caged you up to protect you, only to discover it's killing you," he says, sounding contrite.

"No, it's not that really…it is just that there is not a lot to do but sit and think about Alfred…or my uncle." I say in a hush voice, thinking of my Uncle Jim and the fact that I will never see him again. Alfred had made sure of that. He had made sure that my uncle suffered before he died.

We walk a few steps more before I can say, "It just seemed easier to sleep and not think about anything." I pretend as if the nightmares that haunt my sleep don't exist. "You must've been worried to call Buns."

Reed frowns. "I don't have very much experience with human emotions. This is all new to me. I'm trying to understand your emotions and mine, too. I've felt a different range of emotions since meeting you," he smiles down at me as we continue walking arm-in-arm.

"A different range?" I ask, raising my eyebrow.

Reed studies our clasped hands. "Let me think…" he sighs. "Well, elation is an emotion that I have not experienced for sometime…not since I've been here and I don't remember it being so—intense," he says, smiling and shaking his head.

"What made you elated?" I ask him, breathless as his beautiful smile melts my heart.

"When you told me that you would never love anything more than you love me," he says in a soft tone. A blush of happiness warms my cheeks and I listen intently as he continues. "Desire is also stronger, more—potent."

I nod knowingly, because I share the same unquenchable desire for him.

Reed's eyes darken as he continues, "Well, Power angels are often jealous…but I have never felt that emotion as strongly as when I had to watch you with Russell—thinking that I would have to wait for the next eighty years, until he dies, to call you mine," he says as his jaw clenches. "That was more than jealousy…that was sorrow."

It is my turn to squeeze his arm as we round the far side of the lake. "And then, there is an emotion that I don't ever want to experience again. That one is called agony," he says, scowling a little when he names it. "That's what I felt when I thought you were dying."

I find it hard to breathe all of a sudden and have to take several deep breaths to try to slow down the beating of my heart. I had hurt him deeply when I had tried to give up my soul to save Russell. It has left a mark on him that hasn't quite healed yet. I believe he understands why I did it, that I couldn't just allow my soul mate to be torn apart by fallen angels, but I also know just how separate the head and the heart can be. He notices and stops to sweep me up in a hug that lifts me off my feet.

"And then, there is love," he says in a voice soft with affection, "an emotion I have never really believed existed. But it does exist and it has a name…and her name is Evie." He hugs me tighter. "And I can't live without her, now that I have found her. So tell me what to do to make you come back to me and I will do it."

I wrap my arms securely around Reed's neck, snuggling into him, as I try to formulate the words that I need to say so he will know what he means to me. "I have thought a lot about you and the way that you can hear my heart. You said it sings to you, like the call of the Sirens to a sailor at sea. I think it sings to you because you were listening with your lonely heart and it calls to you because it is meant for you. I'm still here…I would've given up without you. You're why I survived. I just miss my uncle," I say, swallowing hard to get past the lump in my throat.

"I will help and Buns is back, too. She will know what to do. I was so wrong about the Reapers, Buns and Brownie. They've been the best for you," he says, placing me back on the ground.

"No, you're the best for me," I say, taking his hand and walking back toward his house. And I'm going to try to be the best for you, from now on, I promise myself, realizing the pain he has been going through by watching me in my sorrow.

When we arrive back at Reed's house, Buns is already in the game room researching sites on the Internet. "Oh, sweetie! There are several parties going on in Chicago tomorrow! There is one at Navy Pier! They're having 9 different DJ's and a fireworks display at midnight. Evie, did I ever tell you about the fireworks the Song Dynasty set off in the 9th century? I was really young then and I was just beginning to understand why I wasn't blending in very well." She smiles at me and I can't tell if she's teasing, or if she is serious.

I look over at Reed and see him frowning. "Buns, can you find something else…something a little more feasible…tactically?" he asks.

When Buns turns to look at Reed skeptically, Zephyr, who has been sitting close to her, decides to contribute to the discussion. "Buns, honey, that is a bad call. Do you realize how many Fallen will be at an event like that? And Reed is right; it is entrapping terrain, which appeals to me if we did not have Evie. Maybe you and I can go next year and see how many Fallen we can end before the ball drops," he says with a smug smile that has Buns smiling at him.

"We're getting out of Crestwood, that's nonnegotiable," Buns states flatly.

"Okay, but maybe we could avoid huge parties—something with less of a crowd?" Zephyr offers and I catch Reed smiling a little as he watches Zephyr work on Buns and her sense of celebration. "You know, for Evie's sake, not because you are not the best event planner we know." He is really good at strategy. I will have to listen more intently to his dissertations on the matter.

"For Evie's sake," she agrees stiffly, turning back to the computer screen. She pulls up website after website in rapid-fire succession. "Okay, how about something a little more recreational?" she offers, and I see Zephyr's and Reed's faces light up with interest.

"Recreational?" Zephyr asks, squeezing closer to Buns to peer at the screen. Reed drops his hand casually on my shoulder, caressing it.

"Snowboarding?" she says, flashing us an impish grin. "There are a bunch of small hills with ski lifts in this general area that do midnight runs on New Year's Eve. I'm sure there is something going on at one of them where we could either ski or board until sometime around midnight, and then head in to the chalet for a midnight toast," she says, smiling as she watches Zephyr's face light up.

"That is my girl!" Zephyr says possessively, scooping Buns up off of her seat and twirling her around so fast they become just an impression for a moment until he sets her back on her feet.

"It's off the chain, right, sweetie?" Buns asks, turning to me, "What do you think?"

"Sounds amazing," I reply.

"You are truly a force of nature, Buns." Reed agrees, leaning forward and kissing Buns on the forehead, which makes her smile deepen. "Let's decide on the resort we are going to go to so that Zephyr and I can get some satellite shots of it, for strategy. Then, we will plan our assault on the slopes."

I try to keep my face as neutral as possible and not let them see that there is a war going on inside of me. One side is rejoicing at the prospect of getting out of the house and living again; the other side of me is scared to death of what might happen once I leave the house. My heart must have given me away because Reed pulls me into his arms. Hugging me, he says, "It will be okay. Nothing will touch you." He presses his cheek to mine and the heat we generate is intoxicating.

"I'm looking forward to boarding. I can't wait to see how angels can slay a mountain," I whisper in his ear, letting my cheek brush over his in a caress.

"I was created to slay," Reed replies with a smile that almost stops my heart.

"I found it!" Buns's tone is smug as she swivels in her chair to face us. "It's a five star resort a few hours north of here. It says they're booked for the holiday, but we know what that means," Buns laughs, swiveling back.

I glance at Reed's face, then Zephyr's; they both do seem to know what she means by that. "I'm sorry, Buns, does that mean we can't go?" I ask in confusion.

"No, sweetie, of course not. That just means they only have the really killa suites left for the VIPs."

"Oh—are we VIPs?" I ask, trying not to sound ignorant. This makes Zephyr laugh like I have made a joke. His eyes sparkle at me like he is waiting for me to say something else amusing.

Buns smirks, too, and replies, "You know it. Reed, get her a black card."

"Already done. She just hasn't been anywhere to use it," Reed replies.

"What are you talking about?" I ask in suspicion. I think I might know what it is they are saying, because I've seen the black credit card Buns uses to burn through cash like she prints it herself.

"I have a card for you. I don't plan on us separating anytime soon, but you can carry it and use it however you would like," Reed says, and frowns as he watches my mouth drop open. "What did I say?"

"I can't take your money," I reply, watching his face get darker.

"Why not?" Reed asks in confusion.

"Because it's not right," I reply.

"Why is it wrong?" he asks.

"Because it's yours," I reply evasively. Does he really not get that taking his money is completely grody?

"But, when I give it to you, then it is yours," he says, smiling at me because he thinks what he is saying is logical.

"Buns, you get why I can't take his money, right?" I ask, looking for help.

"No…it's just money," she shrugs, and I'm beginning to believe they are printing it somewhere.

"I have my own money, Reed, but thanks," I say in embarrassment.

"Evie, you have a few thousand dollars—that is not money, that is…" he trails off when he sees me duck my head to hide my deepening blush of mortification. My house is for sale, but no one seems interested in it, since the previous owner was viciously murdered in it. Most of our things have been removed and put into storage, for which I will need to reimburse Reed when the house is sold. Although, I don't think he's going to let me. The funeral arrangements for my uncle had probably cost a lot, too, but no one will tell me who paid for it, or how much it cost. "I'm sorry, did I say something wrong?" Reed asks, trying to make eye contact with me.

"No…I just have to start looking into Internet gambling and see if I can beat the odds," I reply, since there is not a lot I can do right now to earn money. Having a homicidal angel, like Alfred, bent on beating the soul out of me is seriously hurting my chances of getting and maintaining gainful employment.

"Evie, we can consider all of this a loan, if it makes you feel better, and you can pay me back later," he says, holding up my chin and looking into my eyes.

"When am I going to be able to pay you back, sugar daddy?" I ask him in a worried tone.

I watch the way his sensual lips curve cunningly as he tries not to smile. He notices I am not smiling, so he says, "Let me take care of you. It's all I want to do."

I sigh. "I've no choice right now but to rely on you for help, but I'm not taking the credit card," I say firmly.

"Evie," Reed's tone is cajoling.

"Reed," I say, as I dig in.

"What's a sugar daddy?" Reed asks me, and then laughs when he sees my blush deepen. "That bad, huh?" he asks.

"Yeah, that bad." I reply. "When are we leaving, Buns?" I ask to try to change the subject away from my waifish existence.

"I'm going to call them and make the arrangements. How long do you two need to plot and scheme?" Buns asks Zephyr and Reed.

"A couple of hours. We'll be ready by tonight." Zephyr replies and Reed nods.

"Yes! We can go tonight and be on the slopes after breakfast tomorrow," she says happily, and then she jets out of the room in an eighth of a second to get her phone and make the arrangements.

"I'll go pack." I say, feeling the mixture of excitement and dread again. I speed to my room in seconds so that they will all think I am just excited.

Alone in my room, I go to my closet to get my suitcase. As I pull it down from the top shelf, a box that had been partially hidden falls down with it. Kneeling on the ground to retrieve the box, I freeze. It is a wooden box with dragonflies encrusted on its lid. Someone must have gotten it from my dorm room when they had brought over my things. My hand shakes as I reach for it.

My touch is light as my fingertips brush over the wood, feeling the intricately carved images covering the surface. Freddie gave me this for my birthday, I think as I lift my fingertips from the box as if I have been scalded by it. He had been telling me what he is with his gift, only I hadn't realized it at the time. He is a fallen Reaper angel with iridescent wings that resemble a dragonfly, not unlike the ones depicted here. I shudder as I recall touching his paper-like wings that had buzzed and vibrated in agitation.

I'm so stupid. How could I have let this happen? Guilt and shame hit me. I open the lid to the box and see the small, silver makeup compact inside; on the lid is etched an ornate dragonfly with inlayed opals that comprise the torso of the dragonfly. The stones gleam evilly in the dim light of the closet.

I didn't see what he was, and as a result, many people had suffered and died including my uncle, I think as my hands curl into fists. This gift is a physical representation of my stupidity. It is a reminder that I have to look at things differently from now on. I can't afford to be stupid and naïve anymore or the ones I love will suffer for it. This is my bitter reality. I pick the compact up, hugging it to my body in despair. I can't fail again because the price is too high.

Feeling the small latch on the compact beneath my fingertips, I flip the compact back over and look at it. Depressing the button, it opens with a soft click, dispelling a small gasp of air that was trapped inside. I raise the lid, revealing the mirror. For an instant, all I can see are my eyes looking back at me. I look haunted: deadened by the thing I hold in my hand. But then a movement in the mirror distracts me from the image of myself. It startles me, so I look behind me to see what could possibly have moved. There is nothing there. I peer in the mirror once again, noticing that the image of me is murkier, less crisp.

Something moves in the mirror that is not a reflection; a truly distorted and shadowy shape shifts within the glass. The longer I watch it, the closer it seems to be coming and the more it takes on a definite form…as if a shadow is running toward me down a long corridor within the mirror that is in no way a reflection of any room I have seen in this house. But, it isn't just a shadow, it's a swarm of flies all working together to form the shape of a man.

Coming to my senses in the next instant, I try to snap the lid of the compact shut, but it is levered open and refuses to close. Tossing the compact away from me, it crashes to the floor. Hissing emits from the mirror, casting a stench in the air that I had prayed I would never smell again. Black clouds of flies come pouring out into the air, billowing from the mirror to sway and undulate grotesquely until their dark mass implodes into a single image of a man—a shadow man. He is like the one I had seen in Coldwater with Freddie. It only takes the shadow man a fraction of a second to grin at me evilly before he lunges forward to kill me.

CHAPTER 2

Road Trip

Only the blink of an eye exists to assess the danger of the shadow man. As he stands in front of me, his lurid form moves and shifts as the dark, disjointed spirit crests and swirls around him. The shadowy entity is almost like a lover embracing the demonic man. Feeling paralyzed by its presence, I fail to evade his attack. He catches me by my throat, picking me up off my feet. His steely grip probably would've crushed me just weeks ago, but I have evolved since then; I am harder to kill now. The demon realizes this; irritation flickers across his face as he brings his other hand up to apply more pressure. Black spots dance in my vision and my eyes dart around the room, looking for a means of gaining my release.

Buzzing registers in my consciousness, and at first I think it must be a result of having the life choked out of me. But as my eyes dart away from the evil grinning creature suffocating me, I see that my bedroom window is covered on the outside in dragonflies. The dragonflies form a dark silhouette of a man, which then morphs into an image I know quite well. It's Alfred and he is hovering just outside my room. His iridescent, bluish-green wings are beating rapidly to sustain his elevation. As he observes the scene inside my room, his mouth turns up with a grin of satisfaction.

My feet dance drunkenly beneath me while I bring my own hands to my throat. I tear at the shadow man's hands, trying to utter the name that I am screaming over and over in my mind. *Reed.* Panic makes my legs swing out further, trying to kick the monster in front of me. Baring his teeth in a feral growl, the shadow man cringes when I kick him as hard as I can. That is all it will take and I know it. The shadow man just sealed its fate with that one tiny sound.

In an instant my door crashes in, and before it has time to ricochet off the wall, I am released from the strangle hold that had me dangling in midair. Dropping to the ground, the body of the shadow man, along with his shadow is propelled backward away from me. I take the first gasping breath of air, feeling it burn a path to my lungs because the shadow man's putrid odor permeates the room. Reed's charcoal-colored wings spread wide as he hurls the demon out into the hallway, where Zephyr catches it. The grotesque popping and tearing sounds of the shadow man being torn to shreds by Zephyr become softer as it is carried further and further away from my door. In the next instant, Reed has me in his arms.

"Al-Fred," I wheeze, trying to tell him that Alfred is outside my window. I turn to look at it and point, but Alfred is no longer there at the window. The coward ran away again when he saw the Powers enter the room to save me.

"Evie, are you hurt?" Reed asks in an anxious tone while scanning me for possible injuries. I shake my head no, coughing as I try to inhale too much air and have it forced back out.

"No," I croak feebly as Reed holds my chin gently in his hand. Tipping it up, he assesses my neck, touching the bruises that I'm sure are going to be ugly for a couple of hours until I heal.

"I don't know how it got in, Evie. Zephyr and I didn't know it was here. It shouldn't have been able to get past us," Reed tries to explain to me through clenching teeth. He presses my face into his bare chest. I hear the powerful drumming of his heart as it pounds against his chest and his wings twitch in agitation.

"Alfred's here, too," I say with a raspy voice, pointing again to the window.

In seconds I am swept up and deposited in the adjoining bathroom with the door firmly closed to my room. Alone, I face the vanity mirror. The shadow man has, indeed, left his mark on me—big black inky bruises that aren't turning purple, yet. I walk to the mirror and am startled by my eyes. They are red with the blood of broken capillaries where they should be white. A monster from a horror flick looks less freakish than I do at the moment, especially since my crimson wings had sprung out of my back at some point during my struggle. They're hanging limply at my sides, protesting the abuse I had just sustained.

The bathroom door swings open and I jump in fear. Buns is at my side in seconds, hugging me to her. "Sweetie, what happened?" she asks. Pulling back from me, her eyes zero in on my neck. She bites her lip as her brows draw together in a scowl. "How?" she asks with menace.

"Shadow man tried to strangle me," I reply.

"What's a shadow man? I didn't hear it. I didn't see it. How did it get in?" she asks me in an angry tone as she gently pets my hair.

"Possessed soul, it came in through my compact," I reply, turning back toward the sink to fill the glass on the counter with water. I take a small sip of it, attempting to soothe my throat that now burns with a raw heat. "Where did Reed and Zee go?" I ask her sluggishly. I'm having a hard time orienting myself to the reality of the situation.

"They flew out the door a second ago like they're chasing the hounds of Sheol. Are they?" she asks me. She runs a washcloth under the faucet, and then presses it to my throat.

"Alfred…at the window. He was probably waiting for my soul to leave my body so that he could reap it," I explain with brevity, feeling the cool cloth ease the ache in my neck.

"Alfred!" Buns hisses while her golden butterfly wings fly out of her back to float effortlessly behind her. She looks like a fairy queen, pacing the bathroom in agitation. "Alfred wouldn't have let it kill you. He probably wanted it to mostly kill you, so that he could then convince you to give him your soul. I don't think he can take it without you giving him permission," she says. "I hope they crush him. He's *so* getting on my last nerve. You said the possessed one came in through your compact? What did you mean by that?"

"The compact, it's in my room. I dropped the mirror on the floor when I saw that thing running toward me in the glass. I couldn't get the lid shut again because it just wouldn't close," I say in exasperation. "And then, it was in my room and it grabbed me by the throat so I couldn't scream." The numbness of my shock is wearing off. My hands shake and I cross my arms in front of me to stop the trembling. Buns disappears for a second, leaving the bathroom door open, and then returns with the compact in her hand with the lid firmly shut.

"Oh, he's so done when I get my hands on him. I don't enjoy killing; Brownie and I consider it beneath us. I go out of my way to avoid it, but it'd be an honor to make him cease to be," she says as she resumes her pacing.

"I don't want you to do that. Just stay away from him. He's really twisted and evil. I don't want him getting his hands on you," I say, imagining Alfred tearing the golden wings off of Buns's back.

Buns rolls her eyes. "Please…Alfred," Buns scoffs at me. "Evie, he's a cretin. I can seriously kick his butt. That's why he keeps getting others to be the heavy, because he's weak and very lame," she finishes with the kind of confidence that makes me want to believe her, even as the memory of Alfred plunging his knife into Russell flashes in my mind and I shudder in revulsion.

"I don't know what I'd do if you were hurt, Buns," I say, feeling something twist inside me at the thought.

"Sweetie, Alfred can try if he wants, but that'd be opening a whole new level of pain for him," Buns replies with confidence. "Now, did Alfred give you anything else—like jewelry, perfume, or anything edible?" she asks.

I frown, thinking. "There is just the wooden box that the compact came in. It's in my closet," I say. She is gone again before I have time to blink. When she steps back into the bathroom, she has the box with her. "What is it?" I ask, because I know now what it's not—it is not a gift; it is a Trojan horse.

"It's a lot of things, but mainly it's a portal." I must look confused because she continues to explain, "It's like a doorway. When you opened the lid, it opened a conduit, like a tunnel, to whoever has the mate to this gateway. Alfred must've given the other compact to the possessed one who watched it, waiting for it to open. When it reached the threshold here, it popped out, and well, you were there for that part," she says, touching my neck. "Some demons use them for escaping Powers. They leave one open in a safe haven, and then carry the other around. If they come across danger, they pop in the channel and go to their safe place. When they get there, they destroy the portal before anything can follow them."

"How does someone enter a mirror, especially one this small?" I ask in confusion.

"Transfiguration," she replies casually.

"Uh huh," I say dully. "You shapeshift?" I ask for clarity.

"Yeah," she smiles at me.

"You can do that?" I accuse her, and watch her nod her head. "Show me," I demand, putting my hands on my hips because everyone is holding out on me.

She shrugs and says, "Okay."

She heads over to the counter and sets the compact and box on it. Turning back to me, she gives me a bright smile as her body begins to shimmer in the light. Within seconds, she explodes before my eyes into a swarm of beautiful golden butterflies, leaving her clothing in a pile on the floor where she had been standing. The butterflies circle and flutter around the bathroom, in no particular pattern, as butterflies will. Then, they all meet up again to form the silhouette that resembles my friend, and like an implosion, Buns is back in her normal form in front of me.

"Holy freaking…Buns!" I say to her in awe.

"Exactly!" she replies, getting dressed again, and all the while smiling at me.

"Will I?" I ask, unable to form the complete sentence.

"Yes," she replies. "At least I think so. I'm not positive because you're both angel and human, but since everything else is evolving like an angel, I can only assume that this will, too."

"Can you take any form you want?" I ask.

"No, that's about all I can do," she says in a casual air. "Brownie is the same. We never really honed the skill too hard because we rarely ever use it. It comes in handy when I want to evade humans and I have somehow gotten trapped, but mostly I can just outrun them or fly away."

I rub my forehead in annoyance. "Okay. I think it's time we started the Angel one-o-one class, so that I can be let in on all of these little pitfalls that I keep stumbling into," I say in exasperation, as I pace the room. "Because now, I have to worry if the chair in the next room is really a chair and not some evil angel waiting for me to sit down in it so it can kill me."

"Evie, we have to transform into something animate. Chairs are safe," she says, chuckling at me.

I put my hands on my hips and glare at her amused face. "Yeah, great, so you're saying every bug I see could be a threat though."

"Well, I wouldn't worry too much about bugs unless you see a horde of them. Then you can worry. If you noticed, I turned into a swarm of butterflies, not just one."

"So scale is important?" I ask.

"Yes," she replies. "And about the Angel one-o-one thing…" Buns says in a tentative voice.

"What about it?" I ask, my tone suspicious.

"Well, we all had a discussion about what to tell you and what not to tell you. Reed made a point and I think he's right that we can't just go blurting out all the secrets of Paradise and Sheol to you. There are laws which forbid us to reveal things to humans, and since you're part human and have a soul, we have to be careful," she says as she watches my face darken. "Don't get me wrong, once their side slips and reveals something, I'm all about explaining it to you. Here's the thing: if your soul does leave your body—I want to make sure it gets into Paradise because I can't bear the thought that I'll never see you again." Her voice has a catch in it when she says, "I'm not heading into the negotiations for your soul having tipped the scales in their favor because I revealed something to you that allows you not to act on faith."

"Buns, I have wings sticking out of my back, what more proof is there?" I ask her gravely.

She smiles at this and replies, "You could just be a freak and I could be lying to you about everything."

"Well, I know I'm a freak, but I'm pretty sure this is all real," I reply.

"Exactly. You're *pretty sure*...but you don't know. So you have *faith* that God exists and that I am a divine angel and that's the part we want to preserve," she says. "I'm not letting you suffer in Sheol because I said too much. But, I love it when Alfred messes up, then I can tell you so much more," she smiles conspiratorially.

"That's not fair, Buns," I say, not wanting to see her point.

"I know, just think how I feel. I have all these secrets I want to tell you but I can't. It's really hard," she replies with agitation over having to keep it all in.

I know I have to let her off the hook because I remember how it felt when I wasn't able to tell Russell what was going on just a month ago. Was it really only a month? It feels like years—like I was younger then and now I feel so much older—at times I feel ancient, like none of this is new to me.

"Do you think they'll get him?" I whisper, and I realize a part of me wants Alfred dead so badly that nothing short of his annihilation will suffice. I want his blood; I want to avenge my uncle. Then there is the other part of me that still can't reconcile the fact that, because of me, Reed is now at risk while he hunts for Alfred. Even though they all say that the risks are minimal, I still feel a nagging fear that something could happen to him and I will lose him forever.

Buns shrugs. "I don't know, sweetie."

"Do you think it's safe now? I want to pack so that we can leave if they get back tonight," I say, walking toward the bathroom door.

"Sweetie, do you think Reed is going to let you go now?" Buns asks, looking sheepish.

"We have to go, Buns! I have to get out of here," I say in desperation. "I can't sit in my room after what just happened staring at the walls and wondering when Alfred's going to finally get me," I add, turning the handle of the bathroom door. I step out of the bathroom right into the arms of Reed. He looks sad; his face is a mask of regret.

"He will never get you—please trust me that I will never allow him to get you," Reed says by my ear.

"Reed, I didn't know you were out here...are you okay? What's wrong?" I ask because he is holding me so tight that I'm sure something else has happened. "Where's Zee, is he okay?" I add with panic seeping into my tone.

"He's fine. Alfred got away," he says, sounding as if he is choking on the words. I exhale the breath, grateful that everyone I love is safe.

"Okay…so we're all fine then," I say in relief.

"I'm not okay," Reed replies, and I instantly panic again. I hadn't seen any wounds on him, but maybe I missed something. I am about to have a complete freak out when he says, "How did the possessed one get by me?"

I sigh, "Oh, well, that was my fault because I didn't know that the compact that Freddie…I mean Alfred gave me for my birthday is really a portal thingy. I guess when I opened the lid, I let it in." I feel guilty for what I'd done, even though I had no idea I was doing it.

Reed releases me before he retrieves the compact and box from the counter. Looking around for Buns, so that she can help me explain, she has already left the room.

"This is it?" Reed asks in an angry voice that he never uses with me anymore. Flinching a little, I lean up against the doorjamb of the bathroom and nod. "Did he ever give you anything else?" he asks, still not very much in control of his anger. Paling, I shake my head no. Reed crushes the compact into a very small piece of metal in his hand. The box goes next.

I flinch, saying, "I'm sorry, I never thought such things existed— I mean, maybe in fairytales, but not in real life. I wasn't keeping it from you. I just noticed it in my closet. It fell down off the shelf when I went to get my suitcase…" I'm babbling, but I can't stop. "I'm just stupid, that's all. I just don't think and I can't seem to stop doing really stupid things…" I have to stop talking because Reed covers my mouth with his index finger. I scan his face to see if my attempt at an apology has had any effect on him.

He still looks angry to me when he says, "This is not *your* fault. This is *my* fault. You couldn't have known what would happen when you opened it. I'm sure it never occurred to you that a demon would jump out of it and try to strangle you. Please do not call yourself stupid again," he finishes, removing his finger from my mouth. He turns and walks to the door of my room, calling over his shoulder, "Get packed. We're getting out of here."

It only takes me a half-hour to pack up what I'll need for our trip to the ski resort. Reed and Zephyr decide that taking two cars is a better idea than going in just one. Buns and Zephyr will take the lead in the black Range Rover. Reed and I will trail them in the red Range Rover I had gotten for Christmas. I guess the strategy is that one car can always divert the enemy away as a decoy, while the other sneaks away with me safely inside.

Reed tosses the keys to me after he loads my luggage in the hatch. I catch them and look at him questioningly for a brief moment, before I smile and rush to the driver's side, sliding into the seat. Buckling my seatbelt, I start the engine and it purrs to life with quiet menace when I touch my foot to the accelerator. Adjusting the rearview mirror, I see the reflection of my eyes in it. They're almost clear again; there are only traces of red in the corners. I breathe a sigh of relief that I don't still look like a freak show. Shifting my chin, I move the scarf I have wrapped around my neck a little to the side to see if my neck looks better. That's subjective; the bruises are now a faded yellowish color. I pull my scarf back up to hide the marks from sight. Reed sits unsmiling in the passenger seat, watching me.

Unbuckling my seatbelt, I crawl over the console and sit in Reed's lap. Wrapping my arms around his neck I press my forehead to his and look in his eyes. "Thank you," I say in a gentle tone. "I know that this outing is a stretch for you. You're probably fighting the urge to pick me up and take me back into the house, or at the very least, to drive the car yourself, so that you'll be absolutely sure nothing will happen to me."

A small smile touches Reed's lips. "I marvel at how well you seem to know me. If only I could know you as well. You seem to know what I'm thinking, whereas I have no clue most of the time of what you'll do next," he says.

"You're wrong…I don't know what you're thinking most of the time, but you seem to have a theme going on lately. It's that 'Evie's Continued Survival List' except you seem to have thrown out the con side. Now you're just focusing on the pros," I say, snuggling closer to him and kissing the place just beneath his ear tenderly.

"There are no cons," he breathes into my hair, and for a second, I believe him. I press my teeth to his earlobe and nip him gently.

"How about now?" I ask, smiling at him and hearing him groan.

"Okay, one con, but I'm sure that will not be a problem much longer," he says, referring to our inability to act on our desire for each other until I'm safely sturdy enough to handle it. "I think Zephyr is waiting for us to go," Reed says, reminding me that we're holding them up. I look over to the other vehicle to see that Zephyr has rolled down the driver's side window and is waiting for us patiently.

"Oh," I say, blushing. "Time to go." I crawl back into my seat, buckling my seatbelt again. I follow the black Range Rover out and we get on the road to the resort. "How long until we get there?" I ask

Reed, while watching the road ahead.

"Depends on how fast you drive. It shouldn't take more than three hours, if you drive the speed limit," he says blandly because I can tell that he thinks driving slowly is a waste of time. There is no danger in it, no thrill. I can also tell that Zephyr agrees with this philosophy wholeheartedly because I have to keep the pedal almost to the floor to keep up with him on the highway.

"You said that I know you very well. On some levels I think you're right. But, on others, I hardly know you at all," I admit as Reed holds my hand casually, not even aware of how perfect he is.

"What would you like to know about me?" Reed asks somewhat guardedly, probably because he thinks I'm after some of his trade secrets that he's not allowed to reveal.

That isn't what I'm after. "Relax, I'm not going to make you tell me why archeologist have found dinosaurs bones if Creation is a true story," I say, smiling at him and watching as his smile travels all the way to his eyes. *I love that.* "No, I was just after a story from your life. Something about you."

"I told you, Evie, I didn't really begin to live until I met you," he says. I roll my eyes at him, not buying it. "You don't believe me?" he asks me, scanning my face.

"No, you're an artist. I've seen all of the beautiful carvings you've created, so I know you've at least had something going on before me," I reason.

"Most of those carvings were done while sitting in some desolate hole somewhere waiting for my prey to arrive," he replies, looking out of the window at the scenery flashing by. "It was something to do when I couldn't read one more sonnet I didn't understand because I had no basis for the emotions being discussed. I travel through human civilizations on the fringes." He glances at me then, probably trying to gauge my reaction to what he's telling me. I school my face, trying not to let him know just how my heart hurts because of his lonely existence.

He is quiet for a little while before he continues. "For the most part, I watch civilizations rise and I see them fall. Once in a while, I try to participate, like I have recently here, but that's not my purpose. I have to be careful that I remain guarded about what I am," he says. "I could tell you about my impressions of Sparta, of the warriors who were torn apart when their civilization was overrun. I can tell you about the Spanish Inquisition and the atrocities all perpetrated, supposedly in the name of God, but I'm merely an observer of the deeds of men. I cannot participate to any great extent, even when I would've felt justified to tear some of those men to shreds." His smile is grim. I shiver, thinking of all the evil he has witnessed.

"I've had to take time off from humans, after seeing some things that have disturbed me." My imagination goes wild thinking of what must have been so bad as to disturb an angel whose sole purpose is to kill and tear apart other angels. I am ashamed when several things come to mind, some events in the not so distant past. "Sometimes, I've been able to stay out of human societies for decades. It's more difficult now, than it used to be, but not impossible."

"When I do participate more closely with humans, I can't form any lasting friendships with them. Sometimes people form an attachment to me for whatever reason." He pauses to glance at me for a moment. "Take, for example, JT and Pete. They don't know why they like me, they just do," he says, smiling despite the grim life he describes. "But, I will only be able to hang around with them for a few more years at the most because they will notice that I'm still nineteen, while they're older." He laughs humorlessly. "So I'll move away and start a new life somewhere else...but now I have you. You can come with me. We can go wherever we desire, wherever you desire," he says, bringing my hand to his lips and kissing it. I place the palm of my hand to his cheek and watch as he closes his eyes, savoring the feel of my skin on his.

Contact...needs...no wonder he always looked so lost when he was near me, when we first met. He was lost...and I found him...and I'm keeping him, no matter what, I think.

"I love you. We can go wherever you want, just as long as we're together," I say plainly, so that there won't be any misunderstanding between us. I have to tear my eyes away from his radiant smile, so that we won't get into an accident.

"It is so strange where my mind goes these days...how I sit and dream about things that may never be," he says.

"What do you mean?" I ask in confusion.

He glances at me for a moment like he has said too much. Like he has revealed something embarrassing and I think he is not going to answer me, but then he says, "I can sit for hours now and dream about all of the places I can take you and how you might react to them. Then I think about what we could do if we went there, but I discard one place for the next dream...it's so satisfying," he says almost apologetically.

"You're saying you daydream about me?" I ask, blushing a little when I think of this fierce warrior thinking of me that way.

"Yes," he says, watching me. "I've never done that before. When

I make plans, they are wholly based on strategy, such as where I will find the most damned. How I can manipulate a terrain to best entrap my prey. How I can turn my enemies against one another. Or, how to comprise the most lethal alliances," he says with assurance. "But now, I find myself thinking about how I can make Evie smile, or what your reaction will be to seeing the pyramids of Giza, or how your hair will look while spread out on the pillow tonight in your room…" he trails off, and my blush deepens in ecstasy.

"Reed, that's just hot," I say, trying to suppress my smile.

"It is?" he asks me in surprise.

"Yeah…really hot," I reply.

"Oh…well, good. I was beginning to think something was wrong with me," he says, smiling at my reaction to his words.

"Nope. I do that too, sometimes. I think about what it'll be like when I'll be able to kiss you and not have any reason to stop," I reply.

"You are right, that *is* hot," he murmurs, touching my hair softly.

"Told you," I reply.

"What else do you dream about?" he asks me in a soft tone. He's definitely into this topic. I clear my throat and think about it for a second, "Hmm…let's see, just this morning, when we had decided that we were going to make this trip, I might've let my mind wander a bit over how I would plan the sleeping arrangements, if given a choice."

"You did?" he asks, raising his eyebrow in inquiry.

"Uh huh. And when I was packing for the trip, I kinda threw in a couple of articles of clothing, just in case you lift that ban on seduction."

"It is unfathomable what you are capable of doing to me with just words," he says, shaking his head. I smile because I feel powerful all of a sudden. Trying to hide my smile, I look out the window at the scenery going by us. We have gotten past all of the major cities in this area and are now just traveling from one small rural town to another in our journey toward Lake Michigan and the resort we plan to stay in. The fir trees around this two-lane road are dense and covered in a blanket of white that absorbs sound almost completely. It's beautiful in the dusky twilight, as the colors of the night push down on the waning sun. It will get really dark here with no streetlights or city glow to illuminate the skyline. But, it doesn't matter because I can now see awesomely in the dark with my angel vision. I probably won't even need my headlights to drive the car, but I flip them on anyway so others can see me.

The phone in Reed's pocket begins ringing. When he answers it, it is Zephyr indicating they have reached the point where they had planned to get gas for the cars. We pull into a gas station with an at-tached mini mart. I park the car next to a pump and see Buns and Zephyr get out of their car and walk over near our car, surveying the scenery around us. Leaning over the center console of the car, Reed kisses me, his lips touching mine like a whisper before he gets out of the car to fill the gas tank. I open my door, stepping out to stretch my legs.

"Sweetie, let's go in and get some snacks." Buns says, linking arms with me. "I'm in the mood for licorice, what about you?" she asks as we walk together a few feet.

Through the windows of the mini mart, the fluorescent lights flicker eerily, illuminating the aisles of snacks lining the interior. I stop in my tracks and pull hard against Buns's arm, trying to get her to release me. Panic grips me as cold sweat breaks out all over my body.

"No...let go of me!" I whisper feebly, feeling Buns release me instantly. Panic makes my whole body shake as I back away from the doors in front of me.

"Sweetie, what's wrong?" I vaguely hear Buns ask me, but my eyes are riveted on the doors ahead of me. At any moment they will swing open and I will be assailed by that vile odor; the one that makes me puke—and Gaspard will be inside waiting for me.

I can't think rationally, as I turn and run from the gas station. I sprint as fast as my legs will carry me, with no thought as to where I'm going or who will observe me. I cross the street, narrowly avoiding a logging semi packed full of huge fir trees. The driver probably never saw me in the road, since I'm nearly invisible to him at the speed I'm traveling. I rush into the forest on the other side of the street. I as-cend a steep hill, maneuvering between the trees so nimbly that not one branch strikes me as I dart between them. Vaulting over large rocks, I keep going, never stumbling, never tiring of the pace that I have set, but continuing as if I will never stop.

Distantly, I hear my name being called. I keep going, farther and faster. The deep drifts of snow are no problem. I pump my legs hard-er, passing through them with ease. Climbing the rocks ahead of me, I jump from ledge to ledge, never wavering in my conviction that my foot will land solidly exactly where I want it to land on the precarious terrain. Again, I hear my name from somewhere further behind me. I pause on a rocky ledge.

Where are you running? my mind whispers. *Away from the Seven-Eleven...to Reed,* my heart whispers back. I still. I can't run away from it. It already happened. I had gone into the store with Alfred and

I had changed Russell's life forever—for eternity—and ended my uncle's life. *I did that and I cannot undo it,* I think as something brutal twists inside of me. I hear my name being called again, this time closer. I turn knowing Reed is approaching.

Reed bursts through the trees with an alarmed expression on his face. He stops when he sees me standing just above him on a rocky ledge. I probably look wild because my jacket had torn apart and was left on the trail below me when my wings had sprouted. I still have on the light sweater that Buns had modified for me. It didn't shred when my wings thrust out because the Velcro flap in the back just pulls away.

"Evie, where are you going?" Reed asks me in a gentle tone, approaching me with caution.

I look around me at the trees and snow because I don't know how to tell him. "I was…running from the Seven-Eleven…looking for you."

Reed is confused, and then I see him put it together. I hadn't tried to run from Alfred once I knew he held Russell hostage and would kill; I had cooperated. Staring at me intensely, Reed's jaw clenches as he strides the last few steps to me, pulling me into his arms. Reed digs in his pocket for his phone, depressing the speed dial button.

"I have her—she is okay—we will be back shortly. Wait for us by the road." He closes the phone. Picking me up off of my feet, he carries me down the side of the steep hill we had just climbed, as if we are walking on a flat, sandy beach somewhere. I am quiet all the way back to the car, feeling several emotions all at once. Just before we leave the cover of the trees, Reed shrugs off his coat and drapes it over my shoulders to hide my wings from sight. Zephyr had moved our car to the shoulder of the road where it's dark. Approaching the car, Reed places me in the passenger side. Zephyr is at his side instantly while Buns comes to my window.

"Sweetie—I didn't realize—it was stupid of me to think you would want to go in there," she says contritely, as she touches my arm through the open window.

"Buns, I don't really understand what just happened, but it's not your fault I freaked. I panicked and I had to…" I try to explain, but can't.

"I went in the store after we heard you were all right and I got you some water and just about one of everything," she says with a nervous smile, indicating the huge bag of snacks on the back seat of the car.

A real smile creeps across my face when I turn back to see the mountain of treats falling out of the bag. "Buns, I don't deserve you,"

I say.

"Are you kidding? Brownie will never forgive me if I let something happen to our girl," she says, reaching in the window to give me a brief hug. "Are you ready to get back on the road now?"

"Yes. I'll see you at the resort," I say, and watch as she goes to the black Range Rover parked just ahead of us.

Zephyr approaches my window. Smiling, he asks, "Enjoy your run?"

Raising my chin a notch, I reply, "Yes, it was refreshing." Zephyr grins, before leaning in my window and kissing me on the forehead.

"Yes, I'll never be bored again with you around," he says, chuckling as he walks back to his car.

I put my window back up as Reed climbs in the car. He sits in the driver's seat for a second, staring at my face. I try to hide my ragged emotions as I say, "I think we're going to have to come up with some kind of signal from now on to indicate that I'm sorry for my actions because just saying, 'I'm sorry' is getting redundant. I don't know how you can buy it anymore. Or, maybe you can teach me the words in Angel. Everything sounds so much better in your language."

"There are no words that mean, 'I'm sorry' in Angel," Reed replies and I have to fight back tears when I hear that little nugget of information. *Of course, what would a perfect being be sorry for?* I think sadly.

"And I couldn't be more pleased that you were looking for me," he says, keeping his eyes on me. "I don't require an apology from you—ever. You always follow your heart, even when it's in direct opposition to logic and your heart was telling you to find me—to make a different choice than the one you made before."

He starts the car and we follow Zephyr onto the road. "Can I ask you something?" Reed asks. I nod, still not trusting myself to speak. "What do you think would've happened if you'd gotten away—if you hadn't gone along with Alfred's plan to give up your soul for Russell and not gone into the store with him?" he asks me. I shrug and look out the passenger side window because I don't want him to see the tears in my eyes.

"How would things have been different?" he asks me relentlessly.

"You might have been able to stop Alfred," I say in a small voice.

"No," he says forcefully. "If you had made it to my home instead, the only difference would have been that you would have remained safe and Russell would be dead. Alfred would have killed Russell immediately, and then he would have left directly to slaughter your uncle. He would have gone to your uncle's home to seek revenge for your disobedience. We would not have known until it was too late. He would not have waited around for me to kill him, if you had evaded him."

"Sometimes I think that a person could die of regret," I whisper.

"What have you to regret?" Reed asks me, probing my response.

"If it weren't for me, Russell would be in Paradise right now, not being protected because I made him a hunted freak," I reply bitterly.

"You *helped* make him a highly evolved being. You made him Seraphim, the highest form of angel in Paradise, and he still gets to be your soul mate. He couldn't be more elite," Reed says, shaking his head. "Russell should kiss your feet for the upgrade."

"Yeah, it's such a great lifestyle, running from demons and angels, we're elite all right," I scoff.

"We will figure something out so that it won't always be this way. Zephyr and I have some ideas about getting the word out about you in my community without exposing you to danger," he says.

"Planning a PR junket?" I ask flippantly.

"Maybe," Reed says, giving me a sexy look. "Can I ask you something else?"

"Of course, I have no secrets from you," I reply, wondering what he would ask me.

His smile deepens at that. "What made you stop running tonight, in the woods?"

"I realized I was running to you and that you were behind me, not out there somewhere," I reply.

"You weren't tired or fatigued?" he asks.

"No, not at all," I say, and watch him grin. "Why?"

"Because I couldn't catch you, you were too fast for me," he replies.

"Really?" I ask him because he has to be joking. He's a Power. He's built for speed, strength, endurance...raw power. "NO WAY!" I say, my jaw hanging open.

"I was going to have to fly to look for you because you had me on foot," he grins. "I followed your footprints and I couldn't believe how far you leapt on the rocks, and your footing—you never slipped or hesitated—it was impressive, and now that I know you are all right—hot. Zee said you were really fast, that day he chased you, but I didn't realize just how fast."

"Really...huh? That's very interesting," I reply, studying him.

"That is your secret weapon, Evie. If you come across an enemy, you run as far and as fast as you can, don't look back just go. We will make sure you always have a cell phone on you. When it's safe, I can call you, or you can contact me and we'll meet up." Reed says with authority.

"So, I'm supposed to run away—like a coward?" I ask, offended by this new plan.

"Evie, there is a difference between evasion and cowardice," Reed says calmly.

"Yeah, one means avoidance and the other means spinelessness and neither one appeals to me," I reply.

Reed counters, "How about obedience, how does that appeal to you?"

"Submission—hmm—not so much," I reply stubbornly.

"Respect, not submission," he says in a rational tone. "Deference that I know what I'm talking about where strategy is concerned."

"I do respect you, you know that." I say, wondering why we are arguing about tactics.

"Then, you'll follow my orders," he says placidly.

"What will you be doing, while I'm running away?" I ask in a dark tone.

"What I'm made to do. I can handle angels. What I can't handle, is living without you, so we have to find a way to keep you safe," he says.

"Why is my safety more important than yours?" I ask, testing his resolve for this new strategy.

"What do you hope to accomplish against a fully evolved Power, Evie?" Reed asks me pointedly. "You would be more of a liability for me in a fight, than you would be an asset. The moment a Power angel realizes how vital you are to me, then we'll have some serious problems."

"I'm a liability," I say in a small voice, studying my hands so I won't have to look at him. "I guess I would be, wouldn't I?"

Reed groans when he sees that he has hurt my feelings by calling me a liability. "Only for now. You will be very powerful one day, if you keep evolving the way that you are and I will have to eat my words."

"Do you promise to choke on them, just a little bit, when that day comes?" I ask, a little salty because I know he's right. But it still reeks like I'll be selling him out if I make a break for it while he stays behind to fight for his life.

"I promise," he says, taking one of my hands and pulling it to his lips. He kisses my palm. I have to bite my lip from the sensual caress.

"Do you promise to listen to me, if I tell you to run?" he asks me, kissing my palm again as I squirm in my seat.

"Fine," I sigh, watching him look at me with his eyes wide, and then a frown pulls his brows down, making his hair slip down over one eyebrow. I hadn't actually said the words "I promise." I think he's catching on to that, so I unbuckle my seatbelt and brush his hair back from his brow. Turning, I rummage through the treat bag in the back seat. "Twinkie?" I question over my shoulder.

"Yes," he says. I retrieve a twin pack from the bag and find a couple of waters for us. Unwrapping the Twinkies, I hand one to Reed.

"So, you were thinking of ways to tell other angels about me?" I ask conversationally, trying to change the subject to something else.

"Yes," Reed replies.

"But, you haven't committed to the idea yet?" I ask.

"No," he replies.

"Are you worried that once you let that genie out of the bottle, there is no going back?" I ask, chewing my Twinkie thoughtfully.

He looks at me in suspicion, "Evie, you're dangerously sharp."

"Well, look at the bright side, we have a new weapon in our arsenal—*evasion*," I say, enunciating the last word as if it leaves a bad taste in my mouth. My smile brightens, however, when I hear Reed laughing as if I had made the funniest joke he has ever heard.

CHAPTER 3

The Resort

The resort that Buns has chosen is magical, or at least it is to me. The angels are not very impressed by it, but since they have probably been in several palaces at different points in their vast lifespan, their opinions have to be put into perspective. The lobby of the hotel is massive and resembles a Bavarian hunting lodge with large picture windows that face the slopes. There are huge stone fireplaces at either end of the lobby that are stoked with enough wood each to burn all night without having to add to them. I wander over to the windows as Buns checks us in. The slopes aren't that large by the standards of most ski resorts around the world, after all, this isn't the Alps, but it is perfect for what I want—a distraction.

As I gaze out the window, I see a group of teenagers snowboard down the hill and meet up at the bottom. Their carefree laughter, as they congratulate each other on the run, is almost shocking to me. I've forgotten that such things exist; that there are people whose only concern is learning a new trick to impress their buddies. I press forward near the glass; I can just make out one of them saying something about the wicked air he caught while freestyling in the pipe. They unstrap their boards and begin walking away toward the lights near the lifts. I follow their progression, my fingers running over the cold glass of the window as I walk across the back of the lobby, trailing them until I run out of window and can no longer see them.

Disappointment hits me when they are gone. They were probably about my age, but I don't feel that young. I want to follow them, to beg them to teach me how to be young again because I've forgotten. I've let that part of me slip through my fingers and I don't know how to get it back. Or, maybe that isn't it at all—maybe it's that I've forgotten what it is to be human—just human. I even call them "the humans" now, like I'm not a part of them. But I'm not, not now, and maybe never again. I'm surprised to acknowledge the sorrow that I feel for the loss of some of my humanity, even as I am grateful to be evolving so that I can keep up with Reed, now that I've found him.

Arms snake around me from behind, and seeing Reed's reflection in the window, I lean back against him securely. "What were you thinking?" Reed asks me as he nuzzles my neck.

"When?" I ask evasively.

"Just now. You looked—lost," Reed replies in a gentle tone.

"I'm not lost. You found me, remember? I was just thinking about how badly I'm going to smoke you out there on the slopes. It could get ugly for you, you really should prepare yourself for the worst." I say, trash talking to cover up for my earlier thoughts.

"Evie, you cannot be serious," he says, smiling.

"Oh, but I am. You don't stand a chance," I reply, resting my head against his chest.

"Against you, you're right—I never stood a chance," he replies, and his words make me smile.

"See," I say and hear him laugh.

"Okay, it's all set," Buns says behind us. I lift my head from Reed's chest as we both turn toward her. "The cottage is ready. We just have to follow this map."

"We're not staying in the lodge?" I ask in confusion.

"No. We thought something more private would be better," Buns explains as we head out to get back in the cars. We follow the map to a private drive that winds in a serpentine pattern through the woods, leading to an incredible cottage in a secluded area. Located just off the backside of one of the more impressive hills, the cottage is like something out of a fairytale. The cedar shake roof is covered in newly fallen snow. All of the doors and windows are rounded at the tops and contain shutters with wrought iron hardware. Each bedroom has its own private deck and there is a central deck in the back of the cottage, complete with an outdoor fireplace.

Reed cuts the engine to the car and I just sit in the passenger seat for a second, unable to move. "It's so beautiful," I breathe, because this cottage is perfect. I couldn't imagine a more romantic setting.

"Evie, you make me want to show you the world. If I get this reaction from you by just taking you to a little cabin in the woods, what will you say when you see the Palace of Versailles?" he asks with affection in his tone.

"I don't know, Reed, but this is pretty sweet," I say, smiling.

The door of the black Range Rover parked ahead of us opens and

Zephyr exits the driver's side. He bolts around to the passenger side, and reaching in, Zee pulls Buns out of the car. Kissing her passionately, he then hoists her over his shoulder. My eyes widen in shock as Zephyr carries Buns to the door of the cottage and disappears inside.

"Did you see that coming?" I ask Reed.

"Yes," he replies.

"Oh. Where have I been?" I ask him.

"You have had a lot on your mind," he responds as he picks up my hand, holding it to his lips.

"I thought that Powers don't really mix well with Reapers," I say, still trying to figure it out.

"Well, we usually have a hard time being around each other, you see, because most divine Reapers are annoying." I start laughing after he says this and he smiles while continuing. "It's true. Reapers want to talk about rainbows and sunshine and shiny, happy feelings. Powers usually don't have shiny happy feelings. We wind up wanting to tear them apart, if left in close proximity to them for extended periods of time. But Buns, she's not like that at all. She can hang with us, talk strategy and tactics and never once mention rainbows," Reed says.

I burst out laughing. "You're kidding, right?" I ask. "Buns would never talk about rainbows and Brownie…there is no way," I say, thinking of Brownie wasting her breath like that.

"No, I'm not kidding. Buns and Brownie are the strangest Reapers I have ever met. They don't seem to be cast in the mold of a Reaper. They aren't annoyingly happy and bubbly all of the time. It makes me wonder about them," he says, as if he is mulling over a particular problem.

"You mean you think there is more to them than they're showing us?" I ask in alarm.

"Evie, Zee would normally rather pluck the wings off of a Reaper than sit with one in the car for a minute. But that's not the case with Buns. He can't get enough of her. She and Brownie are special," he says. "But then, we all behave strangely around you. So, maybe it's a reaction to you."

"We're a very interesting crowd, huh?" I ask him, seeing his brow rise in question. "Let's see…we have a couple of Reapers who don't particularly act like Reapers. There is the Power, Zee, whose forte is strategy and warfare. Russell and I are half-breeds with the high rank of Seraphim and the low rank of human, and then there is you—the most perfect angel ever created that can control humans by suggestion."

"Evie, I'm not perfect," Reed says, frowning. "But you are right, it's a strange crowd," he agrees in a quiet tone. He gets out of the car and comes around to open my door. Before I can get out, he reaches in and cradles me in his arms, carrying me to the door of the cottage and over the threshold.

Reed kisses me passionately before letting go of my legs so that my body slides down his as my feet reach the floor. It's exquisite torture, being held in his arms like this, knowing it is all there can be between us for now. His immense strength could crush me if he is not extremely careful with me. Tearing myself away from him, I notice we are just inside the doorway.

It's so cozy inside the three-bedroom cottage. The hardwood floors are not highly polished, but dull and rough, giving a rustic impression to the pale maple wood. The fireplace in the main room is fieldstone in soft gray tones, cobbling its way up to the exposed beams of the ceiling. The mantle is made from the same rough wood as the floors and it holds several glass bowls with floating candles all lit to illuminate the small space. There is also a small, open kitchen. The kitchen has maple wood cabinetry with wrought iron hardware, tumbled stone tiled countertops, and a porcelain sink.

I walk over to the fireplace and watch the flames of the fire licking at the wood in the grate. For just a moment, I would've given anything to live here with Reed for the rest of my life. I would be satisfied to stay here, safe and protected. We could pretend that we aren't angels and that no one wants to hurt me. We could forget about Alfred and revenge; he would never find us here. I doubt many Fallen would hang here either; they would be after a more exciting venue. But we can't stay here forever, even if it would be perfect. Eventually, someone would notice our inability to age and we would have to leave. No place can be permanent. I sigh as my brief fantasy is shattered by reality.

"What's wrong?" Reed asks.

"Nothing, I was just wishing we could stay here forever," I reply.

"I was thinking the exact same thing," Reed says with a small smile. "I don't think I would need more than this, if you were here with me."

I smile back at him and would've said more, but a crashing sound comes from one of the bedrooms in the back of the cottage. I am startled for a second until I hear Bun's muffled laughter and realize they're okay. I blush a little when I look at Reed.

"Are you hungry, Evie?" Reed asks me quickly.

"Starved," I say, because it is a good excuse to get out of the house and away from the bedrooms.

"There is a restaurant on top of the slope that I think is fairly casual. We just need to head over to a gondola and ride it up to the summit," he says as more noises come from the bedroom furthest away. Zee and Buns are talking to each other in Angel, and by the look on Reed's face, I'm fairly sure that for once, I'm grateful I can't speak their language. "I'll go get the luggage," Reed says, and runs out of the house in an instant.

I choose the room next to Zephyr's and Buns's room. Reed takes the one next to mine on the other side. Showering quickly, I style my hair and change into a casual sweater and jeans with lace up boots that go to my knees. Before much time passes, I meet Reed in the main room. He is seated on the sofa with his iPod blaring, having already changed into a cable knit sweater and some jeans. Putting on the coat I had packed for evening, I wrap my scarf around my neck and mouth the word, "Ready?" He nods and tentatively pulls the ear buds out of his ears.

Taking my hand after he shrugs into his coat, we walk outside and down the lighted path that winds through the trees leading to the slopes. The pine trees are thick and imposing here, like what you would expect in the Black Forest, and it's so quiet with only the sound of our footsteps to break the silence in the night. For a moment I feel like Lucy escaping into the wardrobe and finding herself in Narnia. We emerge from the woods into a snow covered clearing, awash with light from the tall lanterns mounted overhead. The gondola lift is close to where our path through the trees had ended. We walk over to it, joining a line of snowboarders and skiers waiting patiently to catch a ride back up to the top.

Entering a gondola, Reed and I are herded toward the back of the car. We stand there together, braced against the far corner, as riders shuffle and maneuver for space. The lift is soon packed with snowboarders ready to take their next run on the hill. It feels like being on a crowded subway car at rush hour, except the people in this car are all talking animatedly to one another. After squeezing in several more riders than necessary, the doors close and the cable begins pulling the car upward. Pressed firmly against Reed's body, I'm becoming uncomfortably aware that the close proximity is doing crazy things to the butterflies in my stomach.

Desire makes me moisten my lips as my fingertips trail lightly over the fabric of Reed's sweater. I want to run my hands under his sweater, to feel his bare chest under my fingertips. I drop my hands to my sides, balling them into fists. Biting my lower lip, I stare up into his green eyes. He smells like the pine trees we had just walked through and an incredibly masculine scent that is quintessentially Reed. *I can probably find him blindfolded now just by scent alone,* I think as I lean close to him.

The gondola bounces gently, as the car's cable hitch goes over the pulley, causing me to brace myself against Reed for support. I close my eyes briefly, savoring the contact. When I open my eyes, Reed's mouth is dangerously close to mine. My eyes memorize every gentle curve of his sensual lips. There is an ache building inside of me. To be near beauty like this is heaven and it's the kind of torment that I could never have imagined existed, if I had not been subject to it.

Again, the gondola bounces as the hitch goes over the next pulley, but this time Reed shifts aggressively towards me. He presses me firmly back against the wall of the gondola, trapping me there with his arms bracing on either side of me. His face nears and I raise my chin as his cheek gently brushes against mine. Feeling heat radiating off of his skin, he inhales the scent of my hair. One of his hands passes lightly over the curve of my waist and slowly up my body, tracing my shape as if he would memorize my silhouette. My heart beats violently in my chest.

"Evie," Reed breathes by my ear, creating a desperate sense of longing in me.

How are we going to survive this? I wonder as I pull my hands from him to grip the railing that lines the wall behind me. I squeeze the railing tight, feeling the cold metal bar beneath my fingertips give way gently. The sound of metal being crushed registers in my mind; it sounds like a tin can being smashed. My eyes widen and I still for a second, easing my grip from the bar and feeling the distinct ridges of finger impressions.

Reed stills too, seeing shock register on my face. His hand moves from the wall to investigate the railing, and when he feels the imprints I had left in the handrail, I whisper to him, "Sorry, my bad." I look around to see if any of the other passengers had heard the crunch of the bar, but no one is paying any attention to us.

When I look back to Reed, his face registers an even deeper desire than just moments before. "Evie," Reed replies in a whisper, "that would get a high rating on any angel's awesomeness scale."

"Are you telling me that my bending a railing is hot?" I whisper my question near his ear, fascinated by the darkness in his eyes as he looks at me.

"In the extreme," he replies with his sexy voice.

The lift is now entering the gondola house at the summit and people are shifting and jockeying for a better position in which to exit the car. I don't breathe for a couple of seconds because Reed's face is radiant. It's like he's proud of me, which is insane because I've just crushed the metal railing with my fingers. Now we have to try to hide it, so that no one sees my newly developed strength.

The doors open and a rush of cold air enters the car as the vacationers all push to exit the lift. I hide the railing from sight for as long as I can until Reed gently pulls me along toward the exit. He wraps his arm around my shoulder as we stroll casually from the car, as if nothing had happened. When we exit the gondola house, the restaurant is just ahead of us on the crest of the hill, overlooking the lights of the small town below. Walking slowly toward the restaurant, I'm grateful for the cold air swirling around us because it's helping to ease some of the heat that radiates between Reed and me.

Entering the restaurant, I am assailed by the warmth and understated appeal of the Bavarian-style building. It boasts white-washed walls with darkly stained, exposed wooden beams that pitch high above our heads. Reed leads me forward and he speaks in a whisper to the hostess regarding a table. There is a quiet exchange of cash from Reed to the young woman at the podium whose blushing face indicates that she would give him anything he wants without the bribe. I try not to let her physical response to Reed annoy me, because really, who can blame her? But, it does annoy me and I want to snarl at her. *What's wrong with me?* I wonder.

Within minutes, Reed and I are led to a very nice table for two in front of the windows that overlook the slopes and the twinkling lights of the town below. I gaze out at the night sky, seeing all the stars lay out like a mystical roadmap to destinations not yet revealed to me.

"I'm getting stronger," I say, turning back to Reed to see his reaction to my words.

"Yes," he replies with a sweet smile, taking my hand.

"So, does that mean we can lift that ban on the no seduction clause of our contract?" I ask as casually as I can manage.

"No," he replies.

"Why not?" I ask, exhaling deeply.

"You have to ask?" he counters, and when I nod he continues. "The shadow man who attacked you, just this morning, nearly succeeded in strangling you. I am infinitely stronger than he is and he left bruises on you that didn't heal for three hours and fifty-two minutes."

"That sounds like a pretty accurate observation. Did you count the seconds, too?" I tease him. I lose some of my smile when I see that he had counted the seconds.

Our waitress arrives at the table then and introduces herself as Katie before asking us for our drink orders. Reed picks up the wine list. I watch as our waitress plays with the ends of her lovely blond hair, twirling it around her finger while she reviews the wine selection with him, leaning in close to him to recommend something she likes. Her arm brushes up against Reed's briefly when she is pointing out something to him on the menu. She gives him a radiant smile full of flawless teeth when he looks up at her in response.

My eyes zero in on the contact as my mind rapidly pulses through ways in which to kill her. Startled by my inappropriate reaction to the situation, I pick up the menu that she had placed in front of me, holding it up so that I can't observe them. I try not to be annoyed when she doesn't even card him and leaves the table to get the wine he ordered for us. "She's friendly," I say, not looking up from my menu.

"Yes," Reed agrees as he pulls his menu from the table and begins scanning it.

"She seems to know a lot about wine," I say, casually trying to gauge his reaction to the waitress.

"Yes," he agrees distractedly, reading the menu.

Our waitress returns and pours the wine for Reed, giving me an assessing look as if sizing up the competition. When she is finished, she focuses all her attention on Reed as she again leans near him to recommend several different entrees for various reasons. I see her flush hotly when she inhales his scent. Then, her arm accidentally-on-purpose brushes up against Reed again and my eyes focus in on the contact.

A low growl comes from somewhere deep inside of me. It is so low that only Reed hears it and his eyes snap up to zero in on my hand that is twitching on top of the knife in my table setting. Quickly, Reed places his hand over mine, which pins it to the table as he stares into my eyes.

"May I please have the salmon?" Reed asks the waitress abruptly, cutting off whatever it is that she had been saying, while not taking his eyes from mine. "Evie, what would you like?" he asks me, continuing to hold my hand down.

"Same," I reply in a terse tone, trying not to look at the waitress so I won't be tempted to pounce on her and tear her apart.

"Excellent. She'll have the same," Reed says quickly and he doesn't move his hand until the waitress is safely away from the table. Pouring me a glass of wine, Reed studies my face as I raise the glass to my lips to drink. I try to avoid his eyes, and instead, I look out the window, feeling completely lost. "Evie?" Reed asks with concern.

"I don't know what just happened, Reed, but I can tell you, that if she touches you one more time, she's going to wind up with a fork sticking out of her," I say as an explanation, still not looking at him.

"Really?" I hear him ask and his voice sounds strange. Glancing at him, I notice that a smile is creeping up the corners of his mouth, even though he's fighting it. *He's smug!* I assess.

"That is funny to you?" I ask him in a low tone, giving him my full attention. "It probably won't be in about fifteen minutes when she comes back and brushes up against you again. I should leave now, before I hurt her." I say, beginning to get up from the table.

"Evie, please sit," Reed says quickly, "I'll take care of it and make sure that she doesn't touch me again." He watches me sit back down cautiously. I feel aggressive, like I could lash out at any moment. The feeling is so foreign that I have to take another sip of my wine to try to calm down.

"What's wrong with me?" I ask Reed to see if he knows what this is all about. "I feel edgy…like I want to break something."

Reed shrugs, but the smile is still lingering, barely suppressed at the corners of his lips, giving away the fact that whatever it is, he's certainly not unhappy about it. "You are Seraphim," he says in a nonchalant manner.

"And?" I counter.

"And, that makes you extremely protective, even territorial," he says, grinning at me, "when it comes to your affection."

"My affection?" I ask in confusion.

"It's instinctual, the need to protect what is yours," he says in a soft tone, while watching me.

Dread creeps into my consciousness when I begin to understand what he's saying to me. "So you're saying I just had an instinctual re-action to someone I assessed as invading my territory?" I ask, feeling the blush of embarrassment flushing into my cheeks.

"No, I'm saying much more than that," his smile is radiant.

"How much more?" I ask, taking another sip of my wine.

"Much, much more," he replies, and his smugness cannot be contained. "I'm saying you love me."

"Oh—I already told you that," I say, looking at him in uncertainty.

"Yes, you did and I believed you when you told me in human that you love me, but you never told me that you love me in Angel before," he replies, and I still.

"That's how you say 'I love you' in Angel?" I ask incredulously, watching him across the table. He is extremely satisfied judging by the way he sits back in his chair and casually toys with his wine glass.

"That's one way," he replies. "You've marked me as yours, your love, and a growl in Paradise is enough of a warning to another angel that you will not share."

"Seriously?" I ask.

"Deadly serious," he replies. "And, since you're a Seraph, unless another Seraph challenges you, I'm yours."

"But you have a say in the matter. Right? I mean, I couldn't just claim you. Right? You have free will?" I ask, totally wigging out over this new bit of information.

"Evie, I haven't had free will with you since I met you. But, yes, theoretically, I wouldn't have to be your love if I didn't reciprocate your affection," he replies as he picks up my hand again, lacing it through his own.

"Someone could challenge me for you?" I ask, panicking at the thought of losing Reed to some other angel.

"Yes, but I have ultimate say, so you don't have to worry, love," his voice is soothing. "And, it would be rare for a Seraph to fight over a Power," Reed says offhandedly.

"I would fight for you," I reply without thinking, because it would be instinctual for me, like breathing. He is mine and I will always want him.

That sensual darkness enters Reed's eyes again as he replies, "I know. You just demonstrated that so eloquently only moments ago."

"I think I'm experiencing culture shock, Reed. Everything you're saying sounds so primitive…no, so primal," I say.

"Yes, it is ancient…it is animal in its basic simplicity," Reed replies.

I sigh heavily and avoid eye contact when I ask, "Can we talk about something else?"

"Why?" Reed asks.

"Because, I'm growling at the waitress, Reed. At the very least it's considered bad manners where I come from and some people would consider it shady. Being part angel sucks sometimes," I say, taking another sip of my wine, watching Reed's eyes grow large as he smiles at my comment.

"Evie, why would you say that?" he laughs.

"Because, angels are capable of logic and higher thought, but have limited emotions and highly instinctual attraction," I don't even pause to breathe before saying, "and then, there is that whole caste system you have going on that I don't approve of at all. I mean rank and divisions? Please," I scoff.

"What could possibly be wrong with everyone having a job to do and an orderly way of accomplishing it?" Reed inquires.

"Nothing, in theory, but when you say that a Seraph wouldn't fight for a Power, then I don't like your divine system. I can't see any reason for someone like me not to want to fight for someone like you," I reply heatedly. I think I stunned him. He stares at me for several moments, not saying a word.

"No, you don't, do you. You really can't see it, can you?" he asks. "To you, we're all the same. Buns isn't a Reaper, she's an angel. Zephyr isn't a Power he's an angel. The only division you can see is good and bad. Brownie is good. Alfred is bad."

"You're right, except for one other division," I counter.

"What division is that?" he asks, sounding puzzled.

"*My* angel," I reply. "That's you, just in case my growl before didn't clue you in."

"You *are* the most dangerous creature I've ever met," he says, sipping his wine, but he seems happy at my words, maybe even flattered.

I roll my eyes at him and say, "You make me sound like I'm the predator and you're the prey."

I am startled when Reed abruptly gets up from the table and says, "If you will excuse me for a moment, the waitress is on her way back and I don't want you to have to protect me from her."

He strolls away, just as Katie brings out our food. Looking disappointedly at Reed's empty chair, Katie sets down the food and says halfheartedly, "Enjoy."

I watch as Reed approaches our table after Katie leaves. It's impossible for me not to admire the graceful way he moves, like a jungle cat, but I'm not the only one admiring him, I observe as I take a sip of my wine. Several women of varying ages watch as he passes by their tables, their heads turn, marking his progression. Some even stop talking entirely as they lose their train of thought. *No female is immune to him.* When Reed is again seated at the table, I pick up my fork and begin eating my dinner quietly, assessing him.

Reed watches me for a while, then he asks, "Evie, what's wrong?"

"Nothing," I say evasively.

"You look upset," he says as I pick at my food.

I shrug and continue eating. "Please tell me," Reed asks, and because he's so compelling when he uses his sexy voice on me, I have to relent and let him in.

"It's just that I've figured a few things out, and now that I have, I can see that I'm doomed," I say, and watch Reed stop eating, as if alerted to a threat. So I continue quickly, "I figured out that loving someone else is a huge risk. Chances are, that sooner or later, something will happen and it will all end." When I see his eyes pull together in a frown, I regret saying anything. "Reed, I should've protected myself against you, but I didn't and now you live here, inside of me," I say, pointing to my heart. "I won't ever be able to run from the love I have for you. Your name is written on my heart. I can't hide from it and it will wreck me if something happens to you—like it did to my uncle."

"Evie, you're stronger than that. You would survive," he says tenderly.

"I don't think so, Reed, but it doesn't matter—it's too late. That battle would've already had to take place way before now. I already love you, so I'm already lost," I reply.

"Welcome to my world, Evie," Reed says, smiling ruefully at me. "You have been living in my head and my heart for as long as I have known you. I can't stop thinking about you. I'm always wondering what you will do or say next. When you enter the room, I can't help following you with my eyes, studying everything you do. There is risk for me, too. I have to compete with your soul mate who may still be meant for you," he says, unsmilingly. "Thinking of the time you almost died gives me an ache in my core that I can't explain to anyone because it doesn't even allow for words. Sometimes, I think I have made you up just to torture myself—and there are other times that I know you must be real because I couldn't have dreamed such perfection."

It is my turn to be stunned. His risks are greater than mine. How can I have forgotten that? We still don't know if by helping me he's aiding the Fallen in some way. He could have walked away in the beginning and probably still should, but he is here with me now. "Russell is like family to me and I will do everything I can to protect him because I do love him. I love him, but it is not with the same... intensity that I love you," I say, shaking my head. "It's like you occupy the spaces he can't ever reach," I add, trying to make him understand.

I must have succeeded because his face lights up again and he looks perfect: every inch the angel that he is. How could I have not seen it sooner? How did I not realize instantly what he is because the ethereal quality is so transparent to me now and I cannot fathom why everyone can't see it? How did I inspire such devotion from this celestial being?

"Promise me something, Reed," I ask him on impulse.

He smiles then and doesn't hesitate before he responds, "Anything."

"Never doubt that I love you," I say. "You can doubt anything else about me, but never doubt that I love you more than anything in this world or the next."

Reed sits back in his seat, assessing me for a moment. I cannot say why it's important to me that he make me this promise, it just is. I need him to see what I am saying is true, more than I need anything else.

"How can I doubt it when you are now growling at the waitress for getting too near to me?" he asks, teasing me lightly.

"Reed," I say breathlessly.

"Why is it important to you that I promise you this?" he asks, suddenly very serious.

I try to think of how I can explain it to him. "You remember when you said that we weren't in a pond, but a vast ocean and that there were sharks that only a fish like me could attract?" I ask, remembering what he said to me that day at registration.

"Yes," Reed replies, becoming very still.

"Well, I want you to have something to hold on to, in case the currents shift and drag me from you," I reply, watching his face pale.

"I promise," Reed vows.

"Thank you," I smile at him.

"Has your premonition become any clearer to you?" he asks in a low tone. His face is no longer playful, but dangerous and sharp, missing nothing in my body language or any other subtle signal that I'm giving off.

"It's just a nightmare," I say adamantly, trying not to think about the darkness in my latest nightmare. "But, no, I just have a morbid sense of dread and…" I trail off.

"And?" he prompts, his tone indicating he would like to interrogate me on this subject, but he's trying not to push me.

"And this feeling like I'm starving," I say, sounding worried.

"Promise me something," Reed asks.

"Anything," I reply.

"If the currents do conspire against us, know that I will find you… I will never stop looking for you," he says.

"I'm counting on it," I reply honestly. "You're all I want. Just you and me…forever." I stare into his eyes and I see what I am hoping to see, the absence of doubt.

"The waitress is coming back. Let's go before you feel the need to adorn her with cutlery," Reed says, smiling broadly and tossing money on the table.

Once outside the restaurant, I notice that most of the lifts are shut down for the evening. The well-lit slopes are now shrouded in darkness. Only a couple of the gondolas are still working to take diners and restaurant employees back down the slopes. Impulsively, I turn to Reed and say, "Race you down the hill." I don't wait to see what he will do, but bolt through the hard-packed snow toward the cottage.

When I reach the bottom of the hill, I glance over my shoulder to see if I can detect Reed behind me, but I see nothing. With a smug smile, I run toward the trees to where the path leads to the cottage. Just as I am about to pass the first stand of trees, someone steps out in front of me, blocking my way. I can't stop, so I plow right into Reed who catches me gently around the waist, hugging me to his body and laughing.

"Gotcha," he smiles and I notice that his chest is bare and his charcoal wings are extended.

"You cheated! You flew!" I accuse him as my arms creep around his neck.

"I told you that I couldn't catch you on foot, so I had to resort to other methods," he says, and I can hardly think because nothing compares to seeing him like this. So, I don't think, I just act. I touch my lips to his, kissing him gently. I don't care that he's strong and could hurt me; I'll welcome the pain because it'll be a different pain from the one that pushing him away now would produce. But, Reed won't let this go on; he's not willing to take the risk. "Evie," he says as he pulls away from me.

"I know I have to be good, but I really want to be bad," I whisper in his ear, feeling him squeeze me harder to him.

"We need a distraction," he says as he bends down, retrieving his sweater and coat he has stashed behind the tree. Handing it to me he asks, "Ready?"

"Uh…for what?" I ask. He just smiles at me and picks me up off of my feet. In seconds, we are shooting straight up to the top of the tree line, avoiding several of the branches by millimeters. A gasp of pure surprise escapes me upon seeing the night sky stretch out above me. Clinging to Reed's chest, I watch as his wings beat rapidly to maintain the velocity necessary to keep us in the air. The perfection of the night sky, with its dark absolutely infinite depth, couldn't be improved upon if it had been the Caribbean blue of the sky in daylight.

"Reed, you're flying…we're flying! This is so amazing," I breathe, not being able to really put into words just how incredible it is to be held in Reed's arms high above the earth. "You can fly," I say in awe, before I can stop myself.

"Evie, you have known for a while that I can fly," Reed replies, as if I've lost my mind, which I might have because this was so far from reality that I again doubt my own sanity.

"Well, there is knowing and there is *knowing*," I say, emphasizing the last word as I look down at the tops of the trees speeding by below me like an ocean of green. *We have to be several stories off the ground at this moment,* I think as I tighten my grip on Reed. I listen to the sound of his powerful wings beating the air, allowing us to defy gravity's pull and stay aloft, and then I listen to the quiet of just the wind blowing by as we glide along the air currents when there is an updraft.

"Why haven't we done this before now?" I ask him, feeling the wind catch at my hair and stream it behind me as we soar faster.

"To me, it's just a way of getting from point A to point B. But, you find it fun, don't you?" he asks as if this thought amuses him, too.

"Yeah…don't you remember the first time you flew? Weren't you excited and a little terrified and just filled with—I don't know—wonder at feeling the wind beneath you and the power and strength you possess to accomplish such an amazing bit of…magic?"

"Is that what this is like for you?" he asks me, as if I'm the mysterious one conjuring tricks. When I nod, he says, "It's so different looking at things through your eyes. You weren't raised knowing anything about us, so this is magical," he surmises with a broad smile. "To me, it was a rite of passage, I guess, is the best way to describe it, but it lacked any magic, since everyone I knew could do it."

"Oh, that's too bad, you missed out on the exquisite enchantment of this moment then," I say as we begin a rapid descent through the trees. I think that there is a chance that we could crash and burn, so I squeeze my eyes closed tight. The smell of pines alerts me to the fact that we have reached the forest. I peek to see trees whipping by at an obnoxious speed. I quickly close them again because the thrill is leaking into scary territory.

Touching down, I don't want to open my eyes because I don't want it to be over. My feet are on the ground, but I still have my eyes closed. "Thank you," I say, hugging Reed.

He gently strokes my back as he say, "You are the magical one, not me. Thank you for showing me what I have been missing," he replies. Opening my eyes, I'm amazed to find that we're at the front door of the little cottage in the woods. I want this moment to be preserved in my mind for eternity, so that I can remember the way Reed is looking at me, as if I am flawless.

The door to our little cottage swings open and Buns stands just beyond the threshold. "Oh, there you are, sweetie!" she says brightly, bouncing up and down with enthusiasm. "You're just in time, we're almost ready to go for a session."

"Buns, I think you missed out on snowboarding tonight," I say, entering the cottage and taking off my coat. "The lifts are all shutting down for the night." When Zephyr hears this, he lets out a deep chuckle like I've said something funny again.

"Sweetie, we don't need lifts," she says, and to make her point, her wings spring from her back, so that she looks like some kind of wood nymph in front of me. "And we can't really have as much fun in the daylight as we can in the dark. No one can see us out there at night with the lights off. It will be stylin', you'll see," Buns says, leading me toward my room. "Now, get ready and we'll head out."

As I pass by their bedroom on the way by to mine, I glance in and freeze. Every piece of furniture has been knocked over except for the bed that has seen better days, I'm sure. The room is a compete mess. I blush a little and continue on to my room, saying under my breath, "What are you guys, rock stars or something?" To which, the room behind me erupts in laughter as Zephyr and Reed hear my comment.

I quickly change into a snowboarding outfit and put on my soft boots. When I exit my room, I meet the angels in the main room near the fireplace, where they are already outfitted and lounging around waiting for me. Each of them is wearing a long sleeved shirt with some boarding pants, except for Buns, who has on a sweater similar to mine in design that can accommodate her wings in the back. "Okay, this should be interesting," I comment, beginning to feel like I may have trash talked a little too early in the game.

"Don't worry, it'll be fun," Reed says, while walking me to the door of the cottage. On the porch outside, Reed hands our snowboards to Zephyr, saying, "Here, make yourself useful."

"Buns, tell him how useful I can be" Zephyr comments to Buns.

"Sweetie, you're very useful to me," Buns says, beaming at him while holding her board. In an instant, she extends her shimmering golden butterfly wings and launches herself into the air, disappearing from sight.

"See, *very* useful," Zephyr says, taking off his shirt to tie it around his waist. Giving me a wink, he too, sprouts his impressive light brown wings, moving with unrestrained power and agility. Zephyr lifts our boards in his arms, and like Buns before him, springs into the air and is gone in a fraction of a second.

I turn to Reed, watching as he takes off his shirt, just as Zee had done, to wrap it around his waist. "Are you ready?" Reed asks as his head dips to nuzzle my neck, causing the heat to intensify in an instant.

"Mmm," I manage to respond. Reed springs effortlessly into the air, cradling me in his arms. Flying through the dark of night, we seem to be going even faster than before, whirling through the trees following the path we had walked just hours ago. A small squeak of fear bursts from me as a tall, pine tree with a trunk the width of an SUV looms before us. Reed narrowly avoids it at the last possible second. "Let's try not to scare the half-human, okay?" I ask him when I can again speak.

He laughs before saying, "Sorry." We reach the summit of the hill in no time at all and find Buns and Zephyr waiting for us with their boards already on. The snowboarding halfpipe, handrails, kickers and other jumps are all located on the opposite side of the hill. I look around, psyched, because we don't have to maneuver or jockey for a good position, since we're completely alone.

Buns is the only goofy-footed rider among us, since she rides with her right foot closest to the nose of the snowboard, but it's great for me, since I can face her and talk to her without having to fakie on the way over to the halfpipe. All the boards that we have with us are twin tipped, so that the board will ride equally well in both directions. "My board is dialed in, Buns. Reed really knows what he's about when it come to boarding, huh?" I ask her.

"Sweetie, Powers have a lot of time to kill. They have to find ways to fill it when they aren't waiting for their prey to make a move. This is a nice distraction from the boredom," she says.

Standing next to Reed on the coping of the halfpipe, I look down the wall to the flat bottom below. "The snow looks bullet-proof," I say, because the snow in the halfpipe looks super hard.

"Yes," he agrees, giving me an evil grin because he knows it will be fast. "Are you ready to—how did you term it? Smoke me?" he asks, looking down at me, and I know I am in trouble because he is probably stellar at this.

"Yeah, I'm ready. Just keep in mind that I only have four limbs that work, while you have six. I'm working with a handicap here."

"Duly noted. Let's see what you've got, Betty," Reed says, smiling again.

"Okay," I reply, and then turn, dropping into the pipe. Hitting my backside wall first, I traverse the pipe a couple of times just doing poptarts to get a feel for the snow. On the third transition, I pump my board hard, trying to build up speed. When I go vertical and catch air, I perform a trick called a Japan; grabbing the front toe edge of the board with my front hand, I tuck my front knee and pull the board up while arching my back. When I drop back into the pipe,

I have to roll down the windows a little to maintain my balance so I won't do a face plant. Just when I know I have my balance back, Reed who had dropped into the pipe and rode the flat to get to me, sweeps me up off the snow and into his arms.

"Need a ride back up?" he asks, attempting to cover up his over-reaction to the garage sale I almost had on re-entry.

"Sure, but you know that I've wiped out before. I'll survive if I fall down," I say, smiling as he flies me back to the top of the halfpipe.

"You may survive it, I may not," he says effacingly. "That trick was good. What is it called?" Reed asks me.

"Japan," I reply. "I want to see Paradise though, are you ready to show me?" I ask, sizing him up when he puts me down on the wall of the halfpipe.

"It would be my pleasure," he says, grinning evilly again. I have to say that I have high expectations when I watch him drop into the pipe. My expectations do not even touch the sickest part of Reed's session. It is so unbelievable because there are no names for the stunts he can pull off. I think he does a modified version of a McTwist at one point, but there are so many rotations involved, at least 1440 degrees that I can't count them all.

When Reed flies back up to me again, I feel like I am looking at a snowboarding god, not an angel. "Seriously Reed, I'll never trash talk you again. That's just insane what you can do." He must like the praise because he pulls me into his arms and hugs me.

"Evie, he is a poseur compared to me. Watch this!" Zephyr says, dropping in the pipe. Again, I freak out as Zee seems to defy the laws of physics with his tricks. The raw power in the rotations and flips are just plain wicked.

Buns has a different style entirely from the guys. Whereas they're power and precision, whipping out deadly maneuvers, Buns is grace and refinement. Her tricks are all stalled, so that she hangs in the air effortlessly as she gracefully extends her limbs. You can see the supple way she bends her body in intricate moves that makes her appear to be posing in midair. I want to learn how to do what she does, but I don't know if I can ever pull it off because her wings seem to float while mine are built more for raw power and speed, kind of like the Power angels'.

"Buns, that was completely gnarly. It was like watching a ballerina snowboard," I say, because that is the best description I can come up with for what she can do. We sit together on the wall of the halfpipe, watching Reed and Zee defy gravity with their tricks.

"Sweetie, when you can use your wings, you'll make what we can do look grody by comparison," Buns says with confidence.

"Highly doubtful, Buns, but thanks," I say.

"No, Evie, that wasn't an opinion, that is a fact. You are Seraphim, you'll be incredible at everything you do, not just this." I must look skeptical because she adds, "Seraphim are God's personal guardians. You're built for speed, strength, agility, power and cunning. Every other angel wants to be Seraphim and you go one step further. You are endowed with a soul, which makes you one of God's children."

"If I'm so great, why is it that every angel I meet wants to kill me, with the exception of you and Brownie, of course?" I ask.

"You're taboo in a way. You're one of the elements the Fallen wanted all along," Buns replies. When she sees my confusion, she goes on. "Some demanded souls, so they could be like humans, like God's children. In Paradise, angels take care of the souls, but the Fallen thought that we should get rid of the humans and take their souls, so that we can be the children of God." Goose bumps break out on my arms as I begin to understand what she's telling me. "But there were others that were far worse—they craved to be above God. To rule over God and His dominion."

"So some might think that I somehow succeeded where the Fallen had failed," I say. "Or…that the Fallen have succeeded and I'm the product of that success," I say cringing.

"Yes. You cause all sorts of thoughts to fly through an angel's psyche. But I want you to understand something about yourself, Evie. You're so compelling to us and at the same time we find you very dangerous. We do not find you disgusting, but just the opposite, you are ideal—a model of perfection. Some will wonder what will happen to us, the soulless, if you are the new standard of being," she says in a quiet way.

"I think I get what you're saying, angels already have to compete with humans for God's affection. What happens when you add some-one like me to the mix?" I say, and flop back to lie on the ground with my feet dangling over the halfpipe.

I look at the stars above my head, trying to sort it out, but I can't. If this is a debate, there are as many reasons to destroy me, as there are to protect me. *Maybe even more to destroy,* I think as fear leaks into my consciousness. But it's strange that I'm not so much afraid of what could happen to me, as much as I am afraid of what could happen to the ones who would fight to protect me. The size of the problem I face makes me feel physically drained. *How am I going to keep everyone safe?* I think as I lie on the ground.

A yawn escapes me then and I try to cover it up, so that Buns won't see it, but she catches me. "Oh, sweetie, you're tired aren't you?" she asks, while popping up off the edge of the wall. "I'll tell the Powers you need to go back now," she says. She drops in the halfpipe to get them before I can lie and say I am fine.

Almost instantly, Reed is above me, blocking out the stars from my vision. "Hi," I say, smiling up at him.

"I forget you need more sleep than we do. I'll get you back to the cottage, so you can rest," Reed says, scooping me up off the ground and brushing the snow off me like I am a child. I smile at him and think that there isn't anything I wouldn't do for him.

Reed flies me back to the cottage and the bliss of being held by him is enough to keep me awake until we arrive. I don't have much energy left in me for more than a good night kiss at the doorway of my room. I stumble in and change before crashing beneath the warm comforter on my soft bed.

CHAPTER 4

Snowboarding

The angels surrounding me are making me feel off kilter; their actions remind me of lethal soldier wasps, like I am trapped inside of a hive with the swarm. Stirred into a frenzied commotion by an invader, me, these angels aren't even attempting to veil their hostility. But, something's missing—it is the sound that should accompany such a scene. It lacks the humming buzz that would reveal this place for what it truly is, a horrifying nest of killers.

Walking forward, my heart hammers in my chest as a soldier behind me prods me to follow the Power angels ahead of us. They are moving slowly, disturbed by my presence, and therefore, inclined to cast haunted glances in my direction. A low, angry growl escapes from one of them as his eyes fall on me, making certain that I am still following them. He is having trouble reconciling what it is he sees trailing him. Since I am beyond caring about what any of them thinks of me, I ignore him to reserve all my strength for what lies ahead—my execution.

As they lead me further into an exquisite, Renaissance-style reception room, we walk to a set of double doors near the back. These doors, it appears, will take us deeper into the "hive." Glancing around the museum-like chamber, I notice a beautiful gilded mirror encompassing a large portion of the foyer. Spying my reflection within the glass, I pause. I no longer look like me—the image in the mirror isn't a girl—she is a Seraph with crimson wings, fiery auburn hair, and the fierce expression of an avenging angel.

I awake from the nightmare with the worst sense of dread that I've ever felt. The fear that this nightmare engenders can't compare with any that I've had thus far. Even though it lacks any of the gore of the others, there is such an intense sense of loss and finality to it that makes me feel like I'm drowning in grief—rage.

Stumbling out of bed disoriented, I shuffle to the kitchen of the small cottage to get a glass of water from the sink. As I sip it, I rub my hand over my forehead, trying to wipe away the images that still linger from the dream. Wondering how I'm ever going to go back to sleep after that dream, I hear Reed say, "That bad, huh?"

Startled by his voice, I drop my glass. But, the glass doesn't shatter because Reed is in front of me in an instant. He catches it before it hits the ground without spilling a drop of water. "You scared me. I thought you were asleep." I say, recovering from the shock of seeing him defy gravity once again.

"I've already slept, but you've only been sleeping for four hours and twenty-seven minutes so that means you need to go back to bed," he says as he sets the glass on the counter.

"How long did you sleep?" I ask, smiling at the accuracy of my precisely estimated sleep time.

"Two hours and thirteen minutes. I slept in because I was really tired," he says seriously, which makes my smile deepen as I shake my head at him. How nice it would be to be able to consider a two-hour nap "sleeping in."

"Are Buns and Zephyr sleeping?" I ask, because it's suspiciously quiet in the cottage with no noises coming from the back bedroom.

"No, they went out for another session when they got up," he replies.

"Oh, you should've gone with them, instead of sitting around waiting for me to get up," I say, walking over to the couch and sitting down facing the fire. I pull one of the throw pillows into my arms, hugging it for comfort while I stare at the fire crackling in the grate. Reed sits down next to me on the couch with his body angled toward me.

"Why would I do that when you're here?" he asks, sounding serious. "So, are you going to tell me about it, or do I have to drag it out of you?"

"New one tonight—not the same one I've been having," I reply.

"Who are the players?" Reed asks, leaning forward with an intense expression.

"I'm not sure. No one I recognized—just me and a score or more of..." I trail off because I don't want to tell him.

"Of what?" he asks succinctly.

"Powers," I say with reluctance.

"Fallen?" he asks the moment I answer him.

"Maybe, I'm not sure, but...there was no gross smell, you know, like before when I dreamt of them. No, this was different," I say, thinking of how to describe it to him. "It was like being a bee flying into a wasp's nest. You pretty much know you're dead; you're just not sure when or from what angle the sting is going to come."

He recoils a little when I say this. "Am I there?" he asks, sounding tense. I shake my head no and watch his frown deepen into a scowl as his jaw tenses. "Describe the surroundings for me. What is the terrain like? Do you have access to any weapons? Are you restrained in any way?" he asks in rapid-fire succession.

"Renaissance-style reception area with what I imagine are crystal chandeliers and gilded everything. There were exquisite rugs on gleaming marble floors and heavy brocaded curtains. Ceilings that would make the Sistine Chapel look like finger painting. No weapons that I can recall. I'm not restrained," I say, trying really hard to think. "And..."

"And?" he asks in a harsh tone.

"And I'm afraid, of course, and filled with dread, but even more than that, I'm just extremely pissed off," I reply, and anger is in my voice as I feel the residual rage from the dream.

"Pissed off?" he asks as if he doesn't know what the words means.

"Yeah, like 'avenging angel' pissed," I say, staring at him. "Like I might just see how many I can take with me on the way out." I say, feeling again the echoing anger.

"Yes. I know the kind of pissed off you are talking about," he says thoughtfully. The way that he said it, with such earnestness, makes me smile again despite the grimness of the topic. "Is evasion possible?" he asks. "Where are the exits? Are they guarded?"

I try to think again of the scene in my dream. "There are angels everywhere...I don't think evasion is possible. I had guards in front of me and behind, like an unfriendly escort."

"Escort?" he asks, pouncing on the word. "Are they taking you somewhere?"

"More like leading because I'm operating under my own power," I reply.

"Where are you going?" he asks.

"I don't know, but..."

"But?" he asks.

"But, I want to go—I need to go faster. I feel like they're too slow because they keep looking at me like they're looking at a train wreck or something and can't look away," I say, trying to read the looks on the angels' faces in my mind.

"Why are you there?" Reed asks, and I see he is losing the battle to keep the anger from his voice.

"I don't know," I reply with honesty.

"Evie, this scenario doesn't sound like our strategy at all to me."

he says accusingly.

"Our strategy? What's our strategy?" I ask him, feeling stumped.

"Evasion. You, running like the wind away from all kinds of angels," he says slowly, so that I will hear every word clearly.

"Oh, yeah right, my bad, you mean the 'sell out strategy' where I place myself above everyone and everything else—that strategy?" I reply with sarcasm.

"Evie." Reed's tone is harsh as if he can't stop my name from exiting his mouth. I don't want to fight with him so I turn toward him instead, scooting down the couch so that I can lean up against his side. In an instant, his arms are around me, hugging me close to him. "You have to run if you get a chance. I can take care of whatever comes when you are safely away from the situation," he says, and I close my eyes, thinking about what he's saying.

"Reed," I say, "the only way that evasion will work for me, is if I don't have to leave you holding the bag."

"What do you mean by 'holding the bag,'" he asks in confusion.

"If I'm running away and leaving you behind to deal with the threat, then that means I'm leaving you holding the bag—I leave you to face the danger that is meant for me," I explain solemnly.

"I'm a Power, I live for danger—I crave it. It's in my blood. That's why I'm perfect for you. You attract danger and I'll deal with it," he says seriously.

I flinch. "You're in love with me because I'm a danger magnet?" I ask.

"No, I'm in love with you for who you are, which is the most extraordinary being I have ever known. The danger is just a perk," he replies.

"That's really sick, and not the good sick, I mean the bad kind of sick," I reply.

"Why is that sick? I'm just now beginning to see why I might be the one who is truly meant for you, for now anyway, because of what I am. I'm capable of protecting you," he says, holding me close to him.

"How do I protect you then?" I ask, snuggling against his chest.

"I thought I had explained to you that I don't need protection," he says, stiffening.

"Okay…sheesh, don't get offended. You're the scariest angel I've ever beheld who never needs anyone else to defend him. Are you happy now?" I ask in exasperation.

"Yes, thank you," he replies, kissing the top of my head.

"So, you're attracted to the dangerous type? That's very interesting, since I, too, am attracted to the dangerous type," I say, tracing the pattern on his t-shirt with my fingertip.

"See, we're perfect for each other," he replies, and there is satisfaction in his voice. He radiates warmth and I smile sleepily when I realize how nice it is that I don't need to convince him anymore that he is meant for me. He picks me up and heads to my bedroom. "You need to sleep now. There is a big day ahead of us, if I know anything about Buns and her sense of celebration."

"It's New Year's Eve!" I say in surprise. Time just doesn't seem to mean anything to me anymore, since I'm not as subject to it. Learning that I am an eternal being has done funny things to my priorities and concept of what is important. He places me on the big bed in my room and I scoot over immediately so that he can get in next to me.

"I'll fall asleep faster if you stay with me," I smile, watching him deliberate before caving in to my request and crawling into bed next to me. I snuggle next to his side.

"Only if you promise to sleep. Buns will not be held at bay when it comes to the party tonight. You have to be ready for anything," he says, smiling. So I am good and I sleep.

∾

"Sweetie, get up and come out to the kitchen. Breakfast has arrived and I need you to pick out an outfit for tonight," Buns says as she breezes into my room.

"Buns, what are you talking about?" I ask her, rubbing my eyes.

"You'll see," she says, handing me a cup of coffee before leaving the room. I get out of bed, shower and style my hair before leaving my room. A light meal of fruit and croissants is waiting for me in the kitchen. As I eat, I watch Buns roll a garment rack full of dresses toward where I am. I glance at the rack questioningly, and then at Buns. Zephyr chuckles in the main room as the angels all watch me curiously.

"What's this?" I ask as I push away from the counter to investigate the garment rack. Dozens of designer dresses flow off of hangers like silken liquid works of art.

"You have to pick one for tonight. There is a party at the lodge, champagne toast at midnight type thing. Not as exciting as fireworks on the pier, but it'll have to do for now," Buns says blandly.

"When did you have time to shop for all of these, Buns?" I ask, running my fingers lightly over the assortment of gowns.

Buns rolls her eyes at me then smiles. "I didn't shop for them. This is a VIP perk. Concierge Services sent them over when I told them what I needed. You just have to pick one," she says, watching me as I touch the dresses lightly.

"You guys *are* rock stars," I say under my breath, but when Zephyr laughs again I remind myself to stop doing that because they can hear me.

I shuffle through the dresses, which are all very lovely, and when I look up I notice Reed watching me. "Do you have a favorite?" I ask, curious to see if he has an opinion.

He seems surprised that I would ask his opinion. "What would I know about women's fashion?" he asks me as he comes to stand next to me by the rack of gowns.

"I don't know, you're male the last time I checked, so you probably at least know what you like when you see it. Do you see anything you like?" I ask again to see what he will do. His eyes scan over the dresses and there is one in particular that they rest on longer than the others. It's silk and champagne in color with a strapless corset bodice and a long flowing skirt that would hug every curve I have all the way to the floor. "This one?" I ask, pulling it from the rack and holding it up for him to look at. His body stills as he scans it, and then he shrugs, as if he is indifferent to the dress. Something about his demeanor lets me know that he is far from indifferent to this particular dress.

Smiling to myself I head toward the bedroom with it, calling over my shoulder, "Buns, will you help me try this on?"

"Sure, sweetie," Buns says, following me to my room. I change into the dress and I am amazed at my reflection in the mirror. Its effect is elegant and sophisticated, making me look older. The color of the dress is just a few shades darker than my skin so the color doesn't conflict with the fiery tones in my hair. "I don't think you have to try on any more dresses, sweetie. This is it," Buns says. "But, don't take my word for it. Go show Reed," she says, smiling.

I step out of the bedroom and into the main room where Zephyr and Reed are quietly talking about the logistics of security tonight at the lodge. They are near the fire and when I approach the couch, whatever Reed was about to tell Zephyr is clearly forgotten as he stares at me.

"That is a pretty dress," Zephyr says kindly when Reed is silent. Reed growls at Zephyr and my eyes widen as Zephyr cracks a huge smile. Turning toward Reed, he says, "I'm only stating the obvious."

"Do you like it?" I ask Reed, as he rises from the sofa slowly and begins to circle me like a predator casing its victim with cool precision. Feeling the tension and restraint in his movements as he circles me, I can't help the small shiver that escapes me.

"You look exquisite…and delicate," Reed replies, while he approaches me from behind. The heat from his body radiates toward me as he breathes softly on my neck, "Too fragile for your own good," he whispers.

"Are you calling me flimsy?" I ask, and then bite my bottom lip as he runs his fingertip lightly over the top of my shoulder to the slope of my arm.

"No, I'm telling you that you are in jeopardy," he replies with tension in his voice as he lifts his hand from me.

"This dress places me at risk, huh?" I ask in a teasing way. "Do Seraphim angels usually let you get away with talking to them like that, or are you just taking advantage of my generous nature?"

"It is always a risk where Seraphim are concerned, but well worth the danger," he replies.

Buns sighs, saying, "Ugh, I can't wait until you evolve, sweetie, the tension is killing me." She pulls me away from Reed who looks unwilling to let me go. "We have a spa appointment at the lodge and we're not missing it. I'll look after Evie while you guys go and do whatever it is you do," Buns says in a dismissive tone as she leads me back to the bedroom to change.

Buns drives us up to the lodge for our spa appointment, and after being scrubbed, rubbed, plucked, waxed and exfoliated, I sit next to Buns in a big comfy chair and watch as the nail-tech applies a second coat of dark red paint to my toenails. I am suddenly curious about something when I watch the woman apply a coat of gold paint to Buns's nails. "So, JT never had a chance, huh?" I ask, smiling at Buns.

"Poor JT. He's so cute, but a little too breakable for me," she says, smiling. I know exactly what she means. JT is too human for Buns. "Plus, Zee showed up and that was kind of it for me," she says, while leaning her head against the plush seatback of her chair.

"I knew you and Brownie liked him, but I didn't know how much," I say, remembering their rock star bedroom makeover and blushing a little.

"What's not to like, I mean he is a Power…ful guy," Buns replies, looking at the woman painting her nails and trying to be cryptic. "And those blue eyes, have you ever seen eyes that blue?" she asks me. I shake my head, remembering the first time I saw Zephyr's eyes. I had fled from the angels at the Delt house only to find myself alone with Zephyr at Reed's house. Even then, I thought he was amazing looking…for a killer.

"Aren't you worried about him? I mean, if you guys are hanging out with me it could get…interesting if things start *fallen* apart," I say, attempting to be discreet.

Buns rolls her eyes at me and replies, "That is part of why I like him because he understands what you mean to me."

"What do I mean to you, Buns?" I ask.

"You are my family, sweetie: you and Brownie. But, I guess we are going to have to expand it to make room for Russell, Zee and ugh, though I hate to admit it…Reed. He has grown on me. He is not as boring as I thought he was, but I really think it's because you gave him an upgrade," she says grudgingly.

"Yes, we are family," I say with my eyes filling up with tears.

"It took me a very long time to find you guys. I've been alone for ages. I'm not giving you up without a fight. Just keep that in mind, you with the sad eyes," she says in a motherly way. "Maybe when you get past some of this sorrow, you'll be able to see that this is just the beginning, not the end."

"Have you ever had a family before, Buns?" I ask her in a taut voice, remembering that Charlie and Elise are not real people, but Buns's imaginary family that she made up so that I wouldn't suspect that she is an angel.

"No," she says. "I've always had a purpose and that seemed to be enough for me until recently. Brownie and I met at Crestwood and we just connected, like sisters I think, and then you came along and you were special," she says with a wink because "special" is such an understatement. "It's almost like I have a new purpose now."

Our toenails, having received a topcoat, are now being allowed to air dry as the attendants walk away to assist other clients. "Don't you find that strange?" I ask, remembering what Reed had said to me in the car. "Reed said that you don't seem to act like other Reapers."

"Reed is observant…it's interesting that he picked up on something like that. Well, I've always felt like a fish out of water when I'm with other Reapers. Angels of my ilk are often enormously cheerful and never ready to mix it up. I sometimes wonder if I'm really meant to be an angel of death or if there'll be another purpose for me," she says wistfully, and then smiles at me. "Then I met Brownie and we were so much alike—always ready to set if off at a moments notice. I believe we were sent to protect you and so does Brownie. Maybe Brownie and I are meant to be your guardian angels when you need us. I don't know because no one in Paradise is talking to us directly. We have not been called to know what the plan is for you."

"How does that work, Buns? How do you transfer the souls to Heaven if you are not speaking with them directly?" I ask in curiosity.

Buns reaches over and pats the top of my hand with her own. "I can't tell you, but someday you'll see," she says with confidence.

I remember all the souls that had been trapped with Russell and me at the 7-Eleven a couple months ago and I shiver. "I can wait," I say in a low voice. "So you were alone for a long time before Brownie and I came along? What was your life like, Buns?"

"Oh, it has always been an adventure. I feel like an explorer at times. I'm very young by the standards of most angels. I've only been here for a little over a millennium. Zee and Reed have been here so much longer than me…" she trails off, thinking.

"How long do you think it's been?" I ask, trying not to let on that I am wigging out over the fact that she is over a thousand years old.

"I really don't know. It's funny, but time didn't ever mean very much to me in Paradise, and then I got here and it took me a while to adjust to the concept of time. But, I've heard human scientists estimate that the Earth is approximately four and a half billion-years-old," she replies. I think I stopped breathing then, as my eyes grow wide and I stare at her face.

"Are you trippin'?" she asks, trying to hide her smile from me. I just nod because there are so many things about that vast amount of time that disturbs me. "Sweetie, science is not always an exact…well, science," Buns says in a reassuring way. "They thought the Earth was flat for a while, too."

"So you're saying they're wrong?" I ask.

"No, I'm saying they may not be right," she smiles at me when I shake my head in frustration. "You could ask Reed how old he is. He might know," Buns says with enthusiasm.

The ridiculousness of that statement is enough to have me frowning at her as I ask, "When would anyone answer that question honestly? I mean, my neighbor's mom still lies about her age any chance she gets and she is somewhere in her mid forties. I can't imagine anyone willingly telling someone else that they are four billion-years-old."

"I doubt he is four billion-years-old, Evie. He lived in Paradise for a while before being sent here, so he must be much older than that," Buns says pleasantly.

"Buns, stop talking. I don't want to know anymore," I say briskly, trying to wave a piece of paper over my toes to make them dry faster.

"Evie, now do you see just how special you are?" Buns asks as she watches me from the seat next to me. "Can you fathom all of the creatures who have inhabited the Earth along with man throughout time and you are the most extraordinary thing any of us has ever seen."

"What do you mean, Buns? What other creatures have lived along-side man?" I ask, honing in on the bit of information she let slip.

"Let's just say that some fairytales aren't delusions," she says, wiggling her toes to see if they are dry enough to slip on her sandals.

"What?" I ask, shifting forward in my seat so that I can see her face better. "Which fairytales are true?" I ask in an urgent tone.

"Pretty much all of them," Buns says casually. "Don't freak out, Evie. A lot of those creatures are extinct now and some found really remote places to hide." She blows lightly on her toes to try to get the last bit to dry faster.

"Name some that are extinct," I respond, trying to figure out if she is teasing me, but I'm not getting that vibe from her.

"Let's see...gorgons I'm pretty sure are extinct now, but I've seen some pretty hideous women lately that could use a spa treatment," she says, chuckling until she sees that I'm not laughing. "Okay, you are *way* too serious."

"Gorgons...like Medusa? Women who can look at you and turn a human to stone?" I ask for clarification.

"Yes. But they were gone before I got here," she shrugs.

"What else?" I ask.

"Well...we thought the Chupacabra were all gone, but I think maybe a few of them survived because there have been reports of them in Puerto Rico lately.

"You mean the little vicious creatures that people think are aliens?" I ask, looking around to see if anyone was within hearing distance.

"Yes. Not aliens, they've been around for a while," she says with unconcern.

"What's not extinct?" I ask as goose bumps rise on my arms.

"Well, you already met a drude," Buns says, and when she glances at me and sees that I don't understand her she adds, "A drude is a possessing demon from German folklore. In central Africa they are called the mbwiri. You call them 'shadow men,'" she says. I shiver, remembering just how I had met one yesterday. "The Germans and Danish also speak of erlkings who are supposed to be malevolent elfish creatures who inhabit forests and carry off travelers to their deaths...can you say Fallen?" Buns asks. "Just imagine what someone a couple of hundred years ago would think if Alfred showed up in the forest with his wings exposed and attacked them. They would think they were being jumped by a fairy king with dragonfly wings," she explains, and a violent ripple of fear courses through me. "La mojana,

I think is a Columbian folklore about shapeshifting water demons… let's just say, don't drink the water down there."

"Shapeshifters!" I explode and watch as every head in the spa turns in my direction. Buns hands me a fashion magazine while she holds one up to block her face from the other patrons in the spa.

Speaking in a low tone that only I can hear, she says, "Evie, I understand that this is difficult to comprehend, but is it really such a stretch if you think about it. You know that angels exist. If you look at some of the legends of several cultures, they all hold elements that point to our existence. Look closely and you'll see similarities between cultural folklore and all manner of creatures that date back untold centuries."

"How can you say that I am the most extraordinary being if there are shapeshifters out there?" I ask, pretending to look at the magazine.

"Evie. *I* can change my shape. You have seen me do it…the butterflies, remember?" Buns inquires and I am silent, remembering what she showed me yesterday. A blush stains my cheeks. I had witnessed her poof into a swarm of butterflies, but it hadn't struck me as being "shapeshifting." "Are you okay, sweetie?" Buns asks, seeing my reaction.

"Let me try to explain something to you, Buns. Until recently, I believed that I was entirely human. As a human, I accepted that I was the most powerful being on the planet—with the remote exception of running into a bear, mountain lion, alligator, or shark—all easily avoidable in most situations. The only thing I really had to fear was another human," I say.

"Sweetie, you really should've had a healthy respect for weather, too, because that is what usually wipes out civilizations faster than even plagues, which by the way, are scarier than sharks," Buns replies. When she sees the frown on my face she says, "What? I'm just saying that bacteria is not a human's friend either."

"So now," I continue on as if she hadn't interrupted me, "I find out that there could be a giant out there who would want to 'grind my bones to make his bread?'" I ask, quoting the old fable.

Buns wrinkles her nose at that. "Not on my watch," she says. "Plus, you are way faster than any giant. You are gonna be really hard to catch soon and almost impossible to contain. You'll be able to fly, run, shapeshift, and the strength you'll possess will rival the Powers. I would like to see a giant try to take you."

"So you are saying there *are* giants," I reply, cringing.

"Evie, relax—you worry too much," Buns says, kicking back and sipping on the ice tea she had been given earlier.

"Relax? Oh, I'm relaxed. I'll just let you break the news to Russell and see how he takes it," I reply tensely, and the thought of Russell sends a pang of longing through me that I wasn't at all expecting. *I miss him, I think. I forgot that I now have someone who I can share all of this with because he is kind of in the same boat…he is the only being like me in the universe. I wonder how he'll take the news that fairytales are real. Maybe he already figured it out. I wonder how he is taking it. Is he a prisoner to it or will he be carried through it…transcend it?*

A crushing wave of guilt that I have been able to keep at bay since we left Crestwood comes down like a heavy weight on me. I haven't been looking out for Russell. I have let everyone else take care of him while I have wallowed in sadness. I suddenly feel very old again, but not wise. If the situation was reversed, I know in my heart that he would've done a better job taking care of me, than I have done for him.

I can't let go of him, that much is clear. I can still feel what it was like to kneel on the cold, hard tile floor in the 7-Eleven, beside his still body, watching his hands turn blue as his blood seeped out of him. I remember praying to God not to take him away from me. Russell is my family every bit as much as Uncle Jim was my family, but it's different. Russell has *always* been my family in a way that Uncle Jim was not. I don't love Uncle Jim any less than I love Russell; I just have a feeling that I have loved Russell longer…infinitely longer. He is my soul mate. No matter where he is in the world, there will be a piece of me that will always want to search for him.

Buns pinches my arm. "Owa! What?" I demand as she grins next to me.

"Sweetie, are you ready?" Buns asks.

"Yeah. You didn't have to pinch me," I reply, rubbing my upper arm to ease the sting.

"You were so far away I couldn't get your attention. I promised Reed I would have you back this afternoon so he can go boarding with you before we have to change for tonight. He is probably pacing the cottage waiting for you," she says, gathering up all of the products that she had bought. I had laughed at her when she had let the lady sell her wrinkle cream, but I think it's her way of helping out the humans without getting in trouble for it. "What were you thinking about anyway?"

"I was thinking about Russell," I reply, trying hard to hide what I am thinking.

"Ah, I see. You had the sad eyes again," she says, looking at me.

"He's going to be okay, you know? He is a Seraph, which makes him tough. He'll adjust."

"I hope you're right," I say.

"I know I'm right. He'll have to adjust or we'll throw him to the mermaids," Buns replies, clutching an armload of beauty products and walking toward the door. It takes me a second to close my mouth and follow her out.

When we get back to the cottage, Reed isn't exactly pacing, but he does seem relieved to see us. "How was the spa?" Reed asks when I put my packages down on the counter in the kitchen.

"Very enlightening. Did you know that Earth is estimated to be about four point five billion-years-old and fairytale creatures exist?" I inquire, putting my hands on my hips and scanning his lovely face that could maybe pass for twenty, possibly twenty-one at the oldest if I take into account that he has a perfect physique.

"Is that right?" Reed counters as he follows me into the kitchen and wraps his arms around my waist. "So what does that mean to you?" he asks as his lips skim mine lightly, more of a caress than a kiss.

"It means you're scary old," I whisper, leaning into his body that feels firm and strong against mine.

"Yes," he agrees, nuzzling my neck. "I am ancient."

"A relic," I tease as shivers of desire flow through me. "Old enough to know better than to get mixed up with someone like me."

"There is no one else like you," he replies in a low tone, and then he kisses me and whatever it was I was thinking about flies right out the window as my arms go around his neck. "Maybe we should go boarding now. I think Zephyr missed Buns while you were gone," Reed says as he pulls back from our embrace and plants a kiss on my cheek. "Let's go get ready," he says, leading me back to my bedroom.

I change and meet him in the main room. Not long after, I hear the crash coming from the bedroom next to mine. Rolling my eyes at Reed, I say, "I can't wait to wreck the bedroom with you."

"You have no idea the amount of damage we will do. We will have to find someplace that we won't want to return to for several years until the staff gets turned over and they forget about us," he says, smiling down at me.

Walking through the woods, arm-in-arm with Reed, I am assailed once again by the beauty and majesty of the place. The woods feel charmed with all of its old trees and while we wind our way through them, I have no trouble believing what Buns had said earlier, that most of the creatures I believed to be mythical are real.

"Why didn't you tell me that there are other creatures that exist beside humans?" I ask in the muffled silence of the forest.

"Because you were having a hard time with just the angel part being real, so I didn't want to confuse the matter by laying it all out at once," Reed replies, frowning. "Evie, I have a need to protect you that I cannot even explain to myself. I want to make sure you are ready to know about things like that before I just blurt them out."

"Oh," I say, thinking. "That makes sense. It's just that, sometimes, I feel like everyone is holding out on me. Sometimes it's nice to know about things before I run into them. Take you, for example. It may have been extremely helpful to have known you were an angel when I met you."

"You have enough to worry about without adding to it. How many nightmares are you capable of bearing?" he asks with concern.

"I think I can handle knowing some things. I won't know until you tell me," I reply, trying to be logical about it.

"Many legends are created to explain the existence of divine angels or fallen angels. There are names for us in every culture in every language in this world. There are other creatures, it's true, but angels are the deadliest. The Cherokee have several creatures that describe the Fallen. A 'Raven Mocker' is a demon that is said to steal a human soul and devour it so that it can gain immortality. They didn't get it quite right, but they were close, wouldn't you say?" he asks as we emerge from the woods and into the waning light of the late afternoon sun.

"Why did they call it a Raven Mocker?" I ask, puzzled.

"Because angels never grow old and die, so they are never food for the ravens," he explains.

"I see, you could say that we mock a mocking bird. Now that's ironic," I reply.

We make it to the gondola lift and stand in line in front of a group of young girls who can't be older than twelve or thirteen years old. They each carry their snowboards with them. They sit across from us on the gondola as we lift slowly up the slope. I sit next to Reed as he holds my hand in his. I watch the girls stare at Reed and me, giggling and whispering loudly behind their hands about how gorgeous Reed is. I duck my head and bite my lip, trying not to laugh, as Reed's eyes grow wider at their antics. Finally, one of the more vocal girls asks us, "Are you guys models or something?"

"Uh, no," I reply, trying to contain my laughter, so that I won't offend her.

"Are you sure?" she asks in suspicion, giving us both a scrutinizing glare. "Because your boyfriend is even hotter than the other guy that we just rode up with on our last run." I squeeze Reed's hand because I love this little girl. She is hysterical.

Her friend nudges her and rolls her eyes saying, "Oh my God, Stacy." But Stacy ignores her and continues to stare at Reed and me.

"Really? Do you think so? Because I think he is the best looking guy I ever met." I say in a confidential tone of voice and watch as every set of eyes rivets on Reed once again.

"Are you gonna marry him?" Stacy asks me boldly, as she tears her gaze away from Reed to look at me. There is more giggling from the other girls as they continue to stare at Reed.

"Uh..." I stammer, because I am wholly unprepared to field that particular question. I glance at Reed to see that he is studying me, awaiting my answer. "Well, he hasn't asked me to marry him, and since it's traditionally the man's job to ask, I'll just have to wait and see." I explain to them, grateful that we are nearing the top so that I won't have to field many more awkward questions.

My new best friend turns to Reed and says, "Are you gonna ask her to marry you? Because that other guy we rode up with is really super hot. He said he was a model," she says, and I just about die, trying to contain my laughter.

"No he didn't, Stacy. He said he was an angel, not a model," one of the other girls counters her friend. I freeze and out of the corner of my eye I see that Reed stills, too.

"Yeah, don't they model that underwear or something like that?" Stacy asks her friend.

Reed stands up and scans the top of the hill. I sit where I am, hoping that these girls are wrong. Reed turns back to the girls and says, "I am going to marry her, but I need your help. I don't want this guy up here to see her because she is so beautiful, he might try to take her away from me. Can you girls help me out?" he asks them with his sexy voice.

They all agree at once. Reed then says, "When the doors open, I want all of you to run out of the gondola and when you see the angel, I want you to run to him and scream, like he is your favorite pop star and you just have to get an autograph. Can you do that?" he asks them, and they all laugh like it is the best joke ever.

In a low tone that only I can hear, Reed says, "We get to test our new weapon. When we get to the top, wait for the girls and me to get off first, then go in the opposite direction. Run as fast as you can. Don't go back to the cottage. I don't know if we were followed or if this is random," he shoves his phone in the front pocket of my boarding pants, and then he pulls me to him in a bone-crushing hug while kissing my forehead. "Find a safe place to hide and I'll find you. Do you understand?" he asks, pulling me away from his body so that he can look in my eyes.

"What about you?" I ask, because he is going to be the one left holding the bag. What if this is an ambush and I'm leaving him to die?

"Evie, you *will* follow orders, do you understand?" he utters in a low tone again, this time he sounds like the Reed I had first met, the coolly polite, detached Reed.

"Yes," I reply, dying inside because I have put him in danger again, just by existing.

We reach the summit and enter the gondola house. "Here we go ladies, show me this hot model you saw," Reed says, casting one last grim glance in my direction as he leads the way off the lift. I exit not long after them, walking in the opposite direction. I can't help the fleeting look over my shoulder to see if I can see anything happening. Reed is watching the girls as they run toward someone. Turning in the opposite direction from them, I am poised to run when I notice someone directly in front of me.

"Excuse me," I say absently, keeping my head down to avoid being seen. I try to step around the person blocking me so that I can rocket off the summit and be gone before anyone sees me, but as I take a step to evade the person in front of me, the young woman counters so that she remains directly in my escape route.

A feeling of dread registers in me as I glance up at a very chicly clad female figure ahead of me. I have never seen an angel quite like this one before now. I realize that this angel must be a Power, like Reed had described to me. Although she is definitely female, she looks like she can tear down the sun with her bare hands. Her hair is dark and short, almost pixie-like in style, which is probably convenient when battling the Fallen because it doesn't give them anything to grab on to in a fight. She is as tall as Reed, and although she is beautiful, with flawless skin, hazel eyes that have a jewel-like quality to them, and a face that has a perfect sort of symmetry to it, there is an androgyny about her. It probably stems from the fact that she is built strictly as a warrior, and the purpose of being so minimizes her femininity, or it's the derisive look on her face that makes her completely lethal looking. Goose bumps rise on my arms when she whispers breathlessly, "Nephilim."

CHAPTER 5

Evasion

There is only one way I'm going to be able to avoid this Amazonian Power angel, I think as she stares down at me like I am her mortal enemy. *I have to wait for my moment,* I reason. A bead of sweat slides down the side of my face. Only an eighth of a second elapses, but it feels like an eternity is spent gazing up into her eyes that are probably debating my weakest points and killing scenarios.

All of my senses come to life in that moment. I know what an antelope feels while it is staring into the eyes of a lioness: raw fear is pumping my heart in an ever-increasing tempo; the scent of this Power is assailing my olfactory and imprinting in my mind; and my muscles are growing taut in anticipation of flight that will trigger when a strategy can be worked out in my mind. It is all of that, mixed with my surroundings, that makes me feel disoriented.

Standing on the apex of a ski slope, I am aware that the humans around me have no idea that there is anything unusual occurring in their midst. Hearing the happy chatter and garish laugher from people enjoying an outing with their families, I understand that they are unaware of the chaos that is overtaking my world.

I think about my strategy in the fraction of a second I have been given, remembering what I have learned in field hockey about misleading my opponents. The direction of the eye can be misleading. I try to show her the direction I want her to think I'm going by glancing to her right. That direction will take me back down the hill to where we had boarded the gondola. When the girls begin to scream over my shoulder I do not hesitate for an instant. Instead, I put my head down and commit everything I have to going away from where I am looking to the opposite side of the slope. Since she is unprepared for the distraction of screaming adolescent girls, she momentarily loses her focus on me for long enough, that when she does recover, she instinctually turns in the direction I had shown her earlier with my eyes.

Instinct takes over then as I escape from the crest of the hill. There is no thought to what I am doing other than concentrating on running as fast and as efficiently as I possibly can. I make it several hundred yards before I realize that I am running straight down the backside of the hill in the open where I can be clearly seem from above. I revise my path when I see that I am parallel with a dense copse of pine trees. I cut through the first thicket that I find. It is blanketed by heavy snow that deadens the sound so that all I hear at first is the light fluttering movements of my feet and my steady breathing. Moments after I enter under the cover of branches, the loud sound of cracking and pitching comes from the trees above my head. Snow is being flung down from the branches directly behind me. I only spare the briefest of glances over my shoulder to the tops of trees I have just passed to see a figure of an angel skimming a path along the tree line above me.

The breaking of tree branches, so close, drives panic straight into my heart as I feel her all around me, coming for me. Something drops with a heavy thud behind me, but I don't spare a glance over my shoulder to see what it is. Then a whistling sound pierces the quiet woods as something rockets past my ear and embeds itself in the tree just on my right. It is the branch of another tree that had been stripped off and used as a spear in an attempt to impale me.

I whimper as my heart leaps into my throat. My wings fly out of my back, tearing my coat away and leaving it in tatters on the ground behind me. *I have to make it harder for her,* I think as I notice that it is growing darker to the left of me. I turn in that direction, knowing that it is darker because the trees are thicker, and therefore, harder to negotiate from above. Not only that, it cuts off her view of me so it might force her to run instead of fly or she will risk losing me.

My strategy is working well and I know it because nothing has killed me yet, that is until I hear a tree being uprooted about a hundred yards behind me. It is then hurled into other pines near me on my right. A deafening noise careens through the woods, as the enormous branches crash into several more trees, causing them to splinter and snap like an avalanche of falling wood. Huge pines are tumbling down like dominoes and I have to veer to the left sharply to avoid being smashed by the sheered off cap of one of those large trees. Fear bolts through me, causing me to increase the speed at which I flee from her. I'm pretty sure she hasn't seen me and is only hoping to get lucky with a wild pitch because if she had seen me, that pine tree would have flattened me like road kill.

I slow my pace a little when I hear a scream behind me. It is a scream of rage and it chills me, sending shivers down my spine. Then, a feminine voice calls out over the distance that is growing more steadily with every step I take, "I WILL FIND YOU NEPHILIM, AND I WILL RIP OUT YOUR EVIL HEART!" She continues yelling her head off, but I can't understand anymore of what she says because she is now speaking in Angel and getting further and further away as I pick up my pace again.

After that, I don't allow myself to think of anything but the terrain ahead of me. When I need to jump over ledges and streams, I do it, never hesitating or allowing doubt or fear to intrude on my mission. I don't know how long I have actually been running without looking over my shoulder, but it is dark when I do look back to see if she is behind me. Still hidden by a thick canopy of branches above me, I slow to take stock of my surroundings. I faintly hear the engines of cars somewhere ahead of me, maybe a few miles away. If I shadow the road, there could be a place to hide out for a while. I could get a clear read on where I am and then call Reed to extract me—if he is okay. That last thought sends a wave of nausea through me. He has to be okay or it is over for me.

Pushing myself to keep going, I follow the sound of the cars to a snow covered two-lane road. I don't leave the cover of the trees, but trudge along, following the tree line near the road. The cold is beginning to register with me now, and I hug my arms to my body, trying to retain some body heat. My skin is thicker now so it's keeping the worst of the frigid air from sending me into hypothermia, but it doesn't feel pleasant to be out here without my coat, which had been ripped apart and left behind me.

Glowing lights ahead indicate the existence of a town so I stay hidden in the trees until I near it. I have to make a decision whether to risk leaving the woods to find a place to hide, or stay where I am and follow the woods further. The trembling of my hands makes the decision for me. I have to find shelter soon to warm up, and I need to find out where I am so that I can contact Reed. I cautiously leave the shelter of the trees, scanning and mapping every living thing around me. Staying well back from the road, I travel to the town's limits and read the sign that welcomes me to Ames, Home of the Happy Folk and the 1994 State Champion Lumberjack Team. Normally, that would have made me smile, but under the circumstances, I'm just numb.

Right before I near the first streetlight overhead, I become aware that my wings are still out so I pause in my tracks to debate what to do next. I have to get them to go back in somehow, before someone in Ames sees me and alerts the media. Anxiety is not going to make this easy on me. I'm so worried about what has happened back on the hill with Reed and the other angel that I can hardly breathe. Pulling his phone from my front pocket, I notice immediately that it's not on. It must have shut itself off at some point in my escape. I depress the power button and the screen brightly illuminates my face as the display indicates that there are 33 missed calls.

As I scroll through the missed calls, there are several made from my cell phone. Maybe Reed went back to the cottage and retrieved my phone to call me. There are several from Buns's and Zephyr's phones, too. They have been trying to get in touch with me for hours now. I check the time; it is almost nine o'clock, which means I have been running through the forest for at least four hours.

They must be insanely worried, I think, immediately dialing my number and hitting send. It is answered on the first ring, "Evie?" Reed asks, and his voice sounds different. It is his voice, but it has an edge to it that I recognize as the voice that I had first heard when I woke up after Alfred almost killed me.

"Reed, are you okay?" I ask because the pain in his voice scares me.

There is silence for a few moments then he says, "Yes. You?" he asks in a strained tone.

"Yeah. I'm okkkay. I'm in Ames. I jjjust got hhhere. I'm outside of the town bbbecause I can't get my wwwings to cccooperate yet. I'm a little cccold," I say as I realize that my teeth are chattering.

I hear Reed say "Ames" to someone he is with on the other end, maybe Zephyr and Buns. "Are you alone?" he asks in an efficient, military tone.

"Yeahhh," I reply as I quake a little from the cold.

"Why didn't you answer the phone?" he asks, beginning to sound more like himself.

"It was ttturned offff. I didn't know yyyou were tttrying to cccall mmme," I explain with my teeth still chattering. I try to clench them so they won't make any noise.

"Are you sure you're in Ames?" Reed asks me in the military voice again.

"Yesss. It's jjjust mmme and the hhhappy fffolk," I say ironically, scanning the area for the happy folk and not seeing anyone walking around, probably because it's freezing outside.

"The what?" Reed asks, sounding much better than he did a second ago.

"Nnnever mmmind, yyou'll know wwwhen you get hhhere. Wwwhen are yyyou cccoming?" I inquire, shivering.

"I'm already on the way. Zephyr and I are in your car and Buns is following us in the other car. Ames is over a hundred miles away according to our map, and there is no direct route there, so it's going to take us around an hour at least to get there. Is there somewhere you can go to wait for us and keep a low profile?"

It takes a minute for what he just said to register. "I'm a hhhundred mmmiles away ffffrom yyou?" I ask.

"Yes," he says.

"I rrran a hhhundred mmmiles?" I ask again for clarification and wonder just how long I have been stumbling around.

"Yes, you are getting better at following my orders. I said 'run' and you didn't disappoint me," he replies, like he's proud of me. "Next time, turn the phone on so that I know you're alive," he continues, and the strained voice is back.

"Ssure," I agree, feeling numb because I had no idea that I had gone that far to escape the angel chasing me. I bet if it had been on even terrain, I would be two hundred miles away and the thought floors me.

"Evie, is there anywhere you can go to warm up? I can hear your teeth chattering," Reed asks.

I scan the area. "Wwell, I hhhave sort of a ppproblem. I cccan't gget mmmy wwings to go bback in," I inform him, switching the phone to my other hand so that I can put the other hand under my armpit to warm it up a little.

"You just have to relax," he replies unhelpfully.

"Oh," I say because it is getting harder for me to concentrate on what he is saying. "Ookay. Mmmaybe if I jjjust sssit ddown hhere ffor a mmminute."

"NO! Don't sit down!" Reed almost yells into the phone. "Listen to me. You can't sit down. You'll get colder if you sit down," he says in a harsh tone.

"Okay," I agree, feeling the icy air blowing across my exposed skin. It's colder here than it had been in the forest. I stumble forward, trying to stay out of the glow of the streetlamp as I walk toward Ames.

"Are you relaxed enough now?" Reed asks.

"I don'ttt know. Lllet me tttry," I try, but my wings don't move.

"Evie?" Reed asks after a while.

"Wwhat?" I respond in confusion.

"Did it work?" he asks.

"Nnno," I reply, shivering.

"It doesn't matter. Just find somewhere you can warm up and I will be there soon and persuade the humans that they saw nothing," Reed says in a tense tone.

"Mmm nnnot sssupposed ta do dat," I reply, but it doesn't come out the way I think it should. It sounds slurred and mumbled.

"Evie, find someplace. *Now!*" Reed barks at me and I flinch.

"Kkkay." I agree and hang up the phone. I feel disoriented and I don't want to be yelled at so it makes perfect sense to me to hang up. I wander toward the light down the street, but when I get near it, it turns out to be a convenience store. The florescent lights glow evilly, making my head spin with flashes of pain and fear. I have to get away from it so I stay in the shadows across the street from the store and continue walking.

I pass by sandstone buildings with festive holiday displays still gracing the facades. The town of Ames has white, twinkle holiday lights wound in a serpentine pattern around each street lamp with wreaths gracing the tops. Golden bells and garlands are wrapped around wire and strung across the street, making a beautiful archway through the town. As I walk further along the sidewalk, I have to duck into a couple of the shadowy doorways of the closed store fronts to avoid being seen by the cars that drive past on the street. Everything seems to be closed for the night, probably because it's New Year's Eve and the happy folk have parties to attend.

The phone starts ringing. *Someone should answer that because it's getting annoying,* I think drunkenly, as I continue on to the center of town. I must have come upon some kind of town hall because there is a big WWII howitzer on the front lawn along with a Nativity scene, a gigantic lighted Menorah, and a Happy Kwanzaa sign. I approach the angel in the Nativity scene. It doesn't look like anyone I know. *They should get one that looks like Reed. Someone would steal it though...I would.*

Thumping sounds, coming to me from further down the street, distract me from the town hall's menagerie of holiday spirit. As I walk toward it, I ascertain that it is music coming from a club at the end of the street. The yellow-lighted sign outside reads, "Cowboys and Cowgirls–Welcome–Dollar Drafts 'til Midnight."

I duck into the alley near the front of the bar just as a laughing couple turns the corner and approaches the double wooden doors. Peeking around the corner at them, a cascade of warm air swirls outside in a rush when the man politely holds the door for his date. A sultry voice tumbles out the entrance accompanied by a hauntingly sweet guitar as they go inside. It's a man singing something about how he has got to run so he doesn't have to keep hiding. He doesn't want them to catch him—no.

I nod in silent agreement, understanding his problem. "You've got that right, pal," I mutter. "I don't want them to catch me either." The door swings shut again and the song is muffled.

I turn away from the bar and slip down the alley toward a parking lot at the back. *Something smells good,* I think, continuing down the alley and crossing over a darkened parking lot. It is the back door area of some kind of restaurant. Coming closer, it appears to be a diner. The back door is slightly ajar. I stay behind a van parked in the lot, watching an employee from the restaurant carry several large, black garbage bags to the dumpster. Heaving them in, the glass bottles clang loudly as they settle at the bottom of the dumpster. He pulls out a cigarette and lights it; smoking it quickly, he throws it away from him with a flick of his fingers as the ember glows orange.

The man goes back to the door before yelling to someone, "Yo, I'm outta here, see ya suckas next year…Happy New Year Daryl, Happy New Year Karen…Later!" He laughs and walks out the door and around the corner to his car. He fires up an old Pontiac and wheels it out of the parking lot while a loose belt in the engine screams in protest.

After he is gone, I walk up to the back door, feeling a trickle of warm air escaping from the portal he left ajar. It feels delicious. Pulling the door open, I am assailed by heat and the heavy odor of greasy comfort food. My stomach growls while I look around with jerking motions to see if anyone is in the back of the diner. It's a stockroom area and it appears to be empty. I step in and lean against the door to close it behind me.

The grill sizzles several yards ahead of me as someone flips whatever is being cooked with a metal spatula. I want to follow my impulse that is telling me to walk to the front and ask for some French fries. I resist doing that because there is a reason that I shouldn't, I just can't think of what that reason is at the moment. Noticing a door on my right, I push away from the one I was leaning against to open it. The door leads to some kind of employee break area with lockers, a broad laminate table with a couple of ash trays on it, folding chairs, and a small sofa that has been pushed against the far wall. Stepping into the room, I close the door just as the phone starts ringing again.

I have to stop the noise, so I push several buttons on it and say,

"Shh!" It stops ringing and I turn off the light, waiting a fraction of a second while my eyes adjust to the dark room. When I can see really well again, I sit down on the sofa, pulling my knees to my chest while hugging myself for warmth. I shiver violently as I breathe in deep gulps of warm air and exhale them haltingly. It takes me a while to realize that there is a voice speaking from the phone in my hand. I put it to my ear. Reed is saying something to me that I don't understand because he is speaking to me in Angel, in his sexiest voice. Sitting on the sofa, I listen to his voice weave like hypnotic music, calming me like a gentle lullaby.

Reed pauses in his recitation. "Wwhat'd yyyaa sssay?" I ask haltingly, because the violent shaking of my body is making it difficult to speak.

"Evie!" Reed sighs like he is vastly relieved about something. When I don't answer he asks, "Are you there?"

"Uh huh," I manage to say as another violent bout of shivers runs through me.

"Where are you?" he asks.

"Yyyou...ffirst," I reply.

"I was telling you all of the reasons I have for loving you," he says rapidly. "Now where are you?"

"Dinerrrr," I reply. "Ssnuck in ttthe bbbaack rrrrooomm."

"Is it warm?" he asks, sounding almost happy.

"Yesss," I say.

"I'm coming. Just stay there. We'll find you, do you understand?" he asks.

"Uh huh," I nod.

"How much charge does your phone have?" Reed asks.

"One bbbarr," I say after I look at the phone, noticing that it's nearly out of power.

"We will have to hang up then to conserve the battery, just in case we need it later to locate you," he says in frustration. "Just stay put, okay? I'm coming," he says again, and I know that this is somehow way worse for him than it is for me, since he is safe and I'm not.

"Sstaying pput. Sssee yyaa ssooonnn," I say before hanging up the phone.

"Are you cold, honey?" a feminine voice next to me asks. I jump in fear, springing up off the sofa and turning to see who had spoken to me. Just for a second, I thought it was the Power who had chased me down the hill and across country, but I realize that if it had been her, I would never have heard her speak. I would probably already be dead.

"I'm sorry. I didn't mean to scare you, dear. You go on and sit back down, I'm not going to hurt you," the older lady sitting in front of me smiles. She isn't that old, maybe in her fifties, with thin brown hair streaked with silver all pulled back in a French twist. She is wearing the restaurant diner attire of blue jeans, a black top, and a short black apron that has convenient pockets in the front to hold the order forms.

I just stare at her. She smiles again and pats the seat where I had been sitting. I want more than anything to sit back down where she indicated because my legs are shaking and I feel weak. "You're an angel," she says, more as a statement than a question. I nod. "You're wings gave it away," she says, pointing to my crimson appendages that I can't hide. "We don't get many like you around here," she says, and the twinkle in her brown eyes makes me relax a little. "There is usually a blanket in the last locker on the right," she says, indicating the locker by pointing to it. "You should get it. We use it when we do double shifts and there is enough of a lull to take a nap. I'm Brenda, by the way."

I stumble over to the locker Brenda had indicated, finding a folded blanket on the shelf. Pulling it down, I wrap it around me. It smells like French fries, which makes my stomach growl again. "You remind me of my daughter, Jenny. She works here, too, and she is never prepared for the weather either. I tell her she shouldn't leave the house without a coat, but she's young," Brenda says with a shrug of her shoulders. "Here, you have to sit down before you fall down, honey," Brenda says, scooting farther away down the sofa so that I have more room to sit. Tentatively, I sit down on the couch next to her. "Do you have a name?" Brenda asks pointedly.

"Evie," I say, snuggling further into the blanket.

"That's a pretty name," Brenda says. "I never knew anyone with that name. My ex-husband liked the name Jenny…I think he had an old girlfriend with that name, he was kind of a jerk like that," she says, shrugging again. "But that's okay. I like the name Jenny, too. Do you have an ex?" she inquires.

"No," I manage to say without stuttering. I'm warming up.

"Was that your boyfriend? On the phone?" she asks.

I nod.

"Is he coming to get you?" she asks in concern.

I nod again.

"Why were you out alone on a night like this, if you don't mind me asking?" she asks me warmly.

"It was kind of not my choice." I say in relief that I can answer her now without my teeth chattering. "I sort of have a few problems," I add honestly.

"Who doesn't, honey?" she asks conspiratorially. "Is this boyfriend of yours part of the problem, or is he helping you with it?" she wonders aloud.

"He's trying to help me with it but…" I trail off.

"But what?" her eyebrow arches.

"But I don't know if he can. The problem might be bigger than he is capable of handling and the closer he is to me, the more danger he is in." I reply, and being so honest with another person and hearing myself say the words aloud brings tears to my eyes. I remember watching Reed exit the gondola today to face the assassin that would have welcomed him with open arms, had it not been for me. I make them enemies. I make him suspect.

"I can't believe that you're the problem," Brenda says kindly.

"Believe it," I mutter. "I know what I should do to protect him, I'm just not sure I'm strong enough to do it."

"What do you think you should do?" she asks in confusion.

"I should leave him. I should go somewhere that he can't find me so that he will be safe from me. He would never willingly let me go, so I would have to run from him, too," I whisper, and the thought of doing that fills me with a sickness from which I'm not sure I will recover.

"Leaving him would protect him?" she asks, probably for clarification.

"Yes," I state. "At least, he would survive. I don't know if he would live though." If he feels half of what I feel for him, he may survive, but he will never live again.

"Honey, I don't pretend to know your situation, but if you want my advice, I'd be prepared for anything. You may never have to choose the option that you just agonized over, but if the day came when it became necessary, you would have a plan in place to execute and save the one you love," Brenda advises. She tries to rest her hand on my knee in a comforting way, but her hand goes right through my leg like an icy blast of air. I am so off guard that I can only sit and stare at Brenda.

"I tried to do that, you know, at the end. But, I didn't tell Jenny about my plans for her, so she never knew before I died," Brenda explains. "I made a will and left her the house, but my second husband didn't tell her. He kept my house and kicked her out."

I gasp as I realize what she is telling me. *Brenda is a soul. She's dead, why didn't I realize it? I must be really out of it,* I think, staring at Brenda. *Of course she's a soul. I'm sitting in the dark talking to someone who wouldn't be able to see me otherwise. She acted so casual when she realized that I'm an angel, probably because she's seen us before.*

"You didn't know I'm dead, did you, dear?" Brenda asks. I shake my head. "Are you new at this?" she asks with sympathy in her voice. I nod my head.

"Do you have a copy of your will somewhere?" I ask her, trying hard to recover.

"Yeah. I didn't trust my second husband, not after what the first husband put me through. I had more than one copy of it and put it in my locker here at work," she says excitedly, pointing to one of the lockers in the corner. "They didn't find it when they cleaned out my locker because it's stuck between the shelves in the back. Crystal took over my locker, that's her padlock on it. You probably can't get it open," she says disappointedly.

Getting up from the sofa, I drag the blanket with me over to the locker that Brenda indicated. The padlock is a combination. "Do you know her combination?" I ask. Brenda shakes her head in remorse. "Oh well, I guess Crystal is gonna have to make a trip to the hardware store, huh?" I say, before I yank hard on the lock, feeling the metal latch release from the casing without much resistance.

The rest of the lock looks smashed when I open my hand and I smile a little, seeing how strong I'm getting. Opening up the locker, I reach my hand to the back, feeling around until I locate a curled edge of a piece of paper. Gently, I dislodge it from the back of the locker without tearing it. Pulling it out, I scan the legal document, noting it is the last will and testament of Brenda Wilson.

"Which locker belongs to Jenny?" I ask. Brenda points to the one a few lockers down. "Should we leave a note on it?" I ask, looking around for a pen to write with. There are several in a plastic cup on the round table in the middle of the room. Plucking a pen out of the cup, I flip the will over to write on the back of it. I look at Brenda who watches me poised to write whatever she wants me to.

"Please write: Dear Jenny, Mommy loves you from the first day to the last and everyday in between, in this world and in the next." I write it on the back of the document. I go over to Jenny's locker and slip it in through the vent at the top of the locker door. I turn back to Brenda. Smiling broadly, she says, "Thank you."

"You're welcome." I reply.

"God's blessings on you, Evie," Brenda says. "I have to go now, they're calling me."

I can hear the whispering voices of a multitude speaking in unison but in their Angelic language. It is a hum, just a light melody whose vibrations are so soft and sweet that it makes me feel light inside, as if I'm floating, rising and falling gently on the waves of sound. It is compelling and I want to reach out and gravitate to wherever the music is coming from, but it's all around me, engulfing me in its cadence.

Brenda begins to flicker, as if she is a piece of film on a screen that isn't threaded correctly, so that she shimmers in bright flashes of light, and then fades rapidly. Her body maintains the same image of her from the front angle, but I notice when I tilt my head, she seems to be flat; she is no longer three-dimensional, but is now two-dimensional. Her features are fading, but her silhouette remains; it's as if she is made up of stars and galaxies all swirling around with pinpoints of light and dense darkness, like the night sky within the shape that used to be Brenda. The silhouette caves in on itself slowly, disappearing from sight in a pinpoint of darkness. There is no sound now, but I detect a lingering scent, if I can call it that. It's more like the way the air smells after a lightning storm. The smell of energy floats in the air, like pollen on a spring evening.

With the absence of the beautiful melody that had just filled me with feelings of joy and contentment, I begin to feel crushed and broken. Desolation sweeps through me. I have been given the barest insight of what others have referred to as Paradise, and the loss of it is leaving me feeling as if I'm bleeding inside. I feel vulgar and unwanted as if I was passed over like a piece of garbage.

"Evie?" Reed whispers from the doorway of the employee lounge. I want to answer him, but I can hardly breathe from despair. In confusion, I realize I'm lying on the floor looking up at the ceiling. "Evie..." Reed says, lifting me up and holding me in his arms.

"Reed, you smell that?" Zephyr asks darkly, sniffing the air. "It smells of transcendence. Is that possible?" he asks.

"Anything is possible when Evie is around. Can you find water and some sugar?" Reed asks Zephyr just as darkly, placing me on the couch while holding my face, tipping it up so that he can look in my eyes.

In seconds, Zephyr is back with a glass of water and a sugar dispenser. "How much sugar?" he asks, pouring a generous amount of sugar into the water.

"Good," Reed responds, propping my head up while holding the glass to my lips. "Drink this, Evie," he says. I struggle a little to fend off the water glass. I feel hopeless and I just want to be left alone to bleed, maybe if I bleed enough, the voices will come back for me. "You have to drink it, love," he insists before speaking to me in the lovely language he knows so well. I turn my head toward him as I drink the water he holds to my lips. "That's it, drink all of it," he says.

When I finish all of the water, Reed scoops me up again and we are outside under the starry night in a fraction of a second. Placing me gingerly in the front seat of the car, he belts me in. The heater vents are blasting out hot air and they are all pointed at me. Reed speaks briefly to Zephyr who gets into the car with Buns that is parked directly behind our vehicle. I barely notice when Reed pulls out of town, driving as fast as the car can go with no headlights on to alert others of our presence.

Feeling Reed's eyes on me, I look over at him, reaching my hand to place it on his hand. He grasps it tightly, bringing it to his lips, and kissing it hard. "Did a soul transcend in that room?" Reed asks me tensely, watching my face for my answer.

I nod and he closes his eyes briefly, and then he opens them again. "How?" he asks and I shrug. "Evie, it's not easy to be around a soul when it transcends. That is why Reaper angels are so bubbly and enthusiastic, so that when they are exposed to the loss of not going with the soul, it's bearable. You were way too close to it. It's like watching a black hole open up—it pulls energy into it as it prepares for the journey—it will take some of your energy with it if you get too near to it. Did you feel sad?" he asks me and I have to turn away from him, so he won't see how wrecked I feel inside from being denied entrance to the bliss I had glimpsed. I nod because I can't speak.

"Even I would feel sad, if I had been there. You feel left behind— unworthy to be called—that is normal, it just wasn't your time to go… and I'm grateful that it was not your time," Reed admits. I glance at him silently again. "I feel very selfish for saying that out loud, but I don't know what I'd do if you had gone tonight."

I watch him grip the steering wheel tensely, as if he truly does feel shame for thinking that thought. I click the button to release my seatbelt and crawl over the center console to sit in Reed's lap. I rest my head next to his and kiss his cheek softly when I feel his arm wrap around me, pulling me to him.

"I don't want to go anywhere without you," I say honestly, and I feel selfish because I know that if I had gone tonight with Brenda, it would probably be the best thing for Reed. He wouldn't be in danger anymore, well, no more danger than he usually is in while battling the Fallen. He wouldn't be in danger from divine angels, too.

"Good," Reed says in relief. "What do you want?" he asks me in a serious tone.

"You—and some French fries," I say in an equally serious tone as my stomach growls. "And a chocolate milkshake," I add. I want so much more than that. I want him to be safe. I want to be safe. I want the cottage in the woods with Reed and maybe some children and a life—or an eternity and I want Zephyr and Buns and Brownie to be with us always and I want…Russell. And, now that I have felt Paradise, I want that desperately, too. But, if I can only have one of those things, then I want Reed.

I think my answer is so unexpected that Reed can't help but laugh. "You are hungry?" he asks, smiling. I nod. Reed pulls out my cell phone from his pocket and makes a call. "We have to make an unscheduled stop…French fries…" he says.

"And a chocolate milkshake," I remind him and see him smile a little more.

"And a chocolate milkshake. We will park and you order," Reed says. We find a fast food restaurant and Reed parks the car while Zephyr and Buns pull through the drive thru window. In typical angel excess, Zephyr delivers more than I asked for. There are several burgers, sandwiches, pies, and six large orders of fries. I also get my shake, which I am truly grateful for. We don't wait to get back on the road, but are off as soon as Zephyr is back in the other car. I offer some fries to Reed who eyes them suspiciously before taking a few and eating them.

"Where are we going?" I ask, since I'm pretty sure we aren't going to the champagne toast at the lodge.

"Home," Reed says.

"Is that a good idea?" I ask, shivering a little when I think of the hostile Power that threatened to rip out my heart.

"They don't know who we are. Zephyr and I planned for this and did not use plastic or our real identities. Everything was cash and alias identification."

I think about that for a second, about what happened on the hill. Reed is being quiet about it, like he doesn't want to talk about it or something. I eat some more fries, watching him, and then I ask him, "What's a Nephilim?"

The car gently loses acceleration as Reed lifts his foot off the pedal. He doesn't look at me, but straight ahead into the darkness and his face loses all color. He looks furious. "What did you say?" he asks me quietly. I stop chewing my fries and swallow hard because I didn't mean to say the wrong thing, but apparently I have. When I don't answer him, he asks, "Where did you hear that word?"

"The other Power called me a Nephilim right before she told me she was going to rip out my evil heart," I reply, hoping I'm not going to make him angrier by telling him that.

"The other Power? There was one that followed you?" he asks. We are just drifting on the road now, decelerating rapidly. The phone starts ringing, but Reed doesn't make a move to answer it. He pulls to the side of the road and puts the car in park.

I am beginning to get really afraid now. He is freaking out, in the quiet way that Reed freaks out, and it's making me freak out. "Uh huh," I manage. "That's probably why I ran a hundred miles. I didn't want her to rip out my evil heart."

"Your heart is not evil!" he barks at me and I flinch. Then, I jump when I look past Reed's window to see Zephyr standing outside it, looking at us.

Reed rolls down the window and Zephyr asks, "Problem?"

"Evie didn't just run for a hundred miles, she was hunted," Reed says in a quiet tone. Zephyr signals to Buns and she is in the backseat of our car in an instant along with Zephyr.

I turn to look at Buns, but she launches herself into my arms, hugging me fiercely before pulling back and saying, "Sweetie, you're amazing. A hundred miles in the cold and snowy terrain—you're my hero."

"She is my hero, too. She was hunted. What hunted you, Evie?" Zephyr asks in an efficient way.

"I think she is a Power—she looked like a warrior, but she was definitely female. Let's see, she was hot in that androgynous model kind of way: short dark brown hair, hazel eyes, dark brown wings, super strong. She ripped out a tree and chucked it at me like it was a weed," I explain, remembering the sound it made as it crashed and splintered into the trees around me. Reed makes a sound from his seat, but doesn't look at me. He is facing forward, looking out the window. "You can't accuse her of throwing like a girl," I add, trying to get Reed to smile. He's not smiling.

Buns looks pale as she speaks to me. "Sweetie, how did you get away?" she asks me like she doesn't understand.

"I ran and I didn't stop. I stayed in the thickest part of the woods I could find so that she wouldn't be able to see me easily from the sky. I just kept going until I had to stop. I was really cold."

"But, even if you outran her, which I have no doubt you did, since you made it to town, why are you still alive?" Zephyr asks.

"I'm sorry, I don't understand," I say in confusion.

"She wouldn't have stopped. She would've kept going, following your tracks. What else was open in town?" Reed asks in a quiet tone. "Did you notice?"

I try to remember my route into town. "The convenience store was open, but I couldn't make myself go in there," I say, looking down because I'm embarrassed that I can't get over my fear of places like that. "I think there was a bar open on the corner—a country western thing, but my wings were out so I couldn't go in, and then there is that rule about no bars or taverns."

"She does not act like normal prey," Zephyr says suddenly, smiling at me proudly.

"Yes. We would have searched for her in the bar because we would have assumed that she would act like all of the other Fallen. But, she doesn't, so, if the other Power made it to town, she would have gone directly to the tavern looking for Evie," Reed surmises. "How far away was the bar from the diner?" Reed asks.

"I think the back of the bar would've been attached to the parking lot of the diner. They shared the parking lot at opposite ends," I answer, trying to remember the layout, but it's a little sketchy because I was sort of out of it at that point.

Reed turns toward the back seat of the car and speaks to Buns, "Do you think a Power would have felt a resistant soul transcend from that distance?"

"Sweetie, you did help a soul, didn't you?" Buns asks me proudly. I nod. She turns back to Reed and answers his question, "Yes." Then, she asks, "Would a Power investigate something like that, if she was hunting?"

Both Zephyr and Reed look at each other, and then say together, "No."

Buns looks irritated when she asks, "What, is it beneath you or something?" Neither one answers, so the question is answered by default. "So, are we gambling here? Do we hope she didn't see us and that she can't contact her buddies? How many were there on that hill?" Buns asks a little bit pissy, probably because of how Powers act toward Reapers.

Reed ignores her attitude when he answers her questions. "There were at least seven other Powers on the hill when Evie and I got there. They were together. If she contacted them, they would follow her orders, since it's her mission. We operate like she saw us load Evie in the car and head out. We assume she had a phone or was prepared to fly any distance to follow us. We need new vehicles Zephyr. What kind of car would you pick to evade an angel, Evie?" Reed asks me, studying me from his seat and I am surprised he asked me my opinion on strategy. They are experts at this.

Not wanting to disappoint him, I think about all the options, but one just sticks in my head, so I blurt out, "Minivan."

"What?" Zephyr asks me as if he hadn't heard me correctly.

"Get a minivan," I repeat.

"Why?" he retorts, like I have suggested he steal a tricycle.

"Because you guys wouldn't be caught dead in one. It's the perfect camouflage," I reply.

"Yes, but if we are spotted, we have almost no chance of escaping. It will act like fatal terrain. We will have to fight because to not do so would be to die," he explains, and I see the dilemma for them. They wouldn't be fighting Fallen, they would be fighting their own. But somehow, I know I'm right, so I have to argue my case.

"That's why it will work, because everything you do is about performance—how to make something perform to your standards, be angelic—but a minivan is very human. You guys never look twice at them. You see boring human existence, so we will be invisible to them in it," I explain. I have learned a thing or two about Powers over the last few months of living with them. "You're a really good driver, Zee, you'll manage and maybe you'll enjoy it," I stop short of calling him a soccer mom because I know my limits.

Reed pulls out the road map, pointing to a spot on it. "We'll meet here in a half-hour. Torch the car and remove the plate and VIN number," he says to Zephyr.

"See you in a half-hour, sweetie," Buns says, hugging me again and she disappears with Zephyr in the black Range Rover. Reed starts our car and begins to drive evasively, watching the rearview mirror as he makes turns to see if anyone follows us.

I am silent, thinking about what a Nephilim could possibly be to elicit such a violent response from Reed. Glancing at his profile, he is still having trouble with something. His jaw is set and his fingers are leaving dents in the steering wheel. I can guess what it is, but I don't know how to talk to him about it.

"You didn't tell me what a Nephilim is," I say quietly, as he drives very fast down a deserted stretch of road.

"You don't need to know," he says, checking his auxiliary mirror before peering out the sunroof at the sky above us.

I sigh heavily, "Please?"

"You are not a Nephilim so it doesn't matter," he says in a stern tone.

"Okay, I'm not a Nephilim—what's a Nephilim again?" I ask cajolingly, because I don't want to let it go. When someone calls me a name, I, at least, want to know why I should be offended.

"Evie," Reed sighs, too. "Why do you insist on knowing everything?"

He is dug in on this one. He really doesn't want to talk about it. *It must be really bad,* I think as I watch him rub his brow with his hand. I am quiet then. Maybe now is not the time to explore this subject. Perhaps just living through the day to see the New Year is enough. I close my eyes and thank God because it is enough for me. I'm here with Reed and he's safe and that is enough for me in this moment. Reed is watching me with concern when I open my eyes.

"You are right. I don't need to know right now. I should just be grateful that your plan worked so well," I reply in a tender voice as I rest my hand on his shoulder.

"What plan are you referring to, because my plan did not involve you being hunted by a Power without aid from anyone," he asks evenly. "I missed her and I don't know how that happened. You are alive because you are incredibly fast, cunning, and brave—and a maverick who confuses us—not because you had help," he replies in an angry tone.

"Reed, I didn't pick myself up off the ground in Ames. You did that. If it weren't for you, I would still be there and she probably would have found me sooner or later. No, scratch that, if it weren't for you, I would have walked right into them on the hill and that would have been the end of it. Come to think of it, if it weren't for you, Alfred would have a bright, shiny new soul to play with right now when the shadow man was done with me. Shall I go on because I can, you know?" I ask, thinking about Sebastian and formal. "I owe you everything and maybe you should be looking at this from another angle."

"What angle is that?" he asks, sounding irritated with me.

"Maybe you should just be grateful that we get to have this conversation right now. I'm grateful. I'm so grateful that I get to see you—to touch you," I say, putting my hand on the back of his neck lightly. "I get another chance to be with you and I know how selfish that is because you are as big a target as I am when I'm with you. I'm ashamed of myself, but I can't stop wanting you."

Pulling the car over in a deserted parking lot and slamming it into park, Reed reaches over and unbuckles my seatbelt, pulling me effortlessly onto his lap. "I am grateful," he breathes against my mouth before he crushes his lips to mine with an unrestrained passion that is making me cling to him as I straddle his hips. Reed reaches around me, pulling the steering wheel right off the dashboard and tossing it in the back seat.

Reed tears the handle off of the driver's side door, crushing it in his hand. I press my lips to his neck, and then further to his earlobe, nibbling on it teasingly. My fingers dig into the skin near his waist as I try to pull him nearer.

"I love you," I whisper by his ear and hear him groan like he is in pain as he reaches his hand behind the passenger seat, ripping it from the bolts that hold it in place.

"And I, you. You are mine, Evie," Reed says in a voice that sounds like he has lost control of the restraint he normally holds. I ignore the destruction he is doing to the car as I continue kissing him. His hand reaches up and pushes against the ceiling of the car. The sun-roof shatters and cold air and glass cascade down on us from above.

"Always," I reply softly. Reed grits his teeth, pushing against the driver's side door with his other hand, dislodging it from the hinges. It tumbles to the ground of the parking lot. Reed is out of the car in an instant, his wings spread broadly at his sides.

I sit in the driver's seat, looking at him for a moment as he paces back and forth, trying to regain control. He is absolutely awe inspiring with his bare chest and charcoal-gray wings powerfully displayed. I didn't think it was possible, but I want him even more now. I see the sexy way he moves, like a caged panther casing the bars, looking for a means of escape. I turn away from him so that I can get a grip. I rest my hand on the automatic stick near the center console. In frustration, I grip it hard, pulling the lever right out of the gearbox.

Reed is watching me with the darkness of desire still in his eyes. "Evie, don't do that," he says softly.

"Why, you already trashed the car, Reed," I reply in confusion as I crush the piece of plastic in my hand.

"Because, I'm trying to calm down and that is so hot it makes me want you more," he explains.

"Seriously?" I ask with a crooked smile. He nods slowly. "Because I really want to crush something."

"I know the feeling," Reed agrees, smiling a little and looking down. "You want to help me get rid of the car?" he asks, sounding a little better than he did a minute ago.

"I love this car," I sigh in regret, looking at the passenger seat that has toppled into the back seat when Reed had finally let go of it.

"I will get you another one. You can even pick it out this time," he says quickly, like I'm a spoiled child that he has to appease.

I try to reassure him, "It's okay. I just feel shady because it's so pretty and new," I say, getting out of the car and resting my hand on the frame where the door used to hang from the hinges. "How strong do you think I am?" I ask, watching him pull some of our stuff out of the back hatch. Then he pulls the plate off the back and sets it on our cases.

"That is a good question," he says, coming up next to me. He reaches in the car and pops the hood. The nearness of his body makes mine gravitate to him, as if he is a magnet pulling me.

Reed works at removing all of the VIN numbers off the car, even the ones that most people don't know about. When he finishes, he steps back, bracing both of his hands on the hood of the car and bowing his head. He is such a temptation with all of his sleekly defined muscles stretched taut against his perfect skin.

The longing inside of me becomes so intense I don't know what to do, so I turn back to the car and put both my hands on it. Pushing with all my might, two wheels on my side of the car lift off the ground as I pump my feet and give an extra shove. The car rolls over on its roof like an overturned turtle. When that doesn't help, I bring my foot back and kick my beautiful car.

Something is clawing its way out of me and I can't contain it anymore. "I want." I shout, kicking the steel panel of the Range Rover. *I need. I long for. I crave. I am here. I exist. I have a right to be,* I think the words in my head. "I want her to come," I say intensely, continuing to beat on my car with my hands. "I want her to find me, so that I can make her feel the pain I feel. I want to be able to rip out a tree and throw it right back at her. I want to pluck branches off and throw them right at her heart. I will crush anyone who wants to take me from you. Pwnage, I swear it to you," I say, turning toward Reed who is watching me silently. My wings are spread wide and they move agitatedly as I heave from the exertion of pummeling steel with my bare hands.

"Just when I think I can't possibly want you more, you go and raise the bar again," he says quietly, staring at me across the small space. "Don't do that again, I don't know if I can take it."

"You like avenging angel?" I ask him in a curious and self-effacing way.

"Uh huh," he agrees, nodding with a pained expression.

"Why?" I ask.

"I wanted you before this, for who you are—so intelligent, brave— delicate and beautiful. But now, you have power and strength, too. Danger, thy name is Evie. You are something from a dream and I just want…" he trails off.

"You just want what?" I ask.

"Forever with you," he replies, and then he turns to face the street when the sound of an engine grows nearer to our darkened parking lot.

A minivan pulls into the lot and I can see Zephyr's grim expression as the tailpipe rattles a little when he hits a small pothole in the pavement. Buns looks thrilled in the front passenger seat. When they pull abreast of us, she bounces out of the car, throwing her arms around me enthusiastically saying, "Happy New Year, Evie!" She lets go of me swiftly and turns to Reed, throwing her arms around him, giving him the same greeting. I hear a growl from Zephyr when he sees Buns hugging Reed, which makes Buns look at me with eyes as wide as mine. *He loves her!*

Buns seems to glow when she releases Reed, smiling at me and saying, "We may not have fireworks, but we get to have a Car-B-Que. Are you ready to set it off?" she asks. She looks at the car, seeing the destruction and she adds, "You already started the celebration, huh?"

Reed loads our cases and the plates and VINs in the back of the van. In a fraction of a second, he is by the Range Rover, reaching up and pulling the gas tank pipe from its housing, letting the fuel drip down the car. "Evie, you should get in the van now," Reed advises me.

Opening the sliding side door, I catch the look of disgust that Zephyr has on his face as he rips the fake plastic lei down from where it hangs on the rearview mirror of the van, tossing it out the driver's side window. Then, Zephyr tosses a book of matches to Reed through the passenger side window. Buns climbs in the car, shutting her door as I move back to the bench seat behind the driver's seat. We wait as Reed lights the match, throwing it on the gas that drips down the side of the car. The gas ignites and Reed swiftly gets into the van, shutting the door. We are out of the parking lot when the car behind us erupts in flames with a big *bang*.

"Turn your lights on and slow down, Zephyr," Reed says, sitting next to me. "Put on the cruise control, if you have to, but go the speed limit, just like a human." I roll my eyes because humans speed, too.

Twenty minutes after we have been in the car, my eyes begin to get heavy and I struggle to stay awake. I barely hear Zee say something about a fast approaching BMW with its headlights turned off. The car blows by us like we don't exist, not even slowing up a fraction. The angels all look at me like I have solved one of the mysteries of the universe. I give them the see-what-I-mean gesture and snuggle into Reed's side. He strokes my hair softly. Then, he leans down and whispers in my ear, "What are you humming?"

I didn't know that I was humming, so I have to stop and think about it for a second. "It's a the song that was playing at the bar that I passed on the way to the diner. I don't know it; it's old. Um, the man

sang something about running so that they won't catch up to him...
and he's gonna have to keep riding...forever..." I say, struggling to
remember the unfamiliar lyrics.

Reed's arms tighten around me. "It won't be like this forever,
Evie, I promise you," he says, trying to reassure me.

I fall silent and lay my head on his shoulder. "No. You're right," I
whisper. "This can't possibly last."

Russell

CHAPTER 6

Soul Mates

The world is fallin' down on me. I can hardly breathe with Evie so near like this. I have to get out of here. It doesn't help that I can smell her perfume from clear over here, I think as I gaze at Evie from my chair in Reed's library. Lyin' on the sofa with a book open in front of her, she is leafin' through the pages like she is just skimmin' it, but I know she's processin' every word of it with her expandin' angel brain. Her body is curved in the perfect shape, draped on the sofa like a cat. *I can remember holdin' her perfect, naked body in my arms, but not in this lifetime, in our past lifetimes. Yeah, just thinkin' the phrase "past lifetimes" should be enough to question the reality of this situation. How am I gonna survive losin' her? Maybe if I could get away for a while, go somewhere and be alone, I could get a grip on this. Or, maybe Zee will train me—beat up on me some more so I can focus on a different kind of pain for a while—pain that I can handle.*

"Russell, where are you going? Have you finished your assignment already?" Evie asks, smilin' from the sofa. She stretches her arms, archin' her back, seekin' a new, enticin' position.

"I'm not done, but I've read the same sentence six or seven times already, so I'm thinkin' I just need to take a break for awhile," I reply, packin' up my books and shovin' 'em in my bag.

"Are your classes getting easier yet?" Evie asks with curiosity in her eyes. We are halfway through the second semester at Crestwood and I can't wait for it to be over. School is so secondary to everythin' else that's happenin' in my life that it seems almost pointless to me, but I continue to go to class 'cuz it makes Evie feel better 'bout our life.

"Sorta, I understand the math problems in class before the prof gives the answers. I never was any good at math. I knew there had to be an up side to all this," I say, tryin' to make light of the situation.

But, my words have the opposite affect. Her eyebrows draw down in a frown. She's probably feelin' guilty over the fact that I'm now evolvin' into a creepy half-angel, just like her. "Hey, Thing One, stop worryin' 'bout Thing Two—I'm all right. I don't even have to wear my earplugs anymore—see," I say. Turnin' my head, I show Evie that I'm gettin' better at blockin' out all of the noises that my heightened sense of hearin' has been pickin' up. *I only need them when you and Reed start talkin' 'bout how much ya mean to each other. They come in real handy then,* I think, pickin' up my bag to carry my books back upstairs to my room. *Well, the room I occupy in Reed's house until we get Alfred.*

A flare of anger sweeps through me as I think of that little bug. *Now that I'm evolvin', I can't wait for it to be over so that I can go out huntin' that little maggot, Alfred. I want to be the one to kill him, to make him cease to be, as Zephyr explained it to me. Hell can be escaped if he can get what he needs—Evie's soul, or mine now, too, for that matter, since I'm also becomin' an angel-human hybrid. Alfred may not be aware that I'm still alive though, so he is more likely to go after Evie again. He also seems to be in love with the idea of possessin' her soul. As soon as we get him, I can leave. I won't have to stay here and watch Evie and Reed together anymore. To be a witness to their desire for each other is more than I can take, given the memories I now have, since almost dyin' a couple of months ago.*

What an evil thing to have to live through: to be able to recall every lifetime with Evie—every first time I met Evie—every first kiss—every first time she allowed me to run my hands over the perfect curves of her body… Of course, she wasn't always the girl in our past lives, so I have to try to block out those memories, too, because they are disturbin' on so many levels.

"Russell, will you tell me another story—you know, about us?" Evie asks, closin' the book in front of her and lookin' at me with that sexy smile that always hits me in the gut.

"I was just gonna go and see if Zee wanted to do some more trainin'. I need to learn how to fight like them…"*If I'm gonna have any chance of survivin',* I think the last part, but she follows my train of thought because the sexy smile is gone now and re-placed by the guilty look again.

"But, you're still really soft, Russell. What if Zee hurts you?" Evie asks, and then she chews her bottom lip anxiously.

"Well, I guess I'll just have to ask him to be gentle with me, now won't I," I say. I'm tryin' to make light of the fact that I haven't yet acquired the armor-tough skin that's an angelic trait, protectin' them from many of the things that tend to kill a human.

"Zee doesn't quite understand the word 'gentle,'" Evie replies sourly.

"I noticed," I say, rubbin' my jaw where Zephyr had broken it several days ago while tryin' to teach me to keep my guard up. It only took a few hours to heal, but somehow, that didn't seem fast enough.

"Come on, just tell me about one of our lives and I promise I'll leave you alone for awhile," Evie pleads. Her eyes get all shiny with anticipation 'cuz she knows I can't resist her.

"All right, just one—" I start to say, but I'm interrupted.

"Just one if it's a good one. Don't tell me about the ones like last time where we had nine kids and were living in an old fishing cottage and I ended up dying at sea and leaving you to all but starve. I mean nine kids..." Evie says, wrinklin' her nose.

"It's not my fault ya couldn't keep yer hands off me. How do ya think I felt givin' birth to all of them and then havin' to take up with the widower next door just to feed them after you were gone?" I reply defensively.

"You're right, I'm sorry. Just, can you tell me one where we didn't struggle so much...one with a little less pain in it," she asks hopefully. "Oh, and make it one that I'm the girl because it's a little weird thinking of myself as a salty, crusty sailor with a penchant for whiskey..." she trails off with a sheepish smile.

"That was just at the end there, ya weren't always like that—you were sweet and—" I try to say.

"Russell!" Evie say, smilin' at my defense of her...uh him...her... whatever.

"All right, I'll keep that in mind...let me think," I say, skimmin' through memories of our lives together, tryin' to find a romantic one that will satisfy her. "No...no, that one was hot but...no...nope... well ahh...no...okay here's one...shoot, no maybe not..." I say, continuin' to rifle through lives.

"What's wrong, Russell?" Evie asks in a soft tone.

"Well, it's just they all start off nice, but then...ya know...one of us ends up dyin' 'cuz that's how life is—or was—now, I'm not so sure anymore. Supposedly, we aren't gonna die—at least, not a natural death anyway," I say. I'm glad we're alone in the room, so I don't have to make sure no one overhears us. Not that anyone would think anythin' other than I'm a complete mental patient, but still, it's nice that this is a private conversation. Except for the angels, they all know exactly what I'm talkin' 'bout.

"Okay, I think I found one ya might like. You were a very, very, very beautiful lass...yer name was Aoibhe, which in Gaelic means beauty, so it was really lucky that you were so beautiful, or else ya would've been teased a lot. Now ya lived in the Scottish highlands in the year of our Lord 1147, well, that's when I met ya anyway. It was the reign of King David I, so many of the abbeys in Scotland were bein' built and there was lots to do for a man who was talented, like yer Da was."

"I like the way you said that, 'Da' like you were truly there," Evie says.

"I was, Red…and so were you. These are memories, not stories," I reply, somewhat frustrated 'cuz I can tell she's still in denial 'bout the fact that we were really there.

"You're right. I'm sorry…it's just you sounded like you were Scottish there for a moment and it made it so real," she replies. "You know Gaelic then?"

"Yeah, I guess so—twelfth century Gaelic anyway. Now, anyway—where was I… you were a Campbell and yer clan was smack dab in the middle of the Highlands. I was a Duncan, which ya won't know, but we were lowlanders and, bein' the third son of a wealthy family, I was shipped off to foster with my mother's people. They were Campbells as well. Ya startin' to see where we're headin'?" I ask her, seein' the smile formin' on her sensual mouth.

"What do you mean by foster?" Evie asks.

"Oh, that's when ya go to another clan and train as a squire and learn to fight so that eventually you can become a knight," I explain.

"You were a knight?" she asks, her eyes shinin' again and an amused smile is quiverin' in the corners of her mouth. "Like…in shining armor."

"Well, no, the armor we had was different then, not so shiny, not so much metal," I reply, amused myself. "We were more like soldiers."

Evie begins shakin' her head, tryin' to process what I'm tellin' her. "So how did we meet?" she asks.

"Well, I'm gettin' to that—let's see…Oh, so I was shipped off to the Campbell's in the Highlands when I was 'round sixteen and I was not too happy 'bout it, since I had a girl that I thought I was in love with back at home. She was verra pretty, but not like you are. You looked like ya look now, only yer hair was more fiery red and yer eyes were more blue than gray and ya had more freckles 'cuz ya would not listen to yer Da when he said ya should wear a wimple 'cuz ya were a heathen child. But, ya didn't look like that 'til later. Ya were only twelve when I met ya," I explain.

"Russell! What were you thinking, going after a twelve-year-old girl?" Evie asks, lookin' appalled.

"I didn't go after ya! You went after me! I couldn't get rid of ya. Ya followed me 'round all the time—you were always makin' somethin' for me and tryin' to get me to take it from ya. Ya drove me crazy," I say, smilin' at her playfully, rememberin' her at twelve.

"Oh, well…that's a little more understandable…" Evie comments in relief, before she asks, "What's a wimple?"

"It's a piece of fabric ya use to cover yer hair and ya fasten it in place with a circle of metal, called a chaplet," I explain, watchin' her face puzzle over the foreign head coverin'.

"Wow, that's weird—okay go on." she smiles.

"Yeah, well, one day I'd had it with ya. I told ya that ya had to stop followin' me 'round and that I was never gonna take another token from ya. I was in front of all of my buddies, ya see, and it was embarrassin' me. Ya got real quiet and ya said, 'But I love ya.' And me bein' the mean sixteen-year-old kid I was, I told ya I was never gonna love ya back," I admit, raisin' my eyebrows at Evie who is lookin' at me as if I'm an ogre.

"No, you didn't say that to a twelve-year-old girl! You're heartless!" she says accusin'ly.

"Oh, but I did, and ya know what ya said, Aoibhe? Ya said, 'Leander Duncan,' that was my name then, Leander, 'I'll not give ya another thing 'til ya tell me ya love me.' And ya ran away and ya left me alone," I say in a gentle tone, rememberin' that fiery, beautiful little girl.

"Then what happened?" Evie asks when I don't continue right away.

"Well, a few years went by and I went home to my family, so when I saw ya again, ya were 'bout sixteen or so, and oh my Lord, were ya the most beautiful creature I'd ever seen in my life," I say, smilin' ruefully at Evie as she grins at me wickedly.

"Ha, ha, serves you right, Leander! Tell me everything and don't you leave out any details!" she grins.

"All right, so I had come with my Mam to visit with her kin, the Campbell clan, for a kind of gatherin' thing we used to have from time to time back then. I saw ya with yer Da, who by the way, was a blacksmith and he had arms like this," I say, indicatin' a bicep the size of my thigh. "He had to be one of the most intimidatin' men I'd ever seen," I go on, rememberin' the size of Aoibhe's father. "And he was taller than I am now, so ya can imagine someone like me not really bein' intimidated easily by another fella, but he was one scary Da." I watch as Evie tries to imagine what I'm tellin' her. "Anyway, you were with yer Da, and the minute ya saw me, it was like ya had eaten some bad haggis or somethin'. Yer face went pale and yer jaw clenched and ya wouldn't look at me again after that."

"So, what did Leander do?" Evie asks, sittin' forward in her seat.

"Well, I just kinda watched ya for awhile. Every young man in the whole place was watchin' ya, so I was in good company. Ya danced every dance with a new partner, but ya didn't seem to have any particular interest in any one, so I felt it was safe to ask ya for a dance. But, when I did, ya turned me down flat. No explanation, I just said, 'May I have the next dance?' and ya said, 'no.' Then, ya danced with the next fella that asked ya." I watch Evie's eyes sparkle as I continue the story how I remember it. "When it was time for supper, I was sittin' with some of the fellas I knew and the lasses were servin' up trays of food. Y'all were passin' out the bread and ya got stuck with my table, so ya went down the line and when ya got to me, ya skipped me, like I wasn't even there. When I pointed out to ya that ya had missed me, ya know whatcha said?" I ask Evie with a chuckle, rememberin' the response in my head.

"No, what did I say?" Evie asks me with a quirk of her brow.

"Ya said, 'I didn't miss ya, Leander, I skipped ya 'cuz ya told me that yer never gonna take another thing from me again and, guess what? I'll not be givin' ya another thing either.'"

"Hooray for me!" Evie laughs. "Then what did you do?"

"Well, ya tossed down the gauntlet, now didn't ya?" I ask, rubbin' my hands together, rememberin' what I did next. "I had to see just how stubborn you were, so I started off by bringin' ya flowers. That was an easy one for ya to turn down. Then I bought ya a chaplet for yer hair. Ya turned that down, too. Then I bought ya some kid-skin boots, but ya wouldn't take those either, so I figured ya couldn't be bought." I tell her, as I go down the list.

"So, if I couldn't be bought...then what?" Evie asks with a curious smile.

"Well, I had to get underhanded. I followed ya when ya went to visit yer sister in a neighborin' burg. When ya went inside, I ran yer horse off and waited 'til ya came out," I admit, hangin' my head, feelin' a little ashamed at what I had done over eight hundred years ago.

"Russell!" Evie says in shock.

"I know, but I was gettin' desperate and you were so stubborn. Anyway, ya came out and I pretended to have just seen ya. I offered ya a ride back, but ya wouldn't take it. So I had to walk behind ya all the way back, feelin' guilty for what I had done to ya. Ya told me later that ya knew I'd done it, too, so ya walked extra slow to punish me," I say, smilin'. "You were such a mean lass!"

"Me? You drove the horse off," she says, laughin'.

"Anyway, by now, I was so obsessed with ya I didn't know what to do with myself. I had fancied myself in love before, but nothin' came close to what I was feelin' for ya. So, keep in mind I was a desperate man—maybe I shouldn't tell ya this part," I say, gettin' up from my seat and grabbin' my bag.

"Where are you going? You can't leave until you tell me what you did to me!" Evie says, grabbin' one of the throw pillows from the sofa and tossin' it at me. I catch it easily, huggin' it to my body, inhalin' her perfume on it as I sit back down in my chair.

"Okay—just remember—desperate man. So there I was, in love with ya, and I couldn't come up with a way to make ya unbend toward me. So, I followed ya to the loch. Y'all went there to wash yer clothes and, when everyone else left, ya stayed to wash yer hair. Ya only had on yer kirtle, which is kinda like a slip made of linen and when it's wet, well, there's nothin' left to the imagination. So, I took the woolen overdress ya left on the bank and I sat just under the tree with it, waitin' for ya to notice," I say, toyin' with the corner of the pillow.

"What happened when I noticed?" Evie asks breathlessly.

"Well, ya stormed out of the water with yer hands on yer hips. Ya took one look at me sittin' under the tree, and ya started marchin' home. Ya would've had to go right through the center of town in yer wet kirtle, if I hadn't caught up to ya and stood in front of ya, blockin' yer way," I explain, smilin'. "Although, I didn't mind the view from behind ya at all..." I add, and catch the next pillow easily as it sails toward my head. "Anyway, I said that ya had to take yer dress back from me before someone saw ya. Ya said, 'I'm never gonna take any of yer tokens from ya, I'd rather walk through the town naked.' So I said, 'But I love ya.'" I pause, lookin' up at Evie. Her eyes are on me, listenin' to every word I say. "So ya said, 'Good Lord man...finally! I thought I was gonna have to walk through town, nearly as naked as the day I was born, before ya told me that ya loved me,'" I tell Evie, smilin' ruefully. "And then, well, ya kissed me...and it was so sweet and innocent and hot, all at the same time."

"So, Aoibhe married Leander?" Evie asks in a soft tone, bitin' her bottom lip.

"Yeah," I sigh, noticin' she has distanced herself from my memories once again. "Ya already had yer Da make the rings. You were just waitin' on me to get to the 'I love ya' part. Ya always were one step ahead of me," I say, standin' up again.

I start walkin' from the room when Evie asks, "What happened to Aoibhe and Leander?"

I pause, not sure I should tell her this part. "Well, a few years after we were married, I got real sick with what we used to call the morbid sore throat. And there I was, beggin' ya to leave me be and go back to yer Da, but yer stubborn and ya wouldn't go. Ya kept nursin' me and I got better...and ya got sick...and ya didn't get better," I say quietly, 'cuz my throat gets tight as I remember Aoibhe dyin' in my arms. The sorrow of that day still lingers in my soul. "Ya seein' a pattern here at all, Red?" I ask her sadly. "Ya gave up yer life for mine."

"I don't remember being Aoibhe," Evie says in a quiet voice

"I know, but she's there—in yer soul—I kissed her on the beach and she tried to give up her soul for me a few months ago. I know ya don't remember, but yer her and she's you and this is by far the strangest life I've ever had," I say, rubbin' my hand through my hair.

"Just say the word and I'll end it for you and you can be free to go on to your next life," Reed says as he enters the library in his customary stealthy way. I never even hear him comin' and that is irratatin', since I should with my improved hearin'.

"I'll let ya know on that. I was thinkin' of stickin' 'round, at least 'til ya get called back to Heaven. Wouldn't want to miss one minute with ya," I reply, tryin' not to let him get to me.

"Reed...be nice please," Evie says, tryin' to be stern to Reed, which never works 'cuz she always ends up smilin' at him anyway.

"I'll see ya later, Red. I'm gonna go and see if Zee's available to train me. Ya know, you can come, too. I bet he can teach ya how to fight and protect yerself 'cuz yer gonna have to learn sooner or later," I urge her. I want her to figure out that the angels are not always gonna be 'round when she needs them. I shouldn't have to spell it out, since we both barely lived through the inconvenience at the 7-Eleven. Evie needs to, at least, be able to defend herself against a Reaper, like Alfred, 'cuz he is still out there, waitin' to get at her again.

"She is not ready yet, Russell. She hasn't evolved fully and that makes her too vulnerable to train," Reed says as he sits down next to Evie on the sofa.

"Correct me if I'm wrong, Reed, but I don't see the Fallen puttin' things on hold 'til Red fully evolves. Y'all should start now with at least the basics so that she has a chance if they attack her without y'all to protect her," I argue my point adamantly.

"Why would one of us not be with her, Russell?" Reed asks in a quiet tone from where he sits, not lookin' at me, but at Evie.

"Don't tell me that with all of yer life experience and military trainin', ya can't imagine a scenario in which Evie could be facin' those freakin' fallen cannibals without ya." I must have hit a nerve 'cuz I hear him growl a warnin' to me.

"Right now her strength for surviving lies in two areas: persuasion and flight. She needs to try to run first, and then, if that option is unavailable, she is very persuasive in turning angels to her favor," Reed says, takin' Evie's hand in his.

"It wouldn't hurt to give her another weapon in her arsenal. I don't understand ya. Ya say ya love her, but then ya don't even try to help her," I say, but no sooner had the words left my mouth, then Reed is standin' directly in front of me with his hands in fists at his sides. It's freaky how fast he can move in a fraction of a second.

"Never question my motives where Evie is concerned. What you are proposing is an unnecessary risk at this point in time," he says by my ear. He's tryin' real hard not to show the agitation he feels just below the surface. Knowin' this, I press on.

"What are ya afraid of, Reed? Would it bother ya that Evie might not need ya to protect her?" I ask with equal quiet, meetin' his eyes without flinchin', even as my instincts are tellin' me to be cautious. "No, that's not it is it…" I say, studyin' his face for a moment. "Yer afraid—yer afraid she'll get hurt—ya can't stand seein' her in pain." Reed growls again and I can tell I have come close to the mark. "Yer losin' perspective, *general*," I say through clenched teeth. "Y'all have to prepare for every eventuality, isn't that what Zee's always sayin'?" I ask him, lookin' in his eyes.

Evie is right here, tryin' to step between us, which is becomin' more and more of a habit as this livin' situation wears on. "Okay— this is so much fun, you two, I don't know what I'll do when it ends." Evie says with sarcasm. "Russell, I think you're right. I think it is about time I started to learn how to defend myself," she says. I look past her to Reed, who is scowlin' fiercely.

"We've been usin' the dinin' room to train, since Reed already started remodelin' it when you were sick. It's just 'bout perfect for what we need with all the vaulted ceilings and wood floors. We could use some mats if yer gonna train, too," I explain, lookin' at Evie.

"No, we won't because she is not training with you and Zephyr," Reed says with his eyebrows pullin' together.

"I say she is," I reply, defendin' what I believe. Before I know what is happenin', I'm off of my feet and propelled to the back of the library where I come to rest against the wall with Reed's forearm diggin' in my chest.

"Do you want to see her die, is that it?" Reed asks, holdin' me off the floor. "Because it would only take Zephyr a momentary lapse in concentration to snap her in two," Reed says, searchin' my face.

Evie is there in seconds, holdin' on to Reed's arm and sayin', "Reed, put him down, now!"

Reed complies, droppin' me to my feet instantly and steppin' back a few paces. He isn't lookin' at her though, he is lookin' at me. "Reed, listen to me, 'cuz I'm only gonna say this once. I love her, too. I want her to survive probably more than you do." I explain, runnin' my hand through my hair in exasperation. "Here's what I'm afraid of—I'm afraid that, for whatever reason, someone in Heaven is gonna get it in their head that Evie, or me, or both of us, could do all right without the help of angels and decide to call all y'all back to test the theory. If that day comes, wouldn't ya want her not to be at the mercy of the next fallen angel that crosses her path?" I ask him, hopin' he will see reason. "'Cuz I don't think I'm gonna be much help, at least 'til I get my wings, and then, who knows..." I say grudgingly, wishin' I knew when all of this is gonna occur so that I can have a timeline for kickin' some angel ass. "But, I'm gonna do everythin' in my power to be ready for when I can help, and I will protect her with my life, if it comes to it."

"That won't be necessary because I'm going to learn how to defend myself so no one has to die for me," Evie says in a stern tone, lookin' from Reed to me and back to Reed. "I'll tell Zee myself, so there is no miscommunication."

"We need to discuss your safe—" Reed begins, but Evie cuts him off.

"My safety—Russell's right." Evie says with genuine concern. "I can't rely on you to protect me all of the time. I need to be able to defend myself if I can." It isn't sittin' well with her to be just comin' to this conclusion now.

"Yes, I agree, when you are stronger and it makes more sense, but now—" Reed begins again, but is again cut off by Evie.

"I can't marinate in denial anymore, Reed. I need to take care of myself. I can't rely on you to do it for me." Evie says, puttin' her hand on Reed's cheek to get him to look at her.

"You don't need to do this," Reed assures her.

"Reed, I'm over the shock of still being alive. I need to do something to insure I stay that way. When are you training, Russell?" Evie asks.

"Zee?" I say in an even tone. It takes Zephyr less than two seconds to join us in the library. He moves past us to the windows. "Can ya train Red to defend herself?" I ask.

"I was wondering when we'd get to this. Evie, are you ready to learn?" Zephyr asks Evie, lookin' directly at her with his discernin' eyes.

"No, she is not," Reed replies for her.

"I am aware of your thoughts in this matter. I am now asking Evie. I want to know if you are fully awake now?" Zephyr asks Evie evenly.

"What do you mean, Zee?" Evie asks, lookin' down at the floor, tryin' to hide the fact that she already has some idea of what he means.

Zephyr says, "What I mean is that you have so much sorrow in you that you have been walking around like you are asleep half of the time. If we are to do this, I am going to need you to break the shell you have created around yourself, or else, I will end up hurting you."

"I see. I thought I was doing a better job at hiding my emotions, but I guess the only person I was fooling was myself. I'll go change and I'll meet you in the dining room, or is it gonna be the training room from now on?" she asks.

"Are you sure, Evie?" Zephyr asks.

"I'm fully alive now, Zee, and I intend to stay that way," Evie replies, squarin' her shoulders and walkin' toward the library doors like a warrior.

That's my girl, Red, I think, smilin' after her as she leaves the room. Then, I see the dangerous look on Reed's face and I stop smilin'.

"Do you know how long we have been killing?" Reed asks as he continues to scowl.

"No," I reply.

"So long that you would believe it was forever," Reed says with a stern look.

"Oh," I say, tryin' not to look impressed.

"And, do you know what it takes to kill one of us?" Reed asks with menace.

"Yeah. Zee explained that ya have to tear y'all apart for it to be effective," I say, tryin' not to adopt a smart-ass tone that won't help this situation.

"Right. How eager are you to see Evie tear another angel apart? Do you really think that she is ready to do that?" Reed asks me.

"Under the right set of circumstances, I'd say she'd do all right with it. Don't underestimate her, Reed; she is a force of nature and she's had centuries to hone her iron will, even if she doesn't remember any of it," I say as an explanation. "I haven't even begun to go all the way back in my memories and I've already learned that."

"What do you hope to accomplish by telling her all the stories of the past? She doesn't remember your lives together," Reed asks me.

"I don't know, Reed, maybe I'm hopin' to accomplish exactly what yer hopin' I won't accomplish," I reply, exhalin' and rubbin' my neck in irritation knowin' he was listenin' when I told Evie 'bout her life as Aoibhe. It's private. It was when she was mine and I won't share that part of her—of us—with him.

"It's not helping her," Reed says with concern.

"No, what's not helpin' her is allowin' her to live like nothin' can get to her 'cuz we both know that's not the case," I reply in disgust at havin' to say it out loud.

"You think she doesn't know that she is in danger all the time? I want her to feel safe here. I want her to heal and she can't do that if she is afraid. Are you listening to her at night? She has nightmares all the time," Reed says slowly, as if I don't have the wit to comprehend the situation.

"I know that, but I don't think they are all from trauma. Some are 'cuz Alfred is still out there and she's gettin' premonitions 'bout him," I reply as an explanation.

"Yes. I am aware of that," Reed's tone is calm. "That is why we haven't left Crestwood. Zee and I are strategizing ways to induce Alfred into making a move. We believe that by making our ranks seem disordered he might be baited into acting recklessly, but I am unwilling to risk Evie as a lure," Reed says. "We need to find a way to make him feel arrogant again because right now he has lost many of his allies. The Fallen will no longer follow him. They are probably hunting him as well. This will work to our advantage because he will be desperate to obtain Evie's soul. It is his only hope for survival."

"Why aren't we out there huntin' him?" I ask in frustration, thinkin' that Alfred is bein' allowed time to gain more allies and strategize a means of gettin' to Evie.

"We are the superior power. Our strength lies in the fact that we are not fractured. We are ordered while he is disordered. We will await him because we have what he wants. He will come and he will die," Reed replies as if lookin' forward to the day Alfred decides to make his move.

"I hope yer right, Reed—for all of our sakes," I say, and then I leave the library to change for trainin' with Zee.

CHAPTER 7

Trainin'

It doesn't take long to realize this isn't gonna be easy. The first time Zephyr takes a swipe at Evie durin' trainin', Reed loses it and the two of them end up brawlin' for several minutes until Buns and Brownie step in to pull Reed off of Zephyr. In Zee's defense, he wasn't really tryin' to fight back so much as not get killed. But, it effectively highlighted Reed's lack of perspective where Evie is concerned. So he is banned from the trainin' room while Evie is workin', a fact that doesn't seem to sit too well with him, since it's his house. When Evie says the alternative is for us to train somewhere else, he falls in line and mostly just paces outside the room 'til Evie finishes fightin' for the day.

Zephyr starts our trainin' by teachin' Evie and me basic defensive and hand-to-hand combat tactics to get us used to self-defense strategies. He works with us for a full month before he starts introducin' us to weapons. We have been workin' with long poles that resemble javelins and act as an equalizer when confrontin' an angel with the ability of flight. Since neither of us can use our wings yet, Evie 'cuz hers aren't strong enough, and me 'cuz I haven't gotten mine yet, the poles come in handy to ward off an attack from above. I'm not sure where we're supposed to find a large stick when confronted by surprise by an angel, but strategy is not the lesson for the day.

I pause after bein' clobbered, yet again, as Zee easily plucks the javelin from my hand and whacks me with it to make his point. "ZEE! Damn, that hurts! I think ya broke my knuckle...yer as mean as the nuns of St. Vincent," I say, rubbin' my knuckle, attemptin' to ease the ache. Zee chuckles from his position in the air above me. His large wings are creatin' a stir of wind that's fannin' my face as I bend over my hand in pain.

"You let me disarm you, Russell, and you pay the price," Zephyr says, grinnin'. "Does it hurt?" he asks.

"Yeah, a lot," I reply.

"Good. Maybe you won't do it again," he says, handin' me back the stick as he dips in closer.

"Ya know, Zee, the humans have it completely wrong, don't they?" I ask, still holdin' my hand with the other.

"That has been my experience with them, but I'm not sure exactly what you are referring to," Zee counters, anglin' away from Evie while she attempts to impale him with her javelin. She's fast, much quicker than I am, and has an almost innate ability to find a weakness in his defenses. I can hardly track the movement of her javelin as it slices through the air in lungin' thrusts. Her angel speed makes her deadly and accurate. It occurs to me that she's more highly evolved than I am, but still, it seems second nature to her, or maybe she's just meant to survive. I, on the other hand, must struggle.

"I mean the way humans look at angels, as some idealized perfect beings...ya know, like yer all kind and benevolent. All y'all are just mean and spiteful," I say, tryin' to straighten out my fingers.

"Did it ever occur to you that the way you look at us is offensive? I have never ever looked like a child, let alone a baby, and yet, those angel babies are all over. It is insulting," Zephyr says, and then he has to swerve out of the way as Evie manages to knick his wing with her javelin.

"Nice one, Red!" I cheer as a feather of Zee's wing floats gracefully to the floor. I have to check myself from givin' her the fraternal pat on the backside, like I would do to a teammate in football, 'cuz I might just end up with a javelin stickin' out of me.

"You distracted him, Russell. It wasn't fair," she says, but I see the smile inchin' up in the corner of her mouth.

"So ya never were a kid, huh? What did ya look like when ya were created?" I ask, 'cuz it occurs to me that I don't know much 'bout their species for lack of a better term.

"I looked much the same as I do now, except no wings at first. They come later, just like they will for you," he says, dodgin' Evie as she parries then thrusts again with the javelin.

"So, no baby cherubs then, huh?" I ask, thinkin'.

"No, but there is an order of angel that is close to Evie's rank, the Seraphim, that is called Cherubim, but they do not resemble winged babies either. However, it would be interesting to see what they would do to you if you likened them to one," Zephyr says with a smirk.

"So what's their story, the Cherubim? What do they do?" I ask to buy time so that my knuckle can stop stingin' before I have to pick up my stick again.

"They are the guardians to the souls in Paradise. They guard the way to the tree of life and they keep the records of the souls," he says absently, while concentratin' on Evie's ever improvin' form. "You would recognize them by their coloring. Blue wings. Oh, and they are leonine."

Evie lowers her javelin and stares at Zephyr in awe. "What's leonine mean?" I ask.

"Like a lion," Evie says slowly, still lookin' at Zephyr.

"So Cherubim are lions with blue wings that defend the souls in Heaven and keep track of the soul's records?" I ask, runnin' down their dossier. "What kind of records?"

"Sins," Zephyr says, smilin' at me warmly, but his words send a shiver down my spine.

"Like Santa's elves, huh?" Evie says, makin' a joke, which gets a laugh from Zephyr. To me she says, "So be good for goodness sake."

While I pale a bit, Zephyr continues. "But I wouldn't say they look exactly like a lion, more that they have characteristics of a lion and an angel."

"Are we gonna run across any of them down here?" I ask, still not too pleased to have learned that somewhere in Heaven there is a lion-esk, man-lookin' angel tallyin' up my sins.

"Possibly, but it may not be one from Paradise, it could also be one from Sheol," Zephyr replies, and his statement makes my skin crawl. Sheol had been explained to me as another name for what the nuns of St. Vincent would've called Hell. The nuns had also told me, several times, that I might find myself there one day, and I can't help thinkin' how much I hope they're wrong about that one. Havin' the place confirmed as an actual destination gives a whole new spin on the word "sin."

"How can ya tell who's Fallen and who isn't?" I ask, 'cuz it would be nice to see them comin' before they see me, even though seein' a lion man might be a total tip off.

"The Fallen are marked…stained–like a dark smear on them. But even without that you will know when you evolve more—the smell of them is foul, it will burn your lungs like acid," he says. I see that Evie knows what he's talkin' 'bout 'cuz she turns pale from the description. "Some can mask the smell, if it has been a while since they have been called to Sheol, but if they are fresh from there, you will know it."

"This dark smear—is it like an aura or something?" Evie asks, followin' him with little trouble.

"No, it is more of a stain—that is the best way I can describe it. Angels do not possess auras, that is a human trait—a trait of the soul." Zephyr explains, watchin' Evie processin' what he is sayin'.

"So we stick out like sore thumbs, huh?" Evie says as her shoulders droop, understandin' somethin' I haven't gotten yet. "An angel with an aura must be like a neon sign that blinks: 'Evil Freak' on and off like a vacancy sign."

"A neon sign, yes, 'Evil Freak,' no…" Zephyr says, trailin' off.

"Then what does the sign say?" Evie asks Zephyr. I'm glad she asked 'cuz it's important to know what we look like to them.

"Your sign reads: 'Dangerous,'" he replies. Evie's javelin slips through her fingers. She turns away to retrieve her water, trying to hide the fear in her eyes.

I search for somethin' to say that might make her laugh. "Well, I guess that's better than: 'Pansy Ass.'"

"No, it's not, Russell," Evie says, turnin' to me. "If it said that, then we would be left alone. 'Dangerous' to an angel would be almost irresistible for both sides, divine and evil."

"There are so many levels that make you irresistible to us and that is just one," Zephyr says, landin' on the ground and pullin' his wings back to a restin' position behind him.

Evie's eyebrow arches in question. "What would be another level?"

"You are so similar to us, being angels, yet you in no way act like us. You constantly amuse me: how you think, how you feel, what you deem essential and what you find baffling," he explains to us, chucklin'.

"Ah, much like talking to a five-year-old child, huh? Her view of the universe is skewed by her limited life experience, and thus, deemed precious to an adult," Evie says evenly.

"Maybe. I do not have much experience with children. But, I doubt I would find a child dangerous on any level," he counters. "And I would not use the word 'precious' to describe Russell." Zephyr continues, wrinklin' his nose at me.

"You're not very endearin' there yerself, general," I reply, pretendin' to take offense. "The girls don't seem to have a problem with me. Brownie and Buns think I'm fascinatin'."

"Yes. They are used to souls, since they reap them on almost a daily basis," Zephyr replies with a smug smile.

"That's funny, I didn't think it was my soul that interested them— I think they like the angel part, too," I reply with an arrogant smile, and then shift into a defensive crouch instinctively when I hear the low growl comin' from Zephyr. I had momentarily forgotten that Zephyr is highly protective of Buns, a fact that she seems to reciprocate. "Ahh, c'mon, Zee, I didn't mean it that way! I'm just sayin' they don't think I'm creepy, like everyone else does 'round here."

Zephyr sniffs once, seemin' to process what I had just said. I look at Evie who is studyin' Zephyr herself, sorta gaugin' his reaction.

"Are you jealous, Zee?" Evie asks him perceptively, as she smiles a little with her eyes, but keeps her mouth neutral.

"Do not be ridiculous," Zephyr replies quickly, which makes Evie turn to me and raise her eyebrow in speculation. Zephyr picks up the javelin Evie had dropped and begins spinnin' it 'round in intricate patterns and maneuvers, so fast, that it becomes just a blur to me.

"Zee, if you could, would you trade places with Russell?" Evie asks him in a thoughtful way, as if unsure of how to proceed, but I can tell that she wants to pick the scab off of this one and to see if it will bleed.

"Trade places with Russell?" Zephyr scoffs. He stops twirlin' the javelin for a moment. "It is impossible. And what would I need a soul for anyway?" he asks, and then continues to exercise the javelin. "Although, it would come in handy, your soul, if I wanted to draw out the Fallen. They would come to me then. I would not have to forever be tracking them and chasing them. They would be unable to resist the lure of a soul in an angel—the danger it represents," Zee says thoughtfully.

"And that appeals to you?" Evie asks.

"Of course. I am an assassin. It would add to my arsenal. I would be the ultimate dead end for them—an irresistible snare," Zephyr replies with a thoughtful air.

"You would not fear that others would constantly want to end you?" Evie asks him.

"No, therein lies the challenge—they would have to try, would they not?" he replies with a broad smile.

"Wow, Zee! That's slightly psychotic," Evie says with a frown.

"Not psychotic, I am just really good at what I do. I hunt Fallen. This would make it effortless to draw them in," he replies with ease.

"But you would get the comrades on your side worked up, too. How would you deal with them?" Evie asks, studyin' him close.

"I can be very persuasive. Russell will also probably have Seraphim wings. That would help in the negotiations," he says as if he would be unimpressed by anyone who finds his physical presence not to their likin'. "But I would not have that luxury, if I were to take his soul. I would have to make due with being a Power with a soul."

"But what if you had to change places with Russell as he is now, without the strength, power, and fighting skills you possess?" she asks, frownin'.

"I would make the most of it. He will be a very powerful being one day, maybe even as powerful as me," Zephyr says with hubris, grinnin'. I can't help smilin', too, at his arrogance. "And he will certainly outrank me, but he will cease to be if he ever tries to pull rank on me. Since I am training him, I will know all of his weaknesses."

He does know all of my weaknesses, which are too many to count right now. 'Bout to agree with him, I glance at Evie and see her growin' pale. Evie picks up the stick I had dropped earlier and the look on her face is piercing—deadly. I have never seen her look like this before; she looks like Reed did when he was about to kill Sebastian. Lethal. Holdin' the javelin out in front of her, she mimics the whirl of the javelin that Zephyr had demonstrated effortlessly just moments before. She moves in close to Zephyr, before pressing the sharp tip of the javelin to his throat.

Bracing her hand behind the javelin so that the slightest movement from Zephyr will impale him, she asks in a deadly calm voice, "Why are you helping us? What's in this for you?"

"Are you questioning my motives?" he counters in an even tone without emotion.

"Answer the question," she snarls, but she is losin' some of the calm she had just displayed as her hand trembles just a little.

"Evie?" I ask, 'cuz this is so unlike the girl I know that I am startled and confused.

"Nothing is unconditional, Russell." she barks at me with her eyebrows comin' together. Then, she asks Zephyr, "What do you expect to gain from helping us? Because if you ever try to take his soul, I will end you—I promise you." Her hands are shakin' while she scans Zephyr's face. She presses the point deeper into his throat and I watch, shocked, as she scowls at Zephyr like he is an enemy.

She has taken him by surprise with her threat, but he does not pull away or move at all. He studies her face; so close to his own, and replies, "I promise you I will never be tempted to kill Russell for his soul. It is not for me, you see, so I will leave it where it is. I am not evil—and I am not Alfred."

Evie looks like she is desperate to believe him. She loosens her grip on the stick, pullin' it back so that it isn't diggin' into his neck, but she doesn't drop it entirely. "Why?" she asks again.

"Because I am compelled to help you. I do not know how to

explain it. When I was unable to kill you, when we first met, you became the first prey that has ever survived me. Ever. You are my first incomplete mission. You survived because of who you are and I just need to see what happens next…and…" he trails off.

"And, what?" she whispers, her arms are really shakin' now from raw emotion.

"And this is the closest I have come to having a family—which is not what I had expected. Generally, I thought that families were supposed to be kind to each other," he says, but there is a teasin' note to his voice. Evie's lower lip begins to tremble and her eyes are fillin' up with tears. I step forward to hug her, but Zephyr holds up his hand to me, indicatin' that I should stop.

Evie whispers, "I know that you're not Alfred…I'm sorry, Zee…I just can't afford to be wrong anymore." She lowers the javelin. "This has messed me up. I was so wrong about Alfred. I thought he was my friend, but he never really was…you've been so good to me, to us," Evie says, indicatin' her and me with a hand gesture. "I just…I just…" she trails off.

Zephyr pulls her into his arms and lets her cry on his chest. "That was a harsh lesson that Alfred taught you. Evil can disguise itself well. The Fallen are deception incarnate," Zephyr says in a quiet tone. "You will battle with this lesson for a while."

"Alfred crawled inside my head and left me with the feeling that I have to question everyone and everything or he'll win," Evie whispers, her face still resting against Zephyr's chest.

Zephyr gives me a grim look. "Betrayal is hard to overcome. You will need to come to terms with it because emotion is costly. You must be able to look at things from an objective point of view or you will run the risk of making the wrong decision," he says in a gentle voice, pattin' her back. "Now, take this situation as an example. I allowed you to surprise me because I have become comfortable with who I believe you to be and I forgot to realize that you are so unfathomable in your tactics, that when you saw me as a threat, you reacted in a manner for which I was unprepared. I did not see how threatening my words were to you. It is what I said before, you do not act like an angel, making you unorthodox."

"I'm so sorry, Zee!" Evie whispers sadly.

"Evie, that was a compliment. I am proud of you. You found a weakness and you used it. Strategically, that is solid," Zephyr smiles, usin' the slang I have been teachin' him so that he can fit in better with the crowd he's supposed to be part of in the human world. "I'll try not to feel too bad about being skooled by a teenager," he says, quirkin' his brow in question to see if he had said it right. I nod and give him a fist, which he knocks back a little harder than I would've liked, due to the knuckle he had cracked earlier. "Now that I have been duly warned, I'll try to keep it on the up."

"Zee, how much time *are* you spending with Russell because you're starting to sound like him?" Evie asks as she straightens up, wipin' her tears with the back of her hand.

"Too much, it is whack," Zephyr replies, and we all laugh over it. "Do you want to try something new, Evie? I think you are getting the hang of the javelin. I want to try another equalizer. I am going to show you what I want you to do." Zephyr says as he pulls us both to the center of the room. "Do not get in my way because I am going to run."

Zephyr walks to the edge of the room where the floor meets the wall. He places his hand on the plaster wall above the wooden wainscot and begins to run swiftly 'round the perimeter of the room, pickin' up more speed with each pass. When he is almost a blur to my eyes, he steps up onto the wall and begins to defy gravity as he runs up the wall to the center, still completin' circuits, but instead of runnin' on the floor, he is runnin' on the wall. He springs from the wall and ends above our heads flappin' his wings and lowerin' himself to the ground. It is a "holy shit" moment for me and I know that my mouth is hangin' wide open when Zephyr lands.

"Evie, you are faster than me so this should be no problem for you. I will be in the center and when you get going, I want you to spring at me, like you are going to attack me and I will catch you," Zephyr orders.

Evie gives me the sexiest wink as she gets into position by the wall. When Zephyr nods, she shoots off faster than I can track her. She is just a blur to me, much faster than Zephyr had been as she runs up the wall and 'round it several times with no effort. My heart is in my throat as I watch her do what I have never dreamt was possible. But, 'cuz Evie is an overachiever, she does more than Zephyr asked her to do. She must be gettin' bored with just runnin' in the center of the wall 'cuz she switches her position: runnin' straight up to the barrel vaulted ceilin', across it, then down the wall vertically, across the floor, and back up the wall.

When she gets to the center of the wall again, she leaps at Zephyr, coilin' her legs 'round his waist. With her hands, she reaches up to place them on either side of Zephyr's head, showin' us both that she can snap his neck with just a quick twist, if she wants to. Then, she smiles at him and kisses him on the cheek. I think that Zephyr is as stunned as me 'cuz his mouth is open just like mine.

"You are very, very dangerous, Evie." Zephyr breathes as he holds her gently in his arms, descendin' slowly to the ground.

"I was going to wrap my legs around your waist, and then thrust my hips back so that I pulled you off balance, but then I thought, no, I should just snap your neck, you would die quicker. Is that right?" she asks. He nods his head like he is the proudest papa in the world.

"Let's see it again, Evie, but this time, come at me from behind," he says as he places her on the ground again. She runs the wall and ceilin' several more times. She never stumbles or panics, but is solid the entire time and it is like watchin' a deadly dance in midair when she spirals off the wall or ceilin', pouncin' on Zephyr like he is the prey. She takes my breath away and I'm not sure how many pieces of me are gonna be left when she finally slips away from me.

"It's your turn, Russell," Evie smiles when she sits down next to me in the center of the dinin' room, pickin' up her water and takin' a sip.

I grimace. "Yeah, I wish. I hope that part kicks in soon. It'd be nice to run like the wind. It looks like fun and y'all don't even look like you're gettin' a cardio workout from it," I reply. "I just don't know what to do with myself. I feel like the last kid picked for dodgeball 'cuz I suck. I've never been that kid in my life."

"I bet. You were probably the captain," Evie says, smilin' at me. "That's probably why this is all happening. It's your bad dodgeball karma catching up to you," Evie teases me and nudges my thigh with her thigh. "Don't worry, I'll take care of you," she says, and my heart contracts painfully. I want that so much that I am sorry from it. I want her to look after me and I want to look after her. "How is your family adjusting?" Evie asks as she puts her hand on my back like she wants to comfort me.

"I think they're still in shock. I mean, how would ya take it if ya had a son who supposedly witnessed a massacre in a convenience store? They think I'm in witness protection now. They think they were moved to a separate 'safe house' and given new identities for their protection," I admit as my shoulders round. "The money helped, though. I heard from my mom that Melanie is super psyched that they're rich now. The angels laid down some serious cash on them. They think all the cash came from the Seven-Eleven Corporation tryin' to make amends for what happened. There's so much cash, my sister's children's children will never have to work again."

"Their new identities mean they are safe from Alfred. That's what's most important," Evie says as her chin lowers and I see her look of guilt again. I want to kick myself for bein' so honest with her. But it's hard for me to be anythin' but honest with her. I feel closer to her than I've ever been to anyone else in this life or any other life for that matter. If she is nothin' else, she is still my best friend. "What are their new names again?"

"Robert and Hannah Buckingham with their two lovely daughters Sasha and Megan," I remind her, and it is like I am talkin' 'bout people I don't know. "My sisters will always be Scarlett and Melanie to me," I say, wonderin' when I'll see them again. Not anytime soon. Not with the kind of wrath I could bring down on them. I won't ever go there until I can be sure I can protect them.

"Do you know where they are?" Evie asks.

I shrug. "I specifically didn't ask. I can't slip if I don't know." *Or be tortured into telling someone like Alfred.* "I know where they are in general and that's good enough for now. I have their names and will be able to find them, eventually, if it comes to that." Evie just nods 'cuz she knows more than anybody how important it is to keep information like that quiet.

She seems to meditate on what I said for a while, not speakin' until I am 'bout to get up and call it a day. "Zephyr, do you have any swords?" she asks. She looks at me as if she is gaugin' my ability.

"I have many. None of which I brought with me from my home. Reed, however, has many more than I do. He is old-school when it comes to things like that," Zephyr explains.

"Do you think he has something that would be familiar to a person from the twelfth century Highlands?" Evie asks him, but she is still lookin' at me.

"Let me think, Claymores did not come into play until later, but Highlanders always used a longer broadsword than most. They had the build for it, like Russell does," Zephyr says, scannin' me for my attributes.

"I think Russell would be at home with a sword. Is there one he could practice with?" Evie asks Zephyr, and I'm beginnin' to see where she is goin' with this.

"I will see, give me a moment," Zephyr says, leaving us alone.

I turn toward Evie and ask, "What're ya up to?"

"It's really nothing, but I was thinking earlier about what you said when we were in the library and you told me about Leander and Aoibhe. You said you were a soldier in the Highlands," she explains, scannin' my face. "I just thought that you already had some training, you just need to tap into it—try to remember being Leander and maybe you can borrow his insight and apply it to our training."

Somethin' 'bout what she said hit me like a burst of joy in my heart. "So, ya do believe me," I smile, tryin' not to show my elation.

"Of course I believe you. It's there in your eyes—I can see it. I just don't know what to do with it," she replies. She's havin' a hard time with the knowledge.

I want to help her 'cuz there has been too much pain for her in this already. "There is nothin' to do. It is what it is—or was what it was—whatever. Ya want to know somethin' ironic?"

"I don't know, there has been too much irony in my life lately. Will I be able to handle it?" she asks, tryin' to sound teasin', but there is an edge to her words and I can see she's tryin' to protect herself from whatever I might say.

"I think so. When ya were Aoibhe, ya had yer Da make me a weddin' present that ya gave to me on the night that we said our vows. It was a beautiful sword that yer Da worked on for a while. The hilt was very intricate with interlocking Celtic knots that looked as if they traveled inside each other into infinity."

"I gave you a sword for a wedding present? How medieval of me," Evie says with the sexy smile that melts my heart.

"Yeah, ya did. Ya had yer Da inscribe somethin' on the blade of the weapon that I'll never forget…again, I'll never forget it again," I reply, tryin' not to lose myself in her smile.

"What did it say?" she asks, and I can tell she's really interested.

"Well, it was in Gaelic, but the rough translation is this: May what lies ahead of this warrior or behind him never take from me what is inside of him, for it is mine," I recite, and I watch the tears collect in her eyes again. She nods as she tries to keep in the emotion she holds just beyond the surface.

"That is the love that you deserve, Russell. I'm scratched on your heart as you are scratched on mine. I will always love you, but we are different now. You'll always have me to rely on, but there is more to us now. I'm no longer just human and the angel part of me demands something other than what my soul would have and I…" She pauses to wipe a tear away that escapes her eye with the back of her fist. "I'm sorry."

"Yeah. Me too," I murmur, lookin' away from her 'cuz I don't want to see her pain that mirrors mine.

Zephyr returns with a couple of wicked lookin' swords that he props against the wall of the trainin' room. Under his arm, he has a couple of wooden swords of nearly the same length as the ones he had in reserve. Tossin' one of the wooden swords to me, he grins evilly and says, "How does that feel in your hand?"

"Feels right at home, Zee," I reply, and I am slightly shocked that it isn't a lie. The weapon, although wooden and meant to be used for the purposes of practice, is so familiar to me that I am amazed when my hand arcs in intricate movements, wieldin' it as if I had practiced with it all my life. I close my eyes, focusin' on my life as Leander, rememberin' many of the details of that lifetime. I can almost smell the air that he...uh I...breathed then. I open my eyes to see Evie and Zephyr watchin' me as I weave the sword in complicated patterns, slicin' the air like it's my enemy.

I make the wooden blade sing as it beats the air in curving sweeps. I can use both of my hands equally well as I aggressively toss the sword from one hand to the other, testin' my prowess with the weapon. A confidence that I have been lackin' since this whole ordeal began, comes to me in an instant, and it isn't a false confidence. I have earned it...just not in this lifetime.

"Nice," Zephyr says as he wields the other sword, imitatin' the patterns I am slicin' out. When his sword strikes out at me, I am prepared for it. I had anticipated the attack, had known instinctively that it was comin' and how to counter it. A slow smile creeps over my lips as my sword blocks his. I manage to step back enough so that the force he expels propels him by me as I counterattack and slap him with my sword in the side.

Zephyr looks a little disgruntled when he gains his footin' and twists to gaze at my face. "You have had training," he accuses me.

"Many, many, many years of trainin', Zee. Let's try the real ones, shall we?" I grin, tossin' him back the wooden sword. Lookin' at Evie I see that her eyes are shiny, and if I was a bettin' man, I would say she is proud of me. "Damn, Evie, you have it all figured out, don't ya?" I say as a compliment, but I watch as my words have the opposite effect on her again.

"Not quite, but I'm working on it, Russ," she says with a sad smile, and there is somthin' in her eyes that raises a red flag in my mind. I have seen that look before. I know that look. Starin' at her face, I remember the look on Aoibhe's face when I had told her to go back to her Da, when I was sick and I thought I was dyin'. She had that same look...and when I had woken up in the 7-Eleven, after Alfred had stabbed me in the leg. I saw that look: it's her determined-to-sacrifice-herself look.

"What're ya up to, Red?" I ask in an accusin' tone, pushin' away the sword that Zephyr is offerin' me and approachin' Evie with menace.

"What?" Evie's expression turns guilty. Her eyes dart to Zephyr to gauge his reaction to what I had just said. She is up to somethin'— somethin' she definitely doesn't want Zephyr to know about. She tries to hide her eyes from me. I am 'bout to call her out on it when she gazes at me with a pleadin' look. She shakes her head just a little before she glances again at Zephyr who is also watchin' her.

She clears her throat and says, "I'm just wondering if there is a weapon that you can remember from our lives together that I would be good with." It isn't a lie. She is thinkin' that, but she is also coverin' somethin' up. I know her now. She can't hide anythin' from me anymore. She is like an open book to me, since I have known her for so long, longer than she can possibly remember. That's probably why she could never lie convincingly to me before—I can always see through her deception.

Zephyr is watchin' us closely, lookin' concerned. He is watchin' Evie, too, tryin' to see if there is somethin' he is missin' that I'm pickin' up on, but I doubt he can tell, since she confuses the crap out of the angels. There's no doubt that she's up to somthin', but maybe now is not the time to drag it out of her. Not while Zephyr is listenin'. "You were good with a bow when you were Aoibhe, much more accurate than I was and ya loved to make sure I knew it, too," I reply. "Let's see...ya can also try a dagger, scimitar, sling, chakram—"

"What's a chakram?" Evie asks, lookin' relieved that I have taken her bait and not probed further with my questions, but had been diverted by her.

Zephyr answers her, "It is a disk you can throw that has a sharp edge." But he is on to us, I think, 'cuz he comes closer to see if I will say more. Evie turns to Zephyr and asks, "Do you have any daggers?"

"If it is a weapon, then Reed will have it," Zephyr states clearly. "I will choose some weapons for Evie to try. Later, I will show you the weapons room and the security precautions you will need to know to enter." Zephyr is gone then in a blink of an eye. I look at Evie who has casually picked up one of the swords that Zephyr had brought. She tests the weight in her hand as I pick up the other weapon.

"Show me how you hold it correctly," Evie says, comin' up next to me. I hold out mine to show her and when she mimics my stance, I walk behind her to reposition her hand, so that it's choked up more on the hilt to compensate for her shorter arm length.

With my hand on her waist and the other hand on her outstretched arm, I say in her ear, "You want to keep yer grip firm, but relaxed so that you can have flexibility in your movement. If yer grip is too tight, yer movements are more rigid and if yer grip is too loose, ya run the risk of losin' control of yer weapon...what're ya up to,

Red?" I ask again, holdin' her arm tighter and leanin' into her body, tryin' to see her face.

"Shh, Russell!" Evie says, closin' her eyes briefly. She turns to look over her shoulder, to see if any of the angels are close. Not seein' anyone nearby, she says in a whisper near my ear, "We have to talk, but not here. This has to be a private conversation…just you and me. I'll come to your room later tonight, okay?" she asks, lookin' at me pleadingly.

"Yeah…okay," I agree. She's up to somethin' and it is serious— dead serious 'cuz she obviously doesn't want the angels to hear 'bout it.

"Thanks, Russell," she replies, exhalin' a breath. Her hand is sha- kin' a little, so I cover it with my own, tryin' to comfort her.

She's really upset, I think, watchin' her struggle to keep her composure.

Zephyr returns then and I begin to practice with the sword again, while Zephyr shows Evie how to battle with the long daggers. He plac- es one in each of her hands. Slowly, he begins to show her how to use them, but in just a few minutes, Evie is ruthlessly wieldin' them like she had done so all of her life. I am gettin' a fair sense that Zephyr is in trouble when I watch her spin the daggers in her hands 360 de- grees and then catch them in her palms with just a supple flick of her wrist. Then, they begin to spar. Lungin' and twistin' to throw Zephyr off his assault, Evie meets his attack with her own, not givin' him an openin' to go in for the kill.

When Zephyr backs her into a corner, she evades his trap by leapin' over his head, effectively tradin' her position for his. She's lethal, and even if she doesn't remember any of her past lives, she seems to still possess the innate knowledge of those lives. It's the only explanation I can come up with for her ability to fight like a warrior without havin' had trainin' for it in this lifetime.

Evie's speed with the weapons is unparalleled. She is able to swipe the daggers faster than Zephyr can, even with his immense knowledge and experience. I think the realization of that fact is just now dawnin' on him as I see his frown deepen. She presses forward, catchin' Zephyr by surprise as she forces him to the corner he had tried to put her in earlier. Lashin' out, Evie tries to check her swing at the last second, but Zephyr brings his arm up to protect himself from her assault. Evie scores the blade of her dagger over his forearm. Zephyr's blood drips from his arm while the horror of what had just happened registers on Evie's face.

"Oh my God, Zee! I'm sorry!" she says, droppin' the blades on the ground with a clatter. Before either Zephyr or I can react, Evie rushes forward and places her hand over Zephyr's wound. The lights above our head flicker. Lookin' up at the lights and then down again, I hear Evie's soft gasp. Her hand on Zephyr's begins to glow. Her legs buckle out from under her and Zephyr catches Evie with his other arm before she falls.

Lowering Evie gently to the ground, Zephyr follows her, as he seems to need to sit down suddenly. "Evie?" Zephyr groans.

I can see what is happenin': Evie's healin' Zephyr. I know it 'cuz I remember what it felt like when she had healed me after I was stabbed in the chest—the fire that had torn through me hotter than molten lead and my inability to move while I was bein' incinerated from the inside out.

Kneeling by them both, I say in an urgent tone, "Don't struggle, Zee. I don't think she can stop."

Zephyr closes his eyes tight against the burnin' sting that I am sure is tearin' through him. I'm not as worried 'bout him as I am 'bout Evie, since he is healin'; his wound is disappearin' before my eyes. It is Evie that has me feelin' panic. She's beginnin' to bleed in earnest; the blood is seepin' out of the slash that has just broken open on her forearm. In the next moment, Reed enters the room and kneels down next to Evie. His face is grim as he is tryin' to pull Evie's hand off of Zephyr. The heat from the glow between them is scaldin' Reed, but he relentlessly continues to try to break them apart.

"Evie…love, can you hear me?" Reed asks in a gentle tone. Her face turns toward his. "Let go of Zephyr, love," Reed continues, but she doesn't move her hand, she just shakes her head.

"Can't," she manages to say. The glow from her hand is dimmin' now, becomin' less intense, and since Zephyr is showin' no sign of havin' ever been hurt, it's probably almost over—for him anyway.

The second that Evie's hand falls away from Zephyr, Reed has Evie in his arms and is out of the trainin' room. I sit down next to Zephyr and reach my hand out to him to pull him up to a sittin' position. Leanin' back against the wall, Zephyr looks weak, like Evie has stolen all his energy.

"I do not ever want her to do that to me again," Zephyr says in a slow, methodical way, rubbin' his forearm.

"Yeah, it's freaky, isn't it?" I agree, noticin' that my hands are shakin'. "Watchin' her do it isn't as bad as livin' through it, but it's no picnic either."

"She is dangerous," Zephyr states, still rubbin' his arm. "It is like magic, what she can do. Did you see her with the daggers?" he asks me, dazed.

My eyes soften. "Yeah, she was gonna whoop yer ass," I say as lightly as possible. "She was trained in daggers a long time ago. In Egypt."

Zephyr cocks his brow as he glances at me. "Did she guard a Pharaoh?" he asks with a serious expression.

"Sorta, she was the Pharaoh's concubine and he really loved her. He made her his pet and trained her to spar with daggers for his enjoyment. She was really good at it. She was his favorite until she met me and I persuaded her to run away with me—not one of our better lives. We got caught and executed," I admit, tryin' to block out the horrific images of her death in that lifetime. "Ya should've seen her, though—she looks the same except her skin was like honey and so soft...her hair was jet black. Irresistible."

"Personally, I like her wings," Zephyr confides, and I smile 'cuz it makes sense for him to find the angel part of her more attractive than the human side of her. Then he frowns, "Do you think she is okay?" he asks as he struggles to get to his feet.

I nod. "Yeah, it's just a cut. She survived a gapin' chest wound, so the knick she gave ya should be no big deal," I reply as I help him up. It is strange to see him so weak. He looks like he barely has any energy at all. "Let's go check on her."

We find Reed and Evie in the kitchen. Reed is just finishin' up wrappin' Evie's forearm in a gauze bandage. I stop just inside the doorway while Zephyr walks over to Evie, and kneelin' down next to her chair, he gazes into her eyes. "Do not ever do that to me again. I much prefer a flesh wound to whatever it was you just did to me," he says in a military tone. Evie hangs her head in guilt. Reed continues placin' tape over the bandage to secure it in place. When Reed finishes he steps back. "That being said," Zephyr says as he wraps his arms around Evie, pickin' her up off the chair in a hug, "thank you for trying to help me."

"I'm sorry, I didn't mean to cut you," she says, continuin' to hug him.

"She cut you, Zephyr?" Reed asks in confusion as if he hasn't heard her right.

"Yes," Zephyr replies, puttin' Evie back down on the chair.

"How?" Reed asks with a searchin' look.

Zephyr grins. "Daggers. Russell said she was in Egypt—a concubine of a Pharaoh." Zee repeats what I had told him and I see the reaction on Reed's face before I hear him growl.

Reed doesn't like the visual he just got of another man havin'

Evie. *Yeah, try seein' it in yer head, pal. It sucks worse than that when it's a memory,* I think heatedly.

"Show me," Reed says to Evie.

Evie cringes. "No. I don't want to hurt anyone," she says, touchin' her arm lightly. A meaningful look exchanges between Reed and Zephyr. Then, Reed kneels down so he can look in Evie's eyes.

"You have to. You cannot let what just happened sink in. You have to push through it so that you do not hesitate in the future, when you really need to use your abilities," he says, while he touches her hair. My hands squeeze into fists so that I won't attack him for touchin' her. "Show me," Reed says again, before holdin' out his hand for her to take. She puts her hand in his with a little reluctance. I step aside as Reed leads her back down the hallway to the trainin' room. Zephyr and I follow them.

When they get to the trainin' room, Reed picks up the daggers that Evie had dropped and wipes the blood off of the one that struck Zephyr. He hands them back to Evie.

Fear. She's afraid, I think as I see the look on her face. Reed picks up the other daggers that Zephyr has been usin'. He looks like a killer. A shiver of dread runs through me as he faces off against Evie. He isn't playin', but appears deadly serious. "I'm your enemy. Stop me," he says in a soft tone, and then he springs toward her with a snarl on his lips.

Evie has just enough time to spring backward from Reed's vicious swipe that causes the air to whistle. Reed's dagger misses her abdomen by centimeters. I shoot forward to pounce on Reed, but am held by Zephyr who whispers in my ear, "Do not go there. He will kill you."

I struggle for Zee to let me go, but he has gotten some of his strength back, enough to restrain me. My teeth clench as Reed stalks Evie, lookin' for an openin' to strike. She isn't givin' him one, stayin' well back from him, but neither is she attackin' him, which she clearly should be doin' 'cuz she needs to be aggressive. Reed seems to realize this as well and he changes his tactics. Instead of watchin' Evie, his eyes drift to me. A slow smile registers on his face as he switches direction and comes toward me. In the next instant, Evie stands in his way.

"No…"she murmurs to him. He ignores her, his eyes remainin' on me just long enough to let her know he will do whatever it takes to get her to engage him in this fight.

"Yes," Reed replies with menace.

Evie tenses and goes on the defensive, totally engaged now in whatever fight is gonna occur. She cuts off his access to me, and in a blink of an eye, she tosses one of her blades up in the air. As the blade arcs upward, she runs to the wall before the blade even has a chance to start comin' back down. Usin' the wall as a springboard, she pushes off of it, catchin' the blade in midair and droppin' toward Reed with the speed of a bullet. He is just able to evade the full impact of what she would have given him as he lunges to the side at the last instant, so that the blade Evie has extended in front of her doesn't embed itself in his chest. She tumbles on the ground, rollin' back onto her feet in a crouch, before she swivels back to face him.

If Reed is shocked, he hides it well, but Evie doesn't give him much time to contemplate his next move. She is off again, flippin' toward him like a gymnast, but a gymnast who can nearly defy gravity with the speed of a tumblin' cyclone. Reed catches her foot that she would've planted in his chest and flips her back in the opposite direction, which to my amazement, seems to be what she had intended him to do. The change in momentum causes her head and arms to flip back up, so that she is able to twist and stretch out just enough to bring the daggers she still holds within inches of Reed's neck. He catches her intentions at the last second, pullin' back as the blades kiss his neck. The knives leave small, red scratches in his skin, but don't cause him to bleed. In retaliation, Reed kicks out with his foot, connectin' with Evie's abdomen. He pushes her away from him. She tumbles back, but she is on her feet in a fraction of a second, runnin' to the wall. She is up on the ceilin' in the time it takes me to exhale the breath I was holdin', thinkin' she might have been hurt from Reed's kick.

She drops from the ceilin' before I know what she is doin', but instead of evadin' her, Reed drops his weapons. His wings unleash out of his back as he springs up, catchin' Evie in his arms in midair. She wraps her legs around his waist, droppin' her daggers, too. They embed loudly in the wooden floor below them. Evie presses her body to his, wrappin' her arms lovingly around his neck. Reed captures her lips in a passionate kiss that sends ice right through my body.

"Ahh, that just blows," I mutter, feelin' Zephyr release me. I turn and try to push him away, but he is rapidly regainin' his strength, so he just grins at my attempts.

"You were hoping she would kill him?" Zephyr asks me.

"Somethin' like that," I mumble, and I hear him chucklin' as I leave the room.

෧

"Russell...Russ..." Evie whispers as she creeps into my darkened room. Still wide-awake lyin' in bed, I refuse to answer her 'cuz I'm still mad at her for what happened in the trainin' room today. Hopin' she will go away if she thinks I'm sleepin', I don't move. Slinkin' to the foot of my bed, she stands there lookin' at me. Realizin' that she can see me clearly, even though it is dark, I watch her shadowy figure put her hands on her sexy hips. Then she whispers, "I know you're awake, Russell. I can see that your eyes are open."

"Whaddaya want?" I ask her in a surly tone. I don't try to keep my voice low. I can really care less if the angels overhear us.

"Shh!" she hisses at me as she comes 'round the bed to perch tentatively on the side by my feet. "I'm here because we have to talk. I have to tell you what happened when you were with your parents over break. I have to explain..." Her voice breaks as she glances away from me for a second.

All of my senses are alerted to her in that second. *She's really upset,* I think.

Sittin' up, I turn on the lamp beside the bed. Her face is a mask of pain. She looks heart-broken when she whispers to me, "I thought we would have more time. I was hoping we could stay until we took our exams, but we can't. We have to go soon, Russell. I heard the angels talking and they're looking for me—Dominion. We have to go before they kill them. They will think they are traitors. They think we're Nephilim." She is whisperin' so fast and I can't understand half of what she is tellin' me. *What's Dominion? What's a Nephilim? Who wants the angels dead?* I wonder rapidly.

Gettin' out of my bed, I walk over to the desk in my room and retrieve a tablet and a pencil. I come back to the bed. Sittin' next to Evie, I write:

WTF Red?

Evie takes the pencil back from me and writes:

We have to leave, Russell. Just you and me.

I scan her face after I read what she wrote. I want to shout at her 'cuz I have so many questions. I take the pencil from Evie's hand and write:

Why? I frown, watchin' her sad expression.

She takes the pencil back from me and begins writin' out an explanation: *When you were gone over break, Buns, Zee, Reed, and I went to a* resort to snowboard. We ran into some Powers who saw me. I ran from them, but one hunted me. She was pretty specific when she told me what she is going to do to me when she finds me. She called me a Nephilim, but when I asked the angels later what it was, they all clammed up on me and wouldn't explain what it is. They acted like it was no big deal and that she couldn't possibly find us, but everything I know about Power angels tells me they were not giving it to me straight. Powers don't quit once they have a mission. They never quit. To her, I'm a failed mission if she doesn't find me and erase me from all existence.

I take the pencil out of Evie's hand and write: **Holy shit Red! Why didn't anyone tell me? No shit, they don't stop. They are like freaking terminators. They won't stop until you're dead. Why are we still in Crestwood?** I thrust the pencil back at her, hearin' my breath comin' out faster in agitation.

I kept trying to figure that out. Reed and Zee want us to think they're still trying to draw in Alfred, but I think they have put him on the back burner because I overheard part of their conversation last night. I woke up in the middle of the night and I was on my way to the kitchen to get some water when I heard them talking in the library. They were all there: Brownie, Buns, Zee, and Reed. Zee has been keeping an eye on what "Dominion" is putting out on me. It turns out that all the Powers are now alerted to the existence of the Nephilim spotted recently in this area.

What's Dominion? I write after I tear the pencil from her hand. I then thrust it back at her.

I think it's like some kind of military HQ for Power angels. That's what I got from the conversation, but I couldn't ask them because I was earjacking the information. If it's made up of Powers, I'm in big trouble. Evie writes and then she looks at me with eyes that show fear that she has every right to feel.

If those angels are after her, she is in deep—and so am I, 'cuz we're the same, she and I. I gaze 'round my bedroom, seein' all of the monstrous shadows bein' cast on the walls from the lamp on my bedside table. I try to make sense of what she's tellin' me. If Dominion is a military headquarters, then those Powers can mobilize legions of angels to search for Evie. I take the pencil from her hand as another question surfaces in my mind.

Then what's a Nephilim? I write with dread, not sure I want that question answered for me.

She writes: *I don't know for sure. Like I said, the angels all clammed up when I asked them that question. Reed must have said something to Zee and the girls because they all keep insisting I'm not a Nephilim anytime I ask any of them what it is. They won't explain it to me. I looked it up on the Internet. I found out that a Nephilim is supposed to be an offspring of the sons of God, meaning angels, and the daughters of Man, meaning human women. The sons of God are angels, but the ones who fathered the Nephilim are specifically the angels called the "Watchers" or another name is the Grigori.*

That sounds exactly like what you are, Evie. I write. Tears collect in her eyes as she nods.

I know. But I hope not. She writes.

Why not? I write.

Because, Nephilim are said to be the offspring of human women and the Archangels that were sent to watch over humans. They weren't suppose to be able to breed with them, but when they did, they created these evil giant monsters called the Nephilim that God had to destroy in a flood because they were so vile.

"The" flood? Like the one with the big ark? I write the question and watch as she nods her head yes and then a wave of panic grips me. She can't be a Nephilim. They'll never let her live if she is. My hand shakes when I write: **Reed would know if you were a Nephilim. He would've killed you right away if that was the case. There is no way Zee would've let you live either, so we have to trust the angels when they say you aren't one of them.**

The only thing I can think of that points to me not being a Nephilim are a few technicalities. She watches as I quirk my eyebrow, eager for her to explain the loophole that gets us out of being seen as innately evil. Then she writes: *Well, there are three things that we can argue: We don't have white wings like the Archangels. I have red wings and I think you will too, so that clearly means that I come from the Seraphim. We aren't giants either. I'm not even six foot and these creatures were supposed to be huge giants. And finally, we have souls. None of the other creatures were reported to have souls, so they couldn't be redeemed.*

I just thought of another reason: <u>We're not evil</u>. I write, stabbin' the paper with my pencil harshly.

She takes the pencil out of my hand and writes: *I overheard Zee tell Reed that he uncovered the name of the Power leading the mission against me. Her name is Pagan. You want to know why they call her Pagan? It's because her favorite bad humans to smote, back in the day, were pagans. The last time I saw Pagan, she promised me that she would rip out my evil heart, just after she tore a fully-grown tree from the ground and hurled it at me like it weighed nothing at all. She's not going to stop. She's got this Dominion on her side. I heard Zee telling Reed that they may have to move us soon because she has shown up in this area searching for me. They were hoping that she* would believe we would leave the area, but somehow, she has gotten closer than they thought she would. Pagan can't find me with Reed or Zee. I heard Buns say that Dominion will execute them if they're found to be traitors. Dominion could put Reed and Zee on trial for treason if they think they're aiding the Fallen. Her hands are shakin' as she writes the last part. I gently take the pencil from her hand.

We're not Fallen. I write, tryin' to reason with her.

How sure are you that we would be able to convince a bunch of hostile Powers of that fact? Especially when one of them has already reported that we're Nephilim. Do you think they will give us time to explain before they rip our hearts from our bodies? What will happen to Reed and Zee? Will they be able to show the other Powers that we aren't evil before they kill them, too? Evie asks me as she frantically writes out her argument.

She has thought this out. She knows there is every chance that we won't be given an opportunity to speak on our own behalf before they mow us down like any of the Fallen would be when they are discovered. No trial, we're just dead.

He'll never let you go. I write, watchin' her expression turn from determination to anguish. She already knows this.

I can't stay and watch them kill Reed, not when I can save him. I can't exist if he doesn't exist. I have to know he is alive somewhere, or its over for me, too. You have to come with me, for their sakes because Pagan will believe you're a Nephilim, too. <u>Please</u>. We can't ask them for their protection anymore. I'm sorry, Russell. I wish you had time to evolve more before I rip you away from their protection, but if Pagan finds us, then we're all dead and I can't have that. If we stay, it's like we're murdering them. Evie writes, and then she drops the pencil back on the paper and covers her face with her hands. I can feel the desperation comin' from her.

I reach out and pull her to my chest. It feels so right to have her in my arms. She's 'bout to give me what I want most in the world and a part of me is so happy, I can hardly contain it. To have her all to myself is somethin' I want above anythin' else. *It's the only way to win her back. I would do anythin' for that chance. Anythin'*, I think to myself, holdin' her close.

"When do we leave?" I whisper to her, feelin' her damp tears on my bare chest as she cries with what I bet is a mixture of relief that I agreed and the agony of havin' to leave Reed.

"Soon. I've been planning it for awhile—since we got back. It was just an option at first. Someone told me I might need it," she whispers back.

"Where will we go?" I ask her in a low tone, hopin' she has thought this through 'cuz it will be a short trip if she hasn't. Reed is like a bloodhound when it comes to Evie and he won't stop until he gets her back.

"North," she says, and I cringe 'cuz I'm 'bout as far north as I ever want to go. Ever.

"How?" I ask, and listen to her plan as she outlines it.

CHAPTER 8

The Option

Finesse isn't required in my escape from the angels who have been safeguardin' me for months. Buns, Zee, and I have a Poli-Sci class together, well, we have every class together, but Red is right when she says my part in the plot will be easy. Zee and Buns have tunnel vision when they are together. They only see each other.

After parkin' in the campus lot, Zee picks up Buns's bag and begins carryin' it toward our class in the middle of campus. I check my watch. My window of escape is narrow. I have to get away within the next fifteen minutes, otherwise, if Evie is discovered missin' before I get a chance to leave, they might get suspicious and start askin' questions. After we enter the classroom, we take our seats together and I pretend to rummage through my bag for a second.

"Ahh, shoot, Zee." I say with a grim smile as I continue to check 'round in my bag, "I left my Poli-Sci book in the car. Toss me the keys and I'll get it." I hold out my hand for the keys to the new Tahoe we had driven to school.

"Do you want me to get it? I am much faster?" he asks, grinnin' at me arrogantly. His easy smile causes a pang of regret to hit me like someone punched me in the stomach. Zephyr and I are like brothers now. In just a couple of months, I have formed a tight bond with him and it feels like I'm sellin' him out, lyin' to him like this. I have to remember that I'm tryin' to save him from lookin' like a traitor to his own kind.

"Naw, I have to hit the bathroom. I'm gonna be late anyway," I say, still holdin' my hand out for the keys.

"Sweetie, you can use my book. I've already taken this class," Buns chimes in helpfully, lookin' past Zee to me from her seat on the other side of him. Seein' Buns with her fairy queen beauty, I'm sure that I will never meet anyone like her again. I'll miss her too, the way she is always tryin' to mother me now that my family is no longer available to me.

Don't think about that now, I tell myself as I look at her. I want to thank her for everythin' she has done for me throughout this freakin' mess of a life. *I wrote them letters,* I remind myself. *They are in my bag that I'm leavin' here. They should find them after I'm gone.* I can't bring myself to write a letter to Reed, though. I'm grateful for his help, 'cuz without him, my family would probably be toast from Alfred, but he has taken my girl's heart so I say we're even. I am leavin' him somethin', though—the tablet that Evie and I wrote on the other night in my room. It explains why she's leavin' him—I guess I owe him that much.

"I write all my notes in my book so I won't lose 'em," I explain, while Zephyr hands me the keys. "Thanks, Zee." I take one last look at them, tryin' to memorize their faces, and then I turn 'round and walk out of the classroom, hopin' I'm not makin' the biggest mistake of my life. *Well, if it's a mistake, ya probably won't be alive long enough to regret it,* I think as I run to the car and launch myself into the driver's seat.

Backin' out of the parkin' space, I fish in my pocket for the map that Red printed out for me, unfoldin' it as I drive away from campus. We are supposed to meet up at the train station in Coldwater. We are leavin' the car in the train station parkin' lot. Red reserved two train tickets to Chicago on her credit card that her Uncle Jim got for her when she went to Crestwood. It's the last purchase she's ever gonna make on that card, since she isn't gonna be Genevieve Claremont anymore. She contacted the private investigator, Ryan somethin'-or-other, that had worked with her Uncle Jim. She told him that she believes the man who killed her uncle is stalkin' her and she doesn't believe the police can protect her from him. She isn't lyin' technically, Alfred is stalkin' her and probably will until I kill him, which I will as soon as I evolve and find the maggot.

This Ryan knows a guy that makes passports and new identities for a price. I didn't ask her how much it cost or where the money came from to purchase our new names, but I have a feelin' it cost her a lot of the savings her uncle left her. One good thing came of it, though: she finally had a reason to praise the Crestwood Mothers Club. She cut out the pictures from her freshman directory to send him for our new passports and licenses. Her new name is Lillian Francis Lucas. I have been practicin' it in my head so I can get familiar with it, but I have decided I'm just gonna call her Red until I can get the Lillian part straight. Maybe Lily will grow on me, I'll see. She didn't get to pick her new name 'cuz I think they got it from a recently deceased woman. I guess that's how these things work. They gave her Lillian's social security number and created a birth certificate too, but the birth date is doctored so she's only eighteen.

I hate my new name, I think as I scan the rearview mirror for any signs of pursuit. Zee has to have noticed that I didn't return to class by now. Cell phones are probably goin' off if Red managed to slip away too. Not seein' anythin' behind me, I concentrate again on the road ahead of me.

They always say karma is a bitch, but now I know it's true. Evie teased me about my bad dodgeball karma again as soon as she handed me my passport. *Henry David Grant.* My mother would be freaked if she knew my new name; I mean Grant is just too ironic for a guy who grew up with sisters named Scarlett and Melanie. I guess it's lucky for me that I can never contact her and tell her. Not with Reed's ability to persuade humans. I tell her my name and it's all over. He would be on our doorstep the next day. I can't even call them, text them, or email them 'cuz Reed can trace it Evie said. She said we have to go on blackout mode until she can get us some new phones and a new computer. I guess Reed can find us just by the IP address of the computer he gave her. Good thing Red knows 'bout these things 'cuz she's 'bout as crafty as he is.

Henry Grant, I think again as I exhale a deep breath that eases some of the pain that name causes me. It's not even the name that I object to, if I'm bein' completely honest with myself. It's just a name. If Red had given me the most stellar name I could think of it would still suck 'cuz it's not my name. It's someone else's name. I'm givin' up my birthright. It's mine. Russell Marx. Me. It's like I'm givin' up my humanity, too, 'cuz I was nothin' but human when I was Russell. Now I'm supposed to be Henry and he's some kind of freaky half-angel. I have had thousands of names in a thousand different lifetimes, but for some reason, this one, Russell Marx, is the hardest for me to give up. Maybe it's 'cuz I'm not dyin' and movin' on to the next life. I don't know, but the pain I feel is somethin' awful. I clutch the steerin' wheel tight, drivin' faster than I should through the sleepy little towns between Crestwood and Coldwater.

I check my speed and ease up off the accelerator when the next thought occurs to me. Maybe I have been foolin' myself. If I'm bein' completely honest, then I have to admit that a part of Russell died months ago on that convenience store floor. Somethin' else survived, but it wasn't all me. No. I'm different now. I can feel it. There is a new purpose that Russell could never have fulfilled, not as I was. I'm changin' 'cuz I have to. Scannin' the cars behind me again, tryin' to see if any are familiar, I catch my own reflection in the mirror. *I even look different*, I think as I hardly recognize myself in the mirror. Evie fixed my crooked nose when she healed me. I'm also beginnin' to get that angel shine to my skin that sorta creeps me out. It's like someone's backlightin' me or somethin'. A small shiver escapes me when I think of it.

No, I'm definitely different. I used to be eighteen, but I'm not anymore. No I'm much, much, much older than that now. *I was eighteen when I died and I woke up ancient, with memories of things I've never seen with these eyes,* I think, lookin' at my brown eyes in the mirror again. I can plow a field with oxen and a yoke. I can make mead and tell ya just how much honey yer gonna need for each cask. I can make the casks, too, come to think of it. I can thread a needle and spin fibers into thread. I can weave baskets and make candles. I can make fire without a match.

I can build just about anythin' I can think of: from an adobe hut to an engine to the spires on a cathedral. I can hoist a mainsail and navigate a ship by usin' a sextant. I understand a host of different languages, some that don't even exist anymore. And I can kill with bullets, swords, sabers, spears, arrows, axes, chakrams, knives, daggers, slings, rocks, and an assortment of other weapons that I don't even care to remember.

Pullin' into the town of Coldwater, I check the map again, and then follow the posted signs that lead me straight to the train station. Red said to park in the lot and wait for her there. She was very specific 'bout not gettin' out and roamin' 'round without her. I kinda laughed at her at first, 'til she told me 'bout the shadow man she met at the Coldwater coffee shop last semester. When she told me what happened, it made what I did afterward to the firewall seem even worse. Smashin' the crap out of it after she went through so much trouble to get it for me was an awful thing to have done. And knowin' that all along she was alone with that evil whack job, Alfred, makes me feel sick inside.

I locate the train station. Turnin' into the parkin' lot, I find a spot in the back of the lot and cut the engine. I scan the lot for Red, but can't see anythin' but humans wanderin' 'round with luggage and smilin' faces. *They look happy. I wonder where they're goin', Chicago maybe,* I think, watchin' a couple of travelers bustlin' into the station on what is probably a planned trip to a destination of their own choosin'. For a moment, I give into the feelin' of jealousy that makes my teeth clench and my hands ball into fists. I can hardly remember now what it feels like to be completely human and have no clue that angels truly exist. Ha! Even if I had thought they existed, I imagined them so much differently than the reality. How I could've bought that Hallmark version is beyond me. I should've paid closer attention in school when the nuns were talkin' 'bout all the sinners gettin' smoked by the avengin' angels. That's more their speed. Well, the Powers anyway. Not the Reapers—they're nicer…well, the divine ones are anyway.

I check my watch again to see if I'm early, but I'm not. I'm right on time. *Where are ya, Red?* I think to myself as my knee bounces in agitation. I look out the back window to see if she is behind me somewhere. *Maybe she couldn't go through with it,* I think and a wave of anxiety courses through my body. *This is the only way she'll let me back in her heart. She'll never see me if Reed is 'round. He's like a drug to her. A drug she's gonna Jones for when he is not 'round to give her a fix.*

I'm ready for that. I just have to get her through the first few months again, and then she will come out of it. She was comin' out of it last semester, when I kissed her at the lake. She responded to my kiss, at first anyway, then she pushed me away, but she had kissed me back at first. I didn't know why then, but I do now. Her soul wants me, not Reed, me. There has to be a way to get her to respond again. If there is, I'll find it. It's worth the risk. She is worth any risk 'cuz I can't seem to let go of her, just like she couldn't let me go when I was dyin' in her arms.

Somethin' is definitely wrong, I think as my lips flatten in a grim line, lookin' at my watch again. *She's late. Her part in this escape is much harder than mine.* I try to remind myself. She has to get away from Brownie and Reed. Brownie shouldn't be too hard because she trusts Red and isn't tryin' to protect her from every little thing that could possibly go wrong. *Reed, on the other hand, can't keep his eyes off her…or his hands,* I think, frownin'. She wouldn't go over how she planned to get away from him. When I asked her, she said she couldn't plan it 'cuz it was gonna have to be as natural as she could make it and rehearsin' it made her feel sick.

Seein' a train leavin' the Coldwater station just in front of where I'm parked, makes my anxiety level increase. Watchin' the railroad crossin' lights near the street begin to flash, my breathin' increases while the crossbars drop slowly, stoppin' the traffic as the loud clangin' of the bell warns that the train is approachin'. The train crosses the street; its' cars go over the rails between the crossbars one-by-one:

ca-click, ca-click, ca-click, ca-click. The sunlight flashes through the division of the cars as each one passes in front of me. *It's not my train that's leavin',* I remind myself. We're not even gonna take a train. We just need the angels to think that that's what we're doin'.

Red really put a lot of thought into this plan. She is buyin' train tickets to Chicago, but we are headin' across town to the bus station to catch a bus north. She said we need to buy time to get out of here. They might just be desperate enough to go after the train, especially since it's headin' for Chicago, which is sure to freak Reed out and throw him off his game. She said there is no way we can go to Chicago 'cuz it's too big a risk. Reed will be frantic to follow us to Chicago, if he thinks that's where we're headed, 'cuz he will believe we are ridin' straight into the Fallen.

Red has been tryin' to teach me how to think strategically when it comes to angels. She says that to avoid angels, we have to think small towns, no excitement, and no luxury—nothin' fun. Oddly enough, that sounds like a great new life to me. Boredom will be a great change of pace to what we have been through in the last few months. I'll take boredom over the Fallen any day.

I check my watch again when the last train car travels over the tracks ahead of me. *She is officially really late now,* I think, beginnin' to really worry 'bout her. The best thing that could've happened to her is that Reed caught on to her plan and stopped her. The worst I don't even want to think about, 'cuz it has a name, and it's name is Alfred. Panic hits me then and I start the engine of the car before I can check myself. I sit there for a second, with the engine idlin', tryin' to calm down and think rationally. *Should I look for her? Should I call Zephyr and tell him what we're up to? Should I wait and not blow the whole thing she planned for months 'cuz of a little glitch?* My knee is bouncin' up and down for real now as I'm rubbin' the palms of my hands on my jeans.

We have to move soon, if we want to make it to the bus station in time to catch the bus to Mackinaw. Once there, Ryan has arranged to have a car waitin' for us. Red said not to get my hopes up too much 'cuz its gonna be a used beater, which is so much different from the luxury we have been used to the last few months. I expect we are in for some culture shock for a while 'cuz our fortune will drastically change now that we are not gonna be hangin' with the VIPs. I have to admit that I was kinda diggin' all the clothes and stuff Buns and Brownie kept throwin' at me for no good reason other than they were bored and wanted to shop. I had to leave everythin' behind though, so it's back to my old lifestyle of t-shirts and jeans from now on. *I hope I can find stuff big enough to fit me when we get to the U.P.,* I think, tryin' to go over the plan so I won't throw the car in reverse and peel out lookin' for Red.

Unconsciously, I pull out the cell phone that has all of the angel's numbers programmed on speed dial in it. When I notice it in my hand, I flip the phone open and my finger twitches on the power button as I stare at it intently. *If I turn it on and call Zee, then I will effectively be tossin' away any hope I have of gettin' Red back—but if she is in trouble and I don't call them, then I may be killin' her.* Somethin' in my stomach twists as I hit the power button and watch the phone light up. The phone starts ringin' immediately and I look at the caller ID, it's Zee. Just as my finger shifts to answer the call, a soft tappin' on the window makes me hesitate. I look over and see the most beautiful pair of eyes I have ever seen in any lifetime staring back at me from the other side of the glass.

I snap the phone shut and open my car door. Ignorin' Red's sad expression, I pick her up off her feet and hold her in relief. "Uhh… can't breathe…" Red says, tryin' to get me to ease up on the hug. I do, but it's hard.

Murmurin' near her ear, I say, "We have to get phones as soon as possible. I almost called Zee 'cuz I was so worried 'bout ya and I knew ya weren't takin' yers with ya."

"You weren't supposed to take yours either," she say. I set her back on her feet. She turns to the car, and leanin' in, she picks up the phone that is now beepin'. "They can use a satellite to figure out what tower your phone is roaming on. They can find our general location that way. We can't take this phone with us," she says, turnin' it off and tossin' it back in the car.

"I know yer irritated with me already, but I brought it just in case somethin' went wrong and we had to abort the mission," I explain, studyin' her face. She looks sick, like she is havin' a hard time breathin'. "You were late and I imagined all sorts of bad stuff happenin' to ya so I was gonna call in the angels."

"You can't do that, Russell," Red says quietly. "Even when bad stuff happens. We are on our own now: just you and me. We can never call them because they can't be responsible for us anymore… at least, not until we can figure out a way to make it so that they won't be traitors if they help us. If you can figure that out, then we can go back to them, but until that day…" she trails off, tryin' to hide her pain from me.

"Are ya ready to go?" I ask, and I mean leave Reed.

I think she knows what I mean, but she ignores my question and says, "No. I have to go get the tickets inside so the angels actually think we boarded the train. I just wanted to put my letters in the car." She pulls envelopes from the small backpack she has strapped to her back and puts them on the driver's seat. "You wait here, I'll go get the tickets, and then we'll head to the bus station."

"I'll go with ya," I reply, not wantin' to let her out of my sight for a second.

"No, I have to do this fast because we're late. I'll just be a second," she says, watchin' me. She must have seen how concerned I am 'bout her 'cuz she smiles a little and adds, "I'll be fine, Russell—I mean, Henry. I'm pretty tough now." She is gone then in a fraction of a second.

I turn to collect my small backpack I had stashed in the back of the Tahoe. I have one change of clothes and a few pictures of my family, but that's 'bout all I can take to start my new life. I close the hatch of the car and head back to the driver's seat to collect the keys and put them under the seat before I lock the car door. The envelopes are lyin' on the seat in front of me. The one addressed to Reed is on top of the others. It's Evie's final goodbye to him. I pick it up. I know that I shouldn't open it even as I begin readin' her letter, but I must be a masochist or somethin' 'cuz I can't stop myself.

Dear Reed,

I wish that you had taught me your lovely Angelic language, so that I could tell you all of the ways I love you and make them sound like the music of your world. But, I am not of that world and may never be. That fact is no more obvious to me than at this moment, when I have to apologize for the situation you and the other angels are in because of me. I know about Pagan and Dominion. I overheard your conversation in the library the other night. I refuse to destroy you by existing. I will not make you a traitor to the Divine. The only thing I can do is leave so that all of you will be safe. Do not mistake my intentions. It is not you that I am protecting because I am aware that you do not need my protection. It is myself I am protecting because I cannot exist if you do not, so I will do what I must to ensure that you remain alive. My only hope for survival lies in the knowledge that you are somewhere in this world, under the same sky, the same sun, the same stars.

If I had the art to say what I feel inside, then I would be certain that you would believe me when I tell you that I love you, but I am afraid that you will begin to doubt it when I am gone. I think Shakespeare said it best when he wrote: "Doubt thou the stars are fire; Doubt that the sun doth move; Doubt truth to be a liar; But never doubt I love...I love thee best, O most best, believe it."

I have only one prayer now and it is that we will be allowed to be together again one day. I will hold on to that thread of hope until the currents shift again and I can come back to you. God's blessings upon you Reed. Goodbye, my angel.

Always and forever,
Evie

I stuff the letter back in the envelope and place it back on top of the other letters on the seat. I feel ill. She means every word of that letter. Every stinkin' word of it and the jealousy that I feel for Reed is reachin' new heights. *How had he managed to win her heart so completely in just a few months? I've had lifetimes with her and it's like that doesn't even matter,* I think, tossin' the keys under the seat as I lock the car door and slam it shut. I lean up against the Tahoe and close my eyes. *Time. I have time on my side. The more time I can get with her, the more of a chance I'll have of winnin' her back. She is gonna give me the time, so I have to make it work for me. The clock starts now; every moment is an opportunity he won't have,* I think, and I almost smile in anticipation of the day she breaks down and lets me back in.

"You ready?" Red asks me in a soft tone. I hadn't even heard her approach me; she is so stealthy now, just like Reed. They are like cats, one minute they are not there and the next second they are in front of ya, sizin' ya up.

"Yeah, how far do we have to go?" I ask as we start joggin' across the parkin' lot.

"About three or four miles," Red answers, easily keepin' her pace with mine. She probably can run there in less than a minute, but she stays with me as I labor to keep a steady pace. It isn't too hard to run it 'cuz I'm still in good condition from football, but she is not even breakin' a sweat as she casually lopes along beside me.

When we reach the bus station, we purchase our tickets to Mackinaw with cash. The bus is already boardin', so we hurry over to the garage. Findin' two seats together near the back, Red and I stow our bags under the seats in front of us. She takes mercy on me and my long legs, givin' me the aisle seat as she slips in near the window. The seats are cramped and I don't even want to think 'bout the pain I'm gonna be in when we reach Mackinaw 'bout six hours from now.

When the bus pulls out of the station, I look over at Red, seein' tears slidin' down her cheeks. She angles her face away from me, tryin' to hide them from me. Liftin' up the armrest that divides her seat from mine, I put my arm 'round her shoulder. I pull her securely against me and stroke her hair as she cries. It is all I can do for now.

She finally falls asleep a couple hours into the trip. I watch the scenery slidin' by us as I gaze out the window that has a layer of film on it. My head reaches over the seat, so I have a pretty good view of what is happenin' on the bus. We are pretty safe here. It's no miracle that there are no angels here, Fallen or otherwise. This sucks from a travel standpoint. We are all crammed into this bus like sardines. The seats look like someone has been sick on them at least a couple of times, and in general, the bus could use a good ol' fashion scrubbin' to get the layer of grit off of it. I haven't ventured back to the bathroom yet, but judgin' by the smell comin' from behind me, I would rather wait until we stop somewhere to go.

I can see why Red opted to take the bus. I can't envision Zephyr travelin' on this bus if his life depended on it. He told me 'bout havin' to drive the minivan, like it was the hardest thing he had ever had to do. Zephyr was kinda funny like that. He has told me 'bout havin' to sit waist deep in mud, while in a trench in the middle of a monsoon one time, waitin' for a fallen angel he had been huntin' to show up and trip his snare. But, drivin' a minivan is a hardship. I guess when yer huntin', it doesn't matter what ya have to go through. I shiver, thinkin' 'bout what Red had told me 'bout Pagan. *I wonder how big a hole she'll be willin' to sit in to get us.*

The bus makes its first stop in a small depot/convenience store gas station in a rural town. I think 'bout gettin' out and stretchin' my legs, but I don't want to wake Red up. I also have to admit that it makes me uncomfortable to be anywhere near small convenience stores. I haven't told anyone that, but I haven't been able to enter one since that freakin' night with Alfred.

A couple of new passengers board the bus at this station. It is a pair of teenage girls 'round our age, but they are excited to be on the road. It sounds like they are headin' up to Mackinaw to get jobs on the island for the summer. Since it's almost May, the weather is warmin' up and we would have been takin' our exams in a couple of weeks, if we could have stayed in Crestwood. But that probably wouldn't have happened anyway 'cuz Red thought the angels were preparin' to move us so Pagan couldn't find us.

I don't feel that bad 'bout leavin' school. It just doesn't seem important to me anymore. I know I will eventually need to go to school if I ever hope to make any money, but since I have either an eternity, or no time at all, I figure it doesn't really matter. Plus, what kind of office job am I gonna get while lookin' over my shoulder all day hopin' an angel doesn't walk in the office and try to mow me down? Naw, I'll probably have to get some kind of job that has little or no interaction with the public. Somethin' I can do in a back room or hidin' somewhere. Stockboy in a grocery store would be a good job for me. Work at night when the store is closed, so no one walks in on me. *Say "hello" to minimum wage,* I think grimly.

The teenage girls who sit a few seats ahead of us are talkin' so loudly, I hear every word they are sayin'. I shift 'round in my seat uncomfortably when they notice me and begin talkin' in lower voices 'bout me. They believe I can't hear them, but with my new ability, I get to hear every word they're sayin'. I wish I had remembered to bring my earplugs with me 'cuz it's embarrassin' the way they're talkin' 'bout me. Some of the stuff they are fantasizin' 'bout probably isn't even legal.

"You have admirers, Henry," Red says, lookin' at me while sittin' up and stretchin' her arms above her head, tryin' to work out the kinks that sleepin' in one position created. I cringe, hearin' her say my new name.

"Is there a nickname for Henry?" I ask, tryin' to divert her attention from what the girls in front of us were sayin'.

"The French pronounce it, "On-Ree," Red says, smilin' and twistin' to stretch her back out better. She looks sleek and sexy with her hair a little messy from sleep.

"No, that blows." I reply, smilin' back at her.

"Hank?" she asks, thinkin'.

"That could be tough. I would sound like a bouncer in a rough country bar. Hey Hank, toss him outta here!" I say, mimickin' the deepest southern accent I know, testin' out the name.

"You're tough all right, Hank," she replies, lookin' at me. "Thank you for coming with me. I couldn't do this without you."

"You and me, that's how it's always been," I smile, holdin' her hand and givin' it a gentle squeeze.

She nods her head as if she accepts my statement. She frowns then and says, "Listen, I have to start telling you about everything I've been trying to do to make sure you're safe," she says, while adoptin' that tense face that she gets when she's worried and upset. "We have to be really cautious from now on and I want to go over some rules that we need to follow so that we avoid our evil buddies."

"Okay, I'm listenin'. Ya don't have to talk a million miles an hour; we have plenty of time, trust me. I don't think this bus has gone a mile over the speed limit since we've been in it," I reply, tryin' to calm her down a little so she won't stress out.

"Okay, you're right. I'm kinda tweeked right now," she says, takin' deep breaths. "The first thing I want to tell you is that, since we have no way to reach each other right now if we are separated, I want you to know that I set up a covert way for us to communicate, if we lose each other for any reason," she says, watchin' my reaction to her words. I nod, but don't interrupt so she goes on, "I created a profile on Facebook that you can check, if you need to find me. Just look up Aoibhe Campbell. The password to log on as me is Leander. I created a profile for you, too. Yours is Leander Duncan. The password is Aoibhe," she explains. I grin at her because she is so cunning. "You can post whatever you want on yours. If we get separated, you can post where you are and I'll find you. Check mine to see if I posted anything for you. I'll make sure to include a smiley face at the end of whatever I write, so you know it's from me. If there is no smiley face, then I didn't write it and it's a trap. Do you understand?" she asks. I nod. "If there is danger, you can go to any library and use the computer. Do you know how to get on Facebook?" she asks.

"Yeah, I'm not completely useless," I reply with a reassuring grin.

"I know that," she says quickly, like she's afraid she hurt my feelings. "We have to avoid all the things that the Fallen like. So that means we have to stay out of bars. If you get buddies that want to go there, you have to make some excuse not to go because we can't take the risk."

"I don't have a fake ID anymore, Red—well, not one that'll get me in a bar. Henry is only nineteen," I remind her, givin' the excuse I'll use for avoidin' the bar.

"That's right. You left your old fake ID in Crestwood," she says as she bites her lower lip, while I nod again. "Okay, good," she says, tryin' to shake off her sadness. "Um, we need to avoid any big celebrations or things that wealthy people do." When I look confused, she says, "Ah, this is tough because it's a judgment call. Let's say that there is going to be a big fireworks display for the Fourth of July or something. We shouldn't go because angels really like fireworks. You should've seen Buns talk about them, like they're the sickest things ever. I think it's because angels are born of fire," she says casually.

"Huh?" I ask.

"What?" she counters.

"Angels are born of fire?" I ask.

"Yeah. Reed mentioned that once and Buns let it slip, too. I'm not quite sure if it's a literal interpretation or a figurative one, but

I'm betting on the literal because Buns is not very abstract."

"What are we born of then?" I ask, tryin' to understand her.

She shrugs and says, "We are born of the earth…dust to dust as they say."

"So now we are fire and earth?" I ask.

"Yeah, now all we need is wind and we'll be a band," she replies. "Anyway, let me think…oh yeah, try not to do anything that wealthy people do."

"What do wealthy people do?" I ask with a smirk.

"I don't know…don't go yachting," she says flippantly, and I can't contain my laughter at that one.

"Is that an option where we're goin'?" I ask as I see that my laugh has helped her find her smile.

"Yes. We're going to Houghton. It's a port town in the Upper Peninsula on the Portage Waterway in the Keweenaw Peninsula near Lake Superior," she says slowly, as if she is recallin' somethin' she had memorized from a book. "It's a college town, but it's like Crestwood in that it's small enough not to interest the Fallen and big enough so that we can retain some anonymity and try to blend in with the humans. There is nothing too over the top there. I researched it. It used to be a mining town: copper mines.

"Great, maybe I can be a miner," I say, thinkin' that no angel will be lookin' for me down in a huge hole in the ground.

"No," Red says with her brows drawn together. "You're going to take the SATs as Henry Grant, and then you're going to enroll in the technology school in Houghton as a freshmen. You're getting an education, Hank," she says in a stern tone as if I have no say in the matter at all.

"Oh yeah? How am I supposed to pay for that?" I ask, thinkin' we may not even get a chance to take midterms before we have to leave for some reason. We have to be mobile, ready to leave at a moments notice, not tied to a schedule and certainly not throwin' thousands of dollars away on an education we may not be able to stick around long enough to get.

"I'm paying for it," she says quickly.

"How?" I ask with suspicion in my voice.

"I signed my uncle's house over to Ryan. He gave me a fair price for it in a cashier's check. Now I can pay for it and we can live for a while," she explains, scannin' my face.

"Red, I can't let ya pay for me like that," I reply, repulsed.

"I'm not going to argue about this with you. You're going to school and that's the end of it," she stiffens, lookin' out the window.

"No, it's not!" I reply like she has lost her freakin' mind, which she has.

"Yes, it is," she says stubbornly as she turns back again and I see her stiff posture. She is gearin' up for a fight and is 'bout to let me have it. "You have to go to school. I can't live with you being a miner down in some hole all day long. You have to get an education. I insist."

"Why?" I ask, 'cuz there is a shadow behind her eyes that showin' such a need, a desperation for somethin'. When she is silent I add, "Ya better tell me, Red, 'cuz I'm 'bout to dig in and once I do you will never convince me to change my mind."

"Because I stole your future, Russell. I stole your name; I stole your life from you. How can you sit there and look at me like I'm the only person in the world, when I have all but destroyed you?" she asks as more tears escape her eyes. She uses her fists to wipe them away harshly, like she is angry that she is cryin' again.

"Ya didn't do any of those things, Red," I say, watchin' her duck her head and look away from me. "I'm serious. Ya haven't done this to me."

"Then who did it, Russell?" she whispers so low I can barely hear her.

"Hey, that's Henry to you, Lillian," I reply, ignorin' her scowl. "Red, this is somethin' that was meant to be long before I met ya at Crestwood. Ya think ya did this?" I ask her, lookin' at her and seein' her nod. "Well, then, yer stupid and arrogant," I reply.

"Thanks a lot, Hank, I feel so much better now," she mutters.

"Naw, ya are. If ya think yer capable of doin' all this alone, without the help of Heaven, then yer foolish. This is meant. I feel it. I have a mission here, and like it or not, it involves ya. I have no idea yet what we're supposed to be doin', but I'm sure it's gonna be comin', whether we want to deal with it or not and it's gonna be messy, and ugly, and painful," I say, lookin' at her like she is the child and I'm the adult. I am the adult. I'm thousands of years old, and unlike her, I remember every one of them.

"Our only mission, Hank, is to survive long enough to see tomorrow. Then tomorrow, our mission will be to survive until the next day. One day at a time," she says pessimistically.

"Okay, you go on thinkin' that and see where ya get," I reply unsympathetically. "Meanwhile, I'll be lookin' out for the signs that are comin'."

"Do you need a crystal ball for that? I could pick one up for you," she says with sarcasm.

"Naw, I just need ya. That's it," I reply easily.

"So you'll go to school then?" she asks me in a rhetorical way.

"We'll see," I reply, not givin' in to her bossy attitude.

"I'm going to work on you until you agree," she says, like she's tellin' me somethin' I don't already know.

"Yes. I know," I reply, ignorin' her again. *She is torn up inside. Raw,* I think as she sits quietly, watchin' the scenery goin' by outside. She looks so sad that I have a feelin' I'm gonna be promisin' her anythin' in a little while just to see if I can ease some of her pain.

Dusk is upon us when we pull into Mackinaw City. I can hardly stand when the bus comes to a stop at the depot. I put my hand out to Red to help her out into the aisle, and then I take our bags and place my hand on the small of her back as we walk off the bus. I'm so relieved to be off that hunk of metal I can shout it to the world. But, lookin' at Red, she looks ill.

Watchin' in shock, Red bolts from the depot, runnin' in a fraction of a second 'round the corner of the buildin'. I spring forward, tryin' to follow her, panickin' as I wonder what is happenin'. When I round the corner, I find her clutchin' a garbage can and heavin', but since she hasn't eaten anythin' today, she isn't throwin' anythin' up. After a while she stops and uses the back of her hand to wipe her mouth.

"I have to go back, Russell," she whispers to me when she can speak. "I can't feel him anymore," she says, clutchin' her stomach like it aches. "He's going to think I betrayed him. I have to go back," she says again, and her whole body is shakin' like a true junkie.

"Ya didn't betray him and he won't think that ya did. He'll know why ya did it. I left him the paper ya used to convince me to come with ya. He'll know. He'll see," I whisper back.

She groans again and heaves some more with the same result, except this time, her hands crush the sides of the metal garbage can where she is holdin' on to it. I look 'round to make sure no one is nearby to witness it, not like I can do anythin' to stop her. "He is probably way past panic by now. What is he going to do when he can't find me?" she asks, starin' at me with wild eyes.

"I don't know," I say, wantin' to help her, but not knowin' how. "But at least, if that Pagan shows up, ya won't be there to make him a traitor. They'll see that he isn't helpin' ya and he'll be safe."

She nods then, standin' up a little straighter. "We don't stand a chance, Russell," she whispers to me, lookin' grim.

"My name's Henry and I say we do. You are one huge ass kicker, Red, and when I get my wings, I'm gonna make sure every fallen angel I meet ceases to be. Now, straighten up and let's go before we attract unwanted attention," I order, takin' charge. She's a mess and the sooner I can get her to the car the better. Takin' her by the elbow, I ask, "What are we lookin' for?"

She reaches into her backpack then, pullin' out an orange locker key. I locate the locker and when I open it, there are two sets of keys inside and a letter. I take the keys and hand the letter to Red. She reads the letter, and then looks up and says, "Jeep Cherokee Sport, four-door, white."

"Sweet," I say, and mean it. I was afraid I was gonna have to cram my body into some little hatchback, and after gettin' out of that bus, a Jeep Cherokee sounds like a little slice of Heaven. "We'll have to send Ryan a fruit basket."

I nudge Red toward the parkin' lot and we locate the Jeep with little trouble. I open the passenger door for her and help her in the car before roundin' the car and gettin' in the driver's side. I start the engine and let the car warm up while lookin' at Red. It's decision time again. I know this is one of the weakest moments she's ever gonna have, but we have to discuss whether to press on or turn back. We have to do this together, or not at all.

"Who are we, Red?" I ask her, lookin' straight out the windshield.

"What?" she asks, like she is numb.

"Are we Evie and Russell? Or, are we Lillian and Henry?" I ask in a gentle tone. I wait for her to respond, watchin' as people walk by the car, laughin' in their happy human existences.

"We're both," she says in a monotone voice.

"No, we're not. We're one, or we're the other," I say patiently. "So you decide now, so I'll know which way to head, north or south."

She is quiet for so long I begin to think that she is incapable of answerin' me. "I'm Lillian Lucas and you are Henry Grant," she says stiffly, and there is so much sorrow in her words she is almost chokin' on them.

"Okay then," I exhale deeply, puttin' the car in reverse and backin' out of the parkin' space before headin' out to the highway. I turn north and we are immediately crossin' the huge Mackinaw Bridge that connects the Lower Peninsula of Michigan with the Upper Peninsula. It's mad cool and I can't stop myself from askin', "What Lake is this we're drivin' over?"

"It's Lake Michigan," she murmurs as we both marvel at the majesty of the suspension bridge that seems to float in the sky above the beautiful blue water below us.

"Yeah? Well, it is beautiful. I can't wait to see Lake Superior. Is the swimmin' good?" I ask and see her lips twitch in an almost smile.

"Yeah." she says. "If you enjoy being a Popsicle."

"It's cold then?" my brow arches as I smile.

"Cold is an understatement. You'll need angel skin to enjoy it if you try to swim now. Lake Huron is warmer," she says informatively. Payin' the toll on the other side of the bridge, I follow the signs west toward Escanaba. We plan to continue to head west toward Iron Mountain and from there we will travel north to Houghton.

We drive for a while on a two-lane road that winds through a few touristy small towns, and then all of a sudden, the road opens up near the water and the sun is settin' on Lake Michigan. I can almost believe that I am lookin' at an ocean instead of a lake. It is pristine; the sand is almost white as the beach spreads out before us with wild tumbled stones spikin' through the breakers, lookin' as empty as the day it was created. Not a soul is roamin' 'round near it. I can't believe that there aren't mobs of people out there enjoyin' its beauty. "Where are all the people, Red?" I ask her, stunned.

"People don't know," she says, lookin' at the water. "It's so wild, untamed. I expect most people like their water warmer and a little more to do—more tourist stuff."

"Yeah. People are crazy," I reply, watchin' the water on and off until it disappears behind thick pine trees. As we drive on, I become aware of the fact that we haven't eaten at all since breakfast. "You hungry?" I ask. She shakes her head no. "I keep seein' these signs for pasties. Do you know what they are?" I ask.

She smiles a little, and then says, "It's meat and potatoes wrapped up in a dough and baked in an oven. There are different kinds. You can get them with cheese and vegetables in them too, but they're traditionally meat and potatoes."

"That sounds good. Let's stop and get some. I'm starvin'," I say.

I pull over at a small cinderblock buildin' whose sign says, "Fresh Pasties." We both come in to use the bathroom, but then Red heads right back out to the car as I order several kinds to go. The girl behind the counter is chatty and keeps askin' me where I am from because of my accent. I tell her I'm from Alabama, even though I don't sound a thing like someone from Alabama. She can't tell 'cuz we all sound the same to her. Takin' the food back out to the car, I get in and hand Red a pasty that is wrapped in tin foil and a bottle of water. She takes it from me, but doesn't look like she is gonna eat it.

I sigh heavily, not wantin' to have this conversation now, but resolvin' to get it out of the way, I say, "Ya have to eat, Red. I'm sorry it's not oatmeal, but it's the best I can do for now."

"I'm not hungry, Hank," she murmurs.

"Well, pretend that you are and get it down 'cuz I need ya and I can't have ya starvin' yerself 'cuz yer sad. I hate to admit it, but yer stronger than me and I'm gonna need yer help if we get spotted by an angel," I say, reasonin' with her before I take a bite of my food and smile 'cuz it is delicious.

Chewin', I watch her take a small bite of her pasty and chew it slowly, mechanically. I manage to eat three pasties in the time it takes Red to eat a half of one, but I don't rag her yet, since she looks like she is really tryin' to eat it.

Neither one of us speaks again until we reach Escanaba. I keep watchin' the gas gauge on the car go down, knowin' we are gonna have to stop for gas. With no credit card, we will have to pay with cash and that means goin' in the gas station. The feelin' of unease settles in my stomach. *Maybe I can find a full service station or one that doesn't have a convenience store attached to it,* I tell myself, scannin' the streets for somewhere to fuel up. I know it's stupid to be afraid of somethin' as ordinary as a gas station, but the thought of goin' in one of these places now, after bein' in the 7-Eleven with fallen angels and watchin' them dismember those people, makes me feel like ice is formin' in my stomach.

It's dark out now, and since the fuel light is indicatin' that I have run out of time to find a full-service gas station, I pull up to a self-service pump and get out to pump the gas. After stickin' the nozzle of the pump in the tank, I walk back to the driver's side door and stick my head back in the car. "I don't suppose we have anythin' other than cash to pay for the gas?" I ask as casually as I can. She shakes her head no and I grimace. "Shoot," I mutter, rubbin' my sweaty hands on my jeans. She's pale, too. "God, we're a pair, aren't we?" I ask, tryin' to smile at her as the pump keeps tollin' the price of our gas like it is tickin' out the last few seconds of my life. "We're both terrified of florescent lights and snack aisles."

"I hate the glass refrigerators and the coffee machines as much as the snack aisles," she says, attemptin' humor.

"I bet ya do," I reply, 'cuz Buns had told me how Alfred had thrown Red through the glass door of one of the refrigerators in the 7-Eleven before he had dragged her over to me. That's how her wing was broken. Reed had to re-break it when she was unconscious 'cuz it had healed wrong. When I asked Buns how she knew that, she told me that one of the souls told her how it all went down. The souls would know 'cuz they were there, too, I think, shiverin'. "Don't worry, I'll handle this one," I say as the pump clicks off, tellin' me that my time is up. Just then, somethin' funny moves across my back and I look over my shoulder to see what is touchin' me. Nothin' is there.

I shut the door softly and turn to remove the nozzle from the tank. Dread is eatin' me alive as I screw the cap back on the tank and shut the latch. I walk 'round the car toward the double doors. Sweat trickles down the side of my face when I push weakly against the glass door, starin' at the ground as I enter the store.

"Ahh, hell," I mutter as I imagine blood stainin' the floor. I have to hesitate just inside the doorway to steady myself as the room spins on me like a freakin' tilt-a-whirl. I clench my teeth, tryin' to focus on movin' forward toward the clerk. There are a couple of people in line at the counter. I walk by them, pacin', so that I won't just bolt back out the door.

"Did ja see da baseball game o'er at da high school there, Joe?" The clerk asks his customer, not even botherin' to ring up the items on the counter. He is makin' small talk like they're at a tea party or somethin'.

Joe leans on the counter like he is settlin' in and says, "No, how'd da boys do, eh?"

As I pace down the aisle near the back of the store, a shootin' pain tears up my back, makin' me clutch the top of the snack shelf near me. Lookin' 'round the store, I panic even more 'cuz I'm no-where near the front door and escape.

"Ah, da boys did good. Da Eskymos were down for a while, but they fought back, doncha know?" the clerk says slowly as he scratches his chin, watchin' the expression on Joe's face.

Another shootin' pain strikes me and it registers in my head that the pain is comin' from inside of me, not outside. Seein' that I'm near the bathroom, I manage to turn and run to the door just as a grotesque poppin' and crackin' sound resonates in my ears. I slam the door closed behind me, gaspin' as somethin' punches it's way out of my back. It knocks all the wind out of me. I lock the door before I spin 'round to see my jacket and shirt lyin' in tatters on the bathroom floor. Lookin' in the mirror directly across from where I'm standin', I see my reflection and nearly shout, "LORD! What are ya DOIN' to me now?"

Bright red wings are spreadin' out 'round me like a matador's cape. I just stand there, starin' at myself in the mirror, not believin' what I'm seein'. "I'm a Seraph all right," I say under my breath to my reflection as I shake my head. My wings aren't as big as Reed's or Zee's, but they are definitely much bigger than Red's. I try to move my new crimson appendages, but they won't budge at all.

"Ahh, naw! Naw, naw, naw, naw, naw…" I say, panickin' again as I realize the situation I'm in. I'm locked in a convenience store bathroom, in the middle of an escape from the angels, in the heart of the U.P., at night, with Red waitin' outside all alone for me to come out, and somewhere in Heaven, there are freakin' Cherubim, laughin' their asses off while countin' out my sins.

Turnin' on the faucet, I run my hands under the cold water, splashin' it on my face while tryin' to calm down. Everyone is always tellin' Red that her wings won't go back in when she's panickin' or worrin' 'bout somethin'. *I just have to relax*, I coach myself as I jump 'round, tryin' to work off a little bit of the adrenaline coursin' through my body. After 'bout fifteen minutes of pacin' the bathroom, I am beginnin' to calm down a little, so I grasp the counter in front of me with both hands, bowin' my head as I concentrate really hard on tryin' to move my wings. I look up hopefully, but they are still there in the mirror when I catch sight of my reflection.

"Damn. Okay," I say, lookin' up at the ceilin' helplessly. "I can use a little help here, please."

Immediately there is a knock on the bathroom door and Red's shaky voice sounds from behind it. "Hank, you in there?"

Scramblin' over to the door, I unlock it. I open it just a little and pull her through the doorway by her arm. Then, I slam it shut behind her, lockin' it again.

Her face is as white as milk, probably from her struggle to enter the store, but I can tell that is nothin' compared to the shock of seein' me with wings stickin' out of my back. "Russell, you're a freakin' angel!" she gasps as her hand shakes while she reaches out to touch my wing that flutters on its own when her fingers make contact with it.

"Yeah, whaddaya know?" I breathe, 'cuz I had no idea how nice it would feel to have her stroke my wing like that. "Slight problem, though. I can't get 'em to go back in."

Her brow wrinkles. "Uh oh!" she breathes, understandin' my problem immediately. "Okay, this has happened to me a couple of times, too. Let me think for a second," she says, while she continues to pet my wing in a comfortin' way. "I would tell you to relax, but I know that doesn't help at all," she says, thinkin'. "Wait here a second, I'll be right back." She unlocks the door. She is gone and back in less time than it takes me to exhale.

"Here," she says, handin' me a bottle of whiskey that is still sealed.

"Where'd this come from?" I ask as I break the seal and put the bottle to my lips, takin' a deep sip and feelin' it burn down my throat.

"I just knicked it from behind the counter," she replies, and I choke a little on my second sip. "Don't worry, he never saw me take it."

"Yeah, but the Cherubim are makin' another notch on your naughty side," I retort, takin' another sip of the whiskey.

"I'll risk it," she says in true troublemaker fashion. "I left money on the counter."

"So, this whiskey is supposed to get my wings to go back in?" I ask as I chug a little more of the liquor and feel it burn a little less than before.

A look of hesitation crosses her face. "Not exactly," she says. "It's kinda a two part thing. Just keep drinking, and then I'll show you the rest in a few minutes," she adds cryptically. "What happened?" she asks.

"Let's just say it was harder than I thought it was gonna be comin' in here," I reply evasively.

"Yeah…I was freaked waiting for you. I thought you'd ran into Gaspard for sure," she says, turnin' paler still. I hand her the whiskey. She takes a small sip of it, coughin' a little when she hands it back.

"I thought I was supposed to be able to run fast before I got my wings," I say while my eyes search hers.

She bites her lower lip. "I don't know, Russell—Hank, maybe you can run like me, maybe you just needed fear, initially, to kick it in. Mine kicked in when I was running from the Delts. Your wings popped out because you are freaked about coming in here. We can try to run later, okay?" she asks in an anxious tone.

"Yeah, okay," I agree, before sippin' more whiskey.

"You really are something, though," she says, walkin' 'round me like she is proud of me. "I'm so jealous—your wings are so much bigger than mine."

"Thank God for that. I would look really stupid with your delicate wings. They look perfect on you, but on me, with my big body, I would look ridiculous," I say gratefully. If I have to have them, at least they don't make me look disproportionate.

"I never stopped to imagine you with wings. It's funny, but they look like they belong there—like they have always belonged there," she says as if she is in awe or somethin'.

I shrug. "I'll be stoked later when they work and I can use them. Right now, they're a pain in the ass." I reply, but a part of me is psyched that Red likes them so much. It makes me feel better 'bout havin' them. I take another deep swallow of the whiskey, watchin' her standin' on the side of me, playin' with one of my feathers, which is the strangest thing to watch, let alone feel.

"Okay, that's enough whiskey, I think," Red says tensely, not lookin' at my eyes. She drops her hand from my wing, steppin' behind me to sit on the counter in front of the mirror. She holds out her hand to me and says, "Give me the whiskey." I hand her the bottle and she takes another sip of it before placin' the bottle on the counter beside her. Lookin' up at me with her beautiful, gray eyes, she whispers, "Come here."

"Why?" I ask her in confusion, but I step closer to where she is seated on the counter. She looks scared and embarrassed as she takes my hand in hers and places it on her waist, pullin' me forward so that I stand between her legs.

My heart begins poundin' in my chest, feelin' the warmth of her skin through her shirt. She takes my other hand, positionin' it on her other side. The scent of her skin is hittin' me like waves of heat risin' off of hot pavement. Her scent is incredible and my hands tense as I grip her tighter. Reachin' up slowly, she wraps her arms 'round my neck and gently pulls me down to her. I can hardly breathe when her lips brush mine, soft and sweet. Then, somethin' snaps inside of me, like a restraint that I'm always controllin' when I'm near her comes undone. Pickin' her up off the counter, I hold her to me, devourin' her lips with mine. I want to possess her—please her—feel every inch of her body on mine.

Her lips leave mine for a brief moment as she whispers in my ear, "Pull me closer to you, Russell." Unbelievable passion ignites in me as I kiss her neck, causin' her to shiver in my arms. Pullin' her tighter to me, I press her back against the wall, before findin' her lips once again. There is somethin' in the way she said my name that makes me want her to say it again.

My hand slips down her back and over the curves of her body. A small groan escapes me as my hand comes back up to her hip, brushin' against her bare skin where her shirt rides up. Just when I am ready to remove her irritatin' shirt, Red starts pullin' away from me. I glance at her face to see her fingers pressed to her swollen lips, confusion is cloudin' her eyes when she says, "You did it. Let's go."

"Do wut?" I ask, not lettin' go of her as she presses her hands gently against my chest, pushin' me back from her.

She clears her throat, not lookin' me in the eyes and says, "Your wings, they are back in. Let's go. I'll go pay for the gas and get you a new shirt," she pushes harder than I am expectin' and breaks free from my embrace. I watch her slip out of the bathroom door as it gently closes behind her.

I turn 'round and look in the mirror. My wings are gone and I'm back to lookin' human again. *How the hell did that happen?*

My heart is still drummin' in my chest as I walk up to the sink and turn the faucet on again. I splash some cold water on my face, lookin' at my reflection in the mirror again. Seein' the whiskey bottle on the counter, I grab it and drink another big gulp. *Lord, that is harsh,* I think. *Being so close to her like that and havin' to stop is harder than never havin' started in the first place. Painful. I feel burned…scorched on the inside.*

Then I think again of the kiss I just shared with her and it is like my blood is runnin' free in my veins. I feel like I can pick up a car and chuck it, like I can do anythin' and everythin' I never thought possible. I jump when Red sticks her head in the bathroom again briefly and throws a long sleeved t-shirt at me like a missile while sayin', "Sorry, this is all they have. I'll meet you in the car.

I catch the shirt. It has a silhouette of the Upper Peninsula on it with a caption that reads: "If Ya Ain't A Yooper, Ya Ain't Shit!" *Is that right? What the hell's a Yooper?* I wonder to myself as I shrug into the shirt. It is tight on my shoulders and biceps, but otherwise fits me okay.

Pickin' up my shirt and jacket from the floor, I take one last look 'round the bathroom, decidin' to leave the whiskey on the counter. I keep my head down when I leave the bathroom. Makin' it outside, I breathe deeply. I notice that Red is sittin' in the driver's seat of the Cherokee with the engine already runnin'. After I climb into the passenger side, I have to stop myself from leanin' over and pullin' her in my arms for another kiss. She doesn't look at me as we pull out of the gas station without a word.

"Thanks," I say.

She glances at me briefly, and then her eyes dart back to the road. "It was either that shirt or the one that said: 'Say Ya To Da U.P., Eh?'"

She is deliberately misinterpretin' my thanks. "No, I mean, thanks for yer help back there. I know it wasn't easy for ya to go in there," I say, seein' that she is really tryin' not to fall apart.

She shrugs to try to fool me, and replies, "You would do it for me."

"Yeah, I would," I agree, wishin' she didn't look so fragile. "Can I ask ya a question?" I ask, and see her cringe. She doesn't want to talk about our kiss in the bathroom. That is glaringly obvious. It dawns on me that the only reason she did it was so I would be able to get my wings to go back in and the disappointment is crushin'. But she had responded to the kiss. I can tell she started off like she was sacraficin' herself to the situation, but I wonder if it was like that the entire time I was kissin' her.

Her grip on the stirring wheel tenses. "What?" she asks.

"What's a 'Yooper?'" I ask.

Red's face transforms from tense, to relief, to humor. "A Yooper is someone from the Upper Peninsula, the U.P." she explains with a ghost of a smile.

"Are we gonna be Yoopers then?" I ask, wishin' that she would keep on smilin'.

Her smile deepens just a little. "Not exactly. People up here will probably consider us 'Troopers.' Here's the thing: anyone who is from below the Mackinaw Bridge is considered a 'troll.' So, when a troll moves to the U.P. to live, they call them troopers," she clarifies.

"Is that right? It's kind of like that when all of the tourists flock down to live in Asheville. We call them 'snow birds,'" I say, laughin'.

"Yoopers have other names for tourists...let me think, uh...'trunk slammers, 313ers, fudgies...'" she says, until I interrupt her.

"Fudgies?" I ask, grinnin'. "What's that supposed to mean?"

"They make the best fudge up here...Hank. I'll buy you some, you'll love it," she says. I have to look away from her 'cuz the sexy smile she gives me makes me want to touch her again.

"What else do you know about Yoopers?" I ask, attemptin' to distract myself.

"Not much more. I learned most of what I know from the Internet when I was researching towns," Red says. She starts frownin' again, so I try to think of somethin' to ask her.

"So, are there a lot of Lions fans up here?" I ask, and by the look on her face I see that she is amused again.

"No. We are closer now to Green Bay than to Detroit, so most Yoopers cheer for the Packers."

"Really? This is cheesehead country?" I ask in surprise and watch her nod her head. "I'll get ya one of those cheesehead hats, Red, you'll love it," I tease her 'cuz I know how she feels about Detroit.

"You will never get it on me, trust me," she replies, wrinklin' her nose at me.

"Red?" I say, lookin' at her again.

"Yeah?" she asks.

"I know ya didn't want to kiss me back there at the gas station," I say in a gentle tone. Her face grows sad again. "But I want ya to know that if ya ever do want to kiss me...it'll be alright with me," I add, tryin' to make what I am sayin' less awkward somehow.

She glances at me then and her eyes are so sad that I can tell she is thinkin' she is never gonna heal from the scars that are torn open inside of her. "Don't hope for it, Russell. I can't give you what you need…what you want. I just can't," she says, and there is true regret in her voice as tears escape her eyes.

"Don't cry, Red. Yer a Yooper now and they're supposed to be tough, right? What are we lookin' for now?" I ask, grabbin' the map and findin' our position on it. "Do ya want to head toward Marquette or Iron Mountain? It looks about the same distance either way," I gauge, lookin' at the map.

"We have to stay away from Marquette. It's dangerous for us," she replies quickly.

I look up from the map with a frown. "Why?" I ask, 'cuz there is somethin' in the way she said it that has goose bumps risin' on my arms.

"There is a prison in Marquette. The Fallen love prisons, it's like a candy store to them. We have to stay out of Marquette," she explains, wipin' her tears away.

"Okay. We'll head toward Iron Mountain and we're gonna spend the rest of the time on the road talkin' 'bout everythin' ya know 'bout angels and dangerous stuff for us in general. This is gonna be an intel session," I order, and then I listen while Red spends the next few hours goin' over everythin' she has learned in the last few months. I feel sweaty and irritated when she pauses to take a sip of water she bought back at the gas station for us. "Fairy tales are real?" I ask, and I can't hide how annoyed that makes me.

"Reed was pretty adamant about Seraphim, that when we are evolved, we will be the most powerful creatures out there…but, so are the fallen Seraphim, so take that into consideration," she says as a warnin'. Then, she looks at me and adds, "Listen, I researched Houghton the best way that I could. I employed all the resources I had available, which was mainly the Internet and the library. I analyzed the town, the school, and the surrounding area. I tried to think like my enemy and envision them there and everything points to the fact that it should be safe. It should be, but I don't know for sure. I have no spies to check it out for me. I have no way of knowing for sure if we're heading into something awful."

She seems almost apologetic, like she hasn't just pulled off the most amazin' feat of evadin' four ancient, highly intelligent angels with a brilliant plan, which has been workin' like clockwork since we left. "Once we get there, we'll find the apartment Ryan rented for us near the school. We're going to stay together until we feel comfortable with our surroundings."

"Believe me, I plan on bein' the gum on yer shoe," I say in a serious tone. I have a feelin' I won't feel comfortable at all unless I can see her, at least for a while.

"There is one more thing I have to tell you," Red says with a solemn expression. "I'm putting some of the money into a joint bank account, but we will keep a stash of the majority of the cash somewhere safe. If there is trouble, take the money; find a small town that's less than ten thousand in population and nothing exciting that will attract the Fallen. I want you to research it on your own, but don't tell me where it is. If something happens, take the money and leave if you can. If you need an ID, make inquiries on the Internet, don't go to Ryan again."

My eyebrows pull together in a frown. "Whaddaya mean, Red?" I ask, feelin' sick as I grab the water out of the cup holder nearest to me. "Why can't I tell ya?"

"I mean if something happens to me, you should leave immediately. Don't hang around, especially if I go missing," she replies in a monotone voice. It's like she's numb, just operatin' on autopilot. "I don't want to know where you will go, so no one can make me tell where you are. If there is enough pain, I may talk…I would try really hard not to, but the less I know about your strategy for evasion, the better."

"I'm not gonna leave ya. We go down together. You and me," I say, clenchin' my teeth to keep from shoutin' at her.

"Russell, if one of the Fallen gets me, what are you going to do?" she asks in a dull voice. "You have to run. You can't save me, not now," she says evenly as she watches the road.

"Red, believe it or not, I'm not completely useless. I can at least call in the cavalry," I reply, reasonin' with her.

She immediately snaps out of autopilot then, her face growin' dark. "There is no cavalry, don't you get it?" she yells at me and I have never seen her so angry. "What if I'm taken by Pagan? If you call Reed, he will go to war with his own kind to save me and it will destroy him," she says, runnin' her hand through her hair in agitation. "We are on our own now. No safety net. Do you understand?" she asks, starin' at me like I haven't heard a word she's been sayin', and maybe she's right, maybe I haven't. Maybe I've been livin' in denial, thinkin' I could just call for help.

It finally starts hittin' me then just how lost and alone she is feelin'. She knows I'm not gonna be helpful to her in a fight for a while. In her mind, she has to take care of me, but there is no one who can take care of her now. I don't have the strength yet to beat another angel. "Yer right, I can't call them. I get it. That doesn't mean I'm leavin' ya," I say, not wantin' to argue with her, but not lettin' her think I will sell her out like that. No way.

"Do me a favor," she says, holdin' out her hand to me and I reach out immediately to take it in mine. "Do the research on a town. Just in case there is no reason to stay…if I'm dead, you won't be selling me out and I want you to survive—I need you to survive. Okay, please?" she asks, squeezin' my hand.

My throat closes up immediately and I have to look out the passenger side window. *There is no goin' on without her,* I realize. But, I nod to her anyway, not trustin' my voice to speak.

She squeezes my hand harder. "You have had to go on without me before. What do you do when I die first?" she asks me in a soft tone. "What did Leander do?"

"I do what I always do. I pick a fight I know I can't win," I say, lookin' at the stars outside my window, feelin' like I have a noose wrapped 'round my neck, chokin' me. Shootin' pain courses up my back, and in a fraction of a second, my wings shoot out of my back again. Fear and sorrow are a lethal combination when it comes to wings, I'm learnin' quickly, as I lurch forward into the dashboard in front of me. "SON OF A…" I shout, but I manage to stifle the rest of what I would have said at the last second.

Breathin' in shallowly, tryin' to get my lungs to decompress, I push my wings back with my hands, leanin' against them more comfortably. "Damn. I left all the whiskey back at the gas station. I guess I'm just gonna have to settle for part two of gettin' my wings back in," I say, rubbin' my forehead that had hit the windshield when I was brutally thrown forward.

Red immediately squares her shoulders and her tone changes from desperation to one of determination. "You are right, Hank. I am an ass kicker and we're going to be all right. The first thing we are going to do, after we find our apartment, is figure out where we can train without raising suspicion. Then, we have to get creative. Maybe you can teach me some plays from your football handbook. Start thinking about anything that will give us an edge in a fight. We can download some movies, too, like Bruce Lee or sports clips like Mohammad Ali."

"Ultimate fighter," I chime in, thinkin', "oh—Scarface."

"Scarface?" she says, wrinklin' her nose at me.

"We have to get weapons too and whatever we can't get, I'll make," I say, thinkin' strategically.

"What are you going to make?" she asks me with curiosity in her tone.

"Red, I have been makin' weapons for thousands of years. You'd be surprised what ya can do with a sling and a little rock, especially now that yer stronger and quicker than before," I reply.

"Well, Hank, we're going to need every single trick you have up your sleeve. Our biggest issue is time. We have to buy time somehow. The more time we get to train and evolve, the better off we're going to be. Time is going to make us or break us," she murmurs in a contemplative way.

"Then, I believe it's time to get me in the game. No more red-shirt bullshit. I'll get started on it right away," I say, makin' mental lists of things I can make right away and things I'll need to look for.

Red looks surprised for a second, like she wasn't expectin' that I would be much of an asset to her in the defensive strategy part of our life together. Pickin' up her hand, I press it to my lips briefly and say, "I know you don't understand this yet, but I'm not eighteen…I have had so many lives that some of what I know doesn't even have translatable lexicon. My knowledge base keeps gettin' broader, and the more I meander through my memories, the more I study them, the more I recall. I have infinite knowledge stored inside of me. It's like your instincts, but my knowledge is conscious now." Her eyes leave the road as she studies me as if she is seein' me in a new light. "I *will* have your back, I just need to develop my strength and I'll be an ass kicker too, trust me."

"I trust you. You are my best friend," she says without a hint of doubt.

"As you are mine, always," I reply.

CHAPTER 9

Houghton

To say that the first few days in Houghton have been dark for Red would not be a very good description. It is more accurate to say that there has been a complete absence of light for her. She tries to hide it from me, doin' all the things that need to be done to establish a new life, but there is absolutely no light in her. We arrive at our new apartment in the middle of the night, which turns out to be a good thing 'cuz it is less disgustin' in the dark than in the bright daylight. I doubt Red sees it that way 'cuz her eyesight is fierce in the dark, but it is better for me.

Our new digs consist of a two-bedroom apartment on the upstairs portion of a duplex. It must have been a bachelor hang out prior to our movin' in, judgin' by the scars in the peelin' floral wall paper and the lack of cleanin' done when the previous occupants moved out. I seriously doubt they got their security deposit back. Lucky for us, it has hardwood floors 'cuz I can't imagine what the carpet would've looked like if there had been some.

The entrance to our apartment is on the side of the house, and once yer in the outside door, ya have to climb a steep, narrow stair-case that leads to a narrow landin' at the top of the stairs. I have to duck my head the entire time I'm walkin' up them 'cuz they weren't built for someone six foot five inches. When ya unlock the door at the top of the stairs, ya then have to step down one step 'cuz someone mounted the door backwards, makin' it open out instead of in. The door still locks on the inside, so they must've decided that turnin' the doorknob 'round was easier than remountin' the door. I might have to fix it soon 'cuz it's drivin' me insane.

The first night is just plain awful. There is no furniture, so we end up huddling together on the floor in one of the bedrooms without a blanket. I must be really tired 'cuz I manage to sleep for a while. I wake, though, when Red has one of her nightmares. She won't talk to me about it. It must be a bad one 'cuz she can't go back to sleep for a while after havin' it. I can't sleep either, since I drank a half a bottle of whiskey by myself at the gas station and I'm feelin' the after effects of the alcohol.

In the mornin', we check out the first floor of the house and learn that a little old lady occupies it. Her name is Estelle Strauss, but she insists that we call her Stella when we venture downstairs to introduce ourselves. She has a cat named Snowball that she talks to like it's a person. She says she is sad to see the young men from the college go, they were helpful to her from time to time, when she needed somethin' done. She must not have heard them 'cuz I notice she has to turn up her hearin' aid several times in order to hear what we are sayin' to her. She seems like a nice lady and I promise to help her out if she needs somethin' done.

Everythin' we do consists of cautiously planned out missions. Even the most mundane tasks have a written set of objectives. There are parameters, variables are discussed, and recon is to be done prior to the missions.

Our first mission is a grocery store run to get food and cleanin' supplies to make livin' in that apartment bearable. After goin' through a fast food drive-thru for coffee and breakfast sandwiches, we do a drive by of the local grocery store. Houghton has a couple of the big chain stores up here, like ya see everywhere else in the country. But, we opt for a smaller, privately owned grocery to begin with 'cuz it has big plate glass windows linin' the front of the store, which are easy to see through. Pullin' up in the parkin' lot, we start gatherin' intel on the grocery store before either one of us attempts to enter.

Red can see the layout of the aisles through the storefront windows. Every item that is needed is discussed and outlined by aisle for the most efficient use of time while in the store. We do surveillance on the grocery store employees, shift changes are noted, and time frames are established. We know which checkout lane will be fastest, based on the chattiness and efficiency of the cashier.

We watch the store for two days before we determine that it is safe to go inside. Red decides that she is the only one who is allowed to go in the store for now. This pisses me off, at first, 'cuz I'm more afraid of her runnin' into a bad guy than if I do, but she makes a good argument when she says that my wings are uncontrollable at this point.

She says it's better to have me watch the front of the store and signal her if I see anythin' threatenin'. We don't have cell phones yet, so Red comes up with a great way for me to get her attention in the event that I see an angel comin'. She pops out the vanity mirror on the passenger side visor of the car and hands it to me. I'm supposed to flash sunlight on the front windows of the store if I see anythin'.

"Remember, if you see anything, don't get out of the car. Flash the mirror at me, and then go. Drive back to the apartment and wait for me. If I'm not back in an hour, head out of town. Don't hang around. Just go. You can stop in any one of these small towns and check Facebook to see if I wrote to you," she says, watchin' my face for any sign of rebellion.

I scan her. She looks so fragile sittin' in the passenger seat of the Jeep. She is dressed in jeans and a simple cotton shirt that she modified to accommodate her wings, in the event she can't control them from comin' out. She looks to me like someone should be holdin' her hand when she crosses the street. She seems so delicate, even though I have seen how lethal she is, if she has to be.

"How badly do we really need to do this, Red?" I ask her, panickin' a little, thinkin' of her in there all by herself.

"Badly. We're almost out of the toilet paper that was under the sink in the bathroom and I can't stand looking at the grossness that is our apartment. Plus, I can't eat one more meal from the drive-thru," she says, tryin' to hide her frustration with the situation we have been livin' with for the past few days. "I need to take a shower with shampoo and conditioner and deodorant would be nice, too." She goes on, eyein' me, and I have to admit it would be nice to have all of those things again.

"We have enough cash left for this?" I ask her again, cringin' 'cuz it's her money, not mine. My money is gone, which is one of the worst feelings in the world. Bein' dependant is probably the worst part of all of this. Red keeps sayin' the money is as much mine as it is hers 'cuz it was her uncle's money, not hers, and he would want both of us to have it. But, it still blows.

"Yeah, we have enough for this and maybe the mattresses next, but we're going to have to get our bank account straight soon. We have to establish our stash of cash somewhere safe, so we can get out of town fast if we need to," she replies.

"Maybe we should do that first," I say, more 'cuz I don't want her to get out of the car, than that I really care what order we do things in.

I think she sees through me, 'cuz she says, "I'll be right back. We haven't seen any angels here, just humans. It's safe. I'll be as fast as I can."

She opens the door and starts to get out when I say, "Red!" She pauses and turns back toward me. I throw my arms 'round her tight and don't let go for a few seconds. She lets me hug her, and when I let her go, she gives me a brief smile. She steps out of the car and into the bright sunlight, puttin' on a pair of sunglasses and carryin' her small purse. I watch her cross the parkin' lot and pull a metal shoppin' cart from the bay of carts. She disappears through the automatic doors in the front of the grocery store. She reappears again, seconds later, pushin' her cart through the produce aisle while pickin' up fruits and vegetables with the speed and precision of a soccer mom.

I tear my eyes away from her so that I can act as her lookout and make sure that no angels are gonna sneak up on her. We both know that the risks are minimal, even if there are angels nearby. Judgin' by the way we've been livin' with Reed and Zee, they would consider shoppin' for their own food beneath them. I don't know 'bout the Fallen, but I would guess they have a similar arrogance when it comes to the grocery store, but if I'm wrong, the consequences are catastrophic.

I glance back in the store to see Red comin' back up another aisle. She is concentratin' on her list, but she is not goin' unnoticed by the people in the grocery store. Everyone she walks by gives her a second look. Everybody: women included. It could be 'cuz of the sensual way she carries herself, like she's stalkin' a particularly stealthy prey. Or, it could be that she's just the sexiest thing they've seen in this part of the world. Whatever the case, she is definitely not blendin' in well. A growl escapes me when I notice the stockboys followin' her, watchin' her ass as she pushes her cart back down another aisle, not even pausin' while she plucks another item from the shelf.

She looks over her shoulder once or twice, noticin' that the stockboys are followin' her. She knows everythin' that is goin' on 'round her 'cuz of the way she can process information rapidly, but I wonder if she knows why they're followin' her. I doubt she does. She has no idea just how allurin' she is. None.

The stockboys soon have competition from the store manager who notices her as she walks by the customer service counter. The middle-aged man pops his head up from behind the counter and 'bout falls over it in his haste to unlock the door and get out from behind the counter. He hitches up his pants to pull them more securely over his protrudin' belly. Then, runnin' his hand through his thinnin' brown hair, he straightens his tie and smoothes his shirt a bit, waitin' for Red to head back up the next aisle. Just before she nears him, he leans casually against the soda pop display and sucks in his gut a little before he says somethin' to her.

Red smiles at him, pausin' to reply to whatever the pervert is sayin' to her, and then she is movin' to the next aisle. Mr. Manager finds somethin' pressin' to do in every aisle she is in for the last few aisles of the store. Another growl escapes me, seein' him dismiss the boy baggin' up Red's groceries in the fast checkout aisle. He is doin' it for her. My hand twitches on the handle of the car door. I am across the parkin' lot and pacin' in front of the store window in a matter of moments. I'm not even sure how I got here, but I'm here, watchin' the round man eyein' my girl.

Red sees me immediately and I can tell by the look on her face that seein' me here is alarmin' her. She scans the parkin' lot, lookin' for any potential threat that would cause me to deviate from the plan. She absently hands the money for the groceries to the cashier. She starts to help bag the rest of the groceries, nervously castin' glances at me, and then at the parkin' lot.

The manager says somethin' to her, and then he does the unthinkable. He puts his hand on Red's arm. I am in the store with every intention of flattin' the round man into a pancake. Fantasy after fantasy of ways to maim and kill him bounce through my head. Seein' me comin', Red steps out from the cash register aisle. She must be readin' the look on my face 'cuz she walks in front of the manager and breathes nervously, "Hank, you're just in time to help me take the groceries to the car." She catches me 'round the waist, huggin' me to her body. Her grip is like steal and I can't step 'round her to get to the pervert behind her, but he is definitely readin' the intentions on my face. He takes a couple of steps back from the lane, lookin' 'round wildly for an exit strategy.

When I glance down at Red's face, I see her frownin' at me. "I think we're ready to go, are you ready?" she asks.

I try to clear the clouds of black rage from my head that are blockin' out everythin' else. "Do wut?" I ask in confusion.

"I'm done, let's go," she orders. She eases her arms off of my waist. Reachin' back, she pulls the cart, loaded with groceries, from where it is packed up near the end of the cashier aisle. She manages to pull the front of the cart to us, and then she holds my hand and pushes the handle of the cart as we walk from the grocery store with all eyes on us.

Warm air assails us when the automatic doors open up and allows us to exit the store. Red is watchin' me the entire time that it takes to walk back to the car. She notices when I look back over my shoulder at the store and her hand tightens almost painfully on mine. She holds my hand as she opens the hatch of our car, and then she says, "Help me get the groceries in the car."

I pick up a bag, and then I look at her 'cuz she still has my other hand in hers. "You can let go of me now. I'm just gonna load the car up," I say, and when she doesn't let me go immediately, I add, "I promise."

She lets me go, but she doesn't move from her position, which is between the store and me. When I finish, she waits until I get back in the car before she pushes the cart to the cart corral and then comes back. Sittin' in the passenger seat, she is quiet as I pull out of the parkin' lot. She is bitin' her lip nervously like she wants to say somethin' to me but she doesn't know how.

I exhale deeply, feelin' aggressive and pissy and guilty. I totally lost focus on what I was supposed to be doin' when I saw all of those guys followin' her 'round the store. I wouldn't have seen an angel comin' to warn her 'cuz I had been too focused on the humans to care. "Listen, I…I don't know what—that guy touched ya—and they were all followin' ya—I couldn't just sit there and…" I can't think straight. I run my hand through my hair, tryin' to calm down 'cuz I can feel my wings movin' in my back and that's always a bad sign. I think the only thing that will make me feel better is goin' back to the store and beatin' the snot outta that freakin' manager.

"It's okay, Russell," she says, watchin' me struggle with my emotions. "It's an instinct and it's really hard to control it."

My expression grows darker. "An instinct? Explain," I say fiercely.

"I'm not sure what you saw when you were out in the parking lot, but you must have interpreted that someone was getting too close to me. You must also believe that I'm yours." The last part she says like she is eatin' sawdust 'cuz it is hard for her to say the words. "I have been told that our kind, Seraphim, are highly territorial when it comes to attraction and what we feel belongs to us."

My eyes shift to hers for a second, and then it all makes sense and I relax a little. I pull up to our apartment and put the car in park. We sit there not movin' for a second, and then Red says, "You don't seem very upset about what I just told you."

"No. It makes perfect sense to me," I answer. Her eyebrows draw together in confusion so I add, "I'm a guy, we're usually like that, but it's more intense when there's angel DNA to back it up." I see her frown.

"You don't seem to mind it very much," she points out.

"No. I just have to do a better job of controllin' it, but it's not a totally foreign feelin', if that's what yer sayin'. Like I said, it's a guy thing," I reply, gettin' out of the car and openin' up the hatch to get an armload of the bags from the back.

When she comes 'round the other side of the car to pick up some bags, she looks sullen.

"Wut?" I ask, smilin'.

"Nothing," she replies, still frownin' at me like I have lost my mind.

"Seriously, what?" I ask as I follow her back up to the apartment.

She unlocks the door, climbin' the stairs to the landin'. Openin' the door, she steps down a step, so the door won't knock her off the landin'. After she enters the apartment, she goes straight to the kitchenette and places her bags on the counter. She immediately unpacks the bags, and findin' the cleanin' supplies, she opens the refrigerator and starts wipin' it out with soapy water and a sponge.

"Red?" I ask, unpackin' the bags I brought up from the car.

She sighs. "FINE! Why is all of this so easy for you to accept?" she asks, glarin' out her frustration. "Because when I found out what I just told you, it was after I almost put a fork in a waitress, and to me it was a big deal."

"Ya did that?" I ask, tryin' to imagine the situation that led her to do that. She had been with Reed no doubt. Just thinkin' of her havin' that kind of reaction for him makes the aggressive emotions flair back up in me. I try to play it cool though, so she won't see how wrecked that thought makes me. I shrug coolly and continue to unpack my bags. "I told ya, this is all meant to be. Maybe it should be easier for me than for you, did ya ever think of that?" I ask, 'cuz she needs a good fight to get out some of the anxiety that's floatin' 'round in her.

"Why should this be easier for you than me? I was born part angel," she says, her hands on her hips now.

"Yeah, but I had to die to become part angel," I reply as I pick up one of the sponges and dip it in the soapy water, usin' it to clean off the shelves in the cupboards.

She doesn't take the bait I hand her, but instead, she begins cleanin' again and thinkin' 'bout what I just said. "Did you die?" she asks, not lookin' up, but continuin' on with her task.

"Yeah. I think so. I don't remember leavin' ya, but I'm pretty sure I was goin', even as I was prayin' to God to let me stay and help ya," I admit, still workin' on the shelves.

"You're so stubborn. Of course you would stay," she replies. I smile 'cuz she knows me so well. I have no doubt that she would've stayed, too. We finish cleanin' the kitchenette and puttin' the groceries away. Red hands me a local newspaper she picked up at the store and asks me to look for a place to buy a couple of mattresses and box springs. She takes all of the toiletries to the bathroom, along with a couple of new dishtowels she had purchased at the grocery store. We don't have any big towels yet, so we have to make due.

I scan the paper for things we need. Several things come to mind, like tools to fix the door and all the squeaks and loose hinges on the cabinets. Mattresses, bedding, towels, dishes, pots and pans, a garbage can—all of the stuff ya take for granted when they're available, but absolutely miss when ya don't have them. I really want a television, too.

I want cable so I can catch some ESPN and maybe watch some baseball or, shoot, anythin' to do with sports. It makes me feel human to just watch a game. I even got Zee into watchin' some sport shows, like golf. At first, Zee had been skeptical as to why anyone would want to hit a small ball into a little hole, but when I took him to the indoor drivin' range, he quickly became hooked on it. I had to warn him not to break the 500-yard sign with his ball. I also had to tell him that humans would find it scary if he got a hole-in-one on every hole, so when he does get a chance to shoot a round, he should make sure to miss a few times. I miss him. I miss havin' someone besides Red to ask questions about what's happenin' to me.

After dusk, we start our surveillance on the Mattress Carnival, a store in town that sells all kinds of beds and beddin'. "Why do ya suppose they call it a Mattress Carnival?" I ask Red offhandedly, as we sit in the car in the parkin' lot eatin' the apples and grapes she packed in a small cooler she had bought at the grocery store.

"Maybe they want you to think it's as fun as a party buying a mattress here," she replies as a lame explanation.

"Yeah, but carnivals always make me think of clowns and clowns are really kinda freaky, so I really don't want to buy a mattress here 'cuz it makes me think of havin' a clown in my bed." As soon as the words are out of my mouth, Red is laughin' so hard I think she is not gonna be able to breathe. "Wut?" I ask, smilin' at her, lovin' every second of her laughter. "You like clowns in yer bed or somethin'?" I ask her in a soft tone, and tears form at the corners of her eyes 'cuz she can't stop laughin'.

"Russell, stop," she says, tryin' to regain her breath. She can't look at me for a second 'cuz every time she tries, she loses it again.

Finally, she pulls it together after takin' several shallow sips of water and wipin' her eyes. "Maybe they want you to think of havin' an acrobat in your bed," she replies when she can talk.

"Naw," I shake my head. "I can't get past the scary clown image. It's givin' me the creeps." She rolls her eyes at me. "So, what kind of beds are we gettin'?" I ask her as casually as I can.

"I don't need much. A single mattress and box springs will do for me. The advertisement said they will give us a free metal frame with the purchase of a mattress and box springs," she says, lookin' at me. "But you need at least a double bed, don't you? I hope they have a longer mattress in stock for you," she says with concern as she looks at my long frame.

"Don't worry too much, Red. I'm used to my feet hangin' off the end of the bed."

"We can probably get you a queen, and then you can sleep diagonally on it so your feet don't hang off," she says, thinkin' 'bout me.

"That might work," I reply, thinkin' we should just get one big king size bed and share it, but I don't say that out loud 'cuz she is laughin' for the first time since we left Crestwood and I'm not 'bout to ruin that. "I'm comin' in this time. Those mattress salesmen are a little suspect," I continue, watchin' the salesmen millin' 'round the front of the store, waitin' for the next customer to come in.

"I think I can handle the mattress salesmen," Red says, lookin' at me.

"I know, but if I'm there they won't try anythin' 'cuz I look tougher than you even though you can whip us hands down," I say soothingly.

She doesn't argue with me, but continues to watch the storefront, pickin' out subtle hints in the people's body language. She lets me know which bed each of the people like the most as they walk 'round the store. She is dead on with everyone. She also points out that the women mostly get their way on the bed selection, when shoppin' as couples. I laugh and say, "Red, that's a no-brainer."

Her eyebrow arches in question. "What do you mean?" she asks, lookin' at me and smilin'

"Guys don't really care what the bed looks like. We just care 'bout what's gonna be *in* the bed," I explain.

"You mean who is going to be in the bed with you when you're sleeping?" she asks for clarification as she blushes a little. Lord, she is so naïve. It kills me. I'm sure she knows I am talkin' 'bout sex, but since she hasn't had any yet, in this lifetime anyway, she really doesn't have the frame of reference to talk 'bout it. "Can I ask you something, Russell?" Red inquires. The question is impulsive 'cuz she bites her lip after she asks it.

Intrigued, I say, "Sure."

She shakes her head. "No, forget it," she says, and she is quiet.

"Ah, ya can't do that, Lillian! You'll drive me crazy," I smile, usin' her fake name to see if it will spark her into askin' her question.

It works 'cuz she turns to me tentatively and asks, "Why Candace?"

I think 'bout her question for a while, tryin' to see if I can explain why I had dated Candace after Red had told me she was datin' Reed our first semester at Crestwood. I know what she is askin' me really. Candace is a very pretty girl and she wants to know if that is why I had been with her.

"Well, I was attracted to Candace, I'm not gonna lie. She's easy to look at in that All-American beauty sort of way," I say, watchin' Red for her reaction. She is tryin' to play it cool so I go on. "I guess there were several reasons I was with her. I could point out all of her physical attributes, but that wasn't really why I picked her," I explain as I see Red react a little to what I'm sayin'. She seems to flush a little, like she's gettin' irritated with me.

"Why did you pick her, Russell? She is one of the meanest people I have ever met in my entire life," she says, tryin' to keep her emotions in line.

"She's mostly only mean to you, Red, 'cuz she doesn't like anyone who is more beautiful than she is," I reply, and smile when I see her scowl at me. Red didn't believe me when I said she is more beautiful than Candace, but she is. Hands down. No contest. "Naw, before ya say anythin' hear me out. I was with Candace 'cuz I knew that I didn't love her."

"What! Why would you be with someone you don't love?" she asks, like I'm sick or somethin'.

"'Cuz I couldn't be with the girl I love," I murmur. When she closes her mouth I add, "And, I knew that Candace didn't love me either. I knew that she wouldn't be very hurt when she figured out that I didn't love her 'cuz she only really loves herself. I didn't want to pick someone who would be hurt when they found out I couldn't care about them like that 'cuz I'll always love someone else."

"What's wrong with being alone until you find someone else you can love?" she asks me quietly, like there is someone else out there for me.

"There is no one else," I say flatly.

"How do you know?" she counters, and I can hear the thinness in her voice when she asks her question.

"'Cuz I've lived for thousands of years and it has only ever been you, Red. Just you," I reply darkly.

"Well, of course it's been just me," she argues. "Because you're stupid and pick people like Candace when you're not with me. If you picked someone nicer and capable of love, you might find out that I'm not the only entity in the universe you can love," she says all huffy, and I am surprised that she is so pissed off about it.

"Maybe. You'll have to give me back my heart, and then maybe I can try again," I say softly.

"How do I do that?" she asks with a sad look.

"I don't know," I answer her honestly.

Red is quiet as I sit thinkin' 'bout what she said while we watch the Mattress Carnival employees walkin' people through the store. Red makes a few comments 'bout the bald guy bein' the best salesman to go to 'cuz he's the quickest when the decision on a bed is made. He wastes no time gatherin' the stock from the back and havin' someone load it in the car for the customers.

"Red. Can I ask ya a question?" I ask, continuin' to watch the bald man run 'round the store, gatherin' up things for the customer. He is quick; I'll give her that.

"Huh?" she ask absently, but I'm not fooled 'cuz I see the way she sits up a little at my question.

"What's yer nightmare 'bout?" I ask, while seein' immediately that she doesn't like my question, since she bites her lower lip again.

"Which one?" she counters, not lookin' at me.

"How 'bout ya tell me 'bout the one ya had the first night we got here. That one should be extremely significant," I say, watchin' the neon sign make her face glow red, and then yellow as it flashes the alternatin' light on her through the front window.

"I don't think that one is real. I think that one has to be some kind of nightmare, not a premonition," she says quickly.

"Why do you say that?" I probe.

"Because of all the weird stuff in it," she replies in a calm tone. She really wants to believe that, but whether she does or not is another story.

"Weird stuff? Yer gonna have to be more specific 'cuz everythin' we talk 'bout is weird," I point out, askin' her to elaborate.

"Okay, you want me to clarify? Here it is. I'm being carried through a chamber that is right out of some Arthurian Tale. I'm in a massive hall with several rows of Corinthian columns, you know, the really ornate ones and they are carved out of the same dark gray stone that surrounds the room. The ceiling is cavernous, but the only sources of light are coming from several massive stone fireplaces carved into the walls. The fireplaces are big enough to walk into and not have to duck your head and there is light from the candlelight chandeliers that hang from the ceilings.

She's not lookin' at me 'cuz she seems to be there, in the place she's describin' to me. "There is something about the walls of the place. They have a tarnished green color to them that is like limestone, but different…and there is a sweet smell that I don't recognize," she adds. I watch her touch the window of the car like it was the wall of the room she is describin', and then I see her shiver. "Its very beautiful here in a 'welcome to Merlin's House' kind of way. I mean very, very, surreal," she says, lookin' 'round like she's not lookin' at the car at all.

"Is it night or day?" I ask, tryin' to process what she is sayin'.

"I have no idea. There are no windows," she replies.

"You said yer bein' carried?" I prompt her.

"Yeah. I'm puttin' up a big fight, but I'm bound up so it's not working out so well for me," she says. I see goose bumps risin' on her arms and my wings move sharply inside my back.

I squeeze my eyes shut in concentration, tryin' to calm my rapid pulse. "Wait a sec. Don't tell me anymore," I say, knowin' that if I don't manage to calm down, I will be kissin' the steerin' wheel 'cuz my wings will fly outta my back. I take a couple of deep breaths, tryin' to relax. When I think I can handle it again, I open my eyes and say, "Okay, go on."

"There is not a whole lot more to tell. I'm shoved into an ornately carved chair in front of what can only be described as a mediaeval conference table and it looks like we are waiting for someone," she says with some bravado. It makes me frown 'cuz I think she's doin' it for my benefit so I can continue to control my wings from flyin' out of my back.

"You said 'they.' Who are they?" I ask, grindin' my teeth.

"I don't know—they are really strong and fast—angel fast," she replies, like she is rememberin' somethin' that hasn't happened… yet.

"Shit! I was hopin' for dumb ass human bad guys," I say, feelin' frustrated. "So they're angels. Fallen or Divine?" I ask, holdin' my breath. I don't know why it matters; both kinds will get us killed deader than dead.

She doesn't answer me. She looks confused. "I'm sorry, Russell, I have no idea," she says plainly.

"You don't know if they're Fallen or Divine?" I ask.

"No…I don't know if they're angels," she says slowly, and then my head hits the steerin' wheel hard when my wings drive me forward.

᧚

After we establish all of the mundane necessities, like openin' a bank account and gettin' a couple of beds and beddin', we move on to checkin' out the town. We do a lot of recon on places we would like to go to in the future, like the library and the college campus. We are lookin' for angels, specifically Powers or Fallen, but either we suck at recon, or this town just isn't somethin' they are into 'cuz after bein' extremely cautious for three weeks, we don't turn up any enemies.

Things in Houghton have died down since we arrived 'cuz a lot of the students from the school went home for the summer break. There are a sprinklin' of tourists, which helps me blend in a little 'cuz of my accent, but for the most part, Red has accomplished what she had set out to do. She has found us a safe, borin' town in which to exist for a while. All of this should be a good thing, but the less danger we seem to be in, the more despondent she is becomin'.

We locate a place to train. It's a secluded clearin' a couple of miles off the Nara Nature Trail. It is very beautiful terrain, like what I expect a wild sort of Heaven to look like. There are rollin' hills that shoulder thick stands of enormous trees and a rapidly flowin' stream that is still carryin' the icy cold water from the hills above. Some of the trees are in full bloom; the dogwoods and the redbuds each compete with one another to be more impressive. There are also thick stands of lilac bushes burstin' with color and their scent is unbelievable. The open field that we found is dotted with wild flowers that poke their heads out above the long grass. It would make a decent postcard, if I had anyone I was allowed to send it to.

"C'mon," I say in a low voice in Red's ear as she picks up another marble and places it in the sling I had made for her. "I know ya can do this. Ya just have to focus on the target," I coach her, havin' just demonstrated several different ways to use the sling I made for her from some leather scrap pieces and heavy string. We are startin' off by usin' marbles for ammunition. *Maybe I should've started off by usin' golf balls,* I tell myself as I see the marble fall out of the cradle of leather on Red's second swing.

Red groans in frustration.

"All right, listen, yer really strong, so ya only need one swing. You can pick any swing yer comfortable with, the overhead, underhand, side—or I know, watch this one; it's an overhead swing that's kinda like a figure eight. I like this one 'cuz it gains the most momentum," I pull a marble from the hundreds I had bought at the dollar store in town. I demonstrate the swing and hit the target I had set up over a hundred yards away. The tin can all but explodes when the marble penetrates it. A slow smile touches my lips. It's so much easier to do that with my improved eyesight.

I'm able to see things far away now with no problem. I woke up a week ago and the apartment, which we have spent a considerable amount of time cleanin', looked even dirtier than it normally did. I told Red about it and she immediately knew what I was talkin' about. She looked relieved that I now have angel sight, like she had been frettin' about it or somethin'. I guess she is worried about bein' able to protect me.

I made her go out with me that night, so I could walk 'round under the stars. It's like I can touch 'em now 'cuz they seem so much closer and it's mad cool to be able to see everythin' in the dark. I had to reason with myself that I couldn't just reach up and pull Heaven down to me.

Now I can see all of the pollen in the air, floatin' on the breeze and gently dustin' everythin' with its essence. Red watches me with a sour look on her face. "Wut?" I ask, but can't hide my smugness from her. I have finally found somethin' I am better at than she is. *Sucks huh?* I think, pickin' up another marble and doin' it again in a blink of an eye.

"Nice one, Hank. Let's try Bruce Lee now," she says in exasperation.

We had purchased a used television out of the paper and bought a crappy DVD player so we could get stuff that might be able to teach us somethin' 'bout fightin'. Red is particularly good at emulatin' Bruce Lee moves, ah let's be honest, she makes Bruce seem like a little girl. She's more Japanese animae than martial arts. The things that she can do only exist in the cartoon realm.

"Naw, Red. I want ya to learn how to do this. This is the easiest weapon you can fashion in a pinch," I explain, frustrated with her 'cuz she doesn't even seem interested in this.

"Why can't I just pick up a rock and throw it at my enemy?" she asks with her bad attitude showin'.

"'Cuz yer enemy is wicked-fast and you'll need the extra velocity that the sling will provide to nail them," I reply, watchin' her holdin' the sling negligently with her hand on one of her hips and her leg cocked out to the side. She is as mean as a snake lately. I know its 'cuz she's hurtin'. She is always tryin' to retreat inside herself and hide behind the little wall she has created. I won't let her stay behind that wall for long 'cuz it makes me nervous to see her sittin' 'round just starin' into space like she doesn't exist anymore. "If ya have nothin' else, ya just need to find a bit of fabric ya can punch a hole in on both sides. Then, ya just put a string on one side that's a little longer than yer forearm and another one on the opposite side," I say, demonstratin' how I made the slings. "You'll be able to throw those marbles probably faster than if ya shot them out of a gun," I retort a little meaner than I probably should, but she is pissin' me off.

"FINE!" she grumbles, stompin' back to the bag of marbles and pickin' up another one.

"Wait. I'll go set up another couple of cans. I'll be right back," I say, pickin' up two empty soda cans we had brought with us and joggin' out to where I had set up the other cans. Leanin' down, I place the cans on the rock where the others had been. I hear the whistlin' right before pain registers in my head and my leg buckles beneath me. Goin' down on my knee, my hand flies to my hamstring where a marble has hit me square in the back of my thigh. I grit my teeth as I look over my shoulder to see Red holdin' her hand over her mouth. Her eyes are buggin' out of her head. She is behind me in the next second and before she can say anythin' I snarl between my teeth, "Run."

With her eyes wide, Red says, "I'm so sorry, Russell! I didn't think I could actually hit you—I was just irritated at you for being so good at this..." she trails off as my shirt rips off my body, fallin' to the ground in shreds while my wings come flyin' out of my back on their own. I stagger to my feet again and turn 'round.

"You had better run, Red..." I warn her, clenchin' my fists to keep from shoutin' at her. My thigh hurts like it's freakin' on fire and I seriously want to break somethin' and she is the only somethin' around at the moment.

She holds up her hands defensively as I stumble toward her, still holdin' the back of my leg with my hand. "You don't really think I meant to hurt you, do you? I was just—"

"RUN!" I shout at her, watchin' her back up from me. She is keepin' her distance, but she's not fleein' like I told her to.

I launch myself at her and she manages to evade me by mere inches. Turnin' away, she sprints to the top of the hill, but when she hesitates at the top of it, I am close on her heels. Shock registers on her face when she sees me just behind. She turns back 'round, continuin' to run from me. She runs all the way to the stream, and boundin' over it, she stops on the other side of the bank to look back at me.

"I'M SORRY!" she shouts as she sees me runnin' toward her with all the speed I can gather, which is substantial, since I'm now movin' faster than I have ever dreamed possible. The wind is makin' a soft whistlin' noise that is resonatin' in the back of my mind. It's not hittin' me as it probably should 'cuz of the black rage I'm feelin'. I only have one objective in my mind and that is gettin' to Red.

I don't hesitate when I get to the stream, but jump to the far bank near where she is standin'. I must still have a murderous look on my face 'cuz she starts runnin' again like the devil is chasin' her, and in my present mood, it isn't far off.

She weaves in an intricate pattern through the trees, but I have no trouble followin' her. When I lose sight of her for a second, I don't worry 'cuz I can smell her ahead of me. I don't need to see her; my other senses take over to fill in the blanks.

She is ahead of me, and gainin' some distance. I'm losin' ground so I do what I have to do to keep up with her. Scalin' one of the tall pine trees that is in my path, I am up it faster than any primate on the planet could climb it. Makin' it to one of the upper branches, I dive to another branch on a different tree yards away from the one I had scaled. Glidin' with my wings, I manage to catch the tree's limb and swing myself up in it. I dive to the next stand of trees, glidin' on the air currents and catchin' limbs like I've been doin' it all my life. I never even stop to think 'bout what I am doin'. I just want to catch up to Red and wring her neck.

I see a flash of red beneath the tree I'm in. It's Evie. She has sprouted her wings, probably in fear 'cuz she saw I wasn't playin' when I told her to run. Divin' to the next stand of trees, I catch the branch, and then I just let go of it, droppin' at least a story to the ground. Goin' down on my knee, I spring back up, catchin' Red 'round the waist as she tries to run by me.

"WHY?" I shout at her, searchin' her face that is pale and drawn from her flight from me. I don't realize just how much I'm scarin' her until she cringes and tries desperately to twist out of my arms. Her heart is beatin' out of control and when she can't break away from me she shrinks in my arms, tryin' to protect herself from the fist she thinks might be comin' at her from me. It is her fear that registers in my brain, calmin' me down instantly. "OH SHIT! WHAT AM I DOIN'?" I yell, freakin' out and huggin' Red to me. "Shit, Red, I'm sorry—I think I just—I don't know what just happened..." I trail off when her arms come 'round me, huggin' me back.

"I'm sorry, Russell, I didn't mean to hurt you…I can't do this anymore," I hear her whisper as her voice cracks. She presses her face into my chest. "I feel like I'm dying. I can't be an angel anymore. I have to be a human for a while. Please? Can we go back to being human? Please…" she begs me as if I have the power to make that happen. If I did, I would do it in a heartbeat. I would give her anythin' she asks for, anythin'.

"Shh…it's okay. We'll chill for a while. I promise," I say in a reassurin' tone, feelin' her shakin' in my arms. I want to kick myself for what I just did to her. Losin' control like that is so unexpected. It makes me ashamed of myself. I know that, no matter what, I would never hurt her, but she obviously doesn't know that. The way I chased her was probably terrifyin', especially since I had acted just like every other angel who has come upon her has acted. Every angel except for Reed. He never chased her down like she was a common criminal. He did sort of threatin' her, but he never chased her.

"You're really fast," she whispers, still shakin' so I know she is not over the shock of what just happened.

"I was losin' you on foot so I had to try somethin' else," I explain. "I'm not sure what just happened to me—it's like somethin' else took over—I was really pissed when ya hit me with that marble. It was like a part of me was respondin' to a challenge or somethin',' I say hurriedly, tryin' to explain to her that what just happened felt like an instinct, not a conscious choice on my part. "I felt extremely aggressive and I wanted to…" I trail off, tryin' to understand what I wanted to do.

"What? What did you want to do to me?" she asks in a quiet tone.

"A lot of stuff," I reply, 'cuz I really don't know where to begin and I'm not sure I can handle bein' this honest with her right now.

"Please?" she asks.

I cringe. "Ahh shoot, Red—I don't know. Y'all said that angels have a caste system of sorts, right?" I ask, tryin' to think 'bout this logically.

"Yes," she replies.

"And we're supposed to be at the top of that pyramid, right?" I ask for confirmation.

"Right," she replies, pullin' away from my chest to step back and look at me.

"Well, it kinda felt like ya were challengin' me—establishin' dominance or somethin' like that. Showin' me who's boss, so to speak," I say, watchin' her expression to see if she is understandin' what I'm tellin' her. "Well, that was my way of showin' ya that yer not the boss of me."

"Oh," she says, lookin' at me with her sad eyes. "What else?" she asks, after she processes what I've said. I run my hand through my hair a couple of times, then I glance down at my hikin' boots that I had picked up at the flea market the other day, along with several t-shirts 'cuz I'm tearin' through 'em faster than I can buy 'em these days.

"Well, the rest was just male stuff," I mutter, kickin' the dirt 'round, not lookin' at her.

"Male stuff?" she asks.

I rub my brow in frustration. "Yeah, Red. Male stuff," I repeat, lookin' up and surveyin' the terrain, tryin' to think of where we are in relation to where we were.

"I don't understand. What male stuff?" she asks in confusion. She really doesn't know and I want to groan out my frustration at her. How can she not get it?

"I was thinkin' about all the things I wanted to do to ya when I caught ya, and not all of them were painful." I say, tryin' to explain the fact that I want to rip the skin-tight, barely-there denim shorts from her body, press her back into the closest tree, and make love to her for as long as I can last, which wouldn't be long 'cuz it has been way, way too long since I held her in my arms like that...another lifetime.

"Oh," she replies as she gets what I'm sayin'. I see her blush and duck her head like a guilty criminal. I sigh loudly at her reaction to what I just said. The last thing I want is to make her feel guilty on top of freakin' her out by chasin' her through the woods. "Never mind, Red, it's my problem, not yers."

"No. I get what you're saying. You need some companionship. You need some other friends—you need a life. So do I," she says, starin' at me. "Survival can't be our only goal because it's going to kill us." She adds huggin' her arms to her body for comfort 'cuz it is plenty warm now, even in the woods.

I'm 'bout to tell her that I don't want anyone to comfort me but her, but I can see that sayin' it won't help the tension between us at the moment. "What do you suggest?" I ask as she paces back and forth before me.

"What if we got some part-time jobs? Nothing exciting, just something where we could get out and talk to other people," she says hopefully. "We can do recon on the places we apply to and have exit strategies for bad situations. What do you think?" she asks, bouncin' her idea off me.

"You think that's a good idea?" I counter as she pauses and stands before me, seein' my doubtful expression.

"Yes," she says without hesitation. "We can't go on like we have been. I'm slinging marbles at you and you're chasing me through the woods like you want to kill me. Can we seriously afford to go on like this?" she asks in honesty.

"I suppose not," I say with reluctance, but fear runs through me just thinkin' 'bout her bein' out there alone without my help. *What if she runs into a fallen angel and I'm not there?* I think, and then I shudder.

With an expression of remorse she says, "I'm sorry again—you know, about the marble."

"At least it was a good shot. You got me right in the leg," I point out, touchin' the spot where she hit me with my hand and feelin' that there is definitely gonna be a huge mark there for a while until I heal. I come up next to her, takin' her hand and pullin' her back down the hill in the direction we had come from.

"It wasn't that good a shot. I wasn't aiming for your leg," she says sweetly, and I remember I had been bendin' over when she had hit me.

"Yer just cruel. Are ya sure ya got any human left in ya at all? Yer as mean as Zephyr with his javelin," I say, teasin' her.

"I don't know how much human is left in me, Russell. That's why I need this so badly. I need to remember what it is to be human, before it slips away from me and is gone forever," she murmurs, and I'm beginnin' to understand what she means. The more I evolve, the harder it's becomin' to relate with the world 'round me. It's like I'm not human at all, like I don't fit in anymore. I don't. I have bright red wings to prove it, but I'm as desperate as Red is to hold on to a piece of my humanity, if I can. The angel part of me is so dominant, like it wants to blot out the human part entirely.

"Why did ya listen to me?" I ask as we walk through the trees. I see her confusion so I add, "Why didn't ya fight me instead of runnin'? I know yer still stronger than me at the moment."

"I will never fight you," she replies in a stern tone, like I have said somethin' completely ridiculous.

"Why not? You thought I was gonna hurt ya, why not fight back?" I retort, rememberin' how she cringed like I was gonna hit her and the shame of what I just did is back full force.

"You're my best friend," she says, like that is an explanation.

"Yes, but ya thought I was gonna hurt ya so I'd say, at that point, all bets should be off," I state clearly.

"No. I won't fight you for real. Ever. We can practice together, but I can't look at you like you're my enemy. It's impossible for me," she says firmly.

"So you'd let me hurt you, rather than defend yerself?" I ask, like she has lost her mind.

"Yes," she says.

"Why?" I ask again, 'cuz I have to understand her reasons before I tell her how stupid I think she is for havin' them.

"Because you're my soul mate and I love you," she says like I'm dense.

"That's not a good reason to let me hurt you," I reply disapprovingly.

"Reason and love are hardly ever compatible," she explains as we continue to walk. "But maybe it's because I still remember what it felt like when you were dying. I know what it's like to almost lose you and if I ever hurt you again…" She doesn't complete the thought; she just lets it hang there in the air between us.

"Ya didn't hurt me. Ya healed me with the help of Heaven, so stop thinkin' that way," I sigh in exasperation, runnin' my hand through my hair again. "And if I ever come after ya like that again, I insist ya beat the tar out of me," I add seriously. "I can't figure out what came over me, but it freaks me out."

She shrugs and says, "You're an angel now. Instinct is a huge part of it. I know some of what you felt. I have been going through it, too. I've had that feeling of aggression flair up in me. It scares me," she says honestly. She pauses before she says bashfully, "And, Russell, just so you know, I couldn't be your companion in that way right now anyway."

I stop walkin' and make her look at me when I ask, "Whaddaya mean?"

She turns red again and looks down at the ground. "I'm just saying that I would hurt you if we tried to be intimate. I would break you."

Somethin' in me leaps for joy, not 'cuz of what she said, but 'cuz she has been thinkin' about us in that light, like it is a possibility in the future. "I have a feelin' I wouldn't mind at all bein' broken in that way," I reply, and see her blush more. *God she's so beautiful*, I think, takin' her hand again and leadin' her through the trees.

"Do you want to try to run? See how fast you can go?" Red asks me suddenly, and then she stops and turns to me, her eyes wide open as if she is stunned. "Russell, did you fly?"

"Naw. I just scaled the trees and glided between them. I couldn't get my wings to move, but they spread out enough to act like a glider so I could reach the next stand of trees when I jumped," I reply.

"Like a squirrel?" she asks.

"I guess so," I say, smilin', 'cuz that is a good analogy.

"Can you teach me?" she asks, and it feels kinda good for her to ask me for help. She is always the one explainin' things to me.

"Yes," I reply, and she smiles for the first time in a long while. "Now that we know I can move like an angel, will ya teach me Bruce Lee? 'Cuz it's so crazy the way ya twist and flip while lookin' like yer 'bout to beat the snot out of somethin'."

"Sure. I'll race you back." She doesn't wait for me to react, but shoots off like she is the wind. I follow her and manage to catch up to her as we eat up the terrain.

∽

Red goes to work right away lookin' for a job to get her outta the apartment. I'm still kinda nervous 'bout her bein' out of my sight for any length of time, but she is right, we can't continue to lock ourselves away in the apartment forever. We do have to live.

Instead of lookin' for a job right away, I head over to the local high school and check out the intramural basketball leagues. I know that it's hardly fair for the humans to play against me, but I've got to live too, right? That's how I fall into my part time gig. I end up on the head basketball coaches' team in the league. He offers me a job as assistant coach of the summer boys basketball team. The pay is crappy, the hours are crappy, but it gets me out of the apartment a few days a week and I get to work with kids. That's kinda cool, since it reminds me that I'm still part human. Red and I talk about my job and decide it's a minimal risk 'cuz the Fallen don't seem very interested in kids for whatever reason. Maybe it's 'cuz, for the most part, their souls are pure.

I'm uncomfortable with the job Red finds. The job itself is all right. She is a library assistant at the college, or what she terms, a "shelver." Mostly, she restocks the books and assists people in locatin' specific publications. What I hate is the fact that she pulled the late shift. The college library stays open until midnight durin' the weekdays and she stays later to finish puttin' the books back after the patrons leave. I try to find reasons to pick her up after she gets off work, but she's on to me and keeps insistin' that she can walk home, since the library is close to our place. I know she's safe from anythin' a human can throw at her, but still, there is a part of me that sees her as just a little girl who should be protected from the world. She seems a little bit better emotionally, than the day I chased her through the woods. Not good by any stretch of the imagination, but better than the blackness she seemed to be entrenched in since we got here.

Red hooks us up with new cell phones so I can call her now, but she makes me promise not to check any messages on my old number. She's afraid that Reed has them tapped somehow and will get our new numbers from the phone log of the cellular phone provider. I ask her how that is possible and she says, "If the police can do it, Reed can too." I am temped to check anyway, just 'cuz I miss my family so much and I want to hear the sound of their voices, just for a second. I think Red has been feelin' the same way 'cuz I catch her holdin' her phone to her lips while starin' out the window. She looks like she is strugglin' just to take the next breath.

"What are ya thinkin' 'bout?" I ask her, after watchin' her stare out the window for a while like a statue.

"The speed of sound," she replies without lookin' at me. "I was just trying to figure out how many seconds it would take if I dialed a number on my phone to hear the voice on the other end of it," she murmurs in a rare moment of openness. I think I'm catchin' her off guard or somethin'.

I frown. "It would probably only take a few seconds I'd guess, dependin' on where you were callin'," I reply, not really understandin' what she is sayin'.

"Yes," she agrees with a sad smile, walkin' over to me and handin' me her phone. "Take this, please."

"I got a phone, Red, and ya need it so I can call ya if somethin' happens," I say, frownin' and tryin' to give her the phone back.

"Just keep it for today for me. Don't give it back to me until tomorrow. Okay?" she pleads and won't let me put the phone back in her hand.

"Why?" I ask.

"Because right now, in this moment, I can't have that phone," she says and when I look at her funny she tries to explain. "You said a few seconds—like three or four seconds—can you imagine what a temptation that is? To know that if I dialed the number, in three or four seconds I could ease, for just a moment, this ache that I have in my chest? To know that, in three or four seconds, I would be able to take a full breath, and for just a second, not feel like I'm drowning?" Her voice hitches as she holds her hand to her chest like she is tryin' to soothe a pain there. "So please, just keep my phone for me for now, so I can't use it."

My lips flatten in a grim line. "I'll keep it for ya as long as it takes. Ya just let me know when ya can have it back," I reply, seein' pain deep in her eyes. I had thought she was gettin' better, but maybe not. Maybe she is gettin' worse.

Evie

CHAPTER 10

Lost and Found

"Excuse me, Lillian…I was wondering…well, Lynnette and me were wondering that, if it's alright with ya, since it's Thursday night, ya know, 'thirsty Thursday,' and we're kinda invited to this party, well we thought that maybe ya could close the library without us tonight, eh?" Autumn asks, standing in front of the circulation desk where I sit with a worn copy of poetry. She can't help playing with her long brown hair, nervously pulling strands from the back while straightening it out. At the same time, she is casting glances at Lynette who is watching us from the racks of current journals.

I don't glance up at Autumn because I don't need to, since I have already processed the entire scenario and know the outcome within seconds. I have gone over all of the options, and even though I don't want to do any favors for either one of the mean girls in front of me, I'll gladly do this one so that I won't be subjected to Lynnette's sulky stares for the rest of the evening. In fact, I won't have to hear either one of them speak and that's worth any price I have to pay. Normally, Fran works the late shift with me at the circulation desk, but her husband has been sick so she is not here tonight.

"Sure, Autumn," I agree without preamble. Autumn breathes in loudly and then gives a giant exhale as she turns toward Lynette, clapping her hands excitedly. Looking over at Lynnette, I notice that she glances away quickly. She doesn't want to acknowledge that I'm doing her a favor. Lynnette is funny like that; she instantly hated me when I met her for reasons I think I will never know for sure. It doesn't bother me quite as much as it probably would have before, since I'm now very used to being hated upon first sight. Maybe she has a better reason than the angels, doubtful, but maybe. At first I was suspicious of her and thought that she was perhaps a Reaper, even though there is nothing about her that says *angel*. After watching her for a while and doing some recon, I have come to the conclusion that she is just mean.

Anyway, I can get everything done faster if they're not here. I can run through the library, putting things back at angel speed if I'm alone, so it will work out for me as well. "Thanks, eh. We're gonna go buy a case and drink out by the river before we go to the party," Autumn informs me in a rare moment of camaraderie.

She must have forgotten for a second that she doesn't like me, or my 'troll accent,' but I smile a little anyway and say, "That sounds like fun."

"Yeah, well…we thought we'd take off then, so we can get ready, eh?" Autumn says, gesturing with her thumb over her shoulder.

"Okay," I answer with relief that they are leaving. She smiles and hurries over to tell Lynnette the good news. I see right away by the smirk on Lynnette's face that this favor I'm doing for her will not make us friends. It seems to have the opposite affect. She looks smug, like she thinks I'm doing this because I'm trying to get her to like me, which is laughable because in reality, I'm terrified of making any real friends. Being my friend is hazardous to your health, just ask Russell…or Reed.

A stabbing pain twists through my chest at the mere thought of Reed. I have to take shallow breaths. I know better than to let my thoughts stray to Reed unless I'm alone. Searching for a distraction that will keep me from thinking of him, I pick up the copy of the works of Edgar Allen Poe that I had been reading before annoying Autumn interrupted me. I flip the book open to the creased pages of the poem entitled, *The Raven*. Reading the first few stanzas rapidly, I slow when I come to the verses that shock me with their insight.

Then, methought, the air grew denser, perfumed from an unseen censer
Swung by Seraphim whose foot-falls tinkled on the tufted floor.
"Wretch," I cried, "thy God hath lent thee—by these angels he has sent thee
Respite—respite and nepenthe from thy memories of Lenore!

*Quaff, oh quaff this kind nepenthe, and forget this
lost Lenore!"
Quoth the Raven, "Nevermore."*

I reread the stanza of Poe's poem over and over again while mem-
orizing every word. Just like the man in the poem, I crave a nepenthe, some ancient drug that can induce forgetfulness, so that just for
one moment I will be free of the painful memories of Reed. I close
the book and gently place it on the mobile bookshelf so that I can
re-shelve it later.

Looking up from my position seated at the circulation desk, I
watch the young woman who has been researching theories on black
holes get up and begin packing up her materials, putting her notes
in her bag. She had told me that her name is Erin when I was helping
her find books on the subject. She's working on a summer research
project for one of her professors and she seems a little frazzled about
the assignment. Her anxiety makes me want to help her out somehow, but I don't know very much on that particular subject.

As Erin cleans up her space at the mahogany table lined with
reading lamps, the thought crosses my mind that I could tell her
what it is like to be near an ascending soul: the unbelievable pull
and ache when I was left behind to exist without Paradise. I wonder
briefly if that's comparable to facing a black hole. Probably not, since
I was repelled instead of stretched out and pulled into its vortex, but
still, there was significant pain in the rejection. But I know I can't really talk to anyone about that experience, since the best-case scenario
after revealing something like that to a human would be that she
would think I am insane, so maybe it's better to keep my mouth shut.

When Erin finishes, she gathers up the books she was reading
and brings them over towards the front desk. Standing up as she
approaches, I reach for the heavy stack of books, taking them easily
from her arms. "Careful, they're heavy!" she warns, laughing as I set
the books down on the counter.

"Do you want to check out all of these?" I ask, picking up the
scanner and straightening the stack on the counter.

"Um, I don't know—let me see. I want this one and this one,"
she says, picking the top two books off the stack and placing them in
another pile next to the one we already had on the counter. "Ugh,
this one is so boring. I don't want that one, eh," she says, smiling at
me and making a third pile for the rejects.

After she sorts through everything, she hands me her library card with the name of Erin Adams on it. I begin scanning the ones she wants and when I finish I place the ones she doesn't want on my bookshelf cart to return to the shelves later. "Your books are due back in two weeks. If you need more time with them, you can go on-line and recheck them out," I explain, handing her a printout with the list of the books she is taking along with her card.

"I want to thank you for all your help," she says, smiling at me.

"You're welcome," I reply but can't quite manage a smile. I don't know if it is something in my face or what, but Erin pauses before she picks up the books.

"Hey, I'm new here, but my roommate knows everybody. We're supposed to go out to the bar tonight. Do you want to come with us?" she asks as she puts her library card back in her wallet. She doesn't have the accent of a true Yooper, so she must be from somewhere else.

"I can't," I say quickly. "I'm only eighteen and I don't have an ID. But thanks for the invite."

"Oh," she says, looking at me disappointedly. "Well, maybe we don't have to go to the bar. We could just hang out. There's not a lot to do here, but like I said, my roommate knows everyone and we could invite some people over," she adds hopefully. She seems really nice and I miss having a friend who is not involved in the supernatural, someone I can talk to about the movie I saw, or the book I read, or the shoes I bought, and not about what I will do if someone tries to kill me with a chakram.

"I'm sorry, I can't tonight. I have to lock up, and then I promised to be home right after work. Maybe some other time?" I say, because it's stupid and selfish for me to make a human friend. There has been too much collateral damage without adding an innocent human into the mix.

"I understand," she says with a sigh. "Well, if you ever feel like grabbing some coffee or something, let me know. I'm going to be around the library a lot because of this article. Thanks again for your help." She takes her stack of books and leaves through the front door of the library.

With Erin gone, I realize that I'm alone here for the first time here. *No, I think I'm alone for the first time since coming to the U.P.*, I think as I move around the end of the circulation desk.

I walk over the tiled floor of the reception area, looking out the giant windows to the walkway in front of the library. The library is dead tonight. I guess the locals really take thirsty Thursday seriously, since it's only eleven thirty and the place is deserted. I listen quietly, searching for any sounds of breathing or movement from the floors above. After several minutes, I'm certain that I'm alone in the building.

Deciding to begin closing down the library, I wheel the bookshelf cart to the carrels, picking up the randomly discarded books and adding them to my cart as I go. When I reach one of the far carrels, I find a cell phone lying on the ground partially hidden under the desk. Crouching down, I pick it up, noticing that it's not turned on. I place the phone on my cart and continue my sweep of the library, looking for books to put back. When I finish collecting the books on the first floor, I ride the elevator up to the second floor and collect all of the discarded books, putting back the atlases and maps that belong on this floor. I also check the study rooms, but they are all empty.

Pushing the cart back to the elevator, I press the button for the third floor while I study the cell phone sitting on the top shelf of my cart. *I wonder whose it is,* I think as I wait for the doors of the elevator to open. A soft ding indicates that I have reached the third floor of the library. I push the cart forward, bumping over the lip of the elevator. It makes a loud clunking sound as it rattles forward. I immediately go to work re-shelving books, using angel speed to get it done in less than a minute. Returning to my cart, I still as I look at the cell phone.

I pick it up and press the power button. The phone comes to life in an instant. Searching impatiently for the phone number, I find that it begins with a 289 area code. I run to the stairs and I'm on the ground floor in a half of a second. Sprinting to the bank of computers, I log onto the Internet and search for the 289 area code. This cell phone is from someone from Ontario or Toronto, Canada.

Could this phone be traced here? I wonder. Probably. If Reed is monitoring my old cell phone account, he could possibly get the phone log of numbers that call my voicemail account. He would either have to hack into the cell phone company or have paid someone on the inside to get him information, though. If I use this cell phone to contact my old voicemail, he might be able to get this number, but since it's a Canadian number, would he then assume I'm in Canada? Could he figure out what tower I used to make the call and know that I'm in the U.P.?

I tug on my lip anxiously, seeing the risks associated with doing what I so badly want to do. I want to use this phone to call my voicemail. I want to see if I can hear Reed's voice for just a second, to pretend for one moment that he is here with me. I want to pretend that

I can reach out and feel his soft hair and his perfectly smooth skin. It's such a tempting fantasy. My hands are beginning to tremble. *It has been three months. He might have given up by now,* I tell myself, and a crushing weight that I can barely hold up anymore threatens to bury me in grief. This grief is impossible to control and I'm growing so tired trying to survive it.

I could ruin everything that I set out to do in seconds if I make this call…but if I make this call, I could save myself from drowning. Making this call might be the worst thing I can do at this point. Can I handle it, or will it kill me to hear his voice again? Unconsciously, I dial the first three digits of the voicemail number then I slam the phone down on the desk near the computer I'm using. Backing away slowly from the phone, I turn and run to the front doors of the library, locking them all, and then I run back to the desk. I check the time; the cleaning crew won't be here for at least another hour.

I feel like my life is already over; that everything I ever was is twisted out of place. I didn't calculate the cost when I made my plan to leave Reed. I thought that I would have the strength to do this for him, but it turns out that I'm even weaker than I knew. All I can think about every single minute of every single day is him. With my new ability to think, I can process things differently than I could before. If I had thought I had overcome the kiosk in my mind devoted to Reed, I was deluded. One part of me doesn't want to acknowledge that there was ever any danger to him and sees what I'm doing as being cruel. If Reed had left me, for any reason, could I have survived it? I am beginning to realize that things aren't ever going to get better. If they were, wouldn't I already know it?

Picking up the phone, I dial my voicemail number and wait for the phone to connect. I enter my password and the automated voice message service informs me that my mailbox is full. A second elapses in the space of an eternity, and then I hear the most beautiful and most gut wrenching sound I have ever heard in my life. It's Reed's voice. This must have been the first call that he made to me just after I left Crestwood. He doesn't sound anxious, just concerned when he says, "Evie, where are you? Brownie said you weren't feeling well after I left, and when she came back to class, you weren't here. Are you okay? I found your necklace. It was in your bed. The clasp must have opened while you were sleeping. You didn't lose it—so don't worry. Call me back, I'm in the hallway outside of class."

I cringe, remembering the lie I had told Reed that morning. It was after we had taken our seats in the classroom. I had pretended to notice that the necklace he had given me for my birthday was missing. It wasn't hard to pretend to panic over it, since I was panicky and ill over the lie I was telling him. He offered to go and look for my necklace at home, his smile casual, as if it were no big deal that the priceless necklace was missing. He was more concerned about how I was reacting to losing it than the fact that it was missing.

As he had gotten up from his seat next to me, I reached out and grasped his hand. Pulling him back into his seat, I had leaned over and kissed him softly on the lips, breathing against his mouth, "I love you."

"You're worried?" he had asked me with a sexy smile.

"Yes," I had replied honestly with my heart retracting tightly in my chest.

He had smiled at me, his green eyes staring into mine as he had leaned forward and allowed his forehead to rest against mine. "Don't worry. I'll find it," he had said, before getting up from his seat once again. I held on to his hand. He looked at my hand in his—my fingers were holding on too tight. His eyebrow had quirked in question when he again glanced at me.

"Bye," I had uttered, making myself let go of him.

Once Reed had left, it was easy to convince Brownie I was sick. I was sick. I had had to put my head down on my desk for a few minutes while my head spun. Brownie had left quickly to get me water and as soon as I knew she was gone, I left, too.

My legs are shaking now. I listen to the automated voice come back on the line to ask me if I want to save the message. Numbly, I press the save button. The automated voice says, "Next message."

"EVIE, where are you?" Reed demands, and this time he sounds upset. There is a pause as if he anticipated a response, but his next words dispel that thought. "Russell is missing. Is he with you?" Reed asks. He sounds worried about upsetting me with the news that Russell was gone, too. "Call me as soon as you get this message."

I have to sit down, I tell myself, walking feebly to the lounge chairs positioned by the newspaper and magazine shelves nearby that face the window. I lower myself into a seat, feeling my heart pounding in my chest. I save the message when it prompts me.

"Next message," the automated voice says without emotion.

"GENEVIEVE AVA CLAREMONT!" Reed's voice yells into the phone, making me sit up straighter in my seat. "Whatever you have planned you need to stop right now! Turn around and come home. It's too dangerous for you to be out there on your own. Think about Russell. He's totally helpless—you both need protection," he says in a stern tone, like I'm a child who has done something naughty. Then, his tone changes drastically, and he sounds desperate in his next breath. "I can't feel you—are you okay—don't do this, Evie! Please... don't do this."

My palms are slick with sweat as I depress the save button on the message again when it prompts me. It's in the back of my mind that this is torture and not helpful in any way. I should just end the call, but I can't.

"Next message."

"Evie," Zephyr says, and I don't know if I'm relieved or crushed that it isn't Reed's voice speaking to me. "What you overheard us talking about in the library is not as bad as it might have sounded," Zee says in a calm tone. He must have found the tablet that I had used to convince Russell to come with me. Russell said he had left it for Reed to find, so that Reed would know why we were leaving. "It must have sounded grave to you. But we have a plan. We are leaving in a few days. We planned to tell you and Russell tomorrow, but it seems we should not have waited. Evie, you are unorthodox, and although I admire that, in this situation, you are letting your emotions cloud your judgment. The best thing you can do now is call us and tell us where you are. We'll come and get you. You will be safe with us...you are our family," Zephyr says, and something twists inside of me and I can't breathe for a second.

"Next message."

"OKAY, YOU'RE REALLY PISSING ME OFF NOW!" Brownie's voice booms. I have to hold the phone away from my ear. She was trying to sound angry, but there is fear in her voice that she can't mask. "YOU BETTER CALL US BACK RIGHT NOW! WE'RE NOT PLAYING AROUND WITH YOU! CHICAGO IS A REALLY, REALLY BAD IDEA!"

They had bought it, I think, feeling at once grateful and sick for what I had done to them and the dichotomy of the emotions is making me feel dizzy. I save the message instinctively. I don't care if Brownie is yelling at me; I need to know that I can hear her voice again if I need to.

"Next message."

"Sweetie..." Buns's voice says and I close my eyes for a second, picturing her face. "We are all very worried about you. I want you to come back now. We're going to go to an island that Zephyr owns. It's really remote and I bought you the cutest swimsuit that will make you look hot. Reed will be unable to resist you. Tell Russell we are going to arrange to have his family flown out so that they can visit each other for a while. We can't go without you two. You have to come home now…please." I hear the catch in Buns's voice as she tries to reason with me on the message. I save this one, too.

"Next message."

"Evie…where are you? I need…I need you…I can't exist without you—you have to come back to me," Reed says, and the pain that those words contain cannot be measured. I can't see. My tears are blinding me. I save it automatically, but I don't think I can ever listen to that message again. I don't ever want to hear his voice sound like that again.

"Next message."

It is Reed again, but this time he is speaking in Angel and it is different than I've ever heard it before. The sound of his voice is so sad that I burst out in sobs when I hear the melancholy lilt to the beautiful language.

What have I done? I ask myself, almost unable to breathe. *Heaven help the one who truly loves me.* When the message cuts off after an endless amount of time, the voicemail prompts me to save the message, but I delete it. I can never hear that again and expect to survive.

"Next message."

"Sweetie," Buns's voice floats gently through the receiver, "you have to come home. When Reed found out you weren't on the train… he completely lost it. I've never seen him like this—I've never seen a Power like this. It's like he's really sick. He can't sleep—he can't eat—he goes over every detail of the days before you disappeared, looking for clues of where you might have gone. We know that you boarded a bus. He got the surveillance disks, but your trail went cold in Mackinaw. If you care about him at all…it doesn't matter what Dominion will do to him. It can't be any worse than what you are doing to him now…" She pauses, taking a deep breath before she says, "But, if you decide you can't come home, then I want to tell you—I will always love you, too, sweetie," Buns says and it sounds like she was crying. "Brownie and Zee are here and they want me to says that they love you, too. We will always be looking for you, sweetie." When this message ends, I save it.

"Next message."

"Do you remember when I told you that I sometimes believe that you're not real? That I imagined you just to hurt myself?" Reed says softly with a bitterly self-effacing laugh that has nothing to do with humor. "I know now that you have to be real. This kind of pain cannot exist if you were imaginary," Reed's sexy voice breathes. I feel like I could reach out and touch him, he feels that close to me. "I know you exist, but you're like a sunset to me now—beautiful and so distant that no matter how fast I fly, I cannot reach you. You are always on the next horizon," Reed says sadly, and my breath catches in my throat as an unbelievable ache throbs in my chest. "Tell me where you are. I will meet you—wherever you are in the world. I will be there. Just you and me, I swear it. We don't have to endanger anyone else—we'll make sure Buns and Brownie and Zephyr are safe. Just you and me, I promise…I will meet you anywhere at anytime…I will…" The message ends and I can't move, nothing about me works anymore. After a few prompts by the voicemail to save the message, the voicemail automatically saves it.

"You have no unheard messages," the voice says and I slowly pull the phone from my ear. I don't know how long I've been sitting here, but the next thing I realize is pounding rattling the front doors of the library. Looking over at them numbly, I see Russell watching me from outside. He looks scared and I wonder fleetingly how long he has been out there waiting for me to notice him.

Numbly, I get up from the chair, feeling weak. Tears slide down my cheek and I'm almost surprised when my hand wipes at it and comes away wet. Haltingly, I unlock one of the main doors to the building. Russell is inside in a fraction of a second, grabbing me by the shoulders and pulling me to him. "What happened?" he asks with a grim look, holding me too close.

I feel dead, like if I tell him what I just heard I will break apart and there will be nothing left of me to love. *He can't console me…there is no relief.*

"Tell me, Red, whatever it is, we'll deal with it," Russell says near my ear.

"I found a phone," I murmur as I lift my hand and pull back from Russell's chest. I open up my palm for him to see the silver cell phone lying in it. Taking it from me, he looks at it in confusion. I'm beyond the point of being able to explain what I had heard, so I say in a hollow voice, "I called my voicemail."

"Red," Russell says, closing his eyes like he is disappointed in me. His hand closes tight on the phone I have just given him and in seconds he has crushed it into a hunk of metal. He opens his eyes and looks at me, surprised by what he had just done. I'm not surprised. I knew it was coming. His strength will rival my own and that thought is the only bright light in the darkness of my world.

"I want to go home," I whisper, and I see Russell's expression turn sad. He knows what I mean. He knows I mean home to Crestwood, not our shabby apartment in the U.P.

"I know ya do," he says. "But, we can't do that 'til we know we aren't gonna be killin' them by bein' there.'"

"But…I can't breathe anymore," I retort. I break down again, putting my hand to my mouth.

"Hang on, just a little longer…you can do it, Red, I know ya can," he says as he pulls me in his arms again. "Did ya make any other calls?" he asks tensely, waiting for my answer.

"No," I reply, and he relaxes.

"C'mon. Let's go. This place is creepy at night. No wonder yer makin' calls to yer voicemail. Why are ya here alone?" he asks in an angry tone.

I shrug. I can't think. I keep hearing Reed's voice in my head speaking in his language, but with the sadness that tortures me. I let Russell lead me to the circulation desk to get my purse. Taking the keys from me, he holds the door for me and locks up behind us. Passing the garbage can outside, he tosses the crushed phone into it.

◦◦◦

I hardly leave my room the next day. I hear Russell stomping around the apartment agitatedly, but it makes me just want to pull the pillow over my head. I think he wants an explanation as to why I used that phone and almost ruined our new life here, but there is no explanation that won't hurt him. How can I tell him that I hadn't known how unrelenting the pain and loss of the family I had come to count on would be? It never ends, this ache for Reed. Russell is definitely stronger than me. He lost his family, too, but he isn't falling apart. He's adapting. I admire that in him. He is an ass kicker and I'm proud of him, even as I struggle to make him proud of me, too.

After allowing me to stay in bed for a day, he manages to cajole me into training with him the next two days. He has a way of getting me to do things that I don't want to do. I think he knows me too well. He knows all the right buttons to push to get my compliance and it's really annoying to come to that realization. I teach him more Bruce Lee and he instructs me on tree jumping. I'm not nearly as good at it as he is because my wings don't span nearly as far as his. I had a couple of really scary encounters with tree trunks before I figured out that I couldn't glide as far as him.

Russell was given a set of keys to the gym at the high school so that he can open up when the basketball coach is running late. We start going there late at night to train and I show him again how to run the walls. He takes to it with a natural ability and grace that is ingrain in him, using his increasing speed to defy gravity and propel himself onto the wall without much effort. The first time he accomplishes the feat, he jumps off the center of the wall and tumbles directly in front of me, managing to scoop me up in his arms and swing me around like a rag doll. He is so psyched about bouncing off the wall, he is... well, bouncing off the walls.

Russell has also managed to find some swords at a gun and knife show that traveled through the area a few weeks ago. He has gotten us quite a few weapons and when I ask him where he'd found them all, he informs me that the U.P. is a virtual treasure trove for all types of weapons. He says that there is even a slogan that goes: The U.P. is made for sportsmen. I don't know what kind of sport involves wickedly sharp Samurai swords, but I guess I'll have to go with it.

Russell is deadly with a sword. He is also patient, using all his knowledge and finesse to force me into positions from which I can't retreat. Then, when it's apparent that he could easily kill me, he stops and shows me step-by-step where I went wrong, trying to correct my mistakes. He makes it seem effortless, his skill with the weapon. There is something terrifying about watching him move like a powerful storm, coming closer and closer with frightening speed and control, knowing that if he wants to, he can slice me in half without a backward glance. But he never loses focus, never lets the intensity of what he's doing overwhelm him or cause him to act wildly. I think he's constantly conscious of what happened when I hit him with the marble and he knows now that it would not take much to lose perspective.

When Monday comes, I notice Russell watching me get ready for work. He looks apprehensive. "Ya know, Red, maybe you shouldn't go in today. I mean, I hate to think of ya all alone there. Ya never know what those two are gonna do," he says, referring to Lynnette and Autumn. He was really angry when he found out that they left me to cover for them so they could go get drunk before a party.

"They don't bother me...much," I shrug, thinking of the girls. They are more annoying than hurtful, since I really don't care what they think of me.

"Still, why don't ya look for somethin' else—somethin' durin' the day with normal hours?" he asks.

"Why? It's not like the Fallen don't come out during the day or any other angel for that matter," I point out, looking at Russell to see where he is going with this.

"Yeah, I know. I guess I'm just used to the dangers associated with you bein' a girl and bein' human. I can't seem to shake it," he replies, smiling a little. "I always had to run over to Scarlett's friend's house after dark to walk her home. My mom didn't want her out at night alone. I guess old habits die hard."

Something about the image of Russell walking his little sister home at night makes me smile. He is such a lovely person, good for all the right reasons. Even through all of this, he has managed to keep that sweetness about him. It's like he is good all the way to the core, so that it doesn't matter how much of him gets scraped away—there is still goodness underneath.

"I dare any human to attack me. Pwnage, Russell," I say, holding up the butter knife I had been using to spread peanut butter on a slice of bread I'm packing for my dinner tonight. When Russell looks at me skeptically, I chuck the knife across the room, impaling the fly with it that has been annoying me all morning. The knife embeds in the wall at the other end of the room, making a new scar in the wall to blend in with the others.

"Flossin' again, huh?" he mutters, and I look down, smiling a little. "Hey, I was wonderin' if you would come with me on Wednesday. One of the parents of the kids on the team is havin' a little party for all the parents and coaches. It's a cocktail and hors d'oeuvres thing. Blake and his wife Angie will be there and I think I kinda have to make an appearance."

Blake is the coach of the team that hired Russell to be the assistant coach. I have met him a few times after the games. He's funny, the way he whistles at me every time he sees me, like he can't help himself. Angie just rolls her eyes at him when he does it. I know he doesn't mean anything by it, well nothing too bad anyway.

"What does one wear to an event like cocktails and hors d'oeuvres?" I ask him.

"Good question...somethin' sexy..." he replies with a charming grin.

I roll my eyes. "I'll call Angie and find out," I reply. Russell frowns a little. He still hasn't given me back my cell phone and I haven't asked for it. I can see the thought of me having it back is not a good one in his mind. Sadly, I agree with him.

"How 'bout I ask Angie for ya. I'll let ya know what she says," he asks, and his brown eyes meet mine with concern.

"Sure," I reply, packing up my sandwich in a plastic bag and putting it in the little cooler I take to work with me.

"I'll swing by tonight, after you get off work," he says smoothly.

He wants to pick me up. He's worried about me, I realize, and I guess

I'm to blame for that, again.

"Okay," I sigh, because it will probably take a little while for me to gain his trust back. He relaxes a little after that and I go to change for work. Putting on a black pencil skirt that stops just above the knee with a white blouse that I altered to accommodate my wings, I select the black heels that always make Russell stop and stare. He likes them a lot.

I walk to work thinking of the party. When I arrive at the library, I'm disappointed to find out that Fran isn't back from her time off yet, so I'm stuck with Autumn at the circulation desk again. As the course of the evening wears on, I notice Autumn being unnaturally quiet. She is just sitting and watching me while I assist patrons, like she is studying me. The more I scrutinize her, the more suspicious I'm becoming of her behavior. She doesn't seem right to me. Normally, she is chatty and filled with inane observations that make me think that she has never been out of Houghton, or at least she has never been farther south than the bridge. But she's uneasy and twitchy tonight. There is a glassy tint to her eyes. I wonder if they had gotten more than just a case of beer when they were out at the river.

I spy Lynnette later by the photocopiers watching me, too. She looks slightly ill and her pupils are dilated to near blackness. *They are definitely on something*, I surmise. A very petty part of me hopes it's a scary, face-melting, shadows-dancing, demon-frolicking trip.

By the time my shift is halfway done, I am truly creeped out by their behavior. Autumn follows me everywhere I go, even into the bathroom. I just about have to shut the stall door in her face and I can hear her outside the door biting her nails. I breathe easier when I go back out to the circulation desk and see Erin entering the lobby of the library, carrying two cups of coffee.

"Lillian!" Erin says, approaching the desk. "I brought you a cup of coffee as a not so subtle bribe." She sets the coffee down in front of me. She flashes cream and sugar at me, drawing it from her pocket like contraband before balancing it on top of the coffee cup lid, along with a coffee stir stick. "I need your help again, eh. I need to find some more information for my project."

"I would be happy to help you. You don't have to bribe me, but I'm glad you did. I love coffee," I say, relieved to see a friendly face. Autumn is earjacking our exchange with glazed fascination that is almost embarrassing.

Erin, noticing our audience, glances from Autumn and then to me again, making a little face that indicates she thinks Autumn is acting weird. Then she says, "I need to have more documentation on how the Schwarzschild radius can be calculated using the equation for escape speed."

"That sounds gnar gnar. Let's go see what we can turn up," I say, coming around the end of the circulation desk. I have to stop, feeling my Autumn shadow trailing me. I turn to Autumn and say, "Autumn, can you watch the desk while I help Erin find what she needs?" Autumn's gaze shifts to Erin, and then it comes back to me. She nods slowly and I exhale a deep breath when she goes back around the counter and sits down, biting her nails as her eyes continue to track me.

"Is she high?" Erin asks in a near whisper as we walk away from the counter toward the reference computer.

"I don't know. She is acting strange though," I reply, trying not to speculate.

"Hey, I want to tell you that you didn't miss much last week, you know when we went to the bar. It was pretty dead," she says conspiratorially, while I referenced her subject on the computer. "But the most amazing thing happened to me on Saturday night!" she says before taking a quick sip of her coffee.

"Yeah?" I reply, cocking my eyebrow and smiling because she seems eager to tell me her news.

"Yeah. I met the most amazing man!" she gushes. "He is extremely hot and he wanted my number! That's why I haven't been back in to work on my assignment," she says, and it is BFO that she really likes this new man.

"Does this amazing man have a name?" I ask in amusement at the dreamy look on her face.

"Yes…his name is Finn Graham and he has the most *amazing* Irish accent. He is so hot and you might get to meet him because he said he might be stopping by with his brother Brennus," she says with a pretty good imitation of an Irish accent when she said "Brennus." Her anticipation is palatable.

"That does sound…amazing," I reply, trying to be supportive. I feel awkward because it has been a while since I tried to be friends with a human that wasn't in on all of my secrets.

"I know!" she agrees with a little squeal that makes me smirk in delight because it was just so…girly. I locate more books for Erin and help her set up on the main floor of the library at one of the study carrels.

When I go back to the circulation desk, Autumn isn't there. *Figures*, I think, *she's probably watching the dust motes blow around in the break room.*

I begin to organize the mobile cart with the books that I will need to return to their shelves at the end of my shift, but as I lift a book from the shelf, my hand stills in midair. A cold, prickling sensation touches my skin and raises goose bumps on my arms. My entire body stiffens with the awareness that something isn't right. I immediately scan the first floor of the library, trying to pick out anything that might be threatening.

The cold feeling intensifies to an icy chill on my skin as I zero in on the front doors of the library. Two men enter and cross the lobby's tile floor, approaching the circulation desk. They are moving like graceful foxes, stealthy and sharp. They seem to be missing none of the details of their environment, but they appear relaxed and at ease with their prowess—a bad sign for me. Reaching over, I ease the letter opener out of the desk drawer, concealing it in my palm as they approach the desk.

The outside doors behind them close, causing the airflow to shift and make me downwind of them. Immediately, the sweetest scent I have ever smelled assails me...it's floral...poppies maybe, and it's making me want to rub my nose to get the reek out. My heartbeat kicks up. My wings are twitching inside my back, and I strain to keep them in. *What do I do?* I think rapidly. If they were angels, I would know what to do—I would have bolted the minute I saw them, but they aren't angels...and they are not human. *Will they know that I'm not human?* I wonder as the shorter one, who is at least six foot tall, leans with a casual elegance against the counter of the circulation desk.

He is scanning the library in front of him, not really looking at me. His short black hair has a very in-the-now cut that makes him look *tres chic,* just like the taller one. They both have a chiseled, high cheekbone profile that is strikingly similar to an angel and that realization is making me feel ill.

The taller one, however, gives me his full attention as he leans negligibly across the counter. I'm sure that most women find him sexy. His green eyes are piercing; they aren't the deep jewel-tone green of Reed's eyes, but a light watery green that reminds me of sea foam. The contrast against his pale skin is startling. "Me brudder and I were looking ta get a couple of library cards. Can ye help us out wi' dat?" The tall one asks me, while his dark eyebrow rises silently as if it is asking the question.

Irish, I tell myself with dread. I glance over at Erin who hasn't looked up when these two had entered, but is avidly studying the books I had given her. Clutching the letter opener tighter in my fist, I gaze back at the man in front of me, feeling fear twist in my stomach.

"Of course," I say in a soft tone, not moving from my position a few feet away from the desk. "I'll just need to see a license or a student ID card," I add, trying to be nonchalant. A slow, handsome smile moves across his lips as he straightens up, retrieving a wallet from his back pocket. He is dressed casually in a dark t-shirt and jeans, but just like an angel, he makes it look posh, almost elegant, and the awareness of that fact makes me want to run for the door.

The taller one withdraws his license from his wallet, and then he waits patiently for his brother to hand him his license as well while never taking his eyes from me. Reaching out his hand, he extends the cards for me to take. Straightening my shoulders, I approach the desk with reluctance. I reach my hand out warily to take the cards from him, and as my hand nears his, I feel coldness radiate from his flesh. My heartbeat quickens. Trying to keep my hand steady, I watch the man in front of me as my fingers close over the cold, plastic cards. I try to pull them from his hand, but he doesn't relinquish them to me, instead, he is watching me as if I fascinate him.

I continue to hold on to the cards, saying, "I only need to verify that you are a resident or a student of the school, so I can issue you a library card." My mouth feels dry.

"Me apologies," he says in a caressing tone as his other hand comes up to gently cover the top of mine before he lets go of the cards, dropping his hands from me. Astonishment and fear war with my senses as it registers that his touch had been freezing, as if he had just come in from the bitter cold—but it's summer.

Not wanting to be this close to them, I back up a few paces from the counter. I glance quickly at their licenses, taking only a fraction of a second to scan the information because I don't want to take my eyes off the eerie pair in front of me. I'm not at all sure what they are, but if I'm innately afraid of them, then I trust my instincts to know that they aren't good. Fear bleeds into my conscious mind when the names on the IDs register, de Graham...Finn and Brennus de Graham.

Erin has found a supernatural boyfriend of the creepy variety. The license says that Brennus, the tall one, is twenty-four-years-old and his brother, Finn, is twenty-three. That looks about right, but then again, Reed looks nineteen and he is way older than that—*way, way* older. The address on the ID is local, so they must live together somewhere on campus because the street address is Townsend, which is the road where most of the dorms are located.

As casually as I can, I step forward and place the licenses on the edge of the counter, and then I retreat again to say, "Thank you. If you want to go look around, I'll have your cards ready for you in a few minutes. You can pick them up before you leave."

Finn, the shorter one, turns and gives me his full attention. He looks so much like his brother Brennus; they both have silky black hair, pale skin and their eyes have the same kind of iridescent-green shine to them. The intensity by which he is studying me makes me have to repress a shiver because I notice the primal way he sniffs the air around us. He is gathering my scent, cataloging it as I have already cataloged his. I'm beginning to feel hunted as they continue to stare at me even after I have made it plain that they can leave and look around.

My focus is on Finn because he seems to want to say something, but he's holding himself back and looking to his brother—like a beta would wait for the alpha... My attention turns immediately back to Brennus. If there is going to be something coming, it's coming from him—by his order.

Brennus' gaze turns sultry. "Whah is yer name?" Brennus asks me. I want to scream out in frustration because the last thing I want to do is engage the creepies in conversation.

"Lillian," I answer, lifting my chin a little to show them that they don't intimidate me even as my heartbeat drums even louder in my ears.

"Is it now?" he asks in a sexy tone, and I'm not sure if that is his typical response, or just his way of telling me he doesn't believe the lie I just told him. By his expression, he looks like he is enjoying himself, whatever it is he thinks of me.

I nod to him, backing up my lie.

He smiles like he knows a secret. "Dat is a beautiful name, but it does ye an injustice. A lily is soft and sweet—delicate. Ye are someting else entirely, are ye na?" he asks me in a seductive tone, toying with the cards I had given back to him.

Adopting my best librarian tone that I have heard Fran use with pushy patrons, I reply, "If there is anything else, I'll be happy to assist you, but I'm quite busy at the moment. If you will excuse me, I have some things to attend to."

Surprise widens Brennus' eyes at my dismissal, and then he bursts out laughing as his brother watches him in amazement. "Did ye hear dat, Finn? I tink she is not atall inta me," he says with amusement in his eyes. His pearly white teeth are perfect in the grin he gives me. I want to find the nearest door and seal it shut against him. I'm on his radar now and I can tell by Finn's incredulous expression that they are both *very* intrigued.

"Whah Brenn, has dat ever happened ta ye in yer entire life?" Finn asks him, amused too.

"I do na recall, Finn," he responds with his eyes never leaving mine. "But I'm drownin' in da pools of gray. Go, find yer lass...I've found moin."

My eyebrows draw together in a frown. "I'm someone else's lass— sorry," I say in response to their exchange. Finn's eyes bulge out of his head at my softly spoken statement.

Brennus' expression darkens. "Show me dis rival and I will fight him for ye," he says in a deadly tone that does not allow for me to believe that he is joking or being insincere. My heartbeat triples its rate and my wings are begging to charge out of my back. I hold my breath, trying to gain control of them.

Gritting my teeth, I reply, "I fight all of my own battles because whom I'm with is *my* choice."

"Now how can I fight ye for yer affection? Dat sounds impossible, but I suppose I can try anyting once. So ye are saying dat, if I win our mill, den ye're moin?" Brennus asks, and I can't help but feel challenged by him. Like he has just dropped an invisible gauntlet.

"No. I'm saying you and I will never happen," I respond succinctly, hoping to head him off on whatever he is planning because I can see the wheels turning behind his eyes. He seems thrilled and I know that when it comes to supernatural beings, they don't want to leave you alone if you have proven to be a distraction—*why can't I be boring?*

"American lasses are a wee bit stubborn," Finn says to Brennus, but he gives me a nod of respect I wasn't anticipating. It is either respect, or it is a salute to the truly damned. I wait for Brennus to respond, he looks fierce and I feel the letter opener digging into my flesh, cutting my palm a little as I prepare for the worst.

"Do na do dat, Lillian. I do na want ye ta bleed...yet," Brennus says, and I lose my breath completely, like he has hit me in the stomach.

"What are you?" I ask him breathlessly.

"Yer destiny," he replies in a gentle tone as he leans forward to touch my face. I pull back from him quickly so that he can't reach me. "Ye need protection—I am very powerful," he says, looking disappointed and maybe a bit unnerved that I'm not letting him get closer to me.

"Anyone ever tell you that if you have to tell someone that you are powerful, then that means you're not?" I ask warily, inching away from them, looking for my best exit strategy.

"I have heard dat once or twice, but I tink dat it mostly applies ta ladies," he replies, frowning. Then, his face grows darker, "Ye callin' me a liar?"

"Ohh, no—sorry," I say immediately, hoping my apology will calm him down because the realization is dawning now that not many people—uh beings—have stood up to him recently, by the way he is looking at me. *Finn looks impressed with me—that's really, really bad.* "Maybe I should've just said, 'no thank you'—for the protection—I got that part covered."

Brennus slowly shakes his head. "No ye don't, have ye no sense atall?" he asks, disagreeing with me. "Everyone is lookin' for ye—and I mean everyone," he murmurs, and dread seeps into my brain, making it hard to think. "Ye haven't had protection since, whah, ye were in Crestwood, right, Genevieve?"

Nooooooo! THEY ARE HERE FOR ME! Talking done—no more talking. Find an out NOW! My brain screams at me. No longer in control of my wings, they thrust out of my back of their own accord. Leaping over the cart at my side in a fraction of a second, I kick off my black heels in one fluid motion, landing on my bare feet. I race toward the back of the library to the emergency exit. But, I pull up short when I feel the cold, prickling feeling just ahead of me. Lynnette is standing docilely by the back door with two pale men. One of the men is stroking Lynnette's arm intimately, like one would a lover. His head of shockingly bright red hair bends toward her as he nuzzles her neck. The other man's eyes are trained on me. He nudges his red-haired friend to get his attention when he spots me in the hallway. *That loser Lynnette let them in the back door,* I realize as my search becomes frantic for another way out.

Glancing behind me, I see Brennus and Finn walking toward me from the reception area, like they are strolling in the park. The other two are coming toward me from ahead of me. Using the letter opener in my hand, I stab it into the fire alarm at my side, breaking the glass and pulling the handle down in one fluid motion. A piercing siren blares out of every corner of the library. Human patrons begin streaming out of every corner to exit the building, getting in the way of the cold, creepy freaks. I fly through the door of a conference room on my right, slamming the door shut behind me. Picking up a conference room chair, I toss it through the plate glass window in front of me. *I just need to get out in the open and I'll outrun these cold things.*

I rush to the window just as the door of the conference room opens. As I back away to the edge of the window, Brennus and Finn enter with the other two behind them.

Finn's eyebrows rise as he turns to his brother and says with admiration in his tone, "Brennus, she is a wee bit of a hallion."

"She is," Brennus agrees, and then he grins. "Genevieve, ye're na gonna jump now, are ye? We have fellas all around down dere waiting for ye."

"I'll take my chances. Later," I reply, while flipping them off. I turn and dive from the window, gliding smoothly away from the building and touching down gently to the lawn below me. When my feet touch down, I launch myself forward, feeling the wind begin to whistle, but then it ends abruptly. A loud bang echoes and something tangles and ensnares my legs, causing me to do a face plant in the grassy terrain beneath me. I hit my head really hard and I see several shadowy figures coming toward me.

As I kick feebly at the nylon-like netting that is brutally cutting into my flesh, I clutch handfuls of grass, trying to pull myself back up on my feet so that I can escape. No one approaches me, but there are several prickly cold "fellas" standing around me watching me struggle to get free of the binding net.

I gasp for air from exertion and panic as I use the letter opener in my fist to saw at the ropes. Succeeding in getting a few of them to separate, I still when I hear Brennus' voice above me. "Ach! Look at da poor craitur," he says with concern, and it takes me a second to realize he is calling me a "poor creature."

Stiffening, I glare at him with my one good eye that isn't beginning to swell shut from hitting the ground face-first.

"Did we banjax yer escape?" Brennus asks me with a solemn shake of his head, kneeling down at my side and gesturing to the fact that I'm lying on the ground tussled up like a Thanksgiving turkey.

I really don't think I'm able to reason well because I react impulsively to his baiting words. My grip tightens on the letter opener. Before I realize what I'm doing, I plunge the dull blade into Brennus' foot. I think it hurts him because he grimaces as he pulls it out. He holds the letter opener in his hands angrily, wiping the blade on his pants. Then, it is my turn to scream as he uses the blade to slice through the Achilles tendon of my right heel in one clean cut.

He pulls me toward him by using the front of my shirt as a handle and he says, "Dat is so ye do na run off." I hardly hear him because I'm trying not to puke. The last thing I see is his fist hitting my face.

CHAPTER 11

Copper Mining

Delusion. It means a false belief or a mistaken notion. It's different from denial, which is the refusal to face an unpleasant fact or the refusal to acknowledge the existence of something. With delusion, you never see the something coming in order to deny its existence. I have been delusional in believing that I had escaped Crestwood without detection. But delusion seems to be the prevailing problem with all of the beings I have encountered recently. They believe they can make me one of them, and that is not only delusional, it's a myth.

I rouse in agonizing pain. Not only does my head ache from tripping head-first into the grass at top speed, it also aches from being pounded by Brennus' fist. But, that is nothing compared to the pain coming from my severed tendon. It began to heal immediately, but it will be several hours before I can stand on it, which will effectively FUBAR my best means of escape. On top of that, the smell around me is enough to make me ill. It is a sticky, cloying scent that reminds me of being trapped in a bottle of perfume. I think I must have moaned when I came to that conclusion because Finn looks back at me from the front seat of the car to ask worriedly, "Genevieve, are ye gonna boke?"

"Huh?" I ask weakly, because he is kind of hard to understand.

"Retch? Are ye gonna retch?" he asks with impatience. He then turns to Brennus, who is driving the car, and says, "I jus got dis bleedin' beemer, and why is it dat all yous wans do na understand plain Anglish?"

Brennus doesn't answer him so he turns to me for answers. "You will have to tell me what a 'wan' is," I say through clenched teeth as I choke on the pain.

With a look of frustration he says, "Ye are a wan—a lass—a wa-man." Finn draws out the last word, trying to make it more clear.

"A woman?" I ask for clarity.

"'Tis," he responds, like he doesn't have a word that means "yes."

"I'm not familiar with your slang. How long have you been here?" I ask, trying to gain a frame of reference for what they are and how long they've been in the area.

"Longer than ye," Finn answers.

"You know how long I've been here?" I ask as dread consumes me.

"I do," he replies.

"How?" I ask.

"A lil' bird told us," he says cryptically.

"Finn, that's not an answer," I say.

"'Tis," he replies with a sharp nod.

"Not a good answer," I amend, and then I stick my finger down my throat and retch all over his new beemer.

"Ach, Genevieve! Ye banjaxed me beemer! Ye bleedin' hallion," he says in disgust as he sinks dejectedly in his seat. Brennus, however, finds it funny as he peers at me in the rearview mirror, his eyes twin-kling in approval.

Brennus pats his brother's shoulder. "Yer wan can clean it for ye, Finn," he says, placating Finn who opens the window to get some air in the car.

Thank God, I might not be able to stop retching now with the smell of vomit and the "fellas" in the front seat, I think, gulping in deep breaths of warm air, trying to clear my head. We are further away from the water. The smell of pine trees and earth alert me to the fact that we are in the hills for sure. *No!* I think, as it just now dawns on me that if they know how long I have been here, then they probably know about Russell, too. I can't ask about Russell, just in case they don't know about him. Laying my head against the seat, I wonder when he will discover I'm missing. *Will he stick to the plan and leave town? Please, God, protect Russell,* I pray as pain makes everything dark again.

When I become conscious again, Brennus is hauling me out of the back of the beemer. *He is being gentle now, like I'm someone he has found hurt and he is assisting me out of the car, so he can make it all better,* I think scornfully. *I hate it when the supernatural swing from one extreme to the other. It makes me feel unbalanced.* I almost want to tell Brennus to pick a side and stay there because being nice, and then all of a sud-den wigging out is really scary.

With that in mind, I begin to struggle immediately as Brennus swings me up in his cold arms, hugging me to his even colder chest. Seeing that we are heading to the yawning mouth of a cave, I study the terrain around me as best I can, while attempting to get free. The cave is partially hidden by a huge rock that had not fallen from the rock face above, but looks like it has been placed there on purpose to shield the entrance to this tunnel. Trying to gaze around at the terrain behind me, to see where we had come from, I look over Brennus' shoulder and hear him bark, "Ye will na be leaving here, so ye do na need ta know whah is back dere."

I don't answer him, but use my forehead as a battering ram, crashing it into the bridge of his nose. My head aches more, but I don't mind that so much because I get to hear the satisfying crack that lets me know that I broke his nose. Brennus, not making a sound, pitches me forward into Finn. He catches me easily as Brennus walks on ahead of us into the cave. Finn looks at me in shock and says, "Whah, Genevieve, ye *are* a hallion, but na a very smart one!"

"Why? You are going to kill me anyway. I just thought I would get it over with now," I say as Finn signals to the fellas to pick me up and take me inside.

"I won't kill ye. I'm surprised he is lettin' us even touch ye now atall. But ye are right, he will kill ye soon, and after he does, ye are gonna have years to make it up ta him," Finn says. Then, he walks on ahead of us as I fight and hit anyone within range.

I don't get a chance to decipher what Finn is telling me, because after we enter the tunnel, he disappears down a deep hole that is more like a mineshaft. The shape of it is square, like it's man-made and not occurring naturally. I don't have time to study it because the fellas carrying me jump into it, too, and we fall a couple of stories to the ground below. Whoever it is that is holding me does a decent job of absorbing the jolt of hitting the ground. The impact is bad only because it rattles my swollen heel, making me want to retch again. Well, that, and the fact that we fell several stories, and I thought we were going to be flattened for sure.

Immediately the place takes on a familiarity of a well-watched movie scene, only it hadn't been a DVD that I had rented, but a nightmare I had dreamt. It's Merlin's House—Morte Darthur—the cavernous chambers in my dreams. They are dug out of stone...the unusual gray walls that bleed with green are rock and copper...tarnished ore like an old one-cent coin. The walls are an earthy green in spots and in other spots it's brilliantly shiny and reflective as a new penny. The ore runs in veins within the walls, giving a marbled appearance to the stone that is stunning. Gray stone Corinthian columns, as tall as pine trees, reach to the ceiling far above. They are a marvel in this place, so polished and symmetrical, but they appear to have been carved out of the same stone as the walls because they have the same ore within them. Stone staircases branch off in several directions. Some lead up to other chambers and some lead down. I'm interested in the ones that lead up. I have no desire to see what is beneath this hall.

Brennus is nowhere to be found when my entourage carries me to the long, rectangular, medieval wooden table and ornately carved chairs. *It's just like my premonition—I should have known.* Finn is still with us, though. He scans me as I sit with my legs awkwardly twisted beneath the chair. I am still wrapped in the netting that someone had harpooned me with at the library.

"Ye look a mess, Genevieve," Finn says, and he has the decency to look sorry about it.

That is kind of weird, I think. *Why should he care? Freaking monster— can't pick a side.* "Thanks, Finn," I reply, trying not to show how terrified I am at this moment. "You look as fresh as a daisy. Your beemer, on the other hand…"

He smirks at my sarcasm. "Have ye control over yer emotions yet?" he asks. I frown at him, trying to figure out what he is asking me now because I'm clearly not crying. "I will cut da ropes off yer legs if ye promise not to kick me or break me face wi' yer head because I would like to keep it as 'tis."

I think about what he just said. The ropes are cutting into my skin and it would be a relief to have them off of me. "I promise not to kick you while you take the ropes off," I reply.

He looks skeptical, but he bends down, pulling a wicked-looking knife from his boot, and begins cutting at the rope that ensnares me. *Why don't I carry a concealed weapon on me?* I wonder, watching him slice through rope like butter. *If I make it out of here alive, I'm always going to carry a knife on me—I can strap it to my thigh,* I scheme. I try to pull myself back together because my head is spinning and I feel really dizzy. I should be trying to focus on escape. *I think I may have a concussion.* The room spins again and tilts at a strange angle.

"Caul, are ye?" Finn asks when he is done removing the ropes from my legs. I don't answer him, but just stare at him because my brain can't decipher what he is asking me. "Ye are shakin'—are ye caul? Do ye need a blanket?" he tries again.

I'm numb, I have no idea if I'm cold or not, but I think I might be going into shock, I say in my head but I'm so disconnected that I can't say the words aloud.

Turning to a fella by his side, Finn refers to him as Ninian. Seeing

Ninian staring at me with his steely-gray eyes, I shiver in fear before he turns to Finn. He seems to be picking up on all of the nuances in Finn's body language as he speaks quietly to him. I hear the words: Brennus, blanket, and shock. But, things are skipping on me. I'm in and then I'm out again—dazed, and then clear. Ninian disappears within seconds into a stairwell of stone steps that leads up from this floor.

They can move like angels, I think dejectedly. Ninian returns, mere seconds later, with a fur blanket that could be mink or sable on one side and on the other side it is lined with silk. After Ninian hands it to Finn, he steps back solemnly. Finn moves forward, wrapping the blanket around my shoulders and wings gently, careful not to touch me otherwise. I droop against the chair as the heaviness of the blanket covers me.

I should've fought harder, I tell myself as the library comes into focus in my mind. *I should've done Bruce Lee all over them. I could've taken at least a couple of them out. No more evasion…if I get the chance, it is pwnage time,* I promise myself before the room goes black on me.

 ⁓

When my eyes open again, they focus on a blazing fire. It burns in one of the monumental fireplaces that line the wall of the stone chamber I had been brought into earlier. Feeling stiff and uncomfortable, I look down, seeing that I'm lying on the dark, wooden table that I know stretches out for yards. The blanket that Finn had covered me with earlier is still on me. My head hurts like a brick fell on it, so I'm not going to try to lift it up just yet. I just watch the fire dance and cast evil looking shadows all over the room and ceiling above me. My brain is trying to make sense of all of this nonsensical information it's receiving. It's more like jargon than actual fact. *How can this be happening?*

"Is she awake?" a familiar voice asks from somewhere near the other end of the gothic table. I recognize the voice, but I can't quite place it. My heart kicks up a notch, though. Unable to lift my head off the table, I crane my neck up, in an attempt to see the owner of the voice. I stop before finding him, because the shooting pains in my head prevent me. Drawing my legs up closer to my body in the fetal position, I wait for the voice to speak again, so I'll know who it is. He doesn't speak right away, but a rapid buzzing emits from somewhere close by—like a buzz saw or a—I still.

Rage makes my head throb and pound. *Death—Pain—Retribution—Beg! He will beg me, and he will have no mercy. None.* "Alfred—you still out there, sweetie?" I ask like Buns would, not moving at all.

"Did you miss me?" he asks, coming around the table to stand in my line of sight. How kind of him to accommodate me. He is only half-dressed, having taken off his shirt to allow for his wings to expand. They are buzzing sporadically as the excitement of this moment is intensifying for him. I can see their iridescent shine, even in the depths of this sunless chamber. He looks beautiful. He must have really had to try hard to look normal when I met him. I think the Lego hair that he used to sport really had gone a long way in hiding his angelic qualities.

"I missed you everyday," I say with heavy sarcasm. "I was worried that one of the Fallen would find you and shred your wings to pieces before I got the chance to do it. Lucky me, you're still alive."

"Evie! So violent. What have they done to my sweet, innocent, trusting girl?" he asks in faux remorse as he reaches out to touch my cheek.

"HOLD!" a voice at the head of the table barks out, as Alfred is just about to place his hand on me. Looking annoyed, Alfred pulls his hand back, straightening up. "Ye will never touch her. Do ye understand whah I'm telling ye?" Brennus' authoritative tone spits out. Alfred stiffens at the command.

Witnessing the war going on in Alfred's head, I almost smile. In Alfred's mind, I am still his—will always be his, but for some reason, he is with the Irish—but not one of them and maybe not even in charge here. *Interesting.*

"Of course," Alfred says, recovering his smooth demeanor. "I'm just after the soul…you are welcome to whatever is left," Alfred says, and then he smiles at me, appeased a little to see my fear.

I wet my lips that have gone dry. "Brennus, I don't know what Alfred has told you, but I'm unable to survive without my soul. If you allow him to take it from me, I'll die," I announce plainly, so that there will be no confusion.

"Ye will…but den ye will be one of us…ye will be moin," he replies with a thoughtful air.

"What are you?" I ask, wishing I can see his face, but I'm not able yet to lift my head.

"Gancanagh," he replies, like I should know what that is.

I have to see his face. I have to know what is going on here. Slowly, I use my arms to push myself up to a sitting position on the table. Lifting my head, it spins wildly and I don't even believe what I'm seeing is real because the long table is occupied with a dozen or more "fellas" all seated quietly watching me. I haven't heard them breathing because they don't move; they are as still as statues, all observing me with the utmost interest. They all reek of the same smelly sweetness, but it is so thick down here that I hadn't realized they were all so near.

Brennus' face stands out among the others with its masculine lines and striking contours, making me think that there are some angels who would be jealous of his beauty. He is seated at the head of the table with Finn at his right hand. The left hand chair is empty, and I wonder briefly if that is Alfred's seat, but something tells me that it's not. That one is a seat of honor and it wouldn't be given to someone who is not one of them. They are a clan...a family. It's clear by the way they hold themselves. They seem to be a unit.

Alfred knows that I have no idea what a Gancanagh is, so he explains, "Technically, they are faeries, but their species is similar to another that you will be familiar with, I think."

"Oh?" I ask, because he wants me to ask him what's up so he can tell me. He is building up to something and my dread is increasing because Alfred only truly enjoys things that are awful. It must be extremely awful because he looks like he's really, really enjoying this.

"Yes, they're similar to...vampires," he says, and immediately every Gancanagh seated at the table hisses at him menacingly, which is lucky for me, because it's taking me a second to regain my composure. Alfred, holding up his hands in a placating manner, explains, "I'm just giving her an example that she'll understand. I know that you're way different than them, but she has been raised as a human. She doesn't know about other species. She wasn't even aware that she is an angel until she started evolving."

I have their full attention again as they try to envision what that was like for me. Finn speaks next, "Truly, Genevieve? Ye did na know ye're an *aingeal*?"

"No. It took me a while to figure it out," I answer honestly, because I can't see any point in lying, yet.

"Den, ye're not from Paradise?" he asks.

"I don't know...I only know this life," I reply, watching Brennus who is silent, but taking in every detail of the exchange.

"If ye have never been dere, den ye'll never miss it," Brennus says as if he is contemplating my situation carefully.

I take offense to his remark. "I didn't say I've never been there, that my soul has never been there. I just said I don't remember any life but this one," I reply with heat, because he doesn't know me at all to make that kind of judgment.

"Yer friend has…" Brennus begins, indicating Alfred, but I cut him off instantly.

"He is not my friend. He is my enemy and I *will* kill him," I reply as calmly as I can, seeing a slow smile register on Finn's face, but Brennus remains neutral.

"Alfred…" Brennus amends and waits to see if I will say anything, I remain silent so he continues, "has come ta us wi' a plan—a proposition. He tells us of yer troubles—dat ye're hunted by da Fallen and da Divine because of da soul dat ye possess—because ye're human and *aingeal*. He tells us dat he can reap yer soul, but 'twill cause yer death." He waits to see if I will dispute any of this information, but it's factual, so I don't speak up. "Unless…we were ta intervene at da point yer life is ending. I can make ye immortal once again. I can make ye one of us."

I'm numb. *What does he mean, one of them? A freaking faerie?* I wonder. *A faerie that is a lot like a vampire—how much like a vampire?* I speculate, but then the next thought hits me like shrapnel to the chest. *These faeries are not good…I felt it innately at the library. I'm instinctually afraid of them. Do the Divine hunt them, too, like the Fallen? If I become one of them, will Reed then be forced to kill me if he finds me?* A sickness that I have never felt before overcomes me. *They would make us enemies— I would be a demon that Reed would be forced to kill. He would have no choice—he would probably see it as putting me out of my misery.* Looking over at Alfred, I see the glee on his face and I know that I have come to the correct conclusions.

"Are you saying that if I become a Gancanagh, that I'll no longer be hunted by the Divine?" I ask Brennus, because even though I'm not considering becoming one of them, I want to know where they stand in the order of things.

"I am na. I am saying ye will no longer be hunted by da Fallen, and since ye will be of me clan, ye will have our protection from da Divine," he replies, confirming my suspicions. They're bad fellas. The Fallen probably aren't interested in the Gancanagh because they have no souls to sell. They may even be friendly to each other, judging by the fact that Alfred approached them with the proposition.

"Why would you want me to join your clan? I represent a threat to all of you. As you said, I'm hunted. What's in it for you?" I ask him, and listen while they all laugh like I've said something hilarious. I wish that the supernatural would stop doing that when I ask questions. It's starting to irritate me.

I hear Finn say to Brennus, "I will fight ye for her."

"Do na make me kill ye, Finn, I would miss ye," Brennus replies without a smile. To me he asks, "Whah do ye know about Gancanagh?"

I think about telling him that I know they reek, but that is not going to help my situation at all. So, I think harder, and reply, "Well, let's see…the ones I've met have Irish accents and aren't really very interested in picking out books at the library. They like fast cars, but hate it when you puke in the back seat. They live in abandon mines in the hills of the U.P. and their decorating tastes stray toward the gothic, mystical genre. They have bad taste in business associates." I pause, looking at Alfred before going on, "And, they move quickly, like angels. As for strength, I'm sure I'll soon find out." When I end, I watch Brennus for his reaction. He is not amused.

"So, ye know nuting," he says, and I don't dispute it. He is not flattered by my ignorance. "Torin, ask da wans ta come ta us, seeing is easier dan saying."

One of the fellas closest to me rises from his seat. The fellas are all really good looking, in their own way, I think grudgingly as I study him. Torin has a devilish sort of look to him, like he has a secret that is extremely amusing. His brown hair and brown eyes are a contrast to the green eyes and black hair of Finn and Brennus, but Torin shares the same pale skin that I can feel radiating coldly as he passes me. He disappears in a blink of an eye to the stairway in the center of the room. That one leads up.

I can feel all of the eyes of the fellas upon me, studying me and it's beginning to make me extremely uncomfortable. Scooting to the end of the table slowly, I'm being hung up by the blanket that is partially covering me. I manage to get my legs to the end of the table when someone scoops me up. Gasping from the cold chest and unfamiliar touch, I lift my chin to meet Brennus' eyes. As he gazes at me, I want to look away from him because I can see that he's studying me, assessing me.

I can't show him that I'm afraid. I'll lose any edge I have in this if he knows I fear him. Not looking away, I allow him to cradle me in his arms. He carries me back toward the head of the table where he had been seated earlier.

It's harder than I thought, trying not to show how utterly freaked out I am about Brennus holding me so intimately. He is seriously scary. He is somewhere between the size of Russell and Reed and cut just like them. His body is powerful and sleek with a beauty that humans do not possess. His face is extremely handsome, with his black hair, arching brows, and beautiful green eyes. *But, he's cold…so cold.*

He lowers me into the seat that had been empty next to his—the seat to his left. *No!* I think as his hand comes up to stroke my cheek gently. I still feel the bruise from the punch he had given me earlier. I wonder if he regrets it or if he is admiring his handiwork.

"How's your foot?" I ask quickly, because he looks as if he is about to lean down and kiss me. Scanning his eyes, I see them narrow. He is expecting something that I'm not delivering on; he wants something. *Does he expect me to invite his cold kisses?* I wonder feebly, shivering a little at the thought.

"Me foot is almost healed. Yers?" he asks.

"Not bad," I lie as my foot throbs hotter than if someone has put an ember from the fire on it.

"Ye lie," he smiles in admiration, calling me on it.

I am saved from having to say anything else, because the noisy chattering of human females entering the hall distracts him. The young women entering the hall are dressed like—I don't know, a harem—no, a brothel. The lingerie secret is out with these girls. Most of them are very beautiful—very tall, shapely, and curvy. Several of the girls don't speak English, but sound like they're from the Ukraine or some Slavic nation. They seem to be extremely happy to have been invited to our party. None of them expresses any surprise at the atmosphere or the fact that we are in an abandoned mine.

Are they imported? Maybe…it is probably a good idea for Brennus to bring in girls from somewhere other than the small towns of the U.P. If they are illegal immigrants, snuck in via the port in Houghton or the one in Marquette, then no one will miss them if they don't survive the fellas, I think, watching the smiling females. As they come nearer, I notice that a couple of them look a little strung out—like they're on drugs and need a fix.

As the girls scramble to the fellas around the table, a few things are becoming clear to me. The first thing I'm noticing is that they don't seem to be forced to be here, in fact, they all seem grateful to be here…like they are each devoted to the fella they are fawning over. And it's not like the affection isn't reciprocated. The fellas are more than affectionate with their girls. So much so, that I'm becoming a little uncomfortable with it. I watch while a girl saunters over to Brennus, and then she sits on his lap—like a lover. He is watching me close, gauging my reaction. When I just continue to gaze back at him, he frowns. *Does he expect me to be jealous?* I wonder in surprise.

The second thing I'm noticing is that, as soon as the girl, or in some cases girls, finds her fella, the moment he touches her skin, she is in ecstasy—or more like she has taken some ecstasy. *Do they have some kind of thrall—like vampires do in the movies?* I wonder, watching them close. The women that had looked strung out only moments ago with one touch have totally transformed, and now look a little dopey—like they are in a narcotic haze.

Brennus hasn't taken his eyes off of me even though his little girl-friend is all over him like a spring breaker in Cabo. The only thing that bothers me about that is the simple fact that I wish they would take it in the other room, because I don't need to see it. I think it's showing on my face, too. Brennus, turning to Finn, says, "Finn, take her." Finn, reaching out his hand, gently touches the cheek of the girl on Brennus' lap. Immediately, she shifts, going to Finn, like she is responding to an invisible leash that is drawing her to him.

When the girl is off Brennus' lap, he lifts his hand up to touch my face. Pulling away from him, I have to stop when he says, "Do na move." Gently, he rests his hand on my cheek again, stroking his fingers down it all the way to my neck. It's like he is rubbing an ice cube down my face. I don't move, I just stare at him in confusion. He reaches his other hand back to the girl he had just given Finn. Using his fingers, he strokes her cheek, as he had mine, and she shifts from Finn back to him again. She climbs on his lap in a heartbeat, but he doesn't seem happy about it. He is irritated.

He wants me to respond like her. Ha! No way, pal! You're not my type, I think scathingly.

Looking around the table at the other Gancanagh, the passion is building rapidly. As their lust is increasing, something else that I had hoped wouldn't happen does. Lust is giving way to bloodlust. Hearing a distinctive *click*, not unlike the sound that a retractable pen makes when you click it into place to engage the ink, my eyes fly back to Brennus. He is still watching me; his smile is seductive, allowing me to see the fangs that have shot forward in his mouth from a retracted position. Then, I watch with detestable fascination as he nuzzles the girl's shoulder lovingly, before piercing her flesh with his teeth. Her gasp is one of pleasure as a small trickle of blood escapes the powerful jaws of the Gancanagh next to me, to slowly trickle down her shoulder.

Freaking vampire! I think as a shudder of revulsion slides down my spine. My hands are trembling for real as the horror of what is hap-pening is breaking through my denial.

Pulling my eyes away from the feast going on next to me, I glance down the table to the other end. Alfred sits alone, watching my reac-tion. He is enjoying my confusion immensely. Rage and fury shoot through me as something snaps inside of me. *I am sitting across the table from the one who killed my Uncle Jim.* And, as that thought registers, nothing else matters at all. Nothing. Killing scenarios pulse in my brain like well-conceived plots, but I'm immediately frustrated by the fact that they all involve the ability to at least walk.

Slowly, so that I won't disturb any of the frolicking going on around me, I lean forward, climbing up on the table. My eyes zero in on Alfred, who watches me with curiosity. I begin to crawl down the center of the table on my hands and knees, stalking the prey ahead of me. Confusion flickers across Alfred's face as he sees my slow progression toward him. Then, realizing that I'm stalking him, he looks around in a nervous panic, as if he wants to get the attention of the others at the table, but he is unsure of how to do that without angering them.

Slinking down the center of the wooden table, it feels endless in its length and breadth from my target. I manage to get halfway to Alfred. As I come abreast of Ninian, my hand brushes his booted foot he has placed upon the table while enjoying his dinner. I pause then, because I know his dinner—it's Autumn. Autumn must have been in on their little plot tonight to sabotage me at the library. She had followed me around all evening, probably making sure that I didn't leave before they got there. She is enthralled now with the attention she is getting from Ninian, content to be his meal—*cheers Ninian.*

The glint of a knife sticking out of the top of Ninian's boot catches my eye. Not slowing my progress, I pull the knife easily from his ankle strap as I continue slinking down the table.

Pushing his chair back from the table, Alfred prepares for the frontal attack I'm bringing him. His wings are vibrating loudly, making me want to tear them from his back. I want to stop the noise that makes me remember the 7-Eleven, where I had first heard it. Alfred's eyes are wide with concern as they search the room wildly, attempting to find his best escape scenario. I train my eyes on his, seeing if they will tell me which way he is going to go.

Someone clears his throat loudly behind me. I ignore the noise, focusing on the fact that Alfred's eyes are telling me he is preparing to leap up toward the ceiling and fly away from my assault. "Genevieve, whah are ye doin'?" Brennus asks behind me. I can tell by the distance of his voice that he is still seated at the head of the table.

Ignoring him, I inch closer to Alfred, who is riveted by my intensity, but he snaps out of it in the next instant. His muscles tense to make his leap into the air. My muscles tense, too, and I don't feel an ounce of pain as I spring up on my severed heel to follow Alfred into the air. Arcing toward him, I extend my knife. Although I had planned on it embedding itself in Alfred's chest, in the exact spot where he had plunged his knife into Russell's, I miss the mark because I don't have the force necessary due to my damaged foot. I am a little disappointed when my knife embeds itself in Alfred's thigh and I slide down his leg, carving a long, severe slice out of his quadricep. Although, hearing his screams of pain makes my disappointment somewhat easier to handle.

Dropping on the floor, I roll and pivot, trying to catch a hold of his foot so that I can pull him down to me. Nothing is registering in my mind but killing Alfred. Seeing that I can't reach him from my position on the floor, I leap back up on the table, pivoting again to jump to the chandelier above my head. Just before I can spring toward it, someone scoops me up off the table. Brennus is holding me in a bone-crushing hug that squeezes the air out of my lungs, making me see spots.

There are shouts of dissent from all around me. Someone says, "Gawd, why did he stop her? Dat is da sexiest ting I've ever seen in all me life."

"Did ye see her movin' down da table? I tought I would die from na touchin' her," says Ninian, who must have noticed me take his knife.

"Ye will na kill me guests, pet," Brennus breathes in my ear. I would have screamed in frustration, if I could get enough air in my lungs to do it. Looking around wildly, I try to see where Alfred has gone, but he must have fled somewhere else. I guess he thinks that bleeding, while in the company of Gancanagh, is not a clever thing to do. It's that, or he is truly afraid of me. He should be. He should quake when he sees me coming because I am his destiny—his end.

When I don't relent, but struggle harder to get away, Brennus squeezes me so tight I think I might lose consciousness. I don't, I just lose my grip on the knife I had stolen from Ninian. "Right lads—we have a very lethal Seraph. No one underestimate her. 'Til she's one of us, she's na one of us—no matter how fetching she is," Brennus says. He hoists me up in his arms and swings me toward one of the stairwells—the one that leads down. "Finn—ye go see if dere is news about da other. Someting went wrong."

Dragging me down several flights of stone stairs, we reach the bottom, where there are several winding shaft-like hallways. Turning left, Brennus half-drags, half-carries me to what can only be described as cells that line the hallway. Thick steel doors held by thicker hinges gape open in some instances and are sealed shut in others. It seems to be a random choice of cell when Brennus turns and deposits me in one of the small rooms. There is nothing in this room. Nothing.

Just a dirt floor and stone walls. He does not say a word when he backs out, slamming the door closed. I hear him sliding a bolt shut to secure the door. *I must have scared him,* I think as I look around at the cell that is probably no bigger than ten by ten square.

Adrenaline courses through me and I'm rational enough to know that I'm the strongest I will ever be at this moment in my captivity. I turn and push with all of my might against the steel door that traps me behind it. The door bows a little as it groans and protests the abuse. I step away from it when it refuses to give any more. Backing away to the wall, I run at the door, using my body as a battering ram to try to plow through it. The door rattles and a couple of cracks form on the wall surrounding the door, but it doesn't open. I try again, but I'm really hurting myself. My shoulder is fractured for sure and I just can't get enough speed to thrust against the door because of my severed tendon and the fact that there just isn't enough room to gather the speed needed to do it.

Hobbling back from the door, I hold my right arm that is limp from being crushed against the door. Defeated, I collapse to the floor in a heap. I lie there for a while, my legs bent at an awkward angle beneath me. I need to rest—repair the damage that has been done to my body and plan my escape. While I'm at it, I'll start my hit list: *Number one, Alfred—number two, Brennus—number three, Finn...*

෴

After my foot is mostly healed, I pace the cell. It has to be mid-afternoon by now and no one has come back to check on me for over twelve hours. I'm so thirsty. I have sores forming in my mouth from dryness. I think that my need for water has increased because of the healing I've had to do to recover from my injuries. I feel dehydrated and it occurs to me that I shouldn't pace, I should sit down and conserve what little hydration I have left.

At around sixteen hours without water, I'm getting desperate, and my muscles are beginning to ache and cramp. I never imagined I would need water this much. But I do need it. I need it.

It occurs to me that this is just like the first dreams I began having right after I found out what Alfred had done to my uncle. I kept having vague dreams, like I was starving, but there had been no images to accompany the dreams. Maybe that is because I'm stuck down in a dark mine, in a cell with only vague shapes to let me know that I'm anywhere at all.

A while later, I begin to feel detached from all of this, like I don't exist anymore. *They're not coming back,* I think feebly and the sadness of being lost down here forever is stabbing at me like a knife.

I lose track of the time, but an eternity later, a small slat in the door opens and a voice comes through the door, "Do ye want some water, pet?" it asks. I immediately know it is Brennus.

"Yes," I reply in a near whisper because I can hardly speak at this point and I'm desperate. Two small, 4-ounce bottles of water drop in. Brennus doesn't speak again and the slat closes quickly without preamble. Pulling myself up off the floor, I retrieve the bottles of water. I drink the first bottle right away, trying not to spill a drop of it. The second bottle I try hard to ration. With my need for water fulfilled for now, I focus on the strategy Brennus is employing with me. *What does he want from me? Does he want my complete loathing? Well, mission accomplished. I hate him.*

There are several things going on here. I have to break them out in little pieces in order to understand them fully, like Zephyr had been teaching me back in Crestwood. A pang of longing hits me when I think of my friend. *Where are you now, Zee?* I wonder, and I almost begin to cry before I clamp down on my emotions so I can focus on what is really important.

Okay, Brennus wants something from me. My blood? Possibly, he might like to snack on angels. We might be tasty to the Gancanagh. But, why not just take it then? There are a dozen of them and only one of me. He said he wants to make me one of them. He's going to let Alfred take my soul so that I'll die—or almost die, and then he'll do what? Somehow make me one of them. How does that work? Maybe I have to be willing somehow—like Buns said, I have to willingly give my soul to Alfred. Do I have to willingly become a Gancanagh, too?

It seems to me that everything in this life of mine is about choice. I have some choice in what happens to my soul. Now that I know where my soul may be allowed to go, I'm less willing to give it up to a stinking demon. Having felt Paradise briefly, I want it. If I had acted differently than I had before, would Russell be enjoying Paradise right now? Instead, he's trapped in the U.P. near a nest of Gancanagh and Alfred. They're probably all out hunting for him. That is what Brennus had meant about "da other." He was telling Finn to find out what has gone wrong with Russell.

Go, Russell! I think, sending up a silent prayer that he is past Cleveland by now and on his way to anywhere. I know they don't have Russell because Alfred would be down here right now bartering Russell's life for my soul.

༄

It is at least a full day before I hear the slat on my cell door slide open again. It had been at least twelve hours since the water that I had tried to ration had run out. I feel dazed, and not at all sure if I am imagining Brennus' voice, when he asks me, "Do ye want some water, pet?"

"Brenn," I croak, but before I can get any more words out, he slides the slat shut. I want to cry because he is gone and I need water. I need it. Lying on the floor, where I had been most of the day, I try really hard not to cry.

About an hour later, the slat opens up again and Brennus asks me, "Do ye want some water, pet?"

"I…" I try to say that I want to talk to him, but he closes the slat on the door. I bury my head in my arm and cry.

About two hours later, the slat on my door opens and Brennus asks me, "Do ye want some water, pet?"

"Yes," I croak my reply. A 4-ounce water bottle drops through the slat. The puzzle pieces snap into place at the same time and I understand clearly what is going on now. The slat slides closed. Crawling over to the door on my hands and knees, I pick up the one water bottle that he left me. I know that there won't be another one for another day. I also understand what he is doing. He is breaking me—I will receive nothing unless it is from him. It will be at his whim that I'm to receive anything, and if I do not follow the rules as he has given them, I will suffer for it. He is a sadistic demon. *That's it then, game over*, I think as a brutal pain stabs my heart.

I can't win this game. The only way this game ends is with me as Brennus' pet. A cold, soulless, Gancanagh pet that sits like a lap dog by his side and is tied to him for eternity. I have to end it, or somehow change the game and it has to be a conscious choice…and I have to do it now. If I drink this water, I will get stronger for a while, but then I'll become weaker faster. Tomorrow, what will I do for him when I am so weak and he only allows me half a bottle of water…will I then do anything he wants me to do just for some water? Probably. I may not even be conscious enough by then to care. I have to decide now what I want. Do I want to live, and by living I will die and become a Gancanagh and Alfred gets my soul? Or, is it better to die? Hopefully my soul will be allowed into Paradise where I can see Reed again someday...well, at least my soul can...the rest of me will be stuck down here to rot for eternity. Those are my choices. I am not surprised to feel tears slide down my face to drip into the dry, cracked dirt beneath my head.

If I'm not strong enough, and I choose to be a Gancanagh, then one day, when I see Reed again, he will have to kill me because I will have become a demon. If I die now, at least my soul might see him in Paradise one day. It takes everything that I am, not to open the water bottle that I have just been given. Placing it back by the slat in front of the door, I crawl back to lie in the same spot. Another tear slips over my cheek and becomes lost to the cold earth beneath my neck as I wait for death to find me.

෴

Time passes and I can no longer move from my prone position on the floor. I watch an industrious spider spinning its web in the corner of my cell; its dewy, white silken threads are secreted from behind it. Its legs move in intricate patterns, shaping and molding its trap for the next hapless victim to hopelessly ensnare itself. Once the victim walks into the ambush, there will be no getting out. The spider will come and paralyze its victim with its venom, making a snack out of it while it waits for another to come along to take its place in the web.

If I could've gotten up from the floor, I would've crushed the spider. But I can't move, so I wait patiently, along with the spider, to see if anything tasty will come along. Hours pass as I study the spider and I begin to realize that the spider is just doing what spiders do. It wants to survive as much as I do. It is driven by the same instincts that I am. I begin to wonder what I would do to survive, if I were the spider. Would I spin my webs without remorse? Would I feel pity for my victims as I consume their blood with agonizing efficiency? Would I be a monster?

I don't know exactly when I began talking to the spider, but there comes a point when I begin rooting for the spider. I think it's because I want one of us in this cell to make it, to survive. I think I realize that the spider has the better odds.

I am talking at some points throughout the eternity of time. Raving would probably be a more accurate description. Every now and then, I sense something moving around my cell. Turning my head to look at the shapes and shadows, they morph into sinister, skeletal demons. The skin of the demons shows all of their spiny vertebrae as their bones stick out of their backs at sharp angles. Creeping toward me, their frightening jaws and claws look like they are made to tear and rip flesh. I can't contain the screams that are escaping me, even though I know that the sounds won't carry very far. There is no longer much moisture in my throat to help produce sounds. But, it doesn't matter anyway. Even if I beg for help, no one here will help me.

Watching the terrifying images of the snarling beasts growing closer to me, I feel someone grasp my hand and hold it firmly. Turning my head slowly, I have to blink a couple of times because I'm staring into the eyes of my Uncle Jim. The gray and blue of his irises are just as I remember them as he stares back at me serenely, smiling from his position laying on the ground next me. I gasp when I look at his beautiful face, my eyes filling with tears because I have missed him so much.

He speaks to me, his mouth is moving, but I can't hear the words he is saying. It doesn't matter because I can feel him. I can feel his hand in mine and I know he is real. He is here with me. Maybe he has always been here with me—have we always been here? In this place? I would stay here forever if I could, with my Uncle Jim and hold his hand. "I missed you so much," I say with my voice tight and strained. He smiles at me again.

I'm not at all aware of what I say when the slat opens again and the scary voice asks me the question that tumbles around in my head every few minutes. Do ye pet some water? Water some do pet ye? Ye water some do pet? I think I laugh when I hear him ask it the right way—it is the wheezing laugh of a crazy person. Maybe he notices the water still lying on the floor under the door, maybe he doesn't—it doesn't matter. I feel like I'm floating on an ocean of water now and I'm beyond the point of caring if I have a drop of water again. Ever.

⁓

"Ye're a stupid, stubborn *aingeal*," Brennus' voice penetrates into my brain as the pain of his backhand wakes me from wherever I had been...where had I been? I wonder, looking up at him. I'm still on the floor of my cell in the ugly copper mine; except now, my Uncle Jim is gone. Looking around feebly for him, I can't find him. I guess he couldn't stay here with me. A part of me is grateful that he has left because I don't want him trapped here in this hell. The other part of me wants to cry because I wish he could've taken me with him.

I'm not alone anymore anyway. Alfred is pacing back and forth outside the door of my cell. Finn is kneeling by my arm, holding it so that the IV they had stuck in it can drip into my vein. Finn's icy fingers gently rub my wrist as if he is concerned about me. When I realize what the IV means, that Brennus is going to get another opportunity to make me a demon, I immediately try to pull it out of my arm. "Ah, no ye don't," Brennus says, pulling me up by using a fistful of my shirt and glaring into my eyes.

"What did you say, pet?" I ask in delirium.

Brennus looks like he wants to murder me. He probably can't believe that I would rather die than be his pet. *Believe it, freak,* I think, watching the IV drip into my arm slowly. *He's going to bring me back, and then the real fun is going to begin,* I shiver. When the first IV finishes, Finn puts in a second one. Watching its slow drip, it makes me realize I'm probably not going to die today. That thought chills me as much as the cold, prickly sensation of being near the Gancanagh.

"Finn, leave," Brennus orders, and my head slowly turns from the IV to see if I can gauge what Brennus is going to do next. He looks like he would like to toss me through the wall, not nurse me back to health. For the life of me, I can't see why he's bothering to keep me alive.

Finn looks like he doesn't want to go, but he gets up off his knees, handing the IV bag to Brennus. Turning, he heads out the door where Alfred is lividly speaking to him in the hallway about the fact that I had chosen to die rather than submit to them and give up my soul. "Your methods are suspect, Finn. I don't care how many centuries you've been using this method to break the will of resistant beings—we are talking about a Seraph—she has evolved since I've been with her—she is strong—I suggest..."

Brennus' roar is enough to make me flinch when he says, "FINN, GET HIM OUTTA HERE!" Immediately, Alfred is ushered away from the door by Finn.

"You should've let me kill him for you," I murmur. I can't get my voice to rise above a whisper as I look at Brennus who has let go of my shirt so that I can lie back down on the ground. He is still fuming over my resistance to his plan. *Is he surprised that I figured out the game and chose another option?* I wonder.

"Do ye know dat ye've broken a tradition dat dates back older den I can recall?" Brennus asks me in a menacing tone, scanning my face for my reaction. "Dat is how it has always been done—ye submit, and den ye become one of us."

"Oh…so you're saying I banjaxed your tradition? I'm sorry—I thought it was a game you were playing—Master and Servant. I got really bored with it, so I decided not to play anymore," I counter, but I'm becoming more lucid. With reality comes the crushing fear that this is not over, my plan for evasion into oblivion has been prevented. There is still a chance now that I can be turned into a demon.

"Ye are by far the most frustrating craitur I've ever met," he spits out as he squeezes the IV bag to make the drip go faster. He means every word of that statement.

"And you are not the first creature to tell me that," I reply, trying not to let the terror of my situation overwhelm me. I can't let fear control me. My brain is working feverishly, looking for a loophole or an angle to get me out of this. *Maybe I'm taking the wrong approach with Brennus,* I think, watching him frowning at me. *Maybe I should just tell him I don't want to be a Gancanagh.* I moisten my lips and say, "Brennus, what if I told you that, however flattering it is that you and the other fellas want me to be a Gancanagh, I just can't make that kind of…commitment right now?" I ask him, but I cringe inwardly, seeing his eyes darken in anger. *Maybe not such a good idea,* I surmise.

"Whah did ye say?" he asks me. "Do ye know whah I'm offerin' ye?" he asks me, and I think it is a rhetorical question, because he starts to explain. "Do ye know whah any one of da wans ye saw upstairs would do ta get an offer ta be changed by us?" he asks, deeply offended.

"Then, why me?" I ask in an urgent tone.

His eyebrows pull together more. "Ye need protection. How long do ye tink ye'll last out dere alone?" he asks in anger.

"I was doing all right until you showed up," I retort because it's true, for the most part—other than feeling like I'm dying most of the time, I was surviving all right. "And, by the way, I give myself better odds of surviving out there than in here."

"Ye're moin. I want ye and I will have ye," he blurts out pompously.

"Why would you ever pick someone like me, when there is a room full of women upstairs who will line up to be with you?" I ask him, stunned.

"Dis has never happened ta me before. I've never had a wan resist me…a wan of any species. I have jus ta touch whah I want and she comes ta me," he pauses to see if what he is saying is sinking in. "My skin—'tis a toxin—a drug. No one can resist it—but ye, it did na affect ye," he says in frustration. It all makes sense to me now. The women upstairs can't resist them—literally. They're like junkies.

"What happens to those women when you get tired of them?" I ask in a soft tone, watching him shrug as if their lives are negligible.

"We drain dem," he pauses when he sees the look of horror on my face. "'Tis a better death dan if we let dem go. Dey are addicts, dey end up killing demselves somehow when dey figure out dey can never come back." My heart goes out to those women because I know some of what they feel. I feel like a Reed addict and it's exhausting to try to live without him now.

"Can't have the strung out addicts stalking you, huh?" I say, getting a clear picture of why they don't let them go. "A nest of Gancanagh must have its secrets preserved."

"Dere is dat, too," he replies with honesty. "When Alfred came ta me wi' his proposition, he presented me a gift. Do ye know whah 'tis he gave me?"

"No," I croak in response to his question.

"He gave me a portrait of ye. 'Tis ye in a white gown and ye look like a goddess. Yer face…'tis da loveliest face…" Brennus says, and my whole body goes cold. Alfred had bought my portrait from Sam MacKinnon. Of course he did. It makes sense. An anonymous buyer doesn't just show up and buy my portrait. Sometimes, I can be so stupid. Alfred is evil—he used my portrait to entice the Gancanagh. *I will kill him.*

I try to downplay the portrait by saying, "That portrait was just a crazy…art thing. You know—girl gone wild—gotta test the boundaries…" I trail off when his eyes became darker.

His eyes soften. "Ye do na even know how exquisite ye are, do ye?" he asks.

"I can't be a Gancanagh. I can't!" I say in desperation. "If you change me, then I can never see my love again," I say pleadingly. "I can never…" My voice breaks. I can't hold my tears back.

"Ye don't even know whah ye need. It would've been better if I had fought dis lover for ye, but he is na here ta claim ye. Ye will forget him. Ye will never mention his name ta me," he says with jealousy choking him. "Ye're moin now."

"There is only Reed, you do not exist for me," I say viciously.

If I had forgotten for a second that Brennus is a very evil and sadistic demon, he reminds me in the next moment. Feeling the back of his hand slap my cheek hard, it forces my head to turn away from him. "Dat is where ye're wrong, I am da only ting dat does exist for ye," he replies with equal heat.

I will not be able to play to his softer side because there is no soft side to him. If he wants something, then he takes it. He feeds on humans, uses them, and then kills them without a hint of remorse. I'm probably a trophy—a prize to him. If he turns me, I will lose my soul, along with my humanity, and I will become a Gancanagh Seraph: a truly evil half-breed—Reed's enemy.

The game is back on now and it is to the death…his or mine.

CHAPTER 12

Gancanagh

Brennus and I do not speak to each other as the IV drip slowly runs out, signifying that I'm to live another day. He extracts the needle from my arm gently as if trying to prove to me he is not a monster, which is laughable because my cheek is still throbbing where he had just hit me. My stomach twists as he bends down to place a cold kiss on the spot where the needle had just been extracted from my arm. I grit my teeth. Killing scenarios pulse through my head, but I resist them because I'm not strong enough to take him right now. I'm having trouble bending my joints because they are so stiff from dehydration and from lying on the cold, hard ground for so long.

He leaves me alone in my small, stone cell just where he had found me, on the ground staring up at the gray ceiling, and I'm grateful to be alone. I have to think and he doesn't allow for thought when he is present. When Brennus is near, all I can do is keep my guard up and watch him for his next move. When I'm alone, I should study the board, try to anticipate his next move. I need to also look ahead several moves, if I can, because checkmate means I become a cold, dead "craitur." One thing I do know that will play to my advantage is the fact that Brennus is trying to make me his pawn. That makes him the king, which is the most vulnerable man on the board next to the pawn.

What other advantages do I have? I have no weapons, well, nothing physical–although, with this crowd, it already proved easy to get a knife. Ninian didn't even try to stop me. As a matter of fact, no one has tried to touch me. Only Brennus has touched me since I woke up on the table in the hall above. Finn did touch me, but I think that is only because Brennus didn't want me to die of dehydration. Brennus freaked at Alfred when he *almost* touched me. It would make sense, if he feels an ownership where I am concerned, that he wouldn't want another Gancanagh to touch me. They are accustomed to women responding to another after being touched. Their touch does not affect me though, but still, I bet they will all think twice before they try to touch me. I'm Brennus' and it's a habit not to touch what belongs to the master.

I shouldn't count on them not touching me though. I'm a known enemy. There will be new rules for me because Brennus is not stupid. But it will be foreign for them to follow the new rules. Old habits die hard…and I have a feeling these guys are old…really, really old. *Freaky evil faeries.*

The fellas are also used to docile women. Total compliance from drugged women who don't know any better. *How much trouble are they expecting from me? After all, I'm a woman.* I bite my lip a little, realizing I gave them a little sample of what I can do when I tried to kill Alfred. Tapping my fist softly against the hard ground of my cell, I think about what they saw me do with a severed heel. That was not very smart, but I'm having a hard time feeling bad about it because I'm remembering Alfred's scream; and it's warming my heart.

Since I lack physical weapons, I will have to cultivate alliances—allies are key here. Look for the disgruntled. I also need to spot their other vulnerabilities—what can they not resist? They seem to be partial to lust. *Can seduction be a weapon?* I wonder. *Can I seduce them?* That thought is causing ice to grow in my belly, but the more I think about it, the more it makes sense. I have to break up their little party if I want to get out of here. I have to cause dissention and make their ranks fall apart. I have to play my games as covertly as possible.

My warfare cannot be overt. I have to attack where they're unprepared. *I have to get out of this cell. How can I accomplish that?* That's my first goal. To accomplish it, I have to seize the mind of the commanding general and woo him into submission. He wants me now; I have to make him need me. In order to do that, I must find out everything I can about him and the Gancanagh. My enemy can be conquered. I will find a way.

༈

My first opportunity to begin my intel arrives a few hours later, when Brennus comes back with four fellas. The fellas wait in the hall outside my cell while Brennus enters. *Five-to-one. Not good odds for me,*

I think, studying Brennus who is holding metal shackles in his hands. The shackles are thick, steel cuffs with a short chain attaching them, but the chain is much thicker than the standard prisoner issue shackle. It's made for beings like me. I stare at the chains, wondering what kind of a tool could be used to cut through the thick metal.

"Put dis on," Brennus says, dropping the shackles at my feet.

"Why?" I ask casually, not because I don't know it's because we are leaving my cell, but because I want to know where we are going.

"So I do na have ta slice yer foot open again," Brennus says calmly, not solving the mystery of my destination.

Dropping to my knee, I place the shackles on my ankles, clicking them shut, but not very tight. Straightening up, I look at Brennus to see his frown. As I gaze innocently back at him, he sighs deeply, and then he crouches down by my feet, tightening the shackles so there is no play in the cuff. *It's the lock that matters, not the chain or the cuff,* I tell myself to calm the increased beating of my heart. *The lock can be crushed to release the cuff.*

"Come," Brennus says, holding out his hand for me to take. I want to push his hand away, but showing resistance is not part of my strategy. Instead, I reach out and grasp his hand tight, trying not to show him how creepy it is for me to hold onto the ice-cold appendage of a monster. Brennus looks confused. He doesn't know what to think, having gained my compliance so easily. *Your move, Brennus,* I smile, looking at him patiently.

Leading me out of my cell, Brennus doesn't pause to introduce me to the entourage. He turns and pulls me back the way we had come before, when he had dragged me down here several days ago. *How long have I been down here?* I wonder in a moment of dysphoria. *At least six days,* I reason stumbling when I do the math. I have been so focused on escape that I haven't thought clearly about the other issues of survival, namely, food.

Not wanting to focus on things that are beyond my control at the moment, I concentrate on my surroundings. I recognize only two of the four fellas who are with us. They are all watching me intensely and I wonder if they will be permanently assigned to guard me. They all look lethal. I can tell by the way they move; they're quiet and stealthy, hardly making any noise with their light tread.

When we reach the chamber that I remember from my introduction to the clan, I have to shield my eyes from the dim light coming from the chandeliers and gothic fireplaces. My eyes have adjusted to the absolute absence of light in my cell, so now, even this dim light is excruciating. "Brennus, please," I say, pulling gently back on the hand leading me forward. I have to stop, due to blindness, having thrown the arm that's not holding Brennus' hand up to cover my eyes. I feel the cold ones hovering around me as my other senses pick up and compensate for the loss of my sight. I know where several of the fellas are in the room and…Alfred is here, too. He is easy to find because of his body heat and the agitated buzzing of his wings. *It's a good thing I can't see him right now,* I think as tears run down my cheeks. *I need a moment to collect myself so that I don't pounce on him and try to kill him again.*

"Evie…you're like a cat. How many lives do you have?" Alfred exclaims when he sees me enter the hall. I lean closer to Brennus, not because I'm afraid of Alfred, but because I want Brennus to think I'm seeking his protection from Alfred. I think it works because Brennus' arm slinks around me, pulling me to his chest protectively.

"Ye will not speak ta her now, *aingeal,*" Brennus barks out. I have to admit, I'm psyched when Alfred doesn't say another word. After a minute, I try to open my eyes again. It takes a few more minutes of standing around to get my eyes to stop watering enough for me to see again.

"Thank you. I'm ready," I say, straightening up and facing Brennus. He is studying me close now and there is something in his eyes that hadn't been there when we had been down in my cell together. Before I can examine what it is, Brennus turns, pulling me forward again. *You bring corruption with your touch, maybe I can corrupt you with mine,* I think, holding his hand tighter when he begins to lead me by the table.

It's impossible to keep the chain that is dragging on the ground silent, but I try to maintain a graceful gait as I cross the floor. Keeping my shoulders back, I hold my head up. I scan the faces around me, counting and cataloging them as best I can. Finn is here, sitting in his seat at the table. As we approach him, I mouth the words "Thank you" to him while we continue by him. Raising his eyebrow in question, I point to the spot where he had injected the IV into my arm. I see the confusion on his face when he nods his understanding. *Potential ally?*

Brennus leads me to a staircase in the back of the room. This one climbs up to a suite of rooms that has "master" stamped all over them. Elegant and masculine, the only things they lack are electricity and plumbing, but they are more magical without the modern conveniences. Candlelight illuminates the rooms, giving them a softer appearance than I would've expected for a demon's lair. "Your rooms? I ask as I enter. Our entourage does not step over the threshold with us, but remains outside the door like bodyguards. I wonder whom they are guarding, Brennus or me?

"'Tis," he says, leading me from the reception area that has several gracefully carved wooden chairs with tapestry cushions and highly polished tables. He has a writing desk, too, and I wonder what the drawers contain.

We reach another room, which is very obviously his bedroom as proclaimed by the massive bed. It can probably sleep several people comfortably. The sheets are coffee-color silk. It also has a blanket made of a soft chestnut-brown fur with silk lining. It covers the entire expanse of the bed. *I'm calling PETA on him if I ever get out of here,* I think, blushing just imagining what probably goes on in that bed. Brennus chuckles next to me, seeing my reaction to his bed.

"Answer a question for me, pet," Brennus says, and I stiffen at his disgusting nickname for me.

"Hmm?" I respond, trying to hide my reaction.

"Ultan and Driscoll said ye sleep alone in yer apartment, is dat true?" he asks.

"Who are Ultan and Driscoll? How would they know that?" I ask him rapidly. Immediately, I see that I have angered him by not answering his question. Trying to placate him, I say swiftly, "I do sleep alone."

"Ye did na share a bed wi' yer soul mate?" he presses.

"No," I reply, and my blush drains away from my face when Russell is mentioned. *They know about him,* I think as fear makes it hard to remain outwardly calm. *They don't have him,* I reason, *Alfred would have used that card to make me comply.*

"Ever?" Brennus breathes.

"Not in the sense that you're thinking...not in this lifetime," I reply, feeling angry that I have to answer these questions. Alfred would've told him everything about my relationship with Russell. Why is he so interested?

"Den, ye're a virgin?" he asks.

"Yes." I retort because he had asked his question like an accusation. My answer is doing something to him, though, and it's really interesting to watch. He looks a little drunk...like his equilibrium is off a little. "But, da Power *aingeal*..." he trails off in a leading way.

"Is an evolved angel and I am not," I explain, seeing his expression of bliss when all the pieces come together for him. I stiffen because he has just confirmed a piece of what it is he wants from me. A suffocating dread shakes me and I have to beat down the instinct to fight him with everything that I have right now as images of what he wants are taking shape in my head.

"Dis way, pet," Brennus says, leading me away from the bed and into the next room. It's an old-world style bathroom. A very large copper tub adorns the center of the room. The tub is large enough to accommodate two people, I notice, blushing again. A wood-burning stove warms the room and heats large smooth stones in a large copper bin on the stove. Another wood-burning stove holds a copper pot full of water that is emitting steam into the air. It's deliciously warm in here, and as I move toward the heat, I glance over and see my reflection in the full-length mirror in the corner.

I hardly recognize myself. The white blouse that I had put on days ago is almost unrecognizable as having ever been white. It tells the entire story of the struggle I have gone through to reach this point; the grass stains and tears in the fabric melt into the crusted matte of sweat and blood, while streaks of dirt and grime create fascinating patterns of hopelessness on the canvas of fabric that covers my body.

My leg is even more interesting, in a sick, macabre way. The blood that had oozed from the wound to my foot has made a maze of lines over my calf, making it look as if a spider has spun a terrifying web in which to entrap its prey. I look like I have survived some hideous explosion and I'm still walking around, dazed and confused by the sheer fact that I'm still alive, when I know I should be dead.

Not wanting to look at myself any longer, I turn and walk to the tub. Bending down, I dip my fingers in the water already in it, testing the temperature. It's tepid, but it doesn't matter because just getting the dirt off of me will be satisfying enough.

Moving to the stove that contains the water, Brennus lifts the pot off the stove with his bare hands. "Ye will have to tell me when ta stop," he says, beginning to pour the water into the tub, heating the bath water rapidly.

"Isn't that scalding your hands?" I ask in shock, because it has to be scorching hot, touching the copper pot that has just been on the stove.

"Me skin is na very sensitive to heat. 'Twould take an intense flame ta burn me," he replies, smiling at me because of the concerned look I'm giving him.

He continues to fill the tub until I say, "Stop, please." He stops pouring and places the pot back on the stove. *He has to be super strong because he picked up that giant pot of water like it doesn't weigh a thing*, I think dejectedly. "What else is different about you?" I ask.

"If ye get in da tub wi' out fighting me, I'll tell ye," Brennus says, and my eyes widen in fear because I thought he would leave before I take my bath. When he was gone, I planned to rummage around the room and see if I could locate anything that would pass for a decent weapon, but now, I have a new problem.

Everything is an opportunity to begin to turn him to your will, a small voice says in the back of my mind. *Pretend that he's Reed.* I almost snort at that thought. That is nearly impossible because his cold skin is emanating near me like icy currents of air, chilling me. He also does not smell like Reed. His odor is sweet and potent, like a poppy, and Reed's scent is masculine and…sexy.

Slowly I turn away from him. Reaching my hands up to unbuttoned the top button of my blouse, I find that it's missing, along with the next button down. Realizing that the garment is a hopeless mess, I grasp both sides of the blouse, tearing it open. The remaining buttons of the garment make soft twinkling sounds as they bounce and roll across the floor. Allowing the shirt to cascade down my arms slowly, I glance over my shoulder to gauge Brennus' reaction to what I have just done. He is still. His eyes have grown dark and dilated. Fear is making my hands tremble as I reach behind me slowly, unzipping my skirt, letting it fall to the floor in the next instant to puddle at my feet. My underwear is staying on because I won't be able to get them off over the shackles and I don't want to take them off anyway with Brennus watching me. Shielding my breasts with my hands, I turn toward him. I walk slowly to the tub, watching Brennus to make sure he stays where he is and doesn't try to come nearer to me. He doesn't move.

Never taking my eyes off of him, I have to sit on the edge of the tub, and then swing my legs over the edge together because of the shackles. The shackles clank against the metal of the tub as I enter the water slowly. I sit there stiffly, watching him watch me. "Dat 'twas different," Brennus murmurs. He moves back from the tub to lean against the far wall of the bathroom where he observes me casually.

My eyes narrow. "What do you mean?" I ask with suspicion.

"I mean da way ye took yer clothes off…I'm used ta wans tryin' ta entice me in da way dey disrobe, but ye're just da opposite. Ye try na ta entice, try na ta flaunt yer beauty…" he replies with a seductive smile. I feel relief because I think that he is telling me that I didn't turn him on when I took my clothes off. That belief is rapidly dispelled with his next statement. "Da contrast is breathtakingly sexy."

Holding my breath, I duck under the water and stay down there until my air supply runs out and I have to surface. When I come up, he is still here. "You said you would tell me about being a Gancanagh, if I didn't fight you," I say, trying to turn the conversation back to where I want it to go and lead him away from lust for now.

"I did," he replies as he goes to the cabinet that holds a basin of water and a bowl. Opening it, he pulls out a sponge and some soap. Nearing the tub, he hands them to me. Taking them cautiously from him, my eyes meet his. He asks, "Whah do ye want ta know?"

I want to know how to destroy you, I think. "You are a faerie?" I ask, wetting the sponge and using it to scrub the dirt and grime from my body. I watch him return to his former position against the far wall.

"I was," he says, and when I look at him for more information, he replies, "I was a faerie, before I was changed into a Gancanagh... before I died."

"Oh," I say as a million questions resonate in my mind. "How did you die and become a Gancanagh?"

"I was captured, just like ye. We were warriors, Finn and me, a long time ago...in a place ye never heard of because it no longer exists," he says smoothly, crossing his arms in front of him and waiting for my reaction.

I'm startled by what he says. I have no basis for any of this, no insight into what he is talking about, unless I count the fanciful stories created by humans that I have read. But, they don't come close to this because I can feel the coldness emanating from his skin from here. I can smell his sticky-sweet scent, like a tobacco flower that has gone past ripe and is now a little bit rotten and brown around the edges of its petals. I can hear the deepness of his voice and the way his words roll off his tongue, not like a being of this world, but one from another world—or lifetime. I was wrong to think he is Irish. He's not even human and never was—no matter how well he may pass for one now.

"I was turned by da method ye were too stubborn ta follow," he says with anger, and my hand stills in the water.

He endured what I endured, but he was unwilling to truly die, so he was made a demon. I almost feel sorry for him—almost.

"My sire was named Aodh," he says, and I can tell there is not a lot of love between them.

"Was—not is?" I ask, feeling cold despite the warmth of the water.

"He made us his slaves," Brennus says with cool detachment. "There was no will but his and da only means of survival was ta abide his will or perish," he explains. "It was not like it is wi' dis clan—we are united, we are brudders."

"Really? So, what happened to Aodh?" I ask, because I have a feeling Brennus didn't become the leader of this clan because of his charming personality. I also hope he will tell me how he had killed

Aodh, so that I might find a weakness to their strength.

"I defeated him. None of us will be slaves again. I am the leader and dey will all follow me orders, but dey also have freedoms dat did not exist under Aodh—and so shall ye," I shiver when he says that. If this is better than being a slave under Aodh, then Aodh was the devil.

"How were you turned into a Gancanagh?" I ask. "How do you do it exactly?" I try to ask casually, but my heart is racing as fast as my mind.

"Ye will find out soon enough," he says with an easy smile, and I want to scream in frustration, but I keep my face as serene as possible. Washing my hair with the soap that he gave me, I rinse it in the steaming water.

"Do you have a razor?" I ask, and he frowns at me, distrusting my intentions. I raise my legs out of the tub just enough so he can see the stubble on them. His eyes run the length of my legs slowly as a smile inches to the corners of his mouth. He again goes to the cabinet, pulling out a straight razor. Killing scenarios rapidly fire through my head again as he hands it to me. I resist them all because there are four huge Gancanagh outside his suite of rooms, blocking my way to freedom, along with a dozen more in the main hall.

"Thank you," I say, trying to figure out how to shave my legs with an archaic razor.

When I figure out how it works, I look up triumphantly to see that Brennus is watching me, captivated by what I'm doing. "So...a faerie, huh? What's that like? Can you fly...do you have wings?" I ask, trying to distract him from the sensual twist I can see on his face.

"Do ye see wings on me?" he asks in a soft tone as the arch of his dark brow extends a bit.

My eyebrows raise in an innocent expression. "No," I reply, and then I retract my wings instantly. "Do you see mine?" I ask sweetly when my wings have completely disappeared into my back.

Brennus' slow smile travels to his eyes this time. "No," he answers in a low tone. "I had dem, wings, a long time ago, but I couldna keep dem as a Gancanagh. For faeries, dey do na survive death." He must have seen confusion in my eyes because he adds, "Ye are an *aingeal*. I believe yers will survive. Dey will make ye very powerful in death."

I let my wings fly back out because what he just said disturbs me. My wings splash a bit of the bathwater on him because of the powerful way in which they expand. Brennus touches the droplets that have landed on his skin, brushing at the water with his long slender fingers that look capable of anything. "Don't feel bad—about your wings. I can't fly either and most of the time, they're just irritating," I admit, trying to stamp down the compassion that is rearing up inside me for his loss. Instead, I try to concentrate on not cutting myself in front of the Gancanagh. I'm not sure if he has eaten yet today and I don't want him to think of food now.

"Tanks, Genevieve, I'll try," he replies. He seems different now, like he is really trying hard not to smile, but he is losing the battle.

"Can you go outside during the day, or are you nocturnal?" I ask.

"Whah?" Brennus ask in confusion, like he honestly doesn't understand it.

"Alfred said the Gancanagh are like vampires, so I was just wondering…" And I have to stop talking because Brennus is laughing really hard. "Not nocturnal, huh?" I ask in a disappointed way, but when he clutches his side and can't stop laughing, I continue on in frustration, "So, can you go out in the sunlight, or not?" He doubles over and almost falls on the floor. I finish shaving while he tries to pull himself together.

Watching him with the light of humor in his eyes, it is difficult to believe that he is the same monster who had been down in the creepy underworld caverns with me. He is so graceful and sensual in the candlelight. It's making his skin look less like alabaster and more golden and warm. It has to be a trick of the light because there are no redeeming qualities about him. Being handsome should make him more of a monster, not less, because he probably uses it as a lure to trap his victims more easily.

"Whah made ye tink dat vampires do na go out in da daylight?" he asks, and I silently curse Bram Stoker for his lack of vision.

"So, why the lair then?" I ask, gesturing around at the windowless, sunless chambers hollowed out of stone.

"Dis is but one of many homes I have, pet. Dis is a private place, away from humans and other nosy beings," he says, but he is grinning now.

"How do you feel about garlic?" I ask him halfheartedly, and see his smile broaden. "This place is so weird. How did you find it?" I watch the candlelight flicker on the shelves that line the room. It would be romantic if I were here with someone I actually like.

"Da mine was defunct a couple of decades ago. I bought it because of its location near a waterway. We made all of da improvements ta it ourselves," he answers, looking around at the walls of the bathroom. He moves to the wood-burning stove that contains smooth stones. Picking up a couple of them, he walks over to the tub and sets them gently in the bottom of it near my feet. The water slowly begins to get warmer and I move my feet nearer the rocks to enjoy the warmth radiating off of them.

"Who did the columns in the hall?" I ask, because they are like pieces of art, but they make the place seem like it was built in another time—in another world. They have intricately carved gargoyles and other figures carved into the capitals. The rest of the columns are smooth as glass, showing the veins of ore within them.

"We needed ta support the ceiling so Lonan and Driscoll created dem," he replies.

There is that name again, Driscoll. He is one of the ones that has been in my apartment...knows I sleep alone. "Is Driscoll one of the fellas that came up here with us, or is he downstairs?" I ask, because Driscoll will know about Russell. He will know what went wrong with their plans for Russell. He is someone I want to talk to.

Instantly, I can see that I have touched a nerve with my question. Fury...and pain are registering on Brennus' face. "Why do ye want ta know about Driscoll?" he asks between clenched teeth.

Something bad happened to Driscoll, I surmise, trying to keep my face blank.

"I think that what he did with those columns is art and I want to ask him how he carved the capitals," I reply with an innocent expression.

"I will kill him," Brennus says in a deadly tone.

"Driscoll?" I ask, but I know we aren't talking about the Gancanagh. A shiver of fear runs through me.

"Yer soul mate—da other," he says, and fear roots in my heart, flowing like acid throughout my body.

"Russell? Why? He has done nothing to you," I say in a pleading whisper. I grasp the sides of the tub tight, bending the rim.

"He has. He has killed Driscoll and Ultan," Brennus counters, pulling out an enormous towel from the cabinet and unfolding it, holding it up for me. I have no choice but to stand up and allow him to wrap me in the towel. His arms snake around me from behind, pulling me back into his chest. Icy-coldness radiates off of his lips as he runs them lightly on the skin of my shoulder.

"Do you know where he is?" I ask in a near whisper, hoping Russell has escaped far away where they can never find him. Brennus lifts me out of the tub, setting me on my feet. He doesn't let go of me, but holds me to his chest.

"He is here somewhere," Brennus states with certainty.

I close my eyes in dread. *Russell, why can't you stick to the plan and run?*

"He fails to appreciate dat ye're moin now—but he will, he will suffer," Brennus says like a promise. My resolve to try to turn Brennus to my will is tested to nearly the breaking point as I imagine reaching back and snapping his neck.

I don't argue with him, or try to plead for Russell's life. I have learned that pleading with evil is useless. Brennus is a Gancanagh and killing is what he does; it is innate. "Come," Brennus breathes against my skin, and then he holds my hand. The clanking of my chains reminds me that I need to step cautiously as we exit the bathroom and enter his bedroom. Fear is threading its icy fingers through me again as I wait for Brennus' next move.

Brennus is back to looking satisfied and completely confidant while strolling through his bedroom, past the bed, and over to a wardrobe. Inside the wardrobe is an array of women's clothing. Extracting a black silk gown that looks suspiciously like lingerie, he holds it up to me to see the effect.

"Do you have any jeans?" I ask. He just smiles and hands me the garment. Clutching the garment to the front of my body, Brennus tugs at my towel, gently removing it. Before I know what he is doing, he reaches down and tears the sides of my underwear away, letting them fall to the ground. Turning away from him quickly, I step into the black silk gown. It's nearly backless, which is fortunate because I'm unable to retract my wings right now with all the anxiety churning within me.

The silk is clinging to my every curve, ending at my mid thigh. Judging by the darkness in my captor's eyes, I know he likes the effect and I have to hold my hands in fists so I won't use my fingers to claw his face. I straighten my shoulders, glaring back in his eyes, trying to stare him down, but it doesn't seem to be working. He begins to lean closer to me, like he is going to kiss me again. My stomach growls loudly and Brennus pauses when he hears it. I haven't eaten anything in days. I've been living with the pain because it's not as important as finding a way out of here, but I'm becoming weaker by the second. I will need to eat something soon.

"Are ye hungry, pet?" Brennus asks. I bristle because it's so similar to his water question.

"Yes," I say between clenched teeth.

"Den let's feed ye," he replies. I am suspicious when he leads me out of his rooms. Our entourage follows us back down to the hall where I sit at the table in the same chair he had carried me to on my first day here. It's the chair on his left. In minutes, steaming chicken broth and thick bread is placed on the table in front of me by one of the fellas. Brennus, seated next to me, watches me without comment as I devour the food. When I finish the soup, my stomach hurts because I have eaten too much, too quickly.

"Thank you," I say as politely as possible because I'm actually grateful for any kindness the evil, narcissistic monster shows me. But, it's probably not a kindness. He probably has an ulterior motive for feeding me; I just don't know what it is yet. My gratitude, however, is making him look happy so I think it is a good thing anyway.

"Finn. 'Tis time," Brennus says, and Finn is with us in seconds. The other Gancanagh come with him—all of them. I stiffen, preparing for their attack, but they each just wait for Brennus. Glancing at Brennus, I wait, too. Brennus extends his hand to me. I take it immediately, letting him lead me away from the table to the middle of the room.

"Ninian," Brennus says. Ninian immediately steps forward; his gray eyes that are shades lighter than mine seem nervous and apprehensive. Tentatively, he raises his hand, reaching it out to touch my face. His eyes are on Brennus, like he will pull his hand back at the least sign of anger from his leader. The cold fingers of Ninian's hand touch my face lightly. Tearing his eyes away from Brennus, he gazes into mine. I see relief in his eyes, but then there is a flash of something else, too. *Disappointment?* I think in confusion as he continues stroking the back of his hand down my face in a caress, like a lover.

Peeking at Brennus, he is studying me intently with clenched teeth and balled up fists. As Brennus reads the confusion on my face, his hands relax. "Dat is enough, Ninian," he commands. Ninian immediately pulls his hand from my face.

Brennus calls Torin next. When Torin nears me, I see the same trepidation in his brown eyes as had been in Ninian's; the look of dread and fear that I'll react to him and he will be killed for it. Standing still, Torin puts his fingers to my face and the brief look of longing in his eyes surprises me. *Their touch does not affect me, but maybe mine affects them*, I think.

Eibhear, Lachlan, and Goban have their turns next, followed by Keegan, Faolan, and Lonan. None of them make me feel anything other than grossed out from their cold caresses. I take the opportunity to catalog each Gancanagh as he approaches me. I try to scan their attributes so that I can recognize them later and maybe use what I know against them. Alastar uses his left hand to touch my cheek and, perhaps, he favors that hand. This is knowledge that will come into play if I ever have to fight him. Cavan and Declan look like they could be true brothers and Eion is unable to hide the fact that he really likes touching me.

Brennus looks as if he wants to smash something as he watches Eion touch me. This gives me an idea, so when Eion is just about to finish, before he can step away from me, I reach up, and place the backs of my fingers against his cheek. I mimic the caress Eion had just given me; slowly and gently I trace a path over the plane of his cheek. Desire burns in his eyes as he stares back at me. With fascination and horror, I watch as his fangs engage with a sharp *click* from their retracted position, sending a chill down my spine. I glance away from his hooded gaze, to see the stunned faces of all the Gancanagh watching me. They are riveted by what is transpiring between Eion and me. Quickly, I pull my fingers back, seeing the murderous expression on Brennus' face; he is about to explode and I know I have just executed a huge *faux pas* by touching Eion.

In an attempt to avoid Brennus' wrath, I turn toward him, walking the few steps to his side. All eyes are on me as I raise my hand slowly toward his cheek. I focus on the green, iridescent flecks in his eyes as they bore into mine, seeing them smolder while my hand inches nearer to his face. The intense chill radiating from him reaches out to me as my hand hovers just above his cheek. The sensation is electric; it's like feeling him without touching him. Allowing the anticipation that I see in his eyes to build by degrees, at last, I relent, softly touching my skin to his.

His skin is smooth and supple, but that is how it appears on the surface. There is a layer beneath his skin, that my fingertips can feel, that is tougher, more like armor. I have no doubt that it will not be easy to kill him because of it. While my fingertips gently stroke his cheek, his eyes dilate and his lids close slightly as his skin absorbs the heat of my fingers. *He does want me,* I realize as a bolt of fear strikes me, *and I am playing with fire.*

Slowly, I pull my hand back from his cheek, not surprised to see that it's shaking a little. Brennus watches me coolly. I jump when he barks out, "Right, lads! Now ye know dat yer touch is allowed when, and only when, 'tis necessary to restrain me *aingeal.* Ye will do it wi' out hesitation and wi'out fear of reprisals. Da only ting ye should fear is her gettin' away—unless ye touch her in any way other den ta restrain her...den ye know ye will die. She's moin," he says, and everyone in the room understands what he means.

"You should arrange for a demonstration of her strength and skills," Alfred's voice carries from the entrance of the hole we are in. He has just jumped in from the outside and begins to walk casually toward me. I envy him the freedom he has to leave this place at will. "She has been training. It is apparent, since Russell is still out there, walking around."

"Who would train her? She is jus a lass. She is na even fully evolved yet," Finn responds from behind us. He had not participated in the touch demonstration, probably because he has already touched me.

"Bruce Lee," Alfred says, holding up the DVD from my apartment. *I WILL KILL YOU!* My mind screams.

Alfred smirks, "She is deadly. You need to let your men know that. Who is your most skilled fighter?"

Brennus stares at Alfred like he is insane because it's obvious that he is the strongest, or else he wouldn't be the leader of a band of bloodthirsty Gancanagh; he would be dead. "Keegan," Brennus says in a commanding tone and the redheaded Gancanagh, who I recognize from the back of the library, steps forward.

"How is Lynnette?" I ask him, trying to gauge his temperament.

"Delicious," he replies with an evil grin, and I wince.

Alfred gives me a wide berth as he passes me to sit at the table. He props his feet upon it, grinning at me. He wants to see me hurt, after what I had done to him with the knife. He wants revenge.

"I'm hardly dressed for a fight," I point out, because I don't want to show them what I can do. That is not part of my strategy.

"Whah do ye need?" Brennus asks me with a relentless stare, and I shiver.

"I, at least, need some shorts," I reply, because I can't fight like this. I'm wearing a nightgown and nothing else. Brennus nods to Finn and he is gone in a second. It doesn't take him long to come back with a pair of men's sports boxers.

"'Tis da best I can do," Finn says with a grimace as he hands them to me. I must have made a face because he adds, "Dey are clean."

"I'm not going to ask you whose they are," I mutter, and listen to them all laugh. This is a really bad idea. I will gain nothing from this, unless I can somehow get away, but there are no advantages to fighting Keegan for me. They will see that I'm stronger than I look and they will compensate for my strength. I want them to believe that I'm weak, so I need to play scared. I inch closer to Brennus, saying, "Don't make me do this." I let the fear I'm feeling leak into my voice. I am afraid because I have never fought someone for real before and Keegan doesn't look like the type who will play nice.

"Don't let her play you, Brennus. She is more than able to hold her own against Keegan. No offense, Keegan," Alfred says when Keegan turns and looks like he might take a bite out of him. "Seraphim can fight the most deadly warriors. She is created to kill and protect. She is well on her way, trust me."

Brennus stiffens. "Whah weapons do ye suggest, Reaper?" Brennus asks in a strained tone. He thinks I'm playing him, too. I'm about to lose a lot more than an advantage. I bite my lip softly when I look into his eyes, seeing anger there.

"I like knives, they hurt a lot," Alfred says as his trap for revenge springs on me. Fear ignites in me while Alfred smiles languidly at me. Glancing over at Brennus, his face is neutral, but Finn, who is standing next to him, looks alarmed.

Everyone falls back from Keegan and me in an instant. Intense fear is giving way to panic. It's beginning to overwhelm me, so much so, that my legs feel weak. Stripping his shirt off, Keegan reveals his broad, muscular back. Pounding on his enormous chest with his fist, he stirs up the crowd of Gancanagh surrounding us. Then, he turns toward me and gives me an evil leer, while bouncing around in front of me, like he is warming up to butcher me.

Finn comes forward with the key to my shackles. Bending down, he releases me from the chains. He pulls them off, letting them swing in his fist as he walks away without looking me in the eye. *He's afraid for me*, I think, seeing the bend to his back and wondering if I have gained an ally. With shaky hands, I put the boxers on under the nightgown I will be forced to fight in.

Everyone antes-up with his knives and there is quite an array of wickedness to choose from. I know almost nothing about knives, so when Brennus orders me to choose, I have no idea what to do. I look around for help, but no one steps forward to assist me. So I ask for help, "Finn, will you choose for me?"

Finn glances at Brennus and when Brennus nods once, Finn steps forward and scans the weapons. He chooses two long-handled daggers of almost equal size and weight. He must be concerned about balancing the weapons. Handing them to me, he explains in a low tone, "Dis blade is moin; 'tis very old and 'tis anointed by the priests of Gahenna. Dis one is Brennus', and it too, has been anointed. I give dem ta ye freely, Genevieve, but I do na know whah dey will do for ye."

"What do you mean, Finn?" I ask him in an equally low tone, feeling all of the hair on the back of my neck standing up. The knives in my hands feel eerie, in a way that is different than just the fact that they are seriously lethal weapons.

"I mean, dey will na respond to anyone unworthy of dem," he replies in a whisper, making my insides churn.

"Is it faerie magic?" I ask him half-jokingly.

"'Tis," he says with a deadly serious expression. I nod my head slowly, acknowledging his words as I tighten my grip on the weapons. I look beyond him to Keegan to see him prancing around trash talking with his boys.

Slowly, I exhale a calming breath, attempting to slow down my heartbeat because it is racing out of control, and I wonder if they can all hear it. Alfred can and he tries to kick it up a notch when he says, "Maybe, after you get carved up, Evie, you can show us some of the magic that you used to heal Russell."

It is like he has cut me. *How does he know about that? Did he get to one of my angels? Who else knows that information? Just my inner circle and the few random souls that witnessed me heal Russell.* I turn cold, and then hot, but I don't have time to break it down. Keegan's snarl is fierce as he launches himself at me faster than a raging bull. Off guard and unprepared for his speed, I leap back from him, barely avoiding being sliced in half. But, I am too slow. Catching my back, his blade runs diagonally across my right shoulder to my left hip. I pivot away. I can feel that the cut isn't too deep because my wings take most of his thrust away. Beginning to bleed instantly, I hear a dozen or more rapid *clicks* of fangs engaging in the room as the scent of my blood permeates it.

The cut burns like fire. Keegan, who is enjoying this immensely, smiles at me, showing me his fangs while licking my blood off his blade. Taunts are being thrown at us from the crowd of Gancanagh that have formed an arc around us. "Ye shouldn't play wi' yer food, Keegan," someone calls out. Someone else asks if I taste like "angel cake." Keegan, laughing and sneering says, "No, lads—she tastes unbelievable—I've never tasted da like—'tis ambrosia, a gift from God…and I must have more."

Trembling overcomes me when the knowledge that Keegan isn't playing games begins to take root in my mind…he isn't trying to train me, or show me how to perfect a move. He doesn't care that I feel weak, terrified, and broken inside. He doesn't mind that my decision to be brave is deserting me as the state of hypervigilance that I have been in is now breaking me down. It doesn't bother him that I just spent days on the cold, hard floor, while mired in dehydration, in a place that is as close to Hell as I have ever been. In fact, he would probably enjoy knowing that and he isn't going to pull up, if I slip or falter. He is going to come at me with everything that he has and he will kill me if Brennus allows him to, but if he doesn't, Keegan will settle for just hurting me really, really bad.

Keegan doesn't change his tactic the next time he charges me.

So, instead of leaping back as before, I became pliant, folding backward so that he charges right over me. Using his force to thrust him past me, I score my blades across his left side, tearing nice sized jagged lines into him. He bleeds, but I wonder if it's truly his blood, or Lynnette's blood as I crouch to defend myself, watching for him to come back at me.

He loses some of his arrogance and swagger, seeing that he, too, is bleeding. He replaces the swagger with brutality. Trying to use terror to throw me off, Keegan licks his own blood off his fingers, letting it smear on his face repulsively. I'm trying really hard not to let it get to me, but he's just so freaking terrifying as he stalks me, looking for a weakness to exploit, that I want to cry, to plead for help, but I know I will get none. *No one will help me here*, I think, cringing as Keegan begins talking to me.

"Do ye know whah I'm goin' ta do ta yer soul mate when I find him?" Keegan asks me with a harsh sneer, coming at me from the right side and piercing the air with his knife, making me lurch back from him. "I'm goin' to take me knife and split him down his middle, so dat everyting inside of him jus slides out," he says, sounding deranged, and the image of what he just says causes something to shift inside me.

I stop retreating. *He will never get Russell because I will not allow him to live long enough to find him.* All of the terror that has made my heart race in my chest is now being pushed back. Fear is melting away as I'm zeroing in on my prey. Engaging in the fight, I begin to stalk Keegan, circling him and picking out all of the subtle imperfections in his form. *He is strong and fast, but he lacks finesse,* I surmise, watching him swing uselessly at the air. His knives whistle wickedly, but they are not getting near enough to me to cut me.

Seeing an opening in his defenses, I sprint to the column nearest to me. Leaping at it in a fraction of a second, I use my right foot to spring off of it, propelling me toward the column next to it. Landing lightly with my left foot higher on this column, I immediately push off of it, effectively reversing my momentum. This is allowing me to spring back to the first column. Landing higher still with my right foot, I'm ricocheting back and forth between the two columns. Almost to the top now, I tower several feet above Keegan's head. The next time I make contact with the neighboring column, I use it as a springboard. Pitching myself toward Keegan at an arcing angle, I drive my knives downward. Keegan, seeing me coming, pivots his body at the last possible instant. He avoids being impaled by my knives, but he is still too slow to avoid having his chest slashed open.

I tumble hard onto the ground and allow my momentum to roll me safely back from any counterattack Keegan might mount. When I bounce up, Keegan stands watching me, panting and clutching his chest in disbelief. "I'm goin' to cut yer wings off and mount dem on me wall," he says as his teeth grind with menace. Instantly, he throws a knife to the right of me while simultaneously diving to my left. He plans for me to go left, to avoid the knife on my right, where he will be waiting to carve me up. But, I'm faster than he expects. Dodging to the right, I manage to avoid his trap, while only getting a small nick on my upper arm as his knife spirals past me.

In a millisecond, I run to the column in front of me, using my momentum to scale it easily. Reaching the top, I spring from it, planting my feet and pushing off hard against the stone, launching with ease to an adjacent column. Catching the column and wrapping my arm around it, I begin spiraling down around the column. I drop to the ground, landing just behind Keegan. Leaping up on his back before he can react, I coil my legs around his waist, crossing my arms in front of his neck. I pull back hard, drawing the blades of my knives across his neck in an X, cutting him open and allowing his blood to seep out of his body unchecked. His legs crumple beneath him as I unwind myself from him before he hits the floor, landing on my feet. Not pausing to see if he is dead, I spin and throw both of my knives at Alfred. His screams of anguish come to me from across the room as the blades embed in him, impaling him to the chair he is seated in.

Turning and running as fast as I can to the entrance of the cave, I feel my blood pounding in my veins. Leaping to the closest handhold in the rock face, I pull myself up the wall, scaling it without faltering. A pursuit is being mounted behind me, but I know I can reach the top of the cave before any of them can get to me. My elation with that fact is short lived, however, because as I reach the top of the wall, a face of a Gancanagh that I don't recognize looks down at me. He is some kind of sentry for the entrance to the cave. He is not alone either. There are two more who are smiling at me. One of them says, "Well, hallo, *aingeal*."

I'm dead, I think. The guard that spoke to me encircles me in his arms, jumping back into the hole of the cave with me in tow.

Raw, agonizing fear hits me in waves when I see the menacing faces of the Gancanagh. The guard releases me immediately when we land. Alfred is still screaming as someone is prying the knives out of his shoulders to release him from the chair. I want to cry because I haven't managed to kill him. *If I had killed him, it may have all been worth it. Now, the Gancanagh will kill me and this will be over,* I think, feeling terror and relief at the same time. I want desperately for this to be over.

I glance over to where I had left Keegan on the floor of the hall. He is still there, lying unmoving in a pool of blood. My entire body is shaking as I stand listless, staring at Keegan, unable to speak. *I did that...I made him cease to be...I murdered him,* I think as my brain slows down. I should fight the fellas that are gathering around me, or I should try to run again, but I can't. I'm disconnecting from them all.

Staring as the crowd parts for Brennus, I watch him approaching me. I can't read his face. The fellas are all talking around me and I'm catching a few phrases that aren't making any sense to me. "Shell shock," "thousand-yard stare," and "battle fatigue" rattle around in the air from the Gancanagh nearest me.

When Brennus comes close enough to me, I reach out, clutching the front of his shirt. But, my grip is so weak that I can hardly hold on to it. As I look up into his eyes, I murmur to him, "Help me...please."

His eyes soften. "I will...*mo chroí,*" my enemy answers me as he pulls me into his arms. He whispers words in my ear that I don't know, "*muirnin*" and "*a ghra,*" as he nuzzles my neck with his cold lips. I want to push him away, but I'm so weak that I know he is the only thing holding me up. Numbly, I hear something *click*. Before I can react at all, Brennus pierces my skin with his powerful jaws. A soft whimper escapes me as my legs buckle beneath me. Brennus holds me tight to him as he drains my blood. Everything begins to grow dark. I'm not struggling because he is setting me free... I'm dying, and when it's over I will be free of this place, and the Gancanagh, forever.

CHAPTER 13

Bloodlust

I'm not dead, I think as crushing reality begins slamming me in the chest. I'm still very much a prisoner of the Gancanagh. Lifting my head off the silken pillow of Brennus' enormous bed, my head starts pounding. I feel faint, so I rest my head on the pillow again, gazing at the ceiling until the room stops spinning. There is something different about the room. Lying in the soft, seductive warmth of the bed, I try to figure out what it is and it finally comes to me. The cloying smell that clings to everything is—not gone—but it doesn't smell so repulsive to me anymore. In fact, it smells almost pleasant.

My heartbeat speeds up. *He bit me!* I growl as a pulse of anger and loathing sweeps through me. *My enemy made a snack out of me and I let him!* The blood within me rushes to my face and a deep blush stains my cheeks. I run my hand over the marks he made on my neck. Pulling my hand back, I look at my fingertips. They have blood on them. I'm still bleeding from the wound he left. *How could I have allowed that to happen? Do you never want to see Reed again...or Russell?* I ask myself harshly. If I become a Gancanagh, then I can never see either one of them again. I have to fight harder. I just moved into check and I have to get out of it or checkmate is the next move, and then it's game over. I'll be a monster, too—*or am I one already?* I wonder as I slowly sit up in the bed.

Stumbling out of the bed, I have to wait for the room to stop spinning before I lurch to the adjoining bathroom. The full-length mirror reflects my image as I approach it. I open my mouth, tilting my head back to see if I have acquired the fangs of the Gancanagh. Finding nothing out of the ordinary about my appearance, except for the marks on my neck where their leader has marked me as his,

I feel relief.

I'm also grateful to find that I'm still wearing the torn, black nightgown and boxer shorts that I had on before everything had gone black. I look wild in my torn clothing that still has Keegan's blood on it. Nausea rolls in me and I have to swallow hard so that I won't vomit on the floor. Not that there is much to vomit, judging by the hunger that is racking my body with pain, the likes of which I have never felt so intensely in my life.

I stagger to the old-fashion pitcher and water basin that rests on top of the cabinet. Pouring water into the basin, I splash my face and arms repeatedly with the cold water. I strip the ruined nightgown off me, along with the boxers. Finding the sponge in the cabinet, beneath the basin, I use it to remove Keegan's blood from me. When I am done, I retrieve a towel from the cabinet, and seeing the straight razor sitting on the shelf, I pause. My fingers trembling, I pick it up and open it, revealing the blade. *A weapon,* I think as I close the razor, grasping it tight in my fist. Rummaging through the cabinet for anything that can be used to aid in my escape, I find nothing else.

Closing the cabinet, I clean up the area so that nothing looks out of place, before I walk back into the bedroom to look for new clothes to wear. Wrapped in a towel, I begin to pass by the bed. I stumble to a halt at the foot of it, feeling cold, prickly air. Glancing over at it, I see Brennus lying against the pillow I had just vacated, with his arms casually crossed behind his head. My heartbeat slows down, and then bolts as a kick of adrenaline launches into my bloodstream. I hadn't heard him come in! And, where is that smell that always makes me want to stick my fingers in my nose to gain relief from it?

"Brennus! Don't do that! You make me want to jump out of my skin," I scold him in anger, because I had jumped in fright at the sight of him. He may look beautifully angelic, but he has no heart— well, not one that beats anyway.

"Whah did I do, *mo chroí?*" he asks, grinning at me as his black hair falls artfully over his forehead like a supermodel.

"Don't sneak up on me. It's not nice," I say, continuing to the wardrobe and gritting my teeth as I listen to him laugh at me.

"Whah did ye jus say?" he asks incredulously, because we both know it is a ridiculous thing to have said. There is nothing nice about him. Nothing.

"You know what I mean," I reply over my shoulder, rummaging through the wardrobe, looking for anything that does not resemble lingerie. Finding a form fitting white cami and a short, black leather skirt, I frown. This is the closest I'm going to get to "real" clothing. I also find some sexy underwear and a pair of black suede boots that will go clear up to my mid thigh. I put the underwear and skirt on underneath my towel, and then I use the straight razor to cut the back of the cami, so that it will accommodate my wings better. Brennus has already seen the weapon in my hand, so I have to show him a good reason for having it.

"I jus came up here ta see if ye were hungry," he says, playing along and acting like he is innocent of any other motive. He seems pleased by the nice comment. I bet no one ever implied that he should be nice in his undead life.

"I am hungry...starving," I say absently, as I finish fixing the cami. Turning away from him, I drop the towel and put the top on.

His eyes are shiny with humor when I turn back around to face him. *I amuse him...like a pet,* I observe, picking up the boots and going to the bed. Sitting on the edge of it, I bend down to put on the ridiculously long footwear. "How come there aren't jeans in there, or running shoes?" I ask Brennus with a sullen expression, pulling on the other boot.

Brennus' smile is sublime. "Whah is sexy about denim and trainers?" Brennus asks with humor in his voice.

"Ugh!" I reply, slipping the razor in the top of my right boot as covertly as possible. "I should've known."

"I had one other reason for coming up here," he reveals cryptically.

"Don't tell me you missed me?" I ask, trying to sound like I haven't just gotten doused in the black dread that accompanies all of his surprises.

"I did, but dat is na it," he replies with ease.

"Maybe you can tell me after I've eaten," I say, trying to postpone any ugly revelations he has planned for me.

"If dat is whah ye wish," he says with a small sigh. "Whah is da razor for?" he asks as I get up swiftly from the bed to face him.

"Protection," I reply, glaring at him with my hands on my hips.

"No one will dare harm ye now, *mo chroí*. Ye do na need da razor... I will protect ye."

I frown. "Ha! You are the one I need protection from the most," I reply, watching him for his reaction. "I don't appreciate being anyone's lunch, Brennus."

"I do na suppose dat ye do," he replies. "Whah if I said dat I'll let ye bite me back next time?" he asks, smiling.

"I would say, 'keep your fangs off me,'" I counter as a shiver of revulsion escapes me. He just chuckles and lifts his brow, but he doesn't argue with me about the razor.

"Come, let's feed ye," he says as he gets up off the bed, holding his hand out to me. I don't take it, but walk ahead of him into the next room and out into the hallway that leads down to the main hall. The guards are waiting just outside the door for us. I recognize them now by name: Declan, Eion, Lachlan and Faolan.

As we stroll down the stairs to the main hall, I detect a different kind of smell in the air that I'm unaccustomed to inhaling. Now that the scent of the skin of the Gancanagh has diminished for me, probably because I have been bitten and it has done something to me, I can now smell other things that the odor had masked. None of these odors are pleasant. I can't name the scent until I reach the main floor and see the horror for myself. It's the stench of dead bodies. The women who had been used for food are piled in a heap by one of the far fireplaces. Eibhear and Cavan are steadily throwing their ravaged bodies in the fire and burning them.

What I had thought was a dramatic way to light the hall and give heat is turning out to have a more practical purpose for the Gancanagh: the disposal of dead bodies. *This is truly a house of horrors,* I grimace, averting my eyes from the face of a female corpse I had seen alive just days ago. Her face is frozen in a mask of pleasure.

"There usually aren't this many bodies, Evie," Alfred says from the table where he is seated, dining on bread and soup. "It's your fault they all bit it last night," he continues, chewing his bread and laughing at his own pun. "After the show you put on for everyone, the bloodlust couldn't be controlled and all those lovely women had to die...all because of you."

"How's the shoulder, Alfred?" I ask, sitting in the chair that Brennus is holding out for me at the head of the table, next to his own chair. "Hurt much?" I ask, trying to hide the stabbing pain his words cause me.

"Just twinges...nothing to worry about," he replies, but I know he is lying by the way he is having trouble lifting his spoon to his mouth.

A bowl of chicken soup and some bread is placed on the table for me. I'm shocked and a little dismayed that I'm still hungry, even with the rancid smell and the sight of the carnage in the hall. I thank Lonan for bringing food to me, and then I begin eating it as fast as I can. The food doesn't taste as good as it had yesterday. In fact, it tastes awful, but I'm so hungry, I almost can't control myself as I eat it all. When I finish, I can tell that I'm full because my belly feels really full, but the hunger pains aren't diminishing at all. In confusion, I think maybe I will have to wait a little bit for the food to digest before I feel better.

Brennus watches me with a light of expectation in his pale green eyes, but I can't decipher what it is he is waiting for me to do. "Would ye like some more soup?" he asks, raising his brow.

"No, thank you," I murmur, since I know if I eat more, I'll end up vomiting because I will be too full. But, hunger is still a gnawing pain, making me sweat a little because of its intensity.

"Are you sure, Evie? You look really hungry," Alfred teases, and he smirks at me, enjoying the look of pain that is beginning to show on my face. "Maybe she wants something else to eat, Brennus?" Alfred asks with a laugh.

"She is more den welcome ta whahever I have ta give," Brennus replies, and he sounds so sincere that I look up at his face in confusion.

"What are you talking about?" I ask, because I'm smart enough to know they are playing with me.

"Ye have been bitten, Genevieve," Finn says from across the table. He has just come in and has heard what is being discussed amongst us. He looks angry, like he doesn't approve of them toying with me.

"Please explain to me what that means, Finn," I say, staring into the light green eyes that are so like his brother's, but lack some of the intensity that Brennus' possess.

"It means dat ye will crave da blood of da Gancanagh who bit ye. Normally, ye would na feel da intense pain of da hunger because our skin acts like a narcotic and deadens da pain. But, ye do na have dat luxury, do ye?" he asks, looking sorry for me.

"So you are saying, that if I drink Brennus' blood, then the hunger goes away?" I ask Finn. I'm having trouble blinking back the tears that have immediately come to my eyes.

"'Twill," Finn's reply is soft, making something twist in my heart.

"Is that all that will happen, if I drink his blood?" I ask, because I have a feeling that there is something he is not saying.

Finn's eyes drift to Brennus' as he waits for something. When Brennus gives a slight nod of his head, Finn turns back at me with a look of pity. "When ye drink da blood of a Gancanagh, ye will die and be reborn as one of us."

Checkmate, I think as tears brim my eyes to fall onto my cheeks.

"Oh, Evie, don't cry…on second thought, please, do cry. You're so beautiful when you cry," Alfred says, leaning back in his chair, satisfied that I'm sufficiently destroyed by what is happening to me.

Finn's eyebrows draw together. "Ye bleedin' parasite! If ye say another word, I will kill ye meself," Finn rasps in anger, glaring at Alfred. "Dat is a warrior and she will soon be a Gancanagh and me sister," Finn says, pointing to me. "Ye had better be prepared ta leave as soon as she tastes his blood and her soul is released ta ye, because den if she orders me to kill ye, dere is no place under Heaven for ye ta hide." Finn is shaking his head at Alfred, like he thinks he is the stupidest creature he has ever set eyes upon. "If ye had any logic in ye atall, den ye would leave now. Do ye hear whah Brennus is calling her? '*Mo chroí*'…it means 'my heart' where we come from. He will be givin' her anyting she asks for once she is Gancanagh—including yer heart on a stake."

I don't know who appears more shocked, Alfred or me, when Finn is done with his rant. So, that is why Alfred has been made to wait. If I had gone along with the water game in my cell, I would've done anything to have gained relief, even drink Brennus' blood, whether he had bitten me or not. Then, my soul would've been forfeit and Alfred would've been there to claim it. Now, they have found another way to get me to become one of them. They must have reasoned, that since their touch doesn't affect me, I would be in so much pain from being bitten that I would be forced to drink Brennus' blood to end the pain. But, it is still my choice, I can choose the pain, or I can choose to end it and forfeit my soul.

Finn turns back to Brennus, tossing an envelope to him across the table. "I took care of whah ye asked me ta. 'Tis all in dere," he says as he comes to sit next to Brennus. Finn glares back down the table at Alfred, who looks like he is sweating now, too, just like me.

"Tanks, Finn," Brennus says as he pushes the envelope to me and waits patiently for me to ask him about it. I'm trying hard to focus on anything other than the pain I'm in, so I seize the envelope, but I don't open it.

"What's this?" I ask, wiping tears from my eyes with the back of my fist.

"'Tis da ting I was going ta tell ye about when we were upstairs, but now, I can jus show ye," he says, waiting for me to open the envelope. Dread consumes me.

"I don't think I can take any more surprises, Brennus," I say, not opening it and not looking at any of them.

"Dis is a good surprise," Brennus counters in a gentle tone, but I doubt that a demon would know anything about a good surprise.

"What is it?" I ask, and I hear Brennus sigh as he pulls the envelope from my hands and opens it for me. There are documents with my name, my real name, on them. They look like bank accounts and deeds and legal papers. I glance at Brennus in confusion, looking for an explanation.

"Ye defeated Keegan," Brennus says, smiling at me proudly. "Ye get all of his assets. He wasn't dat wealthy—less den a billion pounds, he made some bad investments dat did na pan out so well for him, but do na fret, I have more den enough for whatever ye want," he says, handing me back the envelope.

Looking across the table at Alfred, I see something in his eyes—it's fear. *Finn's right,* I think as my hands begin to shake again. *Brennus is making me his queen and they will all treat me as one of them—a beloved demon.*

Numbly, I put the envelope on the table and push it back toward Brennus. Then, I push my chair back from the table and I begin to walk across the hall to the entrance of the cave.

"Whah is wrong, *mo chroí?*" Brennus calls to me.

Stopping, I turn toward him. "I can't take that," I point to the envelope on the table.

"Why na?" Brennus asks, frowning in confusion. "Ye were livin' like a peasant in dat little hovel. Ye never have ta live dat way again. Ye will be powerful and if someting even tinks about huntin' ye, we'll bring dem down and teach dem da true meanin' of da word 'terror,'" he says. I can see the brutality in his eyes. He means every word of what he just said. He will guard me like a treasure for eternity and I will never be free of him.

"I can't take that envelope because I murdered him—I murdered Keegan. I can't take his money," I say in desperation, putting my hand to my stomach and trying to ease the ache of hunger I feel inside of me.

"Ye did na murder him. Ye defended yerself, and ye beat him like a warrior. He died well," Brennus replies, completely confused by me. "No one can say dat ye're unworthy ta be one of us, after whah ye did. Ye will be an asset ta da clan," he adds, and his words chill me.

Will I be good at enticing humans to follow me into the cave, so that I can feed on them until they are corpses, and then feel nothing for them when I toss them on the fire like a funeral pyre? Will I strive hard to be an overachiever as a Gancanagh? Will I begin to love Brennus? Will I forget Reed? NEVER!

I walk away from Brennus, moving toward the entrance of the cave once more. "Where are ye going?" Brennus calls, but I don't answer him or stop. He is by my side in seconds because I'm not trying to outrun him. I'm just leaving—one way or another.

"I'm leaving," I say, pulling the straight razor from my boot.

"Da only way ye are leavin' here is as a Gancanagh," he says in a soft tone as we continue walking together like we are not in a hurry to reach any particular destination. "Den, we can go wherever ye desire."

"No, I'm leaving now. You take care," I say, not looking at him. He sighs heavily, like I'm trying his patience.

"I can na let ye go, *mo chroí*," he says gently as he steps in front of me, making me stop. "Ye're moin." Fear shoots through me because I'm beginning to believe him—*he is breaking me.*

"Please," I beg him. "Please, don't make me hurt you. I don't want to hurt you." I mean it. I don't want to hurt him and that fact scares me to death because I should really want to hurt him.

A slow smile sweeps over his beautiful lips and face, making the light dance in his brilliant, green eyes that remind me of the sea in a storm. He looks like someone who has just gotten the best news of his life. "'Tis okay...hurt me," he breathes.

Trying to step around him, he stops me by grabbing my arm. He won't let go of it. I'll have to make him let me go if I want to get out of here. Quickly, and without much thought, I slash his arm with the straight razor. Two things happen when I do that. First, Brennus smiles euphorically at me, and second, I am overwhelmed by the scent of his blood seeping out of his arm. My head is spinning and my mouth is watering. It's taking every ounce of will power that I possess just to keep from pouncing on his arm and feasting on his blood like a rabid dog.

Dropping the razor, I cover my mouth and nose with my hand, trying to block out his aroma as I back away from him. "'Tis okay," he says in a gentle way, like he is trying to calm a frightened child.

As I shake my head, I look around with wild eyes for a way out, but Faolan, Eion, and Lonan are blocking the exit. They are standing in front of it, watching us intently. I can't escape, but I have to get away. Turning, I use all of my speed to run back up to Brennus' room. Slamming the door, I lock it, backing away from it quickly. I run into the bedroom, and then into the bathroom. I go to the far wall and slowly slide down it to the floor.

Pain and panic are warring for supremacy and I feel so bad that all I can do is lie my head down on the cool floor of the bathroom and curl into a ball. *I am the stupidest creature. What made me think that I had more game than an ancient warrior who holds all the cards? Conceit, thy name is Evie.*

I don't open my eyes so I can't see him, but I can smell him. He thickens the air I breathe, choking me with his scent...his aroma. I shiver. I have to resist. If I'm not strong, then I will be relegated to the same fate as this predator whose sickness infects me even now. But now, I crave him and he knows that; he has been counting on my need to end the gnawing pain. How he would savor my surrender.

I'm alive, but how much longer will it take until I beg him not to be?

"Ye are so strong, *mo chroí*," Brennus says as he creeps nearer to me. I can't move because I'm afraid that if I do, I'll try to make him bleed.

He isn't openly bleeding right now; he must heal more quickly than I do, I think as he sits down next to me, pulling my head onto his lap. He strokes my hair gently, trying to comfort me. *Pick a side demon.* I try not to relax my guard around him.

His voice is seductive as he says, "I tink ye're looking at dis da wrong way. Why wouldn't ye want ta be one of us; ta be protected and cared for by Gancanagh who will always have yer back?" he asks. "We will never look at ye like ye're scum…like ye do na have a right ta exist." I almost scoff because he is trying to change my existence to fit what he wants it to be.

I wouldn't exist anymore…something else will, but it won't be me, I think.

He seems to read my thoughts when he says, "Ye will be mostly da same, but ye'll release yer soul—it hasn't helped ye at all in dis life—it makes ye a target. Den ye will never be alone again…I will stand by yer side forever and ye will never have ta be afraid," he promises. And there it is…he found something that I want desperately at this moment.

What would it be like to never be afraid again? To never feel the terror of being hunted down by a predator? Or, to never fear that the predator that hunted me would harm someone I love? I would probably be incapable of true love.

"I'm tryin' ta help ye. Let me help ye, *mo chroí*," he coos.

"I don't need your help," I whisper.

"Ye do na know whah ye need. If I were ta let ye go, how long will ye last out dere alone?" he asks, sounding angry that I would rather risk death than choose his eternity of being undead.

"I don't know, let's try it and see," I reply.

He sighs heavily. "Ye can na stop whah's coming. Let me bleed for ye," he says in a gentle tone as he touches his cold lips to my neck. "So strong…so brave…" he murmurs.

"I can't…" I whimper, and saying the words seems to be increasing my suffering.

"Den, bleed for me," he says as he pierces my neck again. I don't lose consciousness this time. I don't think he takes as much of my blood as he had last time. His goal isn't to feed on me, but to inject me with more of his venom, so that I will crave him more—and I do. But my blood is doing something to him that I don't think he expected. He looks drunk…or drugged, much like the human women look after having been touched by the Gancanagh. He looks like the world is turning circles on him as he leans his back against the wall of the bathroom to right himself.

"Ye have ta break soon, *mo chroí*. Da more of yer blood I have, da more I need ye. I would've had ye in me bed already, but I'm afraid I will end up killin' ye before I can change ye if I do," Brennus says as his eyes slowly open and the darkness of passion shows in his lidded stare.

"Are you sure that is the only reason you haven't tried? Because, you should really be a little more afraid that I will kill you, if you try it," I say as anger and something I don't want to look too closely at shoots through my body.

Brennus' laughter resonates through the bathroom. "Ye make me want ta live for eternity, jus so dat I can hear whah ye will say next," he smiles. "I will need eternity because I can na get enough of ye. Yer beauty is agony to me. I will na live wi'out ye…I can na live wi'out ye."

I would've said something else, but I have to grit my teeth as a whimper escapes me. Hunger pains are gripping me hotter and stronger than they had before. I writhe on the floor, trying to curl into a tighter ball to ease the pain. "Dis ends now," Brennus orders, standing up and picking me up off the floor. Somewhere, in the back of my mind, I'm aware that my suffering is bothering him. The information doesn't make any sense because everything that I know about him, up until this point, leads me to believe that he hasn't a care for my suffering.

"Where are we going?" I ask as he moves through the bedroom.

"Da hall. I will have Finn cut me and 'twill be over" he says, pulling me tightly to his chest.

"No…please…I won't be able to stop…"

"'Tis meant, Genevieve…'tis yer destiny. 'Tis," he says in a gentle tone as I shake my head in denial.

When we get to the hall, Brennus sits down in his chair at the table with me on his lap. Alfred has been waiting for us. I wonder if he has been listening to everything that we have been saying. He has excellent hearing, but I'm not sure if it would've extended all the way up to the bathroom.

Looking at us with glee, Alfred says, "Finally, I've been marinating in this cave for weeks now, waiting for you to get her to agree to be a Gancanagh. I have to say, I was afraid that you weren't going to get her to turn, but I can see that your methods are highly effective."

"You should've let me kill him," I murmur into Brennus' neck when he stiffens at Alfred's words.

"Patience, pet, da night is young and I am planning many birthday gifts for ye," he whispers in my ear. I hold my breath a little because I have a feeling that one of my Gancanagh birthday gifts will be Alfred's heart on a stake.

A darkness begins to grow within me. *I want that—I want Alfred's heart on a stake.* Lifting my head off of Brennus' chest, I look him in the eyes. He must see the darkness in my eyes because he squeezes me tighter, raw desire showing on his face.

I don't think that Alfred understands what we are saying. He is so manic that he can hardly contain himself. I study the faces of the Gancanagh watching him intently. They look like they, too, are ecstatic by the way their eyes trail him—like he is a rare delicacy they're going to get the opportunity to taste. I'm starting to see that I have not been the only delusional being in the room. But, Alfred is unaware of any of this and he is also unable to shut up. His need to gloat is something that I remember well from my last encounter with him.

"I have been waiting for this moment, Evie, to tell you something really important," he says, smiling into my eyes. Pacing back and forth near us, he is rubbing his hands together happily. "I want you to be completely at ease in your new life, so this is sort of a gift to both of you—you and Brennus—for your happiness," he says in his annoyingly unsubtle way. How I ever believed that he had an ounce of goodness in him, I will never know.

"I can't wait to hear it," I say in a raspy tone as a fresh wave of pain breaks over me, making my entire body shiver like I am doused in ice water.

"What is it?" Brennus asks with impatience. He puts his hand on my forehead, trying to comfort me as he searches around the room for Finn.

"Reed won't be coming after you, Evie. I took care of it," Alfred says, and then he waits for my reaction.

With my teeth chattering from pain, I stare at him and ask, "What?"

"I let Dominion know where their traitor was and his friend, too—what is his name? Zephyr, is it? They were both arrested," Alfred says, and I can't breathe. "You really did betray them both quite well. I swear, I couldn't have conceived of a better plan," he says, pausing to grin at me. "They didn't even leave Crestwood, probably because they were hoping that you would come back to them."

"You lie!" I whisper, but I know he isn't lying. I know he is telling me the truth and a pain that is more excruciating than anything the

Gancanagh could do to me erupts in my chest. I feel like something has died in me. *I have betrayed them.*

I hear nothing else that Alfred says. He continues to speak, but I can't hear him. My mind is racing...*Are they dead? Would Dominion execute them?*

"How long?" I ask, interrupting what Alfred has been saying. I want to know when they were taken by Dominion.

"A month ago," Alfred replies.

A month—an entire month! Would they have been put on trial? Did they get interrogated—they wouldn't even know where I have been. Would the divine angels believe them, or have they been tortured for information they couldn't possibly give? I wonder as my arms coil around Brennus, hugging him tight to me as I try to anchor myself to reality. My brain, spinning feverously, struggles hard to remain lucid enough to ask Alfred for more information.

"Are they alive?" I ask.

"There is no way—Dominion would never let them..." he says, but I stop listening to him because I just deciphered that he doesn't know for sure.

He doesn't know if they are dead or alive. There is a chance they are alive. I can still save them. How? Brennus said the only way I'm getting out of here is as a Gancanagh. What if I let him make me a Gancanagh? He will let me out then. I will be able to go wherever I want. I could then get away from Brennus and find Dominion. If I turn myself in to the Divine, they could see that I am not a Nephilim. They can kill me and Reed and Zee can go free. I will pretend like I never knew them—I will have to figure that part out later. Right now, I have to get out of this cave and get to Dominion.

Lifting my head from Brennus' chest, I search the room. Alfred is still talking, but I don't care, it's background noise. "Whah are ye looking for, *mo chroí?*" Brennus asks me in my ear as his fingers stroke the side of my face lovingly.

"I'm looking for Finn. He has to cut you so that I can become a Gancanagh," I tell him in a near whisper. "You have to promise me one thing, though," I say when I spot Finn coming toward us.

"Anyting," Brennus replies, and his green eyes are the most brilliant I've ever seen them.

"Alfred never leaves this cave alive," I murmur, tracing his lips with my trembling finger.

"I promise," he breathes, just before I lean forward and press my feverous lips to his cold ones.

"Thank you," I say, after lifting my lips from his. I have to put my head back down on his shoulder because it's almost impossible for me to do anything else now. I'm so weak from pain that I'm having trouble staying focused.

Finn looks grim as he approaches us at the table. Leaning down, he whispers something in Brennus' ear that has Brennus on his feet immediately with me cradled in his arms. He turns toward the stairs that lead down to the floor beneath this one. I look at Finn in confusion. Then, I hear a deep, low growl and a voice that I thought I might never hear again in my life. Tears of anguish spring to my eyes because he should have run! He should never have had to see this place. He should have lived!

"Where do ya think yer goin' with my girl?" Russell calls out from across the hall.

CHAPTER 14

Crashing

Brennus, looking livid as he turns back to Finn, scowls at him like he can't believe what is happening. I have seen him angry, usually because of something I said, but this is different, this is rage. I want to lift my head up to see what's happening, but the cramping in my belly isn't allowing me to move without incredible pain. So, I stay curled in Brennus' arms as we sit back in his seat at the head of the table. I do manage to twist a bit on his lap, so that I can look ahead to see what everyone else is seeing, and the image of Russell walking across the hall is nothing short of breathtaking.

Russell's tawny hair is shining in the light of the fires as he walks toward us from the entrance of the hall. His huge frame is almost dwarfed by his bright, crimson wings as they stretch out like wide, arching symbols of vengeance. The set of his brow is making me think that violence is now an innate instinct to his character. He looks like a Power angel hunting a demon and my breath catches in my throat because he is no longer just the Russell I had met at Crestwood on a walk to a lake. No, he is much more than human now. He is a dangerous and lethal assassin. He is a Seraph.

The Gancanagh have lined up on either side of him, intimidating and hostile, but Russell is walking boldly past each one. He is refusing to give them the respect of making eye contact, which is not the wisest thing to do in the presence of dangerous predators. Russell is looking straight ahead and his eyes are locked on mine. I can tell he's freaking out inside. For one thing, all of the light golden hair on his arms is standing straight up like the bristles of a wire brush. His nostrils are flared from his increased respiration and heartbeat, and his wings are spreading out like he might fly to us. I know he can't fly yet, so that just means his wings are doing it on their own out of agitation.

But, those indications are things that I know, and I'm not sure if the Gancanagh will recognize all of those signs, because other than that, Russell looks relatively cool for someone who has just walked alone into a lair filled with over a dozen undead monsters.

Even though he came in alone, he has a strategy all mapped out. I can see immediately what his plan is and I don't approve of it at all. It's the worst plan I have ever seen! Completely asinine! Tears spring to my eyes because I can't believe he would do something like this, after all we talked about regarding his survival and how important it is to me.

Russell is wearing the pair of jeans that I had picked out for him at one of the local shops in town. They are not designer, but it doesn't matter because Russell can make anything look good. He opted to forgo a shirt, probably because his wings would be out for this mission and it's easier for him not to wear one. That is not to say that Russell isn't wearing anything above the waist, it's just that what he is wearing isn't clothing. Strapped to two canvas, military harnesses that crisscross his body are at least a dozen hand grenades, fastened to him with military reinforced straps. In his hand, he is carrying a hand grenade with the pin already pulled. His finger is resting lightly on the safety clip of the hand-held bomb.

"Bad plan, Russell," I whisper to him as he comes nearer to us. The smell down here must be getting to him a little because he begins to rub his nose lightly with the hand that is not holding the grenade. I feel bad for him because I know how it reeked when I had first woken up in here.

"Naw, Red, it's an excellent plan, ya see, 'cuz both of our souls are gettin' outta here, one way or another," he says in a confident tone, his chocolate-brown eyes scanning me. "I missed ya at the library, Red, I'm sorry I was too late to save ya there," he rasps as his eyes stare into mine. All of the fear and worry that he has been going through since I have been taken is etched in that one look that passes between us. Then his eyes shift from mine, as he looks me over again, coming to rest on my neck. His face transforms into a scowl. Staring at Brennus with sharp eyes, Russell's scowl deepens while he surveys Brennus holding me tight in his arms.

"Ya bit her! Ya filthy vampire!" Russell says in anger as he stops near where we are seated. Brennus stiffens, probably because Russell called him a vampire, and not because he cares at all how Russell feels about him biting me.

"I did. She will soon be Gancanagh, but since she obviously has some feelings for ye, her soul mate, I will allow ye ta leave now. We will give ye a head start, Seraph, and den we will see if she can find ye—ye will make a good first kill," he says, toying with a strand of my hair.

My head is spinning at the thought of hunting Russell. *Will I completely lose all of my heart along with my soul? Will he just be prey to me?*

Russell's expression turns doubtful as he shakes his head. "Ya lie. She has to drink yer blood for her to become a vampire, and since I can still feel her soul, I'd say she isn't that into ya," Russell says as Brennus squeezes me tighter, like he wants to hold on to me. I stare at Russell now because I can't figure out where he got his information, but it's very accurate.

"If ye care for her, and I can see dat ye do, ye will let her ease her pain wi' me blood. Ye can na stop whah is happening to her—she will die wi'out it," Brennus warns, stroking my cheek with his hand.

"That's one thing I really hate 'bout ya stinky devils—ya lie and ya lie and ya lie 'til someone beats the tar out of ya, and then ya tell the truth," Russell says, shaking his head again. "But I think I'm gonna have to wait until my girl is safe before I get to beat the snot out of ya—unless ya decided we're all dyin' here now. Then, I'll just have to move on to the next life with her, and I gotta tell ya, I'm not that upset 'bout dyin' 'cuz she's comin' with me and we'll never see ya again—or smell ya," Russell says, wrinkling his nose and rubbing it with his hand again.

"Where did ye get yer information?" Brennus asks in a calm tone, but I can tell he is completely irate by the way his jaw is clenched.

"Zoltan and Crisco told me," Russell replies with a bored look.

Hearing this, Lonan and Cavan lean menacingly toward Russell. If Brennus hadn't said something to them in his language, I'm sure that they would have attacked Russell, grenade or not. I think that Driscoll and Ultan were like brothers to the other Gancanagh and none of them likes the way Russell has gotten their names wrong. They are warriors and to disrespect them in death like that is really a bad idea, but Russell doesn't seem to care.

Brennus controls his men with whatever it is he says to them, but then Lonan says something to Brennus that I can't understand. Watching Russell, he seems to be listening to them, too. Brennus then says something else to Lonan. Russell tenses, looking over to where Lonan is standing.

"Y'all can try to see if y'all can get this grenade from me and get the pin back in it before it explodes, but I wouldn't take that chance if I didn't have a soul, Lonan," Russell says. All of the eyes in the room get wider. "Ah, all y'all didn't know I speak Gaelic? Yeah, I kinda figured that all y'all thought yer the only ones who understand it when Zoltan and Crisco kept makin' all these plans to escape me with me sittin' right next to them. It was really kinda funny, but I guess ya had to be there," he says, smiling into my eyes. I would have smiled back, if I wasn't in pain. He is such a brave, stupid, and courageous smart-ass. "But, this is gettin' lame and I think it's 'bout time I get my girl home. She needs to take a shower to get the stink off of her. Come here, Red, we're gettin' outta here," Russell says.

Trying to move, I can't straighten up enough to stand. I end up hugging Brennus tighter as a wave of pain breaks over me and I groan.

"Looks like she wants ta stay, *aingeal*," Brennus says, holding me close as he presses cold, soft kisses to my cheek.

"She's not stayin', freak! I told ya, she's leavin' here one way or another," Russell says, but he looks really concerned now.

"Ye would kill her if she chose ta be a Gancanagh?" Brennus asks him with a menacing sneer.

"Naw, I would save her before y'all could make her an undead, evil faerie," Russell replies with deliberate slowness, his finger twitching on the safety clip of the grenade.

He knows what they are! He has gotten some good information out of Ultan and Driscoll. He is just being completely insulting by calling them vampires.

"Den we are no different, ye and me," Brennus says in a thoughtful tone.

Russell's eyebrow arches. "How's that, vampire?" Russell asks.

"We both want ta kill her ta save her," Brennus replies, and Russell goes completely still.

"Ya think ya love her? Ya can't possibly know who she is to have made that kind of leap," Russell says, but he sounds sour, like the thought of Brennus wanting me like that is making him ill.

"Ye tink not? I have tasted her—she is fire and sky—life—she is as ancient as da earth and as new as an archetype—she is da brightest light and da darkest night—her blood tells her secrets—her desires. I will fulfill every one of those desires and I will love no other save her," Brennus says softly, and it wasn't said like a threat, but very, very much like a promise.

"No shit, psycho, get in line, everyone wants her! Y'all think I'm down here for my health? I know what she is. Ya don't need to tell me. But, I'm takin' her now and we can settle this later—man to man—angel to vampire—whatever," Russell says in exasperation. I can tell he is really upset about what Brennus just said.

When Brennus doesn't move to give Russell what he wants, Russell adds, "Ya just tipped yer hand, Dracula. I know ya love her, so ya aren't gonna let me blow us up, 'cuz ya won't get a 'do over' with her, like I will. Maybe we should just play poker for her next time. I'll smoke all y'all, no frickin' game in any of y'all," Russell finishes.

"She can na walk. Ye will need ta come and get her," Brennus says in a low tone. "When I bit her, it caused her extreme pain."

Russell scowls at him. "Yeah, ya love her—ya sick freak," he snarls as he walks slowly towards Brennus.

"Ta ease her suffering, give her blood of anyting—she will begin ta feel better," Brennus says, standing up with me in his arms, but he tenses when Russell reaches out to take me from him. Brennus hugs me to him tight, and then he places a soft kiss on my forehead that feels good to me because I'm beginning to feel like I'm on fire. The venom in my blood has brought a fever that is making me feel like I'm trapped in an inferno with no way out. "I will come for ye...ye're moin, *mo chroí.*"

My body leans towards Brennus' instinctively because the coldness of his touch is more soothing than the heat of Russell's body. Brennus speaks soothingly to me in Gaelic while he works to dislodge my hand from his neck. He shifts me into Russell's arms, being careful not to trip the grenade that Russell is still holding in his hand. Gently Russell cradles me in his arms and I feel his body relax a little when I settle against his heart. But, before Russell can back away, Brennus reaches over and touches Russell's face with his hand, running his strong, pale fingers over Russell's golden sun-kissed skin. Russell stills, taking his eyes off of me to look up at Brennus.

"Give me da grenade" Brennus orders, gazing into Russell's eyes. My heart nearly stops as Russell's hand twitches. I hold my breath because if the Gancanagh skin affects Russell, then he is dead where he stands once they get the grenade away from him. My stomach wrenches, but I'm no longer aware if it's from the poison in my blood or the fear that Russell will obey Brennus.

"Touch me again and yer gonna eat this grenade. Yer not my type," Russell utters with a twist of his upper lip as he slowly begins to back away from Brennus. "He's a creepy one, isn't he?" Russell asks me as he quickens his pace backward.

"You're just going to let him leave with her?" Alfred says from the corner of the room where he has been hiding from Russell. Alfred can't believe the turn of events and to have me snatched away from him again seems to be doing bad things to him. He looks twitchy and crazed.

"I will get her back, *aingeal*," Brennus says without a hint of doubt as he shadows Russell and me until we reach the middle of the hall. He stops there and watches our retreat. Brennus, illuminated now by the roaring fire next to him, clenches his fists as the firelight dances in hypnotic patterns over the planes of his face.

Alfred, hopping mad, literally begins to jump up and down while ranting about the incompetence the Gancanagh have shown throughout this entire situation. Russell shifts me in his arms, ignoring Alfred completely as he focuses on getting us out of the sunken pit we are in. I put my arms around Russell's neck as he turns his back on the Gancanagh. I can see Brennus and the others over Russell's shoulder. I have to rest my chin on his shoulder because I'm having trouble holding it up. Russell is hurrying to the entrance of the cave, but Brennus doesn't move as he calls to me saying, "*Mo chroí*...a gift for ye, before ye go." And then my heart nearly stops when Brennus says, "Kill him."

In an instant, the Gancanagh fall on Alfred like a pack of hounds on a cornered fox. Alfred's flesh is being torn from his body while his screams of agony echo off the walls of the cavern. The feeding frenzy is heightening my senses, as the smell of Alfred's blood assails me, causing my mouth to water. Digging my nails into Russell's back, I try to keep from struggling against him as the darkness within me is urging me to join the family behind me.

While Gancanagh continue devouring Alfred, my gaze shifts to Brennus. He is watching our retreat with longing and need in his eyes. I can't stop the slow smile that creeps to the corners of my lips as I gaze back at him. I'm sure that I look as evil as I feel as I raise my shaking fingers to my lips. I touch them gently together, and then turning my fingers, I blow Brennus a kiss to thank him for what he has just ordered done to Alfred. Raw desire shows on Brennus' face in response.

Russell, reaching the wall of the cave that we will need to scale to get out of the mine, whispers in my ear, "I need yer help, Red. Can ya hold onto my neck and the grenade while I carry ya up this wall?" he asks with uncertainty and anxiety etched on his face.

"I don't know...pain..." I say, panting and trying to remain as lucid as I can in order to help him, but the evil darkness is growing in me and I'm afraid of what I'll do if he hands me the grenade.

"Well, I can't leave ya down here, so do yer best. If it doesn't work out, I'll see ya in the next life...and I love ya, Red...God, I love ya so much," he says, squeezing me tight in his arms and burying his face in my neck. "And I'm sorry it took me so long to come for ya," he breathes against my ear. He's in pain, too. Maybe it's as bad as my own.

"I love you too, Russell. Give me the grenade. I won't drop it. I promise," I whisper through my clenched teeth, beating back the pain. Russell hands me the bomb, waiting only long enough to be sure that I have a firm grip on it and that my arms are wrapped securely around his neck, before he begins to climb the wall.

When we reach the top of the wall, Russell sits on the side of it, pulling me up over the edge. He takes off the belts that were strapped to his chest, dropping them back down into the hole. Then, he reaches for the grenade that I'm holding in my hand.

"No!" I say fiercely, holding the grenade as tight as I can in my hand so that he won't take it away from me and drop it down the hole.

Looking stunned, Russell's hand comes up to cover mine as I clutch the grenade. Staring into my eyes, I think he sees something in them that scares him because he shivers, and then he scowls at me just as fierce. "Ya got that Gancanagh's poison in ya right now, so I know ya don't really mean to let those cold, creepy freaks live. Not after what they did to ya—to all those people who have gone down there and never gotten out."

As I'm shaken by what he says, he uses the opportunity to pull the grenade from my hand, dropping it instantly down the hole. He doesn't hesitate, but uses all of his angel speed to scoop me up off the ground and run with me out of the mouth of the copper mine and into the darkness of the overcast night sky. The ground shakes beneath us in vibrating tremors as the grenade explodes, detonating all of the other grenades that had been thrown down there before it. Clouds of smoke and debris spew out of the hole in the ground. He carries me past several lifeless bodies of Gancanagh that I recognize as being the sentry guards who had caught me on my prior escape attempt.

Russell continues to run through the hills and down the mountainous terrain. We pass through dense maple and oak trees that shroud the graceful slopes. It's all rushing by me in a blur as my head lies against Russell's chest. Reaching a clearing, I see a silver shape ahead of us that is as familiar as the shape of a lover to my mind. It's Reed's car, the Audi R-Eight, and I can't wrap my head around how Russell has come to be driving Reed's car...unless Reed's dead and no longer needs his car.

Before I can ask Russell any questions, he is shoving me into the passenger side of the car and slamming the door shut. Getting in the driver's side, he starts the car and slams his foot down on the accelerator. "How did you…" I begin to ask him feebly, but I have to stop as the smell of the interior of the car hits me. It smells just like Reed and leather. The scent is so wonderful and gut wrenching, that I turn my face toward the leather seat to get closer to the smell of the one I have loved like no other. As the scent overwhelms me, I writhe in pain from the agonizing need to crawl back to the cave behind us. It's a need that would have me give in to my desire to drink the blood of the one who has just professed to love me, and no other, for eternity.

Shrinking against the seat, I hold on tight to it while Russell tries to gain control of the car as it fishtails and skids down the dirt terrain of the old road we are on. The road leads away from the copper mine—away from the family that desperately wants me back.

"Damn, I knew there were more ways out of that hell hole," Russell growls as he sees the cars that need no headlights come into view behind us. Sweat seeps down his brow as he shifts the car into a faster gear, burying the needle when we skid onto the paved road that winds away from the hills behind us. "I thought I had disabled all their cars before I went in, but I guess I missed a couple. They're like a nest of ants with all of their tunnels going clear through those hills," Russell says. Then, he has a massive shiver, like his flesh is crawling at the thought of the Gancanagh. "They shouldn't be able to catch us, Red, they're in SUVs and this car has some balls," he reassures me. The Gancanagh, making it to the pavement behind us, rapidly lose ground to the Audi's engine and aerodynamics.

So many questions are running through my mind, but I'm incapable of asking any of them. Curling up into a ball, I pant as my fever causes scary hallucinations to skip through my consciousness. Russell is talking to me, but he sounds like the old VHS tape I had when I was really little. I had a favorite movie with princesses that I used to play over and over, until one day, the tape jammed in the machine, causing the princess to speak in a dark, deep voice that sounded like the devil had possessed her and all of her fairytale-land friends.

A part of me is attempting to rationalize what is happening to me, equating my reaction to being bitten by a rattlesnake. But then, I glance over at Russell and see his face distorting and shifting in twisted patterns of flesh. I press myself against the door of the car, getting as far away from him as I can in the tiny space. When my eyes focus on the passenger window, I shy away from it, too. Sharp-talon ravens fly against the glass, attacking us. Their black wings beat the windshield like mallets, striking it with shrill cries that scream, "Nevermore."

My half-lidded eyes are blurring in and out of focus as I attempt to maintain my grasp on reality. We drive for an eternity around the inside of a paper cup until we finally shoot out the bottom of it. Lynette and Autumn come floating by riding on the library copier. They are looking in the change slot to see if it contains any money. Sneering at me from outside the car, Lynnette's cell phone is ringing. She tries to hand it to me through the window of the car. I don't want to answer it, but it won't stop ringing. Taking it from her grasp, I hold it to my ear. Keegan's voice begins telling me all of the ways he is going to tear me apart when he gets back from Hell. Dropping the phone back out the window, heavy air comes rushing in, permeating the interior of the car with the scent of water, indicating that we are near the sea…or, the river.

A cacophony is building in waves of vibrations, beating against my chest, while pine trees race by me in a blur of dark shadows. I rest my head against the seatback, staring outside while Cherubim race alongside the car, smiling at me. One has golden hair that flows and streams behind him from the velocity of his powerful wings. His pale blue wings beat powerfully and his leonine features, intensely beautiful to my eyes, relay a message that I can't understand fully… something about Brennus and retribution…it is his misfortune to burn for me as others have burned for him.

As I lean forward to ask this angel what he means, he is gone in an instant and everything stops moving. I become aware that I'm sitting next to Russell. We are in the rear parking lot of the small grocery store where we shop for food. It's the one near our apartment in Houghton. Russell parks the car and I'm trying to listen really hard to what he's saying, but since his face is melting in waxy streaks, I'm finding it hard to focus on the words. Reaching out to me, Russell attempts to hold my hand, but I nearly scream because the slightest pressure from his soothing caress causes me searing pain.

Leaping out of the car, Russell slams the door shut. He approaches the back door of the grocery store, pushing it in with ease as if it is made of newspaper instead of steel. Agonizing moments elapse as I wait for Russell to come back out. When I gaze over to the empty driver's seat, the door slowly opens and Brennus' sleek figure eases into it. With a whimper, I press my back against the passenger door. The handle digs into the small of my back, while I look around hopelessly for a means of escape. Brennus stares at me with mock pity on his face as his teeth *click*, engaging them so that he can pierce his skin. Blood, seeping from deep wells in his wrist, makes my head spin. Reaching out with a shaking hand, I pull his arm to my lips, tasting cold, thick blood that instantly cools the burning in my throat.

I have no control over my reaction as I suck and swallow more and more of the salty, metallic-tasting liquid. But, something begins to happen the more I consume. The voice speaking to me now is not how I remember Brennus sounding. This voice sounds more like Russell's—the slow, southern twang that he uses when he is trying to get me to listen to reason, or when I'm really sad and he is trying to comfort me.

It takes me a few moments to realize that Russell is in the car with me, not Brennus. Russell's strong fingers are holding a straw to my lips, allowing me to sip awkwardly from a large, clear-plastic deli container that they use to dispense potato salad. "That's it, that's my girl. Yer okay…I got ya…just drink this venison blood and we'll go. Yer almost done, Red, just pretend it's a smoothie or somethin'," Russell says. When the straw starts making a loud, slurping noise, he pulls the cup back from my lips and asks, "Do ya need more?"

"I…" Pain grips me again, but it's less intense than it was a second ago. Russell pulls another container from the floor of the car, and taking the lid off of it, he sticks the straw in it and holds it to my lips again. I drink the second one as fast as the first.

"More?" he asks when I finish the second deli quart. Reluctantly, I nod my head as he pulls the third one from the floor of the car. "Can ya hold this one while I drive the car?" Russell asks, looking around the lot for threats. "I want to get outta here just in case there is a silent alarm in the store, or…" he trails off, but I understand that he is not comfortable with our position.

I grip the plastic cup between shaking hands, fumbling to get the straw in my mouth again. "Here, Red, never mind," Russell says, taking the cup back from me and holding it again. I drink it as fast as I can, and when I am finished, he asks if I need more. I'm still in pain, but my anxiety to leave the vicinity of our apartment is more pressing than my need to have total relief from the gnawing pain inside me.

"Go," I whisper, because my throat is too tight to say more. Russell doesn't need me to say more. He chucks the empty cartons out the window and creeps away from the back of the store as quiet as possible. He takes obscure side streets out of town, maintaining the speed limit and turning on his lights, so that we can look like model humans leaving town in a human way.

Russell keeps glancing at me every few seconds, probably to assure himself that I'm actually here with him in the car, as much as to see how I'm doing. He begins talking when he starts to shake. I think he's trying hard not to go into shock because his thoughts are scattered. He is rambling about things that aren't very important, in the grand scheme of things, but I recognize it for what it is, it's the need to focus on something other than the horror he just experienced.

"Angie, ya know coach Blake's wife, told me 'bout how she makes blood sausage. It's one of those sketchy things that the Yoopers make up here. Ya remember how I went over to their house for breakfast a few weeks ago?" he asks, and I nod. "Well, she made some for us and it was kind of nasty, but I ate it because I didn't want to hurt her feelins," Russell says. I nod again numbly because it's just like him to eat something he hated just so he wouldn't hurt someone's feelings. "It was black and had a kind of burnt, piney taste to it. She thought I liked it, so she started to tell me how to make it. She said I would have to go to the meat counter at the grocery store because I needed to get a pint of venison blood to mix in with the meat. I had no idea what I would be doin' with that information this week," he mutters, blowing out a deep breath and shaking his head.

"I've done a lot of stuff this week I never thought I'd be doin'..." he says numbly. "Do ya know why we're here right now?" he asks rhetorically. I shake my head slowly. "That annoyin' door is why we're here right now. If we had been in any other apartment in Houghton, I would be dead and you'd be...well, not here..." he says, trailing off. "They sent two of them to our apartment to get me. I could smell them outside the door, feel the coldness clear through it. Ya know how when ya open the door, it knocks ya back off the step if ya don't know ya have to step back when it opens?" he asks me fast, his speech increasing in speed along with his heartbeat as the adrenaline of the remembered attack comes back to haunt him. "Well, I had been makin' myself some eggs when I heard them creepin' up the inside stairs to the door. I had the fryin' pan in my hands when they just 'bout reached the door to the apartment. I bum rushed the door, sendin' it crashin' open on them, which knocked Ultan into Driscoll and sent them down the stairs. I followed them down and wacked them both with my fryin' pan in the head."

His hand shakes when he brings it to his neck, rubbing it absently as he watches the road ahead and the rearview mirror intermittently. "I knocked 'em both out cold, so I had to carry them back up to the apartment. I tied 'em up—I gathered up some stuff in bags—the money—I threw it in the car. I bolted over to the library to get ya—to tell ya we had to go, but there was a huge crowd millin' 'round outside and I couldn't find ya. You had disappeared. I ran in—I saw that conference room on the main floor—I saw a chair had been flung through the window—I hoped…maybe ya got away—if someone was after ya, and then I got afraid because I thought ya might go back to the apartment—I left the evil freaks tied up there. So, I went back, but ya never came home…" he says, his expression bleak.

"They killed Mrs. Strauss—they even killed her cat. I don't know why they had to kill the cat, too. Maybe it was hissin' at them or somethin', I don't know, but they drained that poor old lady—left her body in her big, green armchair," he says. The grief he is feeling is etched on his face. Then, something changes in him, shifts, and his face hardens.

"Naw…" he says in a soft growl—the look of cold detachment, "I've done things this week that I never could've imagined last week. I thought that there was a lot of human left in me, but I can tell ya, Red, there isn't. I had no mercy for Ultan or Driscoll…even when they begged me…and they begged me, Red—they begged. I had to move them out of the apartment. I torched the place so no one can find anythin' that will lead them to us. I took them to our trainin' spot and worked on them there. They told me everythin'. They told me how they would turn ya—how Brennus probably already had ya in a cell and wouldn't give ya enough water. I was out of my mind, but it took me four days to get that information from them. I had to really hurt them, Red—I did some things to them that made me have to leave afterward and puke my guts out, but there was no way they were dyin' without tellin' me everythin'."

He sits quiet for a little while, driving through the dark night toward Marquette. I can't ask him where we are going. I can't think, even as the pain is slowly receding, I'm still not able to form the words. I just sit next to him, listening to him talk as we both continue to shake from trauma. "I thought I was buyin' those grenades to kill ya, Red," he says in a near whisper, turning to look at me. Raw pain shows in his eyes as tears well up in mine for what he has been through. Reaching out, I find his hand. It's warm and sweaty while mine is ice cold and dry. I feel him squeeze my hand.

"I had to find that gun and knife show that traveled south to Iron Mountain. I found the guy I'd bought the swords from and he knew a guy that hooked me up with the military arms. I told them it was for some minin' I planned on doin', but they really didn't care as long as I had the money," he says with a humorless laugh. "I planned on goin' down there, findin' ya, and settin' us both free. I hoped yer soul had already moved on, but I wasn't gonna let yer body suffer down there alone, so I planned on us just movin' on. If yer soul was with Freddie, then I figured he would have to release it if my bomb blew him to smithereens."

"Suicide mission," I say, and my voice sounds thick and raspy.

"Yeah, I guess so. I thought I'd pick a fight I couldn't win," he says. "It turns out I had a royal flush," he adds with an ironic smile. "That thing loves ya, Red," he whispers as all of the hair stands up on his arm again. "That thing killed Freddie for ya."

"Yes," I croak. "I'm his favorite slave."

"Naw...yer wrong...he is yer slave, he just doesn't know it yet," Russell says. "He's gonna go mad without ya. He's gonna twist and burn for ya, and then he's gonna do anythin' to get ya back...and I don't know if I can stop him alone. I can't believe we've made it this far...there are over a dozen of them..."

"I know—I know them all by name," I whisper. "I killed one... Keegan...I murdered him," I confess, and I know that my face is turning white as I say it.

"What happened?" he asks.

I shake my head, "They made me fight him to see if I'd been training. He cut me...he was going to hurt me and I...he said he was going to kill you when he found you," I explain as a tear escapes my eye. "They gave us knives, so I got behind him and I slit his throat...he didn't bleed like I thought he would...it didn't pump out of his neck, but it seeped down the sides...since I nearly cut his head off...he died."

"Oh my God, Red—they made you fight one of them?" Russell asks incredulously. I nod and watch his lips press together as his breathing increases. "Did he put ya in a cell...did he ask ya 'bout wantin' water?" Russell asks, and I nod again. "Then, how is it that ya still have a soul, Red?" he asks in confusion.

"Figured it out...the game. Decided not to play..." I rasp, my throat is beginning to feel cracked and dry and I wish I had some water.

"Ah, so it was like that, huh? Ya told him ya didn't like his game so you were takin' yer ball and goin' home?" Russell says, smiling a little in the corners of his mouth. I can't smile, but I nod because I guess that is about right. I was taking my soul and going...wherever I'm allowed to go. I want to tell him about my Uncle Jim and how he had been there and held my hand when I needed him, but I can't form the words.

"Put an IV in...brought me back," I say, holding up my arm where the IV had been, but there are no marks there anymore to show him.

"He couldn't stand losin' ya," Russell says in a thoughtful tone, studying me. "I bet they're never supposed to do that. It's supposed to be a choice, accordin' to Driscoll...he said you can choose to die or to become Gancanagh. Driscoll said he never knew of anyone choosin' not to become a Gancanagh. But, Brennus took that choice away from ya...Freddie must've been really convincin'..."

"Portrait...Alfred gave him the portrait," I say, and all of the color drains from his face. Russell knows the portrait that I'm talking about—he used to go visit it daily when it was on display at school.

"So it *is* all 'bout ya. I was pretty sure when I saw ya sittin' on his lap tonight. I kept askin' Ultan 'why us.' I mean, we're not even faeries, which is a big deal to them," Russell says, looking at me in the eye as he explains. "Ultan said, normally, they wouldn't even consider changin' someone unless it's a faerie. He said they usually leave other beings alone–they just feed off of humans. He said that Brennus heard our story, but wasn't gonna bother even checkin' us out—but Ultan said somethin' happened and he changed his mind. He saw yer portrait and he had to have ya," Russell says the last part with bitter conviction.

"I think..." I start to say, but have to clear my throat because it feels like I've been drinking sand. Russell notices and reaches back in one of the duffle bags in the back. Rummaging around while he drives the car, he manages to extract a bottle of water. Handing it to me, I gratefully take it, drinking half of it before I am again able to speak. "I think that, in a messed up kind of way, Brennus is trying to help me," I murmur as a scowl forms on Russell's lips.

"How is makin' ya an undead, evil parasite gonna help ya?" Russell barks in anger. He is still shaking, but his anger seems to be getting that part more under control.

"Without a soul, the Fallen would no longer be interested in me. I would be evil...they would be down with me...the enemy of my enemy is my friend," I say, taking another sip of water while he processes what I'm telling him. "Brennus isn't afraid of divine angels. He's confidant that the family could take care of me if anything hunted me... but he didn't count on an angel coming for me who didn't plan to survive," I say, and my voice sounds hollow. "One that had a soul and was not afraid to choose to die, rather than let me submit to them."

"Yeah...he wants ya to be his girl—*mo chroí*—it means 'my heart,'" he says, and he pronounces it "mo kree" in a perfect imitation of the way Brennus had pronounced it.

"What does *a ghra* and *muirnin* mean?" I ask, and see him grit his teeth.

"*A ghra* means love...like beloved and *muirnin* means sweetheart," Russell says, gripping the steering wheel with both hands and crushing it a little. He notices right away and eases his hands off of it gently. "Those bites on yer neck...they don't seem to be gettin' any better. Did he say anythin' about puttin' somethin' on them to make them heal?" Russell asks.

I shake my head no as my fingertips brush over the bite marks on my neck. They are still oozing blood, not coagulating and crusting like a normal cut. "It must be from the venom...maybe it stops the victim from healing," I say, seeing the grim expression on Russell's face.

"Maybe Buns will know what to do 'bout them," Russell says absently.

I still. "What?" I ask.

"We're meetin' her in Marquette. Brownie's there, too. I called them when I made my plan to go down in the copper mine," he says, not looking at me. He seems defensive, like he is expecting an ass kicking from me for calling them. "I wanted them to know what happened to us. I wanted them to let my family know that I wasn't ever comin' back, but that it was my choice."

"What did they say?" I ask, because I can't ask about Reed. If he is dead, then I am, too.

"They demanded to know where I was, and then they were here in a few hours, drivin' this car and makin' plans to go with me into the mine," he says with a grim expression. "I had to convince them that it was likely that you were now Gancanagh, and that we weren't ever comin' out of the hole...even if they came with me," he adds, and we both are choked up because he had gone down there to die with me.

"Brownie made me promise that if we did make it out, we would meet them in Marquette so that we can discuss what to do next," Russell says.

"What about Buns...what did she say?" I ask.

"She said she would see us in a few hours," he replies as he gives me a half-smile. "She wouldn't even consider that we weren't comin' out of that place. She wouldn't accept it—she just wouldn't."

"Why did you go in there, Russell? You know that I want you to live...why didn't you just go with them?" I ask. It was such a stupid thing for him to do. He had no idea that I was not a Gancanagh before he came down to get me. If they had caught him, they could've made me hunt him, like he's food. If I had been turned, I may have fed on him like he was nothing to me...like I hadn't loved him forever. That thought makes me feel twisted and torn.

"Why did ya come into the Seven-Eleven with Freddie?" he

counters in a low tone.

"That was different…I had to…"

"Yeah, well, I had to, too. I love ya every bit as much as ya love me," he replies.

"Russell…you should stay away from me. I'm no good for anyone. I'm like a magnet for—evil faeries and Fallen and angels that don't know any better than to want me. Until I met the Gancanagh, I thought that I wasn't evil—that I didn't crave darkness—but now I'm learning that…" I stop when he reaches out to take my hand again. I pull it back from him. "No, Russell, listen to me. Do you know what I did when Brennus ordered Alfred killed?" I ask, watching his eyes.

He shakes his head and says, "No."

"I blew him a kiss," I admit, remembering the giddiness and euphoria that had pushed it's way through the pain in that moment. It was the moment when my enemy had been reduced to a feast on the floor of the place he had helped make my prison. It was the moment when my uncle was avenged for what was done to him because of me. I know that a part of me loves Brennus for giving me that gift, and that scares me more than I can say.

"Red…ya got his toxic venom pollutin' yer body. It's distortin' yer reality. You just spent some time in hell and they worked ya over pretty good down there, I can tell," Russell says, trying to reason with me. "Freddie killed what was essentially the only parent ya ever had and terrorized ya for months," he adds, and when I won't look at him, he grabs me by my chin so that I have to look at him. "He planned yer total annihilation and I'm glad he's dead, and if I could've been the one to do it I would've enjoyed it, but it would've taken me longer 'cuz I think he died too quickly. He should've suffered longer and that doesn't make me evil. That makes me an angel."

"It was Alfred, Russell…he turned in Reed and Zee. I betrayed them. Alfred couldn't turn them in while I was with them because then he wouldn't get my soul. But, when I left them, I took that reason with me," I say. I can't look at Russell because the shame I feel is strangling me. "Are they dead?" I whisper.

"Red, this is not yer fault…" Russell begins.

In a rough voice, I repeat, "Are they dead?"

"I don't know," he admits. "The girls are having trouble gettin' any information because they aren't Powers so…"

"So, they don't have the rank to pull," I say, finishing for him.

"Yeah," he frowns. "We're gonna take Zee's plane to his island. Once we're there, we're gonna work on findin' out where they are. In the meantime, Buns has some contacts that are gonna…"

"No," I murmur.

"No?" he asks. When I don't answer him he asks, "No to what?"

"No, I'm not going to the island," I reply.

"Yer not?" he asks, and I shake my head. "Then, where are we goin'?" he asks in confusion.

"I'm going to Dominion," I say. "You are going with the girls to the island."

"THE HELL YA ARE!" Russell yells at me as he buries the needle of the car and turns the headlights off so that humans won't see us. He is breathing hard and staring at me like he would like to strangle me. "How is goin' in there gonna help them, Red?"

"I haven't worked that part out yet, but I can't let them die for me. I have to try," I reply.

"Yer just gonna make them look like traitors. You will confirm what they are suspected of," he says, trying to reason with me.

"I'm not a Nephilim. There is a gray area here that we can exploit. We're different...what did Brennus say...I'm as new as an archetype. If you have a new model of something, you wouldn't necessarily know what to do with it. They could've been studying me to see if I'm evil...not protecting me, but protecting the world from me," I say, looking at Russell. "Until they decided if I needed to be destroyed."

"No," he says, and then wipes his hand against his mouth. "You don't even know if they will let ya in the front door before they attack ya," he points out, talking through his clenched teeth again. "It's the worst plan I've ever heard."

"How can it be worse than your last plan?" I counter.

"Because there's no way out of it for ya," comes his dark reply.

"But, other than that, it's a good angle, right?" I say with a calm I don't feel.

"How's tradin' yer life for theirs better?" he asks.

"Two for one," I reply.

"Or, all three of ya dead," Russell says with pessimism.

"Maybe they won't kill me. You know, I'm like a danger magnet and they love that. They eat it up for breakfast," I argue.

"Red, do me this one solid and just get on the plane when we get to the airport in Marquette. We'll come up with somethin' that isn't a suicide mission," he says, really angry now.

"It makes sense, Russell," I say in a whisper.

"How does walkin' into a room full of assassins that have been huntin' for ya make sense?" he asks, not at all sorry that I'm having a hard time arguing with him because I feel like I'm dying.

"You said yourself that you don't know if you can stop Brennus from getting me back all on your own. He's going to find me, Russell—you know he will. Brennus has so much money it's sick and he will use all of his resources to find us." I have to pause to take a few panting breaths. "He has tasted me and he wants me—and I know for sure that I won't be able to resist him next time," I admit, beginning to shake again with fear as I remember the terrifying trip I just experienced. It had felt like I was slowly losing my mind. "We need Reed and Zee if we are going to survive. If they don't survive, then all of this was for nothing," I say, working the angle that I know he will be unable to dispute. "Brennus is going to come after you now, too. He wants you dead because you killed Ultan and Driscoll and because you are my soul mate. I can't stop him alone and I don't think the Reapers will fare very well against the touch of the Gancanagh. It will probably affect them and there is no telling what they will do to our girls."

"But—" Russell says as he watches me shake.

"Russell, he is ancient and I don't even know if he is from this world. Do you hear what I'm saying? If the initiation into their little family is that brutal, what is it going to be like when they really want to torture us?" I ask harshly. "If I go to Dominion, at least we have a shot," I add, wrapping my arms around myself. I'm crashing, just like a junkie coming off of a drug and my body is reacting like I'm detoxing. I'm sweating and trembling with hot and cold flashes. Laying my head back against the seat, I smell Reed all around me.

"If yer goin', I'm goin'," Russell states firmly.

"No, they don't know about you," I reply. "It might freak them out if they think I can make more of us."

"Can ya, do ya think?" he asks in a serious tone.

"I don't know and I wouldn't try because I wouldn't wish being hunted like this on anyone—except maybe Alfred, but he's not doing much of anything anymore," I reply, and I begin to laugh hysterically because I'm no longer in control of my emotions. Tears spring to my eyes as I try to stop the inappropriate laughter that is bubbling up inside of me. *I must sound possessed*, I think, wiping tears away from my eyes that the laughter brings on.

"Why can't ya ever listen to me? Why can't ya just do what I tell ya?" Russell asks me with lassitude in his tone. Slumping his shoulders, I hear him say, "I just can't figure out how to save ya…why won't ya let me save ya, Red?"

Those are the same words he said to me before, when he had woken up on the floor of the convenience store after Alfred had stabbed him in the leg. "You can't save me, Russ. God, I wish you could," I whisper. "I wish that I could crawl into yer lap and just rest there forever. I would, you know, if it were that easy—I think I was very happy there once—but I can't now—that's not my destiny anymore," I want to sob, to cry my heart out because I miss him and us.

"Yer exhausted, Red, and sick," he says with a sad look in his eyes.

"You know, I just want a home—a family, somewhere that I belong—there isn't any place like that, is there? I can't hide anymore. There is no place to hide because something bad will always find us. Remember when you told me that this is all meant and we can't stop what's coming?" I ask, seeing him nod. "Well, I believe you. We can't stop what's coming."

Seeing pain in his eyes, I know that there is nothing I can say that will stop it. I crawl over the console, breaking his grip on the steering wheel as I curl up in his lap and rest my head against his chest. I begin to sob big choking cries because my body aches everywhere and I'm so afraid. "Thank you for saving me, Russell," I say as I snuffle and weep into his chest. "I didn't want to die down there."

His arm wraps around my waist, pulling me tighter against him. He rests his chin on the top of my head. "It's all right...everythin' is gonna be all right," he murmurs in a soft southern drawl, trying to reassure me, but we both know he is lying. He holds me in his arms as he drives through the night, my ear pressed against his chest. I fall asleep listening to the steady beating of his heart.

CHAPTER 15

Goodbye

The private airport in Marquette is small; it's just one airstrip with a couple of hangars to house planes, or any other aeronautic vehicle one might possess. When we pull up to a hangar that Buns has designated as the rendezvous, it's little more than sheets of pressed metal riveted together to form a frame for the concrete floor and tin roof to enclose.

However dilapidated the hangar is, the contrast of the vehicle that the hangar houses is shocking, if one is inclined to be shocked by the strictures of angels. I'm not at all surprised that Zephyr's plane is turning out to be a jet. Unfolding myself from Russell's lap, I crawl back into the passenger seat of the car and stare at the sleek lines of the aircraft that is painted a high-glossed, jet black. *What else?*

"Can ya walk, Red?" Russell asks me as he opens his door and the dome light turns on in the car. I shield my eyes from it because they are still used to the darkness of the cave and firelight.

"I don't know—" I begin to say, before I am interrupted. My car door is wrenched open and I am unceremoniously dragged through it and group-hugged by Brownie and Buns, whom I never see coming.

"You are in so much trouble, Evie," Brownie says as a tear escapes from her eye when she pulls back to look at me. "If you ever do that again, *I* will kill you," she says furiously, before hugging me again. Buns doesn't say anything. She just sniffles and hugs me tighter. "Come here, Russell," Brownie orders. When he nears us, she pulls his arm so that he will come closer, and then grips his shoulder to pull him into the group hug. "You did it, Russell! Good job," Brownie whispers to him.

"Had I known I would be surrounded by three beautiful females, I would've called y'all sooner," Russell says, hugging back and pressing a kiss on the top of her platinum-blond hair, and then one on Buns's honey-blond head. Then, he says in a serious tone, "Thanks for the car. All y'all were right, we needed it. I don't know if we were followed or not, so we had better get on the plane. Where should I put the car?" he asks.

Brownie and Russell break away from the hug, but Buns doesn't let go of me as she continues to hug me tight to her, crying softly into my hair. I cry too, even though I'm amazed that I have any tears left to cry, since I thought I had cried them all into Russell's chest on the way here. Russell gets back into the car, pulling it into the hangar as Brownie guides him in. He parks it next to the jet, leaving the keys in it, and then he begins to pull out the bags he had stowed in the trunk. Presumably, it's our money and some of our things from our apartment, but I don't ask him.

Finally, Buns pulls back from me and scans me from head to toe. Her eyes come back up to my neck that I'm aware is still bleeding. Self-consciously, I touch the puncture marks that brand me as Brennus', just as if I were his cattle and he had branded his mark into my flesh.

"Sweetie, those boots are hot, they make your legs go on for miles," Buns says, referring to my black, thigh-high, suede boots that hug my legs like stockings. Buns bites her bottom lip to stop it from quivering.

I clear my throat so that I can answer her. "Thanks," I say, trying to take a deep breath, but it hitches a little as I go on, "the Gancanagh have an evil eye for fashion."

Buns's eyebrows come together in a scowl. "I'm going to carve Alfred into a thousand pieces and feed them all to the griffins," Buns says in anger as another tear escapes her. She dashes it away with the back of her hand.

"Too late, the Gancanagh already ate him," I whisper, and see her eyes grow wide.

"Oh my God, sweetie! What happened?" she asks, and then she notices me sway on my feet. She clutches me under my arm, leading me toward the shiny black jet in front of us.

Silently, we enter the aircraft and I don't know why I was expecting it to be like a commuter plane with rows of seats crammed in it, but it's nothing like what I had expected. The décor of the plane is black and camel with accents of butter cream and off-white. It's elegant with large, graceful seats clustered in several different areas. The seats are covered in black leather that's so soft and supple, that I can imagine falling asleep in one of them if I'm not careful. But there is no reason to sleep in a chair because the plane has a couple of bedrooms with large beds that can be used for that purpose.

Buns leads me by a kitchen. It's equipped with stainless steel appliances and highly polished dark wood cabinetry, which makes it seem very sleek and masculine. The bathroom in the back of the plane, which is inside the master suite, is just as impressive as the rest of the place. Under different circumstances, I would've felt elated by it, but instead, I feel like I'm an intruder on a plane owned by someone I have bitterly betrayed.

Turning on the shower to warm it up for me, Buns pulls out toiletries. She rests a towel on the sink, along with a black silk robe that is several sizes too big for me. "After you are finished in the shower, I have something that we can put on your…cuts," she says, instead of bites. I just nod, not looking her in the eyes because I don't want to start crying again.

Before she can walk away, I blurt out, "Are they alive?" I know that she doesn't know, but I want to see if she still has hope that they are alive, or if she has lost hope.

"Yes," she says fiercely, her hands balling into fists.

"Good. Take us to Dominion and I'll give Zee back to you," I say in a low tone as a war begins within her cornflower-blue eyes.

"We are going to Zee's—" Buns begins, but I cut her off.

"No, I'm not going to Zee's island. I'm going to Dominion. You can take me, or I can take Reed's car now and try to find them on my own, but I'm going with or without your help. I'm going to take a shower now, and when I get out, you can tell me what you've decided," I say with authority. I strip off my Gancanagh clothing and hand them to Buns, saying, "Burn these for me." Then I get into the shower and try to wash the stink off of me as Russell had suggested earlier.

I let the shower wash away the sticky, sweet smell that has been clinging to me for days, but there is no water that will wash my soul clean of my memories, however much my spirit is desperately wishing for it. I had let Brennus break me and I would have given him whatever he wanted if Russell hadn't shown up to free me from him. I have to cover my mouth so that no one will hear the racking sobs that are tearing out of me. Slowly, I gain control of myself. I watch my blood mix with the water going down the drain from the bites on my neck that won't heal.

Turning the shower off, I step out, tying the belt of the robe that Buns has left for me. When I walk out into the bedroom, I find Russell lying on the bed. He looks like he had probably sat down on the end of it, but had fallen back on it in exhaustion because his feet are still on the floor. One arm is shielding his eyes from the light that is on overhead. I walk to the switch, turning it off so that it won't wake him up. Walking toward the door that leads out to the common area, I plan to ask Buns if I can borrow something to wear, but I stop when I hear Russell speak.

"Red, what can I say to make ya change yer mind and not do this?" he asks, his voice sounding pained.

"I have to go. You know that, don't you?" I reply as I turn and approach the bed.

"Knowin' something with yer head is very different than knowin' it with yer heart...or yer soul," Russell says without lifting his arm from his eyes. "My head knows why yer doin' it...but my heart can't see it. I love Zee like a brother, but if he comes back and ya don't..." he doesn't say anymore because he doesn't have to, I know what he means.

"Russell...I...I can't do anything else. I have to go." When I see his look of anguish, I crawl up on the bed next to him and press my wet head against his chest. His arm snakes around my waist, pressing me closer to him. "If it was you in there, I would go...I would give you whatever I have and whatever I am to protect you...we are linked, you and I, but I'm also linked to Reed. I owe it to him, too."

"He's not gonna thank ya for goin' in there and riskin' yer life for his. He's gonna be really pissed off," he says, and I believe him. Reed will probably be extremely angry. I betrayed him, and then I show up to "protect" him...*yeah, he's going to be livid.*

"I'm not operating under any false hopes, Russell," I reply as I lie perfectly still, listening to him breathing. "You think I don't know what those guys are going to think, if they are still alive? They are going to think I betrayed them and they are going to be hostile toward any attempts that I make to help them because first and foremost in a Power's mind is that they don't need protection," I say as the thought of what I'm about to do causes my stomach to tighten painfully.

"Yeah, well that might just be a male trait 'cuz I felt the same way when I saw ya in the Seven-Eleven with Freddie," his says in a stern tone.

"Yeah, but you got over it," I say.

"Red, ya almost tore yer heart out for me, it was kind of hard for me to stay mad at ya," he replies as he sighs heavily. "But, I wanted to be mad at ya."

I lift my head thoughtfully, looking him over to fix his image in my memory. This is the first time I have seen Russell without his wings since before the Gancanagh took me. His sandy hair is a mess and needs to be cut, falling well past his eyes, but it looks sexy anyway. His skin is so smooth now, angelic in every way, tough and luminous. He could probably use a shave, but the scruffiness he is sporting just makes him look more rugged and powerful. He looks so young without his wings, but looks are so deceiving, because although his body is young, his soul is old.

"How old are we, Russell?" I ask tiredly, lying my head back down.

"Old," he says.

"Have we always been human, I mean, before this?" I ask, because now we are both human and angel, but what could we have been before…now that we have proof that there are other beings out there just walking around and breathing the same air.

"Ya know, Red, that's a good question…I'll have to look and see, but later…when I can think. I've been up for days and I'm havin' trouble thinkin' right now."

"Oh…okay…I feel really old…ancient…" I say drowsily. Hearing Russell's heavy breathing, I know that if I continue to lay here for even one more second, I will be asleep too and I can't do that yet. Pushing myself up off Russell's chest, I crawl off the bed. Standing up, I feel light-headed.

Tightening the belt of the robe more securely around me, I push the bedroom door open to the common area. Buns is curled up in one of the big chairs that faces the bedroom. She probably heard our entire conversation, but it doesn't bother me because I have no secrets from her anymore. Now that the worst has happened, I can see no reason to ever lie or mislead her again. She watches me take the seat across from hers. "Where's Brownie?" I ask as the plane begins moving forward, taxiing the runway of the small airstrip.

"She's going to fly us to Quebec," Buns replies, getting up and going to the bar to pour me a glass of water. "I would take you up there, but she's really upset about where we're going, so I think we had better leave her alone for a while until she calms down."

"Thank you," I say as she hands me the glass, and then she picks up a lap blanket from one of the other chairs, wrapping it around my shoulders.

"What's in Quebec?" I ask her before I down my water, watching her sit back in her seat across from me.

"Dominion is in Quebec—well, a private island in the Gulf of St. Lawrence. There is an estate there where Pagan and company took Zee and Reed after they left Crestwood. As far as we can tell, they are still there, but our intel is not very good because Powers are really good at keeping secrets," she says. "Almost as good as Seraphim are."

The water I just swallowed almost chokes me, but I manage to get it down. I set my glass on the beautifully polished wood table between us and look into her eyes. "I'm sorry, Buns—I never meant for anything like this to happen. I thought I could protect you all if I left and it turned out that—I was so blind—I tried and..." I stop talking because I can feel that the thread that ties us together is still there, but it's stretched taut and frayed. She isn't trying to be cold to me, but I have hurt her by what I have done. "If there is a way to bring Zee back to you, I'll find it, I swear it."

"The only way I'm ever going to forgive you, is if you come back," she says, sniffling again. "Because Brownie is really hard to live with since you've been gone, you know," she says, rubbing her eye. "She just checks the email constantly and she has kept up with all of Reed's monitors. She caught your call to your voicemail and she even figured out the tower it originated from right before we got the call from Russell."

"You would have found us?" I ask.

She nods. "Reed thought you would call your voicemail sooner or later. He would sit at the computer all day and night waiting to see when you would make that call. When Pagan came, he managed to wipe all the computers clean, but he made Brownie promise him that she would keep watching for you," she says as tears leak down my face.

"I can't be too late, Buns—if I'm too late, then—I can't be too late," I plead with her, like she has the power to change the circumstances of the situation.

"Evie, you're wrecked. You need to go and get a few hours of sleep because you're going to need it. You can't walk into their compound like this," she says, indicating my stressed out appearance. "These are Power angels. They despise weakness. You have to go in there like you are the authority there. You are the Seraph. You outrank all of them and they must listen to you, otherwise you're all dead," she says harshly, but it's not because she is mad at me. It's because she is freaking out in a way I have never seen her freak out. I have never seen her anything other than at ease and in complete control of her environment.

Her demeanor strikes a cord in me and I clamp down on my emotions. If I have to lock them away and never bring them out into the light of day again, I'll do it. I'll do whatever it takes to be successful in this mission because this is the most important mission I have ever had. "I hate that angel caste system. It reeks and I doubt that they will see me as the superior rank, but I will sell it for all it's worth, if it means getting what I want…what I need," I say tonelessly.

"Most Powers, not our Powers, but most Powers only respect strength. They are attracted to beauty and you have that in spades," Buns says. "We are going to milk that for all it's worth. If we have to use every weapon we have on those tools, we will. I have some things we can do, but I'm serious about you going to sleep now. We have a few hours before we make it to Quebec City. We have to land there and boot Russell and Brownie off the plane. Russell can't come with us to the St. Lawrence. Dominion can't know about Russell," Buns says.

"Agreed," I say with relief that they already have a plan to take care of Russell.

"Brownie is going to charter another private plane and take Russell to Zee's island. He can see his family while he is there and you won't have to worry about him, we'll take care of him," she says.

I know that Buns is really telling me that she and Brownie will continue to take care of Russell for me if I don't make it back. I almost start to cry again because I'm so grateful to her for that, but I don't allow myself the luxury of tears. I can cry all I want when this is over…or never again, which will be okay, too.

Buns continues, "We may have some problems when we get to Canada because we didn't file a flight plan for this so we're going to fly below the radar until we get there. Then, we're going to have some explaining to do. I'm leaving all of that up to Brownie, because if there is one thing she is good at, it's handling humans."

My mind is racing, thinking of how the authorities are going to respond to a jet full of illegal "teenagers," but I have more on my mind to worry about than the Canadian Mounties. "Brownie can handle anyone," I agree tiredly.

"Evie, go rest. You're exhausted. I'll wake you when we near Quebec," Buns says, trying to hide her worry.

I nod to Buns before stumbling to the bedroom. I crawl onto the bed with Russell. I wake up when we are landing, held tight in Russell's arms. I fit there like I had been created to be there. I can't deny that. Seeing the misery in his eyes, a poignant ache is engulfing me because this is goodbye—neither of us knows if we will see the other again. I have crossed lines with Russell that I shouldn't have crossed. I should have protected him more. I should have been a better friend to him. I should have given him what he needed. He has paid a steep price for loving me, but maybe, when he is not forced to be at my side, he will be free.

"Russell…" I begin to say.

"Don't," he says, closing his eyes.

"Don't what?" I ask.

"Don't say whatever yer gonna say," he says stiffly.

"How do you know what I'm going to say?" I ask, a little ticked off that he's not letting me tell him goodbye.

"I can see it in yer eyes and I'm not havin' it," he says roughly. "Yer comin' out of there. If I didn't believe that ya are the most stubborn woman I've ever met, who always manages to get her own way, then I'd never let ya do this."

"I'm not stubborn," I say with irritation in my tone.

"Red, yer like a cat. Ya can't make it do anythin' it doesn't want to do," he says, and I can tell he means every word.

"I thought you are all about herding cats," I reply.

"Naw, I said it's pointless to try," he replies as he leans down and brushes his lips against mine. When I respond, he deepens our kiss. His hand snakes through my hair, pulling me toward him, while I press against his side. A storm blows up in me, I want to pull him closer and push him away at the same time. Unable to do either, I decide, that if he is not going to let me say goodbye with words, I will say it this way.

I kiss him until he pulls back and looks in my eyes. "You are always sayin' how things are never unconditional. Well, yer wrong. My love for ya will always be unconditional, so ya have to come back, no matter what." I pull him to me and bury my head in his neck and he holds me until we hear a knock on the door.

"Sweetie, you should get dressed. We are getting a police escort to the hangar and I'm sure we're in for some interrogating from SQ," Buns says when she pops into the room.

She gives us a brief cover story while I change out of the robe and into jeans and a t-shirt. We are supposed to pretend that we are rich kids on summer break from school, party hopping across the country. We thought we would head over and check out Quebec, since it's so close. She tells us to play dumb, which is harder than I thought it would be because I have never been a rich kid, so I have no idea how I'm supposed to act.

As it turns out, the Canadian Mounties don't have anything to do with us. The Surete Du Quebec, which means Quebec Security, or SQ, however, is all up in our grill for our unscheduled stop in their city. Russell, being led out first by the police escort, has most of the officers milling around him. I think they are a little nervous about him, due to his size. Watching the rain dampen his t-shirt, he bends down deeply in order to avoid hitting his head on the roof of the police car when they load him in the back. A moment of panic sweeps through me as his car drives away. I'm afraid for him. Maybe I should've gone to Zee's island first, and then left from there to go to Dominion, but it's too late to second guess my decision. I feel an urgency to get to Dominion as soon as possible and I have to rely on my instincts now as much as I can.

The inspectors at SQ separate us all into different rooms before they ask me leading questions like, "What are da bomb sniffin' dogs gonna find on yer plane, eh?" and "Why doncha tell us why yer really here, eh?"

It's strange to listen to the investigators speak because they speak French in Quebec, but since I don't speak French, they speak to me in English that is a mixture of a French-Canadian accent. At least they aren't evil faeries, so I can deal with the strange accents. I pretend to be Lillian Lucas, since that is the passport that Russell had thought to pack for me on the day I was taken by the Gancanagh. He is pretending to be Henry Grant and we are barely able to tell Brownie and Buns about it before we are separated.

Sitting in a room that contains a faux wood laminate table and metal folding chairs, I realize that it's no bigger than the cell the Gancanagh had locked me in just days ago. But, since the SQ investigators don't have fangs, or toxic skin, and they are giving me all the water I need, not to mention breakfast, I'm having a hard time taking them seriously. In fact, I fall back asleep for a while when they leave me alone, presumably to check out my story. Picking at my breakfast, I can't really eat it. The best I can do is eat the dry toast, but it's sitting like a lump in my stomach, churning like I have eaten grease.

My neck is a source of suspicion. I can't get it to stop bleeding, and even though Buns had given me a silk scarf to wrap around my neck, after six hours of being detained at the airport, it begins to show through the scarf. I tell the police that I have a blood disorder that makes my blood thin so that I have trouble clotting when I cut myself. This garners me some sympathy from the police and they seem to act nicer to me after that.

After over ten hours in the airport detention area, Investigator Crawford, a burly-looking man with a penchant for pulling his pants up too high, lets me out of my interrogation room. He leads me to an area where I see Russell and Buns sitting together on an anemic looking bright red sofa. They are speaking in voices that are too low to be overheard by the humans. It sounds like Russell is filling Buns in on what he saw while in the cave with the Gancanagh. Hearing him mention Brennus, a burst of fear shoots through me, causing me to stumble a little as I approach them. Seeing me, Russell stands up, moving down the couch so that I can sit between them.

"Are ya okay, Red?" Russell asks in a cautious tone as he watches my beefy-looking police escort walk away once I had taken a seat. He doesn't wait to hear my answer, but pulls me closer so that he can check me out for himself.

"Yeah, I fell asleep and my neck hurts from waking up slumped over on the table, but other than that, I'm fine," I say as my eyes evaluate him to see that he looks no worse for the interrogation. "How'd it go?" I ask.

He reaches up and rubs my shoulders for me while he says, "I like Canada. Nice police—too nice. They gave me breakfast," he says, cracking a smile. *I love his smile, it's so honest and encompassing,* I think as I try to memorize his handsome face.

I want to smile back at him, but anxiety that has been building in me for the past few hours has me wanting to pace the room and claw the walls to get out. Reed and Zephyr aren't in the custody of the nice police that will feed them breakfast. They are with the Powers who don't dispense mercy to anything they believe to be their enemies. Dire consequences…that's what Reed said he faced if he helped me when I first met him. I should have listened to him. I should have left school when he told me to, but I was too selfish to do that.

Buns smiles, saying, "You bet they're nice, but don't think everyone gets this treatment. They think we're rich kids on holiday who are more than willing to wire them all the money in fines that they're extorting out of us," Buns says, shrugging. "Once they saw everything basically checked out, they started adding up our punishment."

"Where's Brownie?" I snap at Buns. "We have to get out of here. We're wasting time!"

"She's filing a flight plan for us to go to the Gulf of St. Lawrence. She's also getting in touch with a private charter so she can take care of Henry," she says, referring to Russell by his fake name. "Chill, sweetie, we can't do anything but wait right now." Something catches her eye. Leaning towards me, she touches my neck below the scarf where a trickle of blood trails down to darken the edge of my t-shirt. "Sweetie, this isn't healing," she says with her eyebrows drawing together in worry.

"It's fine," I respond, waving her hand away irritably. "It doesn't really hurt anymore," I lie as the puncture wounds throb. "Have you heard from your contacts at Dominion? Do they have any new information?"

Buns looks over my shoulder at Russell who is pulling tissues from the box on the table near him. I feel him press the tissue softly to the side of my neck and try to mop up my blood. My hand comes up to take the tissues from him and finish the job he started.

"Why, are you planning on starting a war?" she asks.

"Yes. If that's what it takes," I reply. "I'll burn that place down if they don't give me what I want."

"Where's your army?" Buns asks, wrapping a piece of hair around her finger.

"I'm a Seraph. I have the right to command and I will not allow them to deny me," I say, pissy now because I feel physically awful and the anxiety of being held here for hours while being unable to find out any information on Reed and Zephyr is doing bad things to me.

"Ass kicker," Russell says under his breath, and I don't know if he is proud of me or disapproving, but Brownie shows up then, looking irritated. The investigator with her smirks at us and then he walks away, presumably to cash Brownie's checks.

With her hands on her hips, Brownie says, "Lillian, I'm going on record as saying your plan sucks! Powers suck! The SQ sucks! And, you should get on the plane and go to Zee's island, so that we can beat the Kappas next semester in field hockey. BUT, since I KNOW you are not going to listen to ME…" she says as her lower lip trembles, "I'll have to just pray that you come back to us," she finishes gruffly.

I get up off the couch and launch myself into her arms. "You have to take care of Buns and Russell for me, okay?" I whisper in her ear, feeling her squeeze me tighter.

"No, you'll have to do that yourself," she whispers back. Pulling away from me, she says to Russell, "Are you ready to go, Henry?"

Getting up off the couch, Russell pulls me into his arms. Hugging me and lifting me off of my feet, he says into my hair, "I can't let ya do this—I thought I could, but I can't—please, Red," he whispers. I squeeze him tighter—my best friend—the best friend I have ever had and will ever have.

"I'll never make it if I don't do this. I'll die by degrees…in pieces and you won't be able to pick up all of those pieces, no matter how good you are at loving me," I say in his ear. "I love you, Russell. Goodbye." I feel the crushing strength and sorrow in his embrace.

"Now, I want to say somethin' to yer soul," Russell whispers brokenly to me as he leans down and speaks to my heart. "You can come back and haunt me, if ya want. I love ya and I always will and I'll always be lookin' for ya…no matter what."

Something twists inside of me and my eyes well up with tears. He doesn't look at me when he sets me down on my feet, but turns to Brownie and follows her out of the open door of the security office. I stand immobile, watching Russell's back as he walks away from me until I can no longer see him anymore. He never looks back.

"Are you ready to go?" Buns asks, next to me. I immediately snap out of the trance I'm in.

"Yes," I nod stiffly.

"Sweetie, the more I think about this plan, the more I think Brownie's right. It reeks of desperation. We don't even know for sure that they're in the Dominion compound I'm taking you to. I could just be delivering you to your execution," she says. When I turn to look at her, her cornflower-blue eyes show the agony that she feels. "Brownie's right, I won't be able to get you out of there once I let you go in. They won't even let me in the front door, that's how it is for us."

She means, that is how it is to be a Reaper and not a Power, and that irritates me. "Ugh. It sounds like some snotty country club," I say. I wonder what they will think of a half-breed walking in the front door of their elite domain. "Buns, do you think I have a shot at getting in the door or will they kill me out in the open?" I ask, and I watch her pale as she looks around to see who is nearby to overhear our conversation.

"I don't know, sweetie," she says, taking my arm and leading me out of the door of the security offices. "This is the worst plan! Let's see if we can catch up to Brownie. We can go with them, and then come up with something else. Russell is right. This is a suicide mission and I'm an idiot to have thought it would be okay."

"Buns," I say, stopping just outside the glass doors to the security area. "I'm doing this with or without your help, but I have to tell you that I really, really need your help. Please do this for me. I promise, I'll never ask you for another favor."

"That will be an easy promise for you to keep because I will probably never see you again," she says as tears escape from her eyes.

"You said that you have some weapons that we can use against them. What are they?" I ask, not letting her see me waver for even a moment. If she believes that I'll do this alone, which I will, then she may still help me.

"I do. I have them on the jet. We have to find a car to take us back there," she says, wiping her eyes. I don't try to comfort her because I can't afford to start crying, too. If I do that, I may never stop. It doesn't take us long to locate someone willing to drive us back to the jet.

Once on board, I have an instant of panic when I realize that our pilot has just left to take a charter flight. "How are we getting there Buns, can you fly?" I ask.

Buns nods. "Of course, sweetie, but I'm not nearly as good at it as Brownie," she says. I think about the way she drives the Golden Goose, her huge gold-color car back in Crestwood, and then I send up a silent prayer that we will make it to the Gulf of St. Lawrence.

"So, what are the weapons you brought?" I ask, hoping that I will be able to learn how to operate them quickly and efficiently. "Do you think that the SQ found them and confiscated them?" I ask as I think about how they have been all over this plane with dogs and high-tech equipment.

Buns gives me a sheepish look as she says, "Sweetie, these aren't the Power angel kind of weapons that Zee had you training with. These are more of the 'feminine' kind of weapons," she says, watching my reaction.

"Huh?" I ask.

"Sweetie, most Powers are male. You happened to get a hunter that's female, but they are rarer than you think," she says. "We are going to make it really hard for them to kill you," she says, and when I don't say anything, she blows out a deep breath. "Okay, these are angels from Paradise. It's been a while since most of them have been there, so we are going to try to remind them of what they have been missing."

"What are you saying?" I ask.

"We are going to tease them," she says.

"How?" I ask, completely puzzled by what she is trying to explain to me.

She bites her bottom lip and goes to the closet in the master bedroom of the plane. When she comes back, I see what she means by what she has in her hands. The outfit Buns gives me to put on is nothing short of indecent, unless you are on the beach in Brazil, but this isn't Brazil. The top she hands me is a gold metallic mesh of metal tight woven to produce a supple kind of chain mail. It clasps at the neck with a wide gold metal collar and the chain mail only reaches to just below my ribs. It ties behind my back with a thin gold metal chain, leaving my back completely bare and exposing the sides of my breasts because it barely covers me in the front, too. There are matching underwear and a skirt, if you can call it that, because it's really just a large square of meshed metal chain mail in the front and the equal square of chain mail to cover the rear. Leather buckles woven into the metal squares are used to affix the sides of the garment, leaving the sides of my hips exposed.

"No way!" I say when I see my reflection in the bathroom mirror. "I feel like I'm going to fall out of this top at any minute!" I lift my arm to watch the sides of my breasts strain to get out. "I look like I belong in some kind of elfin army," I observe scathingly.

"Uh huh," Buns says, looking pleased. "It's perfect. I have some gold sandals to go with it. This is what I was going to wear if they let me in the front door, but they wouldn't."

"Don't you think I look a little ridiculous?" I ask, thinking I belong in a Hollywood back lot dressed like this.

"What do you think they will be wearing in there, sweetie, jeans and t-shirts?" she ask wearily. "They are divine angels in a place where they are allowed to be themselves. Some of them won't be wearing anything at all, I guarantee it."

"So, I'll be overdressed?" I ask, and when the visual of what I'm walking into hits me, a blush creeps up my body and I have to look down to avoid eye contact. I haven't thought about any of this and now it's making my hands sweat.

"Don't worry, they have been on Earth a really long time. Most of them will be wearing something—sarongs probably," she says, and then she shakes her head at me. "If you can't handle that part of it, then we are in huge trouble."

"I can handle it," I snap at her, and she backs off.

"You are still bleeding," Buns says as blood drips down my neck. The golden collar hides my wound now. I fold up a tissue, pushing it under the collar to stop the blood from showing.

"It's fine," I say, avoiding the skeptical look she gives me.

I don't say anything when she adorns me with thick gold cuffs around my upper arms and ankles. She works on my hair next, pulling some of the strands from the front and weaving them into a halo around my head to meet in the back, securing it with a gold clip while letting the rest of the length flow down my back. When she touches my face to brush a wisp of hair back from it, she pauses, and then places her hand on my forehead with a frown, "Sweetie, you feel hot...you have a fever."

"I think it's just residual effects from being bitten," I reply, trying to shrug it off. I don't want her to know I'm beginning to feel worse because I need her help, and if she thinks I'm sick, she may change her mind. I manage to placate her as she applies a minimal amount of make-up to me.

Buns steps back and looks at her handiwork. "That's it, now you have to figure out how to use the weapons I have given you," she says with a sad smile. "You should try to eat something before we get there. It shouldn't take more than an hour. I haven't told them that we're coming, so they are going to be hostile when I land the plane on their airstrip," she says in a very serious tone.

"Good. I bet they haven't had a good fight in a while and this will definitely break them out of their boredom. They can't resist a challenge," I reply.

"Sweetie, you have changed," Buns says, looking at me close. "You aren't the same girl I met a couple of semesters ago."

"So much has happened since then. We should go," I reply, because I don't want to think about all of the things that have happened since I believed myself to be just human.

She nods and we go together to the front of the plane. Buns prepares everything for take off and I sit in the seat next to her as she talks to the tower. She taxis the plane and we wait an eternity on the runway for the tower to give us the green light to take the plane into the air.

Once we are in the air, I leave Buns to fly the plane as I try to eat something, but the most I can manage is a dry croissant and some water. It tastes like dust in my mouth. I wonder if I will ever be able to eat anything normal again after being bitten by Brennus. The thought of him sends a shockwave of fear through me. The terror I feel at ever seeing him again makes the fear that I'm facing now seem small in comparison. The worst that the Powers can do to me is kill me, but Brennus can torture me, and then make me an undead creature—and his lover. Goose bumps cover me from head to toe and a shiver runs down my spine at the prospect.

I go back to the cockpit in time to hear Buns talking to someone on the radio. The voice is speaking French, and judging by the sternness of his voice, he isn't too pleased with whatever she had said to him. She pulls the microphone back from her mouth and covers it. "They are telling me I can't land on their airstrip," she says, watching me close.

"Tell them that you have something for them, something they have been hunting for and tell them in Angel," I say. Buns's face changes. She looks afraid. I know that she is thinking that the moment she tells them that, there will be no going back. She will be essentially sealing my fate.

"Sweetie…"

"Do it," I urge, putting my hand on her shoulder and squeezing it. "And, if they still won't let you, tell them you have the Nephilim they have been searching for."

Buns, turning white, pulls her hand back from the microphone and begins to speak into it in Angel. When she finishes, there is silence on the other end of the radio. We wait for several minutes before the voice returns to bark out commands to Buns.

"They are ordering us to land the plane on their airstrip now," she says in irritation as she looks at me. Just the expression on her face makes me see what she thinks of their arrogance and I can't help smiling at her.

"If I ever get like that, Buns, you have my permission to shoot me," I say wryly.

"No problem," she replies, taking off her headset and giving it her middle finger.

We circle the landing field once and the altimeter bobs from one side of the horizon line to the other as Buns brings the plane in for a rather rough landing. She gives me the "oops, sorry" look. I shrug because we made it in one piece. Stopping the plane at the end of the runway, she looks at me with indecision because no one has told us what to do once we land.

"Do you think they'll think this is an ambush?" I ask.

"Probably, they are really paranoid, but I guess it wouldn't be a very good strategy to just come waltzing up to a plane when you have no idea what it could contain," she says grudgingly.

"I should probably go then. I don't want them storming in here like a freakin' SWAT team. Can you open the door for me?" I ask. I see anxiety in her eyes. "It's going to be all right—you should have Zee back soon and you two can go to his island together," I say, trying to sound hopeful.

"Do you feel him, sweetie?" she asks. I know she is asking me if I can feel the butterflies that Reed always gives me when he is near.

"No, but we're still kind of far from the building," I say, shaking my head.

I look through the windshield of the plane, seeing the sprawling estate ahead of us down a grassy hill on the edge of the water. The sun is going down now. The water is reflecting the light like diamonds as it surrounds the brownstone chateau on three sides. Brownstone turrets, topped with beautiful terracotta tiles, push their way toward the heavens. Dark, overcast clouds, hanging heavily over the chateau, are being offset by the bright orange glow from the setting sun on the water. It's causing the silhouette of the massive building to glow like the supernatural beings it houses.

The building looks like it could have come right out of the Italian Renaissance period. The watermarks on the stones remind me of pictures I have seen of Venetian buildings along the canals that show the changing water levels over the passage of time. I don't know why this is the furthest thing from what I expected their headquarters to look like. I think I was expecting a much more military looking outpost, but then, it's sort of a castle, which is a military fortress by it's very design, so I shouldn't be at all surprised.

Buns rises and I walk with her to the door of the plane. She opens the door and lets down the stairs so that I can debark. "I'll go with you, sweetie," Buns says, but I shake my head.

"No, stay here. Make sure you are ready to leave at any moment, just in case you have to get out of here in a hurry," I say. I hug her because I can't wait any longer. "Thank you for everything, Buns."

"You have to come back, sweetie. If you see Zee, tell him I miss him," she says, squeezing me tight.

"I will," I say, and turning, I step off the plane alone. Facing the Chateau de Pompous Power Angels, I square my shoulders and I walk steadily toward the massive building. The breeze coming off the water is stirring the feathers of my crimson wings. I wish futilely that my wings would work so that I could use them for this mission, but when I try to move them, I succeed only in spreading them out a little.

The scent coming off the water is seductive; it reminds me of Arden Lake in Crestwood with the sun just setting on it like two lovers reuniting after a long day apart. I have to force myself to walk slowly toward it and the chateau. I need to give the angels enough time to assess that I'm not armed and that I have come to them alone, but everything in me is urging me to rush as fast as I can to find Reed and Zephyr.

After walking down the grassy hill, I travel along a cobbled pathway that leads to several sets of windswept stone steps. The steps climb sharply toward the massive structure in front of me. I pause at the last set of stone stairs that lead up to the wooden doors. Before I put my foot on the steps, I realize that twenty or more hostile-looking Powers surround me. They appear soundlessly without my detection. The hair on my arms rises when I hear several low growls, and for some reason, I don't think they are telling me that they love me. I think that maybe I should say something, but I'm at a loss as to what I should say. "Take me to your leader" sounds too stupid to say out loud so I improvise.

"Hi. I'm here to see Pagan. Can you let her know I'm here? I don't have an appointment, but I feel fairly sure she will see me," I say as I let them hear the sarcasm in my voice. I'm here to pick a fight, might as well start now. "Just tell her the Nephilim is here to see her."

CHAPTER 16

The Chateau

Just because I'm at a loss for what I should do next, the Power angels, who are surrounding me on the steps of the Chateau, don't suffer from the same problem. Several of them are barking orders to me in Angel, which of course I don't understand. I stand there for a few moments, trying to figure out what they want me to do, but then I give up and say, "I'm sorry, I don't speak your language. I only know English, well some Latin and Spanish, but I'm really not in the mood to try to figure out what you are saying, so, does anyone speak English?"

A towering Power with pale, blond hair says, "Come this way. If you attempt to escape, we will end you."

"Sounds fair," I reply coolly.

This silver-haired Power seems to be their leader. He has wings just like Zee's; they are a soft, light brown. Since he is wearing the sarong that Buns warned me about, his wings seem even more impressive for the lack of attire. I push my shoulders back and face the front doors. I'm trying really hard not to let my heartbeat kick up a notch because I can't let them know that I'm afraid. If they know that, they might crush me and I can't let them kill me, yet. They have to see that there was a gray area to Reed and Zee helping me. After that, they can do whatever they want with me.

We reach the top of the stairs and I walk ahead of most of them into the Chateau. I almost stumble when the strong sense of déjà vu hits me. As I gaze around, I find that I'm in the Renaissance reception area from the dream I had while at the resort with Reed. *This is the place. The crystal chandeliers are just as I had been shown*, I think. There are intricate marble floors with inlayed designs and richly woven carpets of reds and gold that match the gilded framed artwork and mirrors that cover the beautiful plaster walls.

The angels around me are just like the waspish angels from my dream—a room full of killers, who by my very presence, are stirred up and ready to cut me down at any sign of disobedience from me. *Nice,* I think with sarcasm.

All eyes follow me as I walk into the center of the room, waiting next to the silver-haired angel who pauses to speak to a group of other intensely threatening divine beings. Their eyes are boring into mine, daring me to make a move. I stare back at them because I can't show them weakness if I intend to help Reed and Zephyr. Anger and fear are almost overwhelming me as I think of Reed being held by these condescending soldiers who have already judged me as being evil.

In an attempt to look unafraid, I scan the room, pretending to be like them, even though I have no idea what they are like when they are together as a unit. When we don't move for several minutes, I begin to get more irritated because I need to start gathering information and no one is talking to me or talking in a language I can comprehend.

"Excuse me," I say to the tall, silver-haired angel in charge. "What is your name?" I ask him politely. He glares at me for a moment before he promptly ignores me.

Oh, so it's like that, is it? Can't talk to the evil, half-breed, I think as I watch him pretend to ignore me. *I should make it harder for him to see me as an object. I need to be seen in a different light, one that makes me seem more normal, less evil.* I chew my lower lip, trying to think of a way to do that.

"My name is Genevieve," I say, and something flickers in his eyes. "Will Pagan be coming soon?" I ask, trying to get something out of him so that I can begin to plan what to do next.

He continues to ignore me, so I ignore him, turning to face the angel who is standing on my other side. This one has blond hair as well, but much darker tones and his wings are light gray and they are shorter than the others are. Maybe that means he is younger than the rest of them.

"Hi," I smile at him, seeing his startled expression. He hadn't expected me to speak to him. "My name is Genevieve. What's yours?" Immediately, a vise-like grip clamps on my upper arm.

The silver-haired Power grabs me ruthlessly. He leans near my face and says between his teeth, "You will not speak unless you are spoken to."

My eyebrows draw together in pain. I lean even closer to his face, so that we are a mere hair's breath from each other, as I reply between clenched teeth, "Or else, what?" I already feel physically horrible, my fever is getting worse and I'm running out of time to explain myself. I can tell by the dryness in my throat that I'm in big trouble as far as this sickness goes. It's coming back on and I may not have much time before I start trippin' again. I need to say what I have to say soon, before I can't say anything at all. "I already know that I'm going to die here. I would just like to get on with it. I have some information for Pagan that I need to relay, and then you are more than welcome to make good on whatever it is you are planning to do to me."

He seems taken aback when he replies, "Everyone is gathering. It takes time. It's like everything else—hurry up and wait." He doesn't look as angry as he did a moment ago as he holds my arm less tight than before. Buns is right, they respect strength and despise weakness. I have to be strong or they will crush me.

I nod my head, grateful for the information. "Thank you," I reply, but I can't hide the relief in my eyes. He nods coolly to me, dropping his hand from my arm.

I shift and fidget for a while, trying really hard not to think of Reed, because when I do, the anxiety that I'm feeling builds to excruciating levels. I can't feel him. If they have hurt him, I will take as many of them with me as I can on my way into oblivion.

I pass some of the time waiting by marveling at the intricately painted ceiling. It depicts angels battling among the heavens. The fresco is fairly gruesome in some respects because it shows, in minute detail, what divine angels are programmed to do to the fallen angels, but I can't help being impressed by the artistry, even as I cringe inwardly. I'm not able to look at the ceiling for too long, however, because I keep losing my equilibrium and swaying on my feet. Unthinkingly, I reach out, grasping the silver-haired Power lightly, so I can right myself after dizziness almost makes me fall over. He looks alarmed when my hand touches his arm. I release it immediately.

"What is wrong with you?" he asks like an accusation, narrowing his eyes.

"Nothing," I say quickly.

He scans me and hones in on my neck, just below my golden collar. "You are bleeding," he states.

He can't see Brennus' marks because they're hidden, I think. "It's just a scratch. I got it earlier—rough landing. We all can't heal as fast as you do," I say, trying to brush it off. He looks puzzled by this, but doesn't comment on it further.

I would have watched him closer to gauge his reaction to what I just said, but I still when a small flutter dances in my abdomen. It is so slight that I think for a second that I must be mistaken. I wait agonizing moments to see if something else will happen and I am rewarded with another small flutter stirring to life inside of me. I can't contain my reaction. My hand presses to my stomach and I exhale a gasp of air. I look up at the angels around me unable to suppress the pure joy I'm feeling. *He's alive...my angel is alive!* I think as exaltation is reigning within me. *Reed's here! I'm not too late.*

I smile radiantly at the silver-haired Power angel. He is staring back at me as if I'm possessed, but the fluttering is building within me, so he is easy to ignore now. I begin walking away from my entourage, following the pull of the fluttering magnetism. I want to find him. Reed is here, so close now, but when I would've opened a broad set of doors that the invisible line to Reed indicates I should follow, I am stopped by a curt voice behind me.

"Where are you going?" It is the voice of the silver-haired angel. I hesitate in front of the door as I place my hand on its flat surface, wanting so badly to push it open and run as fast as I can toward Reed. But, I know I probably won't make it more than a few steps before someone ambushes me, so I lean my forehead against the door.

Don't be afraid to break the rules. They aren't your rules and there is no justice in them for you. Do what you must and do it now, a voice inside me says.

I turn back toward the angel and ask again, "What is your name?"

He hesitates, and then he says, "Preben."

I smile at his answer because it means he sees me as more than just an evil spawn. "Preben, I'm ready to speak to Pagan. I can't wait any longer." I say, pulling my shoulders back and opening the door. Instantly, Preben is at my side and there are several angels in front of me.

"In a hurry to die?" Preben asks, but he doesn't stop me. He nods to the divine beings in front of me. They turn and begin to lead the way down the darkened corridors. All of the hallways we march through contain exquisite paintings that can only have been achieved by the sure hand of an angel. They are intricate and the brush strokes contain power and majesty, but I can only give them cursory glances. The fluttering in my stomach is becoming more pronounced. I know that Reed is near and I'm savoring the delicious ramp up to the extreme high that will come the moment I see him.

After marching down endless corridors that wind throughout the Chateau, Preben leads me into a round, vaulting room; it's enormous in size and scope. They can have an aerial battle in this room and not hit anything because there is no ceiling on the room. The room is capped by a glass-domed rooftop; it covers this particular turret several stories above our heads. As I look above me at the stars speckling the sky, they seem to be just beyond the glass panes in the dome. I feel awe at seeing something so lovely. "That's amazing," I whisper to Preben as I inch forward into the room. Preben's silvery-blue eyes fill with confusion as he attempts to figure me out.

I ignore Preben's stare and scan the room for Reed and Zee. Reed must be really close now, but there are so many angels in here, that finding any one person is difficult, even with the fluttering radar I possess. This is an arena with hundreds of seats that line tier after tier of balconies almost all the way up to the glass-dome rooftop above. Scores of angels are flying back and forth from tier to tier, industriously conversing in their language, so that the room is filled by several different symphonies all playing at the same time. Beautifully woven tapestries cover the walls in vivid hues and depict scenes of epic angelic battles on Earth and in the skies, making the Bosch paintings I admire so well look primitive by comparison.

As we walk further into the room, the symphonies all cease and growls erupt from every level of the hive. The hair on my arms stands up again, but instead of fear, I mostly just feel angry. Being instantly reviled is getting old, so I'm anxious just to say what I have come here to say and be done with it. My head is pounding now with an ache from the fever, but the fluttering in my stomach is helping me get through the physical pain that is seizing the rest of my body.

"It would have been better if we had waited longer in the reception area. Now you have to listen to all of them," Preben says near my ear. He scans the crowd; it looks a little hostile in some quarters, and in others, the angels are registering shock and haunted stares.

"You mean, they are growling at me?" I ask with faux shock. "Maybe they are just fashion critics and don't like my outfit," I say in an easy tone.

"What's not to like?" he asks with an appraising smile, before leading me to the middle of the room where there is a raised platform for the "accused." It's somewhat dramatic, but since it is their drama, I will have to play along.

Preben continues to stand by my side, along with several other Powers. We are waiting around for presumably the seats on the raised platform, higher than our own, to be filled. It's shaping up to be some kind of tribunal. I'm a little surprised because I thought I'd be speaking just to Pagan, but apparently that is not the case.

"Am I on trial, Preben?" I whisper. He shrugs noncommittal

about my status here. "What are my rights?"

A grim smile forms on Preben's lips. "You don't have any rights," he replies in a solemn tone, not looking at me, but facing forward.

It feels like he just stabbed me in the chest. "Even the Geneva Convention has rules to handle prisoners of war," I whisper back, watching him frown.

"There are rarely prisoners in our war and those few have only one right: the right to pray for death," he states.

"Ugh. Why couldn't I be born entirely human? In my next life, I'm insisting upon it. No more of this evolving crap. No one listens to you and everyone thinks you are evil. It's exhausting, Preben," I say wearily, and I see by the way he is smiling that he is finding my rant comical. "You know what I hate the most, Preben?" I ask him. His gray eyes dance and he shakes his head. "I hate when all you guys laugh at me like I'm making some kind of joke. It's not funny."

Several of the Powers guarding me begin laughing, but Preben tries hard not to show the smile creeping up in the corners of his mouth. I make up my mind then to stop asking questions. It's pointless, anyway. They aren't going to tell me anything.

I'm still getting occasional growls from above, as I scan the arena for Reed, but he is not up there. I'm sure of it. Even though I'm sure he is close. *He must know that I'm here. He can probably feel me, too. I wonder what he's thinking right now.* I close my eyes and focus on the fluttering inside me.

A stir of musical language comes from the balconies as several angels fly in to take their seats at the bench in front of me. It happens so fast that one second they are not there and the next they are seated and staring at me. In a situation like this, I expect to see some elderly men and women sitting before me to judge my crime. But, instead, to see the youthful, beautiful faces of angels before me is really quite staggering.

They look more like the elite, popular panel of student council members, there to discuss the decorations for prom, than to decide whether I'm a Nephilim and part of the Fallen army or something else entirely. Well, that is not entirely true, because the student council would have more clothing on than just sarongs. They are more like the elite male swim team, seated in front of me, adorned in towels.

I count the all-male panel and come up with nine. They are all Power angels, judging by their wings that are varying shades of grays, browns and greens. One thing is clear about them all as well: none of them look the least bit bored. I whisper to Preben, "Who are they?"

He has lost his smile and looks deadly serious now. Preben's eyes rake the panel from left to right before he says, "That is the war council."

"What are their names?" I ask. Preben's eyebrows pull together—he doesn't know if he should tell me their names.

"It's best that you let them ask the questions. Just try to be quiet until they speak to you," he mutters, like I'm a child who is trying his patience.

I frown. "Fine. See if I help you out at your next trial," I reply snidely, watching him suppress another grin. He seems to think about what I asked him, and then he shrugs.

"The one on the far left is Yesan," Preben says, indicating the angel with pale skin and dark brown wings. "Next to him is Andor, and then Alvar," he says. These two look almost identical in an elf-in way. They both have long blond hair, tied back, and deep brown eyes. Their olive green wings have khaki stripes in the primary feathers, giving them a camouflage appearance. It makes me think that they would be wickedly stealthy in the forests where I used to train with Russell. We would never see them coming and maybe that is the point. I would think that they are twins, if I didn't already know that they are created, not born as humans are born…as I was born.

"Ursus is next," Preben continues without hesitating. Ursus is as big as the bear he is named after. His skin is dark, but it's so smooth and perfect that I bet other divine beings are jealous of his beauty. His wings are soft gray at the base of the feather, until a couple of inches from the edge, where they turn dark grey, making the contrast between his skin and wings startling and lovely. "Followed by Gunnar and Cillian," he says.

Preben pauses, and then looks down the right side of the platform, saying, "That is Reign, then Shaw, and last there is Rio." Reign and Shaw both have varying degrees of brown hair with light brown wings, but Rio is striking. He has black hair and charcoal-colored wings that may even be a shade darker than Reed's. His eyes are dark brown and his skin is sun-kissed golden brown, making him appear Latin or Spanish.

"Thank you, Preben," I murmur, trying really hard to memorize all of the names of the angels on the war council.

The council waits for the room to become quiet, and when it does, the angel in the center of the platform begins speaking in Angel. I listen to the beautiful cadences that his lilting voice weaves, but I have no idea what he is saying. My fever must be getting worse because I feel disconnected again, like I could float away from all of this and leave it behind. A small nudge from Preben makes me look up at him. I frown at him in response to the frown I see on his face.

Preben scowls then, saying in a stern tone, "Cillian asked you for your name."

I try to focus on the panel in front of me as I clear my throat and say, "I apologize for any misunderstanding, but I do not speak your language. My name is Genevieve Claremont."

Immediately, I see that they think I'm lying. They believe that I can understand their language because Cillian again speaks to me in Angel. I listen really hard to him, trying to decipher something, a phrase, or a word that I know, but it just sounds like music to me. I drift away again and receive another nudge from Preben. When I look at him questioningly, he says, "They want to know how old you are and where you come from."

"Oh. I'm eighteen and I come from a suburb of Detroit, Michigan...the planet Earth," I reply to the council. Every one of the council members scowls at me. I ball my fists to keep from cowering. They have to respect me and if I show them weakness now, they will squash me and I will never save my angels.

Cillian is again speaking to me in Angel and I stand on the platform in growing frustration because I really hate when supernatural beings think I'm lying. I glance to Preben to translate, but before he can say anything, Cillian speaks again in English. "You say you are eighteen? Eighteen what?" he asks in anger.

"Eighteen years," I reply, and by the expression on his face, I see he is having a hard time with this answer as well. *They think I'm a big, fat liar,* I surmise as they discuss me in Angel.

Another panel member is addressing me in Angel, but by the look on his face, he seems like he might be telling me off. The language is so beautiful, however, that I really can't be upset about whatever he is saying. When he finishes, I look at Preben who has a grim expression on his face. "What did he say?" I ask.

"He said that if you persist in lying to them, they will be forced to sheer off your wings." I pale instantly, feeling like he kicked me in the stomach.

Maybe I was wrong to think that the only thing that the divine angels will do to me is kill me, I think with a grimace.

"What is his name again, Preben?" I ask as calmly as possible.

"Gunnar," Preben replies.

"Gunnar, you are welcome to any part of me that you desire, as long as you hear me out first," I say through gritted teeth. "Until several months ago, I thought that I was just an ordinary human. I grew up in a small town and nothing much ever happened. I went away to school and I started having nightmares…premonitions, and then all of these frightening things started happening to me. My hearing became acute and my eyesight became enhanced, and suddenly, I could run like the wind. Then, the most amazing thing of all happened: I sprouted these red wings out of my back. I don't know where I came from, other than I had a human mother, who died at my birth, and a wonderful human uncle that raised me." I pause to see if he will say anything, but he is silent so I go on.

"I met a couple of divine angels who didn't want to help me. In fact, they wanted to kill me at first. I couldn't tell them who my father is, because I have never met him. I don't know if I'm some sort of fallen offspring, or if I could be something else. So, they watched me… to see if I'm evil. They said they have never seen anyone like me. Maybe I'm an archetype—something new. I don't know what I am. You will have to judge for yourselves what I am. But, the divine angels really only helped to protect me from fallen angels. The Fallen find me dangerous and some of them really want my soul." At this, the room above us erupts again in the beautiful symphonies of sound as what I said is being discussed among the multitude.

I wait for everyone to quiet down. "I don't know what a Nephilim is exactly. Pagan called me one and she said that she's going to rip out my evil heart, so I ran from her, because I didn't want to die." I explain. I'm trying to focus, but the room is growing hot and I feel it spinning a little. "But, now I know there are worse things than dying. So, I came here. The angels that you think are traitors were just watching me to see if I'm evil. They would have protected the world from me, if I hadn't escaped them."

A discussion ensues between them and I wish I had some water because my throat feels cracked and dry. When they are finished discussing whatever they were discussing, they all focus on the doors behind us. An instant later, Pagan springs onto the platform next to me, scowling right into my face, while she scans me from head to toe. She is just as I remember her, with her pixie-like short brown hair, and brown wings. She is several inches taller than me and as buff as her male counterparts. The outfit she is wearing is similar to mine, but hers is more of a steel mesh, which is probably stronger and tougher than gold.

My eyes narrow at her as I lean nearer to her face, scowling back at her and daring her with my eyes to take a swipe at me. *I'll Bruce Lee her right off this platform,* I think, focusing on the best killing scenario from the ones that are pulsing in my mind. Preben must see my intent because his hands go around my upper arms to hold me back, just in case I decide to attack Pagan.

Pagan looks a little surprised and I'm not sure if it's because she realizes I'm ready to kick her butt, or if it's because of something else about me. She takes a step back from me and turns toward the council. As Pagan speaks to them in Angel, I watch the faces of the council while they hang on her every word. Then, they all stare at me with amazed expressions. I look at Preben who is trying hard not to smile again as he loosens his grip on me, but he hasn't released me entirely.

Preben leans near my ear and asks in a low tone, "How does someone as small as you, outrun a fully evolved Power?"

"You would be surprised what you can do with the proper motivation," I mutter, and see him grin at me.

Ursus directs a question to me—this time in English. "Your story does not make sense to us," he says with authority, his dove-gray wings twitch in agitation. "If you have evaded all of the Powers, then why did you come here today?" he asks, and I realize that I have to be really careful of what I say here because it's a very fine line I'm walking. I can't let them know that I love Reed and that he is the reason I'm here. It might make him look bad.

"I'm here for a couple of reasons. The first reason I'm here is because I wanted you to see that I'm not a Nephilim. I want you to see how confusing I can be for any angel who encounters me," I explain, watching their faces to see if they understand me. "Most of your first instincts are to kill me, but then, when you look deeper, you see that with the danger, there is something else, something compelling," I add, using Buns's words that she spoke to me at the resort. "Can you really blame another angel for not knowing the protocol to follow where I am concerned?" I ask, listening to the murmuring voices from the galleries above.

They digest this information, and then Ursus asks, "What is the other reason that you are here?"

"That is a little harder to explain, Ursus, but let me see if I can make you understand. When I left the blanket of the divine Powers that were protecting me from the Fallen, I failed to realize that one of the Fallen followed me. His name was Alfred and he was a Reaper. He has been after my soul for a while and he found a way in which to obtain it. He told a clan of Gancanagh about me and they decided to make me one of them, which would release my soul so that Alfred could have claimed it." I pause because you can hear a pin drop in the place, it's so quiet. Preben's hands tighten on my upper arms and I look back at him to see the scowl on his face.

Since no one says anything, I continue, "I managed to escape the Gancanagh, but I'm not delusional anymore. I'm sure that they will find me, and I know that if I am bitten again, there is no way I will be able to resist becoming one of them. So I reasoned that if the Gancanagh catch up to me, I'll become a cold, soulless monster and have no chance of getting into Paradise. I will also be the enemy of the angels who once tried to help me." I pause for a second, and then I say, "I know that you have been hunting for me and that I couldn't ask you for your protection, but then I realized that if I came here, you will kill me, and then at least my soul will have a chance at making it into Paradise. You see, either way I'm dead. I just thought that this way, my soul would have a chance at Paradise, instead of Sheol." The crowd above me breaks out in pandemonium again and this time the council has to wait a long time to get them all to calm down.

When things become relatively stable again, the council discusses what I said, "So, you are asking us to set your friends free and kill you?" Ursus asks in a contemplative way.

I exhale the breath I have been holding, turning my head to smile at Preben. He doesn't return my smile when I say, "Finally, Preben, someone is listening to me."

Pagan speaks up then, assailing the council with melodious words that tumble out of her mouth like a cantata.

"What did she say?" I ask Preben.

"She basically just called you a liar," Preben replies, looking at me with anger.

"Do you have proof that the Gancanagh exist? We have not seen them in some time," Gunnar spits out, clearly siding with Pagan.

"Proof. Yes…I have proof," I reply, pulling the golden collar down enough so that the council can see the puncture wounds in my neck that refuse to heal. They must look really bad because the council scowls at me and I blush, embarrassed by what I had let Brennus do to me. "They won't heal. I normally heal right away, but these marks just keep bleeding…I'm beginning to feel ill again, just like I felt right after I was bitten."

"How long ago were you bitten?" Rio asks me, his dark gray wings still as the words shoot from him with force.

"I'm not sure. I think it was yesterday…sometime last night." Goose bumps rise on my arms as I remember what happened to me less than twenty-four hours ago. No matter what, I much prefer this hell to that one. "Brennus bit me twice because I wouldn't drink his blood. It's painful for me to be bitten by them because their skin doesn't seem to affect me, so when they touch me, I don't react to it,"

I explain, wiping my hand over my neck and seeing the large amount of blood on my palm. My blood has been seeping down and I'm surprised that no one noticed it until now. "I know that I will drink his blood the next time he bites me…the hallucinations alone will make it impossible for me to resist."

"Where is their home?" Yesan asks me, his brown wings spreading out like he will leave to hunt the Gancanagh as soon as I tell him where they can be found.

Things are getting a little fuzzy for me, but I try to stay lucid to answer their questions, "It's just outside of Houghton, in the Upper Peninsula of Michigan. I can locate it for you on a map. They tunneled in an old copper mine and transformed it into a cozy little nest. I think they imported their human victims by using the waterways in Houghton and Marquette. You will be looking for Brennus de Graham." I hold back and do not name Finn. I cannot name him…I will not name him.

The whole panel erupts then and everyone begins firing questions at me about the Gancanagh. Some of their questions are in Angel and other questions they ask are in English. Pagan's voice rises above the rest when she asks me, "Why would the Gancanagh want to change you? You are not even a faerie."

I focus in on her, seeing the way she rakes me with her eyes, like she would tear my heart out if given the chance. I decide to answer her question. "Pagan, I thought a lot about that very question when I was locked down in my prison cell. 'Why me' I asked myself, 'why would they want me?'" I say, noticing that the room is again quiet.

"I asked Brennus 'why me' and he asked me how long I thought I would last out there in the world without his protection. He said he could change me, so that I could be a friend to the Fallen. He said that any divine angel who dared to hunt me would know the true meaning of the word 'terror.' He wants me to be his undead lover." Every angel in the room is listening raptly to what I'm saying. "He believes that he is dispensing mercy to me by changing me, since I am loathed by most angels, he would change me into something else. He taught me something I didn't want to learn. He taught me that the only mercy I can expect is the ruthless, painful kind. I learned that lesson well, so I think I'm finished answering your questions. I brought a Reaper with me that I would like to have negotiate for my soul, if it's all right with you. I'm tired and I'm feeling really sick and I just want to go now. So can we just…" But, I can't finish because I feel butterflies in my stomach increasing as someone steps into my field of vision.

"Reed," I whisper his name like a prayer.

He looks fierce and wild, like he might tear me apart as his eyes scour me from head to foot, taking in every inch of my attire and honing in on my neck that is still bleeding ceaselessly. His bare chest, scored with cuts and scratches, is also bleeding steadily. My hands shake fiercely as I assess that the slashes are possibly from a knife or some other sharp weapon. Reed takes his eyes off of me to sweep Preben with a ruthless sneer, seeing that my guard is still holding me by my upper arms. A low growl issues from Reed while his eyes lock on Preben. I notice for the first time that Reed is clutching a knife in his hand. In a fraction of a second, Preben pushes me behind him, facing Reed head on by using his towering body to protect me from my angel.

"Wait!" I entreat in desperation. I step back in front of Preben and hold my arms outstretched so that they won't attack each other. As I turn my back on Reed, I look at Preben frantically. "It's okay! Reed won't hurt me," I assure him before spinning back around and seeing for the first time that Zephyr is with Reed. They are both bruised and cut and Zee is courageously facing down about twenty or so Powers that are cautiously approaching them from the left and from the right. Reed, however, isn't looking at any of them, he just has me in his sights—his expression is lethal.

I hold up my trembling hand to the Powers who are trying to circle Reed and Zee and plead with my eyes for them to stop for a second. Without looking back, I say, "Preben, please call them off for a second and I'll fix this." I don't wait to see if he gives them an order, but I move forward with cautious steps toward Reed. He looks primal, as if he has no higher reason and is now just operating on instinct alone.

His heavy breathing registers in my mind first. It sounds like he can't get enough air in his chest because of the pain he is experiencing. The agony I see on his face is nearly breaking me as my trembling hand reaches out to him. Without me seeing him do it, Reed grabs my outstretched hand and pulls me to him, crushing me in a vise-like embrace.

"You are not going anywhere without me," Reed says in my ear.

He must have heard what I have been saying…has he been listening somewhere nearby this entire time? I wonder.

"How much did you hear?" I ask, hoping he was spared from having to hear about Brennus.

"All of it," he says, squeezing me and burying his face in my neck. I hold him tighter, trying to erase the images for him in his mind, but just like mine, I can't get rid of them.

My eyes lock on Zephyr's blue ones over Reed's shoulder. He looks wrecked, like he has given everything that he has to get to this point. He is breathing hard as he inches back to where Reed and I are standing. I reach out my hand to him and he takes it in his, hugging Reed and I together. "Zee, Buns is here. She is waiting for you in your plane. She wants me to tell you that she misses you. Maybe they will let you go, now that they have me," I murmur.

His blue eyes look very sad, but he doesn't comment one way or the other. He lets go of us then, but Reed still has me crushed to him. Absently, I hear Pagan speaking in low tones to the council. She is arguing some point with them. Reed continues holding me in his arms while his body tenses and his eyes narrow to slits. He is listening to Pagan, observing her in a predatory way. It's as if he is stalking her in his mind, gathering all of her weaknesses and compiling them into neat categories. "What is she saying?" I ask Reed, holding him firmly so that he won't attack Pagan outright.

"She is arguing for her death," Reed says in an even tone, and it is the cool detachment that I hear of calculated thought. He is recovering his sanity and now his mind is taking in every detail of our situation. He is watching several things at once: the council, Pagan, the tiers of Powers, Preben and my entourage behind me who haven't moved to break us up, yet. Preben is focused on Pagan, too, and he is frowning over whatever she is saying.

Pagan looks smug. The war council is discussing something and none of them look very happy about whatever it is. In fact, Cillian and Gunnar are arguing heatedly with one another over it. I glance at Reed and attempt to gauge his reaction to what is being said. He, too, has a smug expression on his face as he continues to scan Pagan with growing aplomb.

"What is it? What's happening?" I ask Reed, but he just pulls me tighter to his side, stroking the feathers of my wings hypnotically, which is starting to do really crazy things to me.

Gunnar wins his argument with Cillian and speaks directly to Pagan. A cold, calculating stare replaces her smug smile as she turns from the council to assess me. She is looking at me in the same predatory way that Reed had been assessing her only moments ago. Goose bumps rise on my arms as I shiver. Then, I narrow my eyes at her and begin to assess her in the same way, trying to pick up on any weakness I can find.

Reed speaks in Angel, addressing the council for the first time. Since I can't understand anything they are saying, I look at Zephyr's face, trying to see if I can decipher what he thinks regarding what Reed is saying. Zee is completely ecstatic. I glance at Preben, who is assessing Reed with what looks like growing respect and amusement. Pagan, on the other hand, has lost her confident demeanor and now looks ill as she listens to Reed.

Cillian smiles at Reed, nodding, and at the same time, Gunnar looks really annoyed. Then, without warning, Reed yells out something really loud. It startles me and I flinch because I didn't expect him to do that...he had called out a word in Angel. I have no idea what it means, but Zee also calls it out, right after Reed. Preben shouts the same word, which makes Reed's head snap up as he growls at him menacingly, holding me closer to his body. Preben doesn't seem threatened by this. He just smiles and winks at me. And then, the strangest thing happens. The whole place suddenly explodes with the word that Reed had used. It comes to us from every level and from all sides.

Reed looks a little bewildered as he scans the room, but then he turns to me. As Reed sees the complete confusion on my face, he gently holds me by my shoulders and explains, "You have been challenged by Pagan to fight hand-to-hand in this arena for your life." Panic courses through me as I look over at Pagan who doesn't seem to be smug anymore. Reed pulls my chin back so that I will look at him again. I focus on his beautiful green eyes and try to concentrate on what he is saying.

"She has the right to challenge you because she has been the one hunting you. It's her mission and she refuses to give it up, even though it has not been proven that you are evil. However, since you are a Seraph, you have the right to chose a champion to fight for you, because you outrank a Power and you are not a fallen angel," he says, smiling at me and tucking my hair behind my ear.

He has found a loophole in their laws that I slide through. I'm not Fallen and they can't prove right now that I'm evil, I surmise. "Oh. I can choose anyone to fight for me?" I ask in confusion, but he shakes his head.

"No, you can only choose me," he replies in a gentle tone.

Preben breaks in and says, "She may choose whoever called out 'champion.' I believe that it was just about everyone in the room, so she may choose anyone," he clarifies for me.

"No," Reed refutes with authority, pulling my chin back so I'm looking at him. "You may only choose me. I have earned the right to fight for you. I will not let you put your life in someone else's hands. You must choose me," he says, and my whole body goes cold.

"Maybe I can fight her...if they let me rest a little bit. I've been training and I'm getting pretty good—" I say as I wobble a little on my feet. The room is spinning and nothing feels that real to me anymore, like this is all a silly nightmare and I will be waking up any moment. A look of alarm crosses Reed's face as his hand goes to my forehead. It feels so cool to have it there that I never want him to take it off of me.

"Genevieve," Reed's voice is stern as he shakes his head at me. He is absolutely adamant about fighting for me. I look over at Zee and he nods to me, indicating that I have to pick Reed if I know what's good for me.

"But...I can't live without you. I tried and it was like I was dying a little more every day," I whisper to Reed, and see that my words make his eyes soften. He crushes me again in his embrace. "What do I need to do in order to choose you?" I ask him in a soft tone.

"Just say my name," he breathes against my neck in the sexy voice that I can't resist.

"And, they will kill me if you die?" I ask for clarification, because I need to know that I will be following him if he leaves me.

"Yes, but I won't lose," he says with assurance.

After closing my eyes and praying, I call out the name of the one who means everything to me. "Reed," I say, feeling his body relax against mine. All of the tension is leaving him as he holds me close. Then, lifting me in his arms, he places me in Zephyr's waiting embrace. My heart refuses to beat properly as it rests against Zephyr's chest. I can hardly breathe; I can only get air in shallow gasps. Zephyr is trying to calm me down by speaking to me softly in Angel while petting my hair.

This is worse than anything I could have imagined. I would rather be facing Brennus again with Faolan, Goban, and Declan ready to carve me up, than to be standing here while Reed takes on the extremely agile and fatal Power who wants us dead. *God, this is so painful,* I think as Zephyr pulls me back from the center of the room. Zee is eyeing all the other angels suspiciously while his arms remain around me. Preben stays close to my side as well. I'm not sure now if he is guarding me from escaping, or just making sure nothing happens to me. He keeps looking at me with a concerned expression, but I can't focus on him while Reed and Pagan are listening to the council speak to them, probably giving them their instructions.

Weapons! I cringe, panicking as Pagan selects a battle-axe and a spear-like weapon. This weapon has a wicked blade on the end of it, made to pierce and slice. I don't even have a name for it because I have never trained with something so gruesome-looking. Holding my breath as Reed selects his weapons, I am confused, seeing him pick two small knives that look very much like spades on a deck of cards. Although these knives are sharp, they are no bigger then the palm of his hand. They don't even have traditional handles on them, but small, notch-like, horizontal holders that fit between his fingers. Zephyr grunts when he sees Reed's choice of weapons.

I pale and look at Zephyr's face. "What, Zee?" I ask, because I need to know what he's thinking.

"Reed is avenging you," Zephyr says with approval in his voice.

"Why do you say that?" I ask, as my lips turn grim. My eyes skim over every muscle and contour of Reed's perfect shape. The white, Egyptian-like sarong that he has on makes his charcoal-gray wings stand out in deep contrast.

"His weapons are very intimate. He will have to get very, very close to her to kill her and it will be extremely painful and...personal," Zephyr explains. Reed remains still and calm, not even flexing his muscles to display his strength. I can't read anything about him. I don't know what he is thinking or which way he plans to attack Pagan. I can't tell if he is weary, or if his chest is troubling him from the cuts and bruises that mar his perfection. He is blank—incomprehensible.

When Pagan faces off against Reed, I find that the space around me is becoming too small for me to exist in it. The vastness of the space is caving in on me. I feel like the air is too heavy for me to abide, so I have to retreat into myself, to a place where I can detach from the outside world. In this place the noise around me is muffled and the colors are dimmer and nothing really makes much sense. I can watch what is happening from this place because it's surreal and there is less emotion attached to any of it. It just is and I am not.

The signal, given by Gunnar, means the slaughter instantly begins. Reed melts into the air with a quickness that I can hardly follow. I think that Pagan is not expecting the velocity of his attack either. When she does manage to launch into the air, Reed is there above her, knocking her back to the ground with a slashing blow that leaves a long, jagged slice along her left cheekbone. The blood from her wound seeps out as she tumbles and pivots on the ground, coming back up to her feet only to be knocked back down to the ground by Reed. He slashes her other cheek, causing her to drop her axe from the cruelty of the blow.

Pagan, slashing desperately at Reed with the spear while prone on the ground, catches him in the forearm, tearing open his flesh. He doesn't even flinch when his arm begins to bleed; he just moves back to evade the next swing.

Something becomes clear to me in the next instant. I realize as Pagan stands, using her spear to try to pierce Reed's left side while he counters the move by gripping the spear in his hand, tugging her to him and cutting a deep, painful rend into her side, that Reed is by far the superior warrior. It's no contest at all. He is killing her slow, in pieces and by inches. He is paying her back for every branch she threw at me in the woods, when I ran for my life because I had no ability to do anything else. He is paying her back for chasing me over a hundred miles through the snow in freezing temperatures while I cringed in terror that she would rip out my heart. He is paying her back for every day that we spent apart because I was afraid that Reed would be taken by Dominion. He is paying her back for what the Gancanagh were able to do to me without his protection to aid me. He is killing her in the most ferocious and merciless way because that is what she would've done to me, if she had been allowed to fight me now. As I gaze around at the faces of the angels, I see that they feel that this is justice.

I push away from Zephyr and stumble toward Reed in the middle of the room. Zephyr is at my side in an instant, holding my arm back to stop my progression and gathering me to him to pick me up in his arms, but I look in his eyes and I shake my head. Zephyr won't let me go any closer to the fight, so I call out to Reed across the room, "Mercy...please Reed, mercy...please..." I beg him. Reed stiffens and stills over Pagan who is now barely able to fight back and bleeding from a multitude of wounds. He is owed her death, but the brutality of it is more than I can take. Her pain is killing me.

I learn then that "mercy" to a human means something entirely different than "mercy" to an angel. In the instant between me saying the words to Reed and what happens next, I feel certain that no one would have been able to explain the difference to them. After Reed hears my plea, he kneels down beside Pagan, slicing her throat, effectively dispensing angel mercy in the form of death. Zephyr explains to me in my ear that Reed can't allow Pagan to live. The council will demand that he finish her and the other angels will see him as weak. Reed has to send the message to everyone that if they hunt me, they will cease to be because Reed will protect me by any means necessary and there will be no other mercy for them except death.

CHAPTER 17

Binding

The war council reconvenes after Pagan's body is carried away. There is nothing poetic about her death. I find nothing noble in it and I grieve inside because I can't make sense of it. I'm truly grateful to Reed for fighting her because I know that Pagan would have killed me without hesitation or remorse, but I just cannot comprehend why it had to come to that. Maybe I'm still too human to understand their world. I have to keep reminding myself, that although I see myself as being on their side, it is not how I'm viewed by most of them. *I should remember that I'm a pawn in this world,* I think, standing between Preben and Reed with Zephyr on Reed's other side. We are near the middle of the room now, but we are no longer on the raised platform, just near it, which somehow feels less conspicuous than being on it.

I can't understand anything they are saying because they refuse to speak English. Reed and Zephyr are answering a stream of endless questions. I'm fairly sure that I wouldn't be able to follow the exchange, even if it was in English, because they talk to each other so rapidly that I hardly know that there is any pause between one of the council members speaking, and then Reed's or Zephyr's reply. Every once in a while, they all pause and look at me with baffled expressions on their faces. I don't shrug when they do this because I know they hate shrugs.

I have to fight hard to stay alert and focused on what is happening now because I'm at a loss for what to do next, since the plan that I had made before I came here has already been executed. My plan, to last long enough for the divine angels to see why Reed and Zee could be confused about me, has been carried out successfully. Well, I think it's been successful, because they all look confused about me now, except for Reed and Zephyr, because they are used to me.

Coming here, I didn't have any hope beyond that, no plan B. I thought that if I achieved my plan, it would be enough. Whatever happened after that would be okay because it would essentially be over. No more running, no more hiding, no more endless days of trying not to think of Reed from one moment to the next. No more Gancanagh or Brennus...no more of anything. That had seemed peaceful to me on my frantic journey from the cave of the Gancanagh to the island of the Chateau. But now, I feel warmth radiating off of Reed next to me. I smell him; his sensual scent is in the air, on my hair, all around me and I find that I crave more...I want so much more, but I didn't negotiate for more. I didn't negotiate for my life. *How much time do I have left? Will they let me say goodbye?*

Slowly, I become aware that everyone in the place is looking at me again. Reed, standing just next to me, has a pained expression and Zephyr looks worried, too. *Is my time up?* I wonder as Reed's fingers tense in my hand. "The council would like to question you further about the Gancanagh. They need specific information: how many Gancanagh did you see, how do they operate, who is their leader, and they want to know if you have precise locations?" I nod to him, because I have that information. "The council realizes that you were injured in your struggle to get away from the Gancanagh. They want you to tell them as much as you remember. Can you do that?" he asks, and I nod again.

"May I have some water?" I ask, because my throat is as dry as it was last night right before I started trippin' out. Luckily, the extreme hunger isn't back, in fact, I don't have any appetite at all. I just want to crash on the floor and not move for a long time.

I am given some water, and then the questions begin. I answer as many as I can as thoroughly as I can, but I don't name Finn. I know it's a small point in this because he will be wherever Brennus is, but I feel something for him—a messed up sense of loyalty for the help he gave me when I needed it, and I can't overlook it despite his hand in my capture.

I also don't mention Russell because I have to protect him. I tell the council that I managed to get a grenade from their arsenal and I threatened to blow them all up if they didn't let me go. It sounds plausible enough and no one seems to notice the lie except for Reed who studies me with tightness around his eyes. His jaw goes rigid when I explain the cell and not being given enough water for days, but when I talk about my fight with Keegan, he has to pace the room until I finish. He is deathly still when I speak of Brennus, hanging on my every word and studying the marks on my neck when I am again asked to show them to the council.

Maps are brought out and I try the best I can to pinpoint the location of the cave and describe the entrance. I tell them that I had dropped the grenade back down the hole once I had escaped, destroying that way out so that the Gancanagh couldn't follow me immediately. I indicate that there are several ways into and out of the tunnels, but the only way I had been shown was by the big rock that looks as if it has been placed there to hide the cave entrance.

I know that there are several holes in my story that are going to come back and trip me up later. When they analyze the fact that I had been bitten twice and wouldn't have been in any condition to walk, or do much else, I hope that they will think, that because I do not share the same physiology as angels do, it will make my story more plausible. Maybe they won't expect me to react like one of them to a bite from a Gancanagh because I'm also human. Reed knows something is not right about my story and I can only hope that he realizes that I'm protecting Russell.

It's apparent from the way the war council is barking out orders that they are mobilizing to check out my story. Units are being assembled as I notice angels that appear to be officers, getting their orders from Cillian and Ursus. For the moment I am forgotten and that is just fine with me. I drift off into a daze again while things heat up around me.

I come crashing back to reality when I feel a Power behind me grasp both of my arms, hooking them together. There are several more Powers approaching me in a casual mien. Reed argues with them in Angel, like he is trying to reason with them. As I look around with wide eyes, I see concern on Preben's face as he watches me being held, but he doesn't try to stop the Powers swarming around me. Intense fear radiates through me when I see Zee turn away so he doesn't have to see what is coming.

My breathing become erratic as I hone in on the Power angel coming toward me. His face is not registering any enjoyment, rather, he looks like he is here to do a job and the quicker he gets it over with, the quicker he can be doing something else. Killing scenarios pulse in my mind when he lifts the knife in his hand. He has pulled it from a brazier that a couple of the other divine beings had brought in. The knife blade is glowing evilly and his intentions are clear to me. He is going to kill me with that freaking hot knife. I struggle to get away from the Power holding me—I can't hear anything now but the pounding of my heart. *I didn't get to say goodbye,* I think, watching the blade coming closer to me.

Then, something in me snaps and I stop futilely pulling my arms forward. Instead, I use all of my strength to flip my legs up so that I launch my body up and over the head of the angel holding me. I straighten my arms while in the air and manage to wiggle out of his grasp by using velocity and force. When I come down behind him, I plant my foot in the middle of his back and thrust him toward the knife-wielding angel in front of him.

Preben catches me just as I try to evade another angel coming up on my left side. I attempt to roundhouse kick Preben, but he catches my leg easily, scanning its length as he holds me to him. A deep growl sounds from behind me as Reed approaches us. "Who has been training you?" Preben asks, continuing to hold my leg, while he smiles.

"Zephyr trained me...and Bruce Lee," I reply in a stilted voice, trying to pull my leg back, but Preben won't let go of it. His face is registering humor and something suspiciously like desire.

"Let her go," Reed orders Preben. Preben's eyes lock on mine. He lets go of my leg gently, allowing his fingertips to tail up my calf as my leg eases down to the ground.

Reed pulls me into his arms. Everyone is watching us again, but I don't care because I only have a couple of seconds before someone else tries to kill me so I have to say goodbye. I grasp Reed tight around his shoulders, burying my face in his neck. "I'm sorry, Reed—I don't want to be a coward, but I didn't get to say goodbye to you—I just need to say goodbye. Then it will be all right...I have to tell you... how much I want to...that I need..." I breathe, but my throat is too tight and I can hardly talk, but this is too important to fail at so I try again. "I want to tell you how much I..." the tightness in my throat gets worse so I have to whisper the rest, "I love you."

Reed's arms tighten on me. "Shh—they weren't going to kill you, love—it's okay—I've got you. No one here will ever call you a coward, Evie," Reed says quickly, trying to soothe me as he rubs my wings gently, making my legs feel wobbly beneath me.

"But, I thought..." I say, choking on my words.

"Shh—it's okay..." he hushes me, leaning his forehead against mine. "They want to fix the Gancanagh bites on your neck. The wounds will not stop bleeding on their own. We will have to sear them so that they close, and then they will heal," he explains, continuing to hold me tight.

"So, they aren't trying to kill me right now?" I whisper, because it doesn't make any sense to me. Why are they going to keep me alive?

"No. You are proving to be too intriguing to kill," he says in a soft tone.

"What about you? Are they going to let you and Zee go?" I ask.

"They have not ruled on that, but it looks promising," he says. My arms tighten on him as hope surges within me.

"We have to take care of your bites now, Evie," Reed whispers in my ear, pulling back from my embrace to look in my eyes. There is worry and pain in his eyes because he knows that this is going to be painful for me. "Zee. Can you help me?" he asks over his shoulder.

Zephyr walks behind me to gently embrace me by pulling me back against his chest. He leans down near my ear and says in a low voice, "This will hurt, Evie."

"How much?" I ask feebly.

"More than healing me…less than healing Russell," Zephyr says with concern.

Swallowing hard, I gaze at Reed. He manages to get all of the Powers near me to step back. Then, walking over to the brazier, Reed extracts another hot knife from it. Zee unlatches the gold collar from my neck, holding it in his hand while he holds me immobile with his other arm crossing my chest.

"You know," I say, moistening my lips as I see the glow of the knife, "maybe we don't have to do this now—I'm starting to feel better," I lie.

Reed frowns. "We shouldn't wait any longer. You have a fever and you keep losing blood. We have to do this now," Reed says with sympathy.

"But the council might have more questions for me—I really should focus on that instead of just…" I trail off as Reed walks toward me. "Okay—that looks really hot and I think that the cure might be worse than the pain I'm in now so let's just stop and talk about this rationally," I argue, because I can feel the heat from where I'm standing a few feet away and it's clear that this is not going to be fun for me.

"I'm sorry," Reed says between his teeth as his hand comes up to cover my eyes. He pushes my head back gently against Zee's chest, turning it to the side to expose the bites.

"Me too," I whisper, right before the searing heat of the knife sticks to my neck, engulfing it in writhing pain. I can smell my skin burning, the stench of it sticking in my nose worse than the reek of the Gancanagh. I can't hold back the scream that tears from me, even though it would have been nicer for Reed and Zee if I had. Then, every bad word that I have ever heard while growing up comes tumbling out of my mouth like a torrent of sound. My knees buckle, making Zee the only thing holding me up when Reed pulls the knife away from my throat. He drops the knife, picking me up in his arms. My throat is throbbing like he is still burning me, which makes it hard for me to croak, "I want to go home." I try to hold back my tears because I can't show weakness.

"Soon," Reed promises, taking something from Zephyr's hand and rubbing it on my neck. It's some kind of salve that is slick and sticky. After he finishes rubbing it on me it stings painfully, and then it burns more than before he put it on. I dig my nails into Reed's back, trying to get past the pain of it. Finally, the pain eases a little to a manageable level.

"Next time you do that, I want some cognac first," I pant when I am again able to speak. Zephyr and Preben laugh like I have made a joke, but I'm completely serious.

"Would you like to rest for a while, Genevieve?" Preben asks. I nod, but I have to stop almost immediately because it stretches the skin on my neck painfully. "I will take you to a room where you can sleep until the council wants to speak to you again."

"I'm staying at the Chateau?" I ask him, because I hadn't expected to be a guest of the Power angels; I just expected to be executed.

"For now," he replies, looking satisfied.

"Am I a guest?" I ask because I want to try to gauge my status here.

He grins again, like I said something amusing, and then he replies, "If you like."

What does that mean? I wonder, and then I ask, "Can I leave?"

"No," Preben replies, and I start to get the picture.

"Is Reed staying?" I ask, holding my breath. Part of me is hoping that he doesn't have to stay—a very small, noble, and pure part of me. The rest of me wants him to have to stay with me.

"I don't know. I'm not involved with his issues, just yours," Preben replies, and then he turns to Reed and says something to him in Angel, so that I can't understand him. It is intentional and it instantly irritates me.

"What did he say? I ask Reed, holding onto him tighter.

"He said that I should convince you to go with him now, so that you can rest and he will make sure that you are unharmed. I am to stay here and answer more questions, but you need to rest," he indicates the massive strategy meeting that is going on at the platform between the warlords. The whole place is in an uproar, which is taking the focus off of us.

"I'm fine, I want to stay with you," I reply, holding on to him tighter.

"You need to rest and I am fine. I will see you in a few hours, I promise," Reed assures me, while caressing my cheek.

"Of course *you're* fine, but what about Zee—he might need me and I just can't leave him because I promised Buns that I would give him back to her. She will kill me if anything happens to him," I say, changing tack and seeing Zee's smile go all the way to his eyes.

Zephyr walks to me and pats my head. "Go rest. I am tired of worrying about you and I have to see if I can get them to let Buns in here. Either that or I have to get them to let me go out to the plane for a while," Zephyr says with a grin that makes me blush.

I understand everything that they are saying, and under normal circumstances, it can be seen as a reasonable request for obedience that I go with Preben and sleep. I'm aware that if I don't lie down soon I'll fall down. It's also quite clear that everyone with authority here is used to getting his own way, for the most part. They have reasonable expectations that whatever they say will be heeded implicitly. I don't have those expectations, but as Preben moves closer to me, I hold on to Reed tighter. After Preben realizes that anything short of prying my hands off of Reed is not going to make me come with him alone, he arranges for Reed's escort to come with my escort to my room.

I do my best to walk out of the vaulting room unaided. No one has to tell me that it's crucial to hide all of my weaknesses as best as I can, even though these angels are highly skilled at assessing all of those weaknesses. None of the divine beings that I pass growl at me. I'm not sure if I won some respect from them, or if it's because I'm walking with Reed by my side, but they are not openly hostile now. Mostly, I'm stared at as an oddity or maybe something else. Maybe the outfit that Buns had given me is enchanted because it's making some of the angels kind of dopey.

As we walk through the opulent passages of the Chateau, I can hardly focus on the intricate pieces of art that line the halls and alcoves of the extensive fortress because I cannot keep my eyes off of the perfection that is walking directly at my side. I barely know that there are others still with us. It's like they are walking in the shade and I'm walking next to the sun, but as we continue our progress, I begin to feel fragile with Reed at my side. I can't read what is going on in his mind. He is giving nothing away, even as I try to enter his thoughts through his eyes. I wonder if he knows that he is the one who can bring me to my knees in a way that the Gancanagh and the council of Powers cannot.

When we reach the ground floor of another vast turret, it is clear by the way that many of the members of my entourage launch into the air that we are heading up. Everyone but Reed looks at me funny when I remain on the ground, looking up in wonder at the tiers of balconies that go all the way up to the rooftop. It's making me feel like I'm trapped in a lavish wasps' nest. A horde of angels are flying around in pursuit of whatever it is that they pursue and it's not much of a stretch for my imagination to picture what a war between these angels and the Gancanagh will look like. It will be just like wasps attacking a nest of army ants, the images of which are making me feel faint all of a sudden.

Something inside of me hurts and I don't know why. The Gancanagh are evil, but they offered me a place in their family—well, maybe "offered" is not the right word, maybe it is better to say they "insisted" I join their family. Now, something dark within me feels like I just betrayed them. *He will pay me back for my sedition,* I think as Brennus' beautiful image comes to my mind and I feel cold inside. *What did Finn say? He called me a hallion and said that I will die, and then, I will have all of eternity to make it up to Brennus.* Something twists inside of me. It's the part of me that had urged me to join them when I saw Alfred being torn apart in front of me. *It's the aching evil part of me that I can never show these angels, or they will end me without hesitation,* I think with fear, because I know now that this evil part of me exists.

Reed sees something in my eyes before I am able to shutter them to the outside world. He watches me close, but he doesn't say anything when he puts his arms around me, embracing me as he makes the leap into the air. We follow Preben up to one of the uppermost balconies of the turret. *These balconies are all lined with doors, almost like individual cells for larvae.*

We land on one of the balconies and I am ushered to one such door, but when it opens I don't find any sticky larvae inside, but a beautifully appointed, if very masculine, bedroom. I tread slowly into the room, feeling enchanted by the fact that it's the opposite of what I expected. I had thought I would be given a sparse room with a militaristic type bed and little else. Instead, I'm treated to an alluring space with a large bed covered in the softest sheets and blankets. The room has it's own bathroom and shower that has every amenity except for a bathtub. A rosewood writing desk and chair are situated on a beautifully woven carpet and the far wall has glass-paneled French doors that lead to a small balcony overlooking the water far below.

On my way across the room to the balcony doors, I pause in the middle of the room. One of the plaster walls contains a gilt framed oil painting depicting a landscape of a place that can't possibly exist because the contours and images created within it are flawless and mystical. Some primal emotion triggers within me as I unconsciously switch direction, creeping nearer to the artwork on the wall. I have no words to describe what some of the things are in the painting beside the frolicking angels. There are also colors in the painting that I have no names for because they do not exist in the human spectrum. As I move toward it, I have to hug my arms to my body. I am afraid that if I don't, I will reach out and touch the painting, which seems blasphemous.

Only Reed and Preben follow me into the room and they are both watching me silently as I study the painting before me. I don't realize that I am crying until I feel tears fall from my cheeks to drip on my forearms. When I touch my shaking hand to my cheek, there are goose bumps on my arms.

"What do you call that, in your sky?" I whisper, because I can hardly speak, but I manage to gesture toward the image near the points of light. They both answer me in Angel, since there is no word for it in any human language. I just nod because they have just proven to me how very inadequate my words are.

"I think that Brennus was wrong," I say in a soft tone, continuing to analyze the landscape. "He told me that I could never miss what I have never had, but I think that, perhaps, I can."

Reed's voice sounds less than musical when he turns to Preben and says something to him. Preben begins arguing with Reed in Angel, but when he scans me with his discerning eyes, he finally nods. Then, Preben says in English, "I will be just outside, if you need me. Do not attempt to leave," he orders, looking at the balcony doors meaningfully.

I nod to him in an absent way, my gaze still riveted on the painting, but the moment he closes the door behind him, I launch myself into Reed's arms. One of Reed's hands comes up to cup the base of my head, while the other hand is planted firmly on the small of my back, pulling me to him as our lips meet in a kiss that makes my knees feel weak and my whole body flame with heat.

A small sound of pleasure escapes me as his lips slip from mine to move along the uninjured side of my neck. My arms feel heavy as I wrap them behind Reed's neck to keep from crashing, even though I'm aware that he is pressing me to his body so that I won't fall. My fingertips lightly dance over the corded muscles of his shoulders and back, feeling raw power beneath them.

His lips find mine again as he lifts me off of my feet and walks me slowly to the bed. The mattress cradles me as Reed lays me across it. His hand rests beside my face, pooling my hair around my head while his other hand is on the bed near my waist. He pulls back from me and the desire I see in his eyes is nothing short of thrilling as his knee presses forward into the mattress between my knees. My hands search the contours of his upper arms, remembering him in a primal way by his touch and his scent and the taste of him.

Reed leans his forehead against mine. "I have to go now," he says with regret. I don't understand what he is saying right away. My body is acting on it's own, rising up to meet his as he hovers so near above me.

"Hmm?" I manage to say, tilting my head to the side so that I can nuzzle his earlobe.

"I have to go back now. I was only allowed to come here with you briefly, but I…" he has to stop for a second as he exhales from the passion building between us. "I have little authority here. I believe that I can rectify that now, since the war council has seen you. It will take some negotiating, since I refused to cooperate with them when I was brought here."

I hesitate. "What do you mean you refused to cooperate with them? They are freaking killers. How do you refuse to cooperate with killers?" I ask as what he said is taking shape in my mind. What must he have endured because of his refusal to tell them what they wanted to know about me? They threatened to shear off my wings just because they *thought* I was lying to them, when I was actually telling them the truth.

"Well, pain is subjective—physical pain is preferable to me than… they were careful not to kill us when they questioned us." He looks away and doesn't say any more, but I understand him. The torture that he has probably been enduring daily for the past month is preferable to the pain that I have put him through when I left him.

I squeeze my eyes shut and turn my face away from him. I can't look at him because of what I did to him—to Zee, too. Tightness grips my heart and compresses it. "How is it that they didn't kill you?" I ask, because I need to know how he survived this nightmare to be with me now.

"They didn't have proof of you, except for what Pagan was ranting. I also have a high rank within the order, so they have to be cautious where Zephyr and I are concerned," Reed answers, pulling my chin back to face him.

"What are you, a general?" I ask, trying to contain the sorrow overwhelming me.

"Not exactly—I rarely lead others—I'm more special ops," he

says, smoothing my hair back from my face.

"Lone assassin?" I ask as he lies next to me, staring at me as if he has never seen me before, while a smile appears at the corners of his mouth.

"I missed you," he murmurs, picking up a piece of my hair.

"Why? All I do is hurt you?" I ask in a choked voice, putting my arm over my eyes.

He pulls my arm away from my face, making me look at him. He can't be more handsome in this moment. His hair is in disarray from the combat he has endured to save me. His perfect skin is smeared with his blood and my blood. He has a myriad of cuts and bruises in various stages of healing, their colors ranging from black to yellow, but it's the intense desire in his eyes that makes him look fierce when he says, "Because you are my reason to live."

"And, you are mine. I would've lost my soul if it weren't for you," I admit, moving to him so that I am on top of him, straddling his hips and gazing down at him. "I realized when I was in the cell, that if I let them take my soul and change me into a Gancanagh, I would never be able to see you again…that one day, if we ever did meet again, you would have to kill me," I whisper as he brushes my hair back from my face.

"You give me too much credit, Evie…I wouldn't be able to kill you. I would probably beg them to change me, too," he says with a sad smile as he touches my cheek tenderly. "I have tried to live without you…I won't try anymore."

"You can't do that, Reed," I retort.

"Why not?" he asks in a low tone. "You are the only thing I have ever needed and I won't give you up. The only being who will keep me from you is you," he says with conviction. "You are where I draw the line. They can have anything else that they want, but they cannot have you—not when I have breath in my body to prevent it."

"You are insane—you should run—I'm a time bomb just waiting to go off—I'm a magnet for evil…I'm…" I say, but Reed sits up so that our chests are pressed together. He kisses me tenderly as his thumb strokes my cheek and his other hand holds my back.

He leans his forehead against mine again, and then he asks in a whisper, "How bad did he hurt you?" His whole body is tense. I know he is asking me about Brennus. I hesitate, because I have already made him bleed physically for me, I don't want him to bleed inside for me as well. His jaw goes rigid at my hesitation. "Please, tell me," he says.

My throat squeezes closed again so I have to whisper my reply.

"He broke me." Reed's arms tighten as I continue quietly, "Russell saved me…if it wasn't for him, and a dozen or so grenades, I would've been one of them. I couldn't stop the pain from his bites. It would've been only a matter of time. Drinking Brennus' blood was ceasing to be an option and becoming more like a necessity. If I had done that, he would've made me his undead lover in due course."

"Then, he hasn't made you his lover?" he asks, hardly breathing.

"No, I was spared that because he was afraid he would kill me before he could change me," I reply. "But it would have happened…I was beginning to crave him and I know that I would have eventually done anything he wanted me to do," I admit, and the shame that I feel is making me break down and cry on Reed's shoulder. "I feel so weak."

"How can you say that, Evie?" Reed asks, holding me in his arms. "You endured more than any one of those Gancanagh did when you refused to comply. That means you are strong, stronger than any of them," he says, but I don't feel strong, I feel small. Reed speaks to me softly in his musical language, trying hard to comfort me while he rubs my wings.

"Brennus gave me a gift before I left…do you know what it was?" I ask Reed between sobs, but I don't wait for him to answer me before I go on. "He ordered the fellas to kill Alfred. They ripped him to shreds on the floor of the copper mine and I…I enjoyed it."

Reed's fingertips are gentle as he brushes a tear away from my cheek. "You are an angel, that kind of vengeance is innate in you. Do not expect to react like a human when you see a fallen one destroyed," Reed says in a soothing tone, not at all surprised or repulsed by what I told him.

"No, it was more than that…Alfred told me he turned you in—that when I left you he was the one that called Dominion to tell them where they could find you and Zee. He bought my portrait and used it to induce Brennus into taking me. He killed my uncle, and if it were not for Russell, I would've joined them just so that I could tear him apart with my bare hands," I say in anguish, because I know that it proves that I'm evil.

"Again, all perfectly acceptable emotions for Seraphim," Reed replies like a caress as I sniffle on his shoulder. "Shh…you are safe… I'm here."

I shake my head at him adamantly. "No…I'm not safe. He is in me. Brennus' poison is in me and I still crave him…like a narcotic, and I don't know what I'm going to do when he finds me because he will," I reply, beginning to tremble in Reed's arms. Reed strokes my wings soothingly, but I can't slow down the words that tumble from my lips. "He told me he would be coming for me because I'm his and I believe him—he will come for me. He calls me his pet and *mo chroí* and you should've seen what my blood did to him when he drank it...it was like a narcotic for him, too. The Cherubim said it is retribution—that he will crave me as others have craved him," I say as I continue to weep. Reed picks me up, placing me on the pillow of the bed while he arranges the blankets over me. He lies down beside me and pulls me to his side and lets me cry until I quiet.

"He is wrong about so many things," Reed says, gazing into my eyes. "You are mine and you will be avenged."

"*No!*" I say in a squeaky-rasp. "He wants to fight you because I told Brennus that he will never exist for me because I love you. He wants to kill you and I can't—"

I can no longer get the words out. I can hardly breathe, but I have to make Reed understand that this can never happen. He can never wage that war because I can't lose him, not when I've just gotten him back. Black spots dance in my field of vision because I can't get enough air in. Reed looks alarmed, speaking to me rapidly in Angel, but I'm too disoriented. The melody of his voice is having no affect on me and it only takes a few moments more until everything goes black.

༄

Slowly, I awake to the sunlight streaming in the bedroom from the open balcony doors. A gentle breeze stirs the feathers on my back as a sheet covers the lower half of my body. As I lie on my stomach, I stretch, feeling the softness of the bed beneath me. It takes me a few seconds to notice that I'm not wearing anything but the sheet. Puzzled by this, I glance over to see that I'm not alone in the bed either. Reed is lying next to me and it takes me another few seconds to realize that he is sleeping. I have never seen him asleep; since he requires so little sleep, he is always awake when I'm awake.

I think for a second that he must have stayed with me last night until I see that he has taken a shower and changed into a different sarong, this one is blue and he smells incredible. It has been so long since I've seen him that I don't waste any time, but let my eyes fall over every beautiful piece of him that is visible above the sheet. With the sunlight falling on him like a finger of heaven, I have no problem seeing all of his characteristics that I have missed so much.

As my gaze roves over his wings, something catches my eye. It is the smallest speck of white jutting out gently from the edge of one of Reed's feathers on the interior of his wing. Reaching out, I gently use my fingernails to grasp the edge of the white and when I pull it, it proves to be a small scrap of paper. It has been folded several times to make it small and the edges are curled. I unfold it and iron it out. My hand shakes a little when I see my own handwriting etched on it. It's a piece of the note I had written him when I left with Russell months ago.

I read the quote I had included in it for him from Shakespeare: *Doubt thou the stars are fire; Doubt that the sun doth move; Doubt truth to be a liar; But never doubt I love...I love thee best, O most best believe it.*

"That is mine," Reed says with a voice low from sleep. He reaches out and takes the scrap of paper from my hand. With military efficiency, he folds it back up, hiding it again between the feathers of his wing.

My eyes widen in surprise. "They let you back in here?" I ask stupidly, because it's obvious that they did or he probably wouldn't be here now.

He gives me a sleepy smile. "Yes. You can have visitors. They are just concerned about you leaving. There are guards posted at both exits. Preben and his men are patrolling outside as we speak and they come in here every few hours to check on you," he says with a tired look.

"I'm sorry I woke you...how long have we been asleep?" I ask in an attempt to recover from finding hidden messages secreted on his body.

Reed glances over at the clock on the desk and says, "You have been sleeping for thirteen hours and nineteen minutes and I have been sleeping for six hours and forty-seven minutes.

My jaw drops when I hear this. He never sleeps more than a couple of hours a day. *He must be sick,* I think with a worried frown, reaching out automatically to place my hand on his forehead to check. Reed says with a sweet smile, "I'm not sick. I have not been sleeping well lately. I think I just needed to catch up." He takes my hand from his forehead and kisses it.

"Why do you have that paper hidden in your wing?" I ask with admiration for his cleverness in concealing what I wrote to him right under the noses of the angels who wanted to find me and prove that I exist.

He smiles again, but this smile can also be seen as a grimace when he says, "You asked me last night how I could refuse to cooperate with killers. I kept that for the times it became difficult not to comply." I stiffen when I hear his reason.

"What?" I murmur, because the note that I had left him frustrated me to no end. It doesn't contain the depths of emotion or longing or passion that I have for him. "You should've complied. You should've told them anything they wanted to know about me," I say, shaking my head over what he has gone through because of me. "I can't believe that you kept that note. You have no idea how frustrating it was to leave that note and not be able to tell you just how much I love you and just how badly I wanted to stay."

"You should have stayed," he says, and the pain in his eyes hurts me.

"I know that now," I reply, dropping my eyes from his. I worry the sheet between my fingers before looking into his eyes again. "I'm so sorry...I thought that I was doing what was best for everyone."

He frowns. "You thought that being without you was best for me?" Reed asks.

My throat feels tight. "I thought that it would save you from being seen as a traitor," I explain. "But, I was losing the battle to stay away from you. Right before Brennus showed up, I called my voicemail because I had to hear your voice," I tell him honestly.

Reed's smile is intoxicating. "You did?" he asks with tenderness, like my weakness for him is a good thing.

I nod as I stare into his eyes. "I couldn't help it. I can't be without you. I missed you every day."

Desire shows in his eyes as I slowly lean over to him, focusing on his exquisite mouth. I graze my lips over his, feeling their firmness beneath mine. When I rest against his chest, I instantly become aware again that I'm not wearing anything at all. A small sound of pleasure slips from me as Reed pulls me closer, wrapping his arms around me.

He nibbles my lower lip gently as he tugs it with his teeth teasing me. Then, he groans a little, releasing my lip to whisper against my mouth, "We have to talk."

"No...let me show you how much I missed you," I whisper, and I am gratified by a sexy growl from him.

He tries to hide his desire behind a serious expression. "The war council—" Reed starts saying, but stops when I rain soft kisses on his chest. Slowly and deliberately, I let my tongue touch his skin. An instant after that, I am flat on my back with Reed hovering above me looking like he might devour me.

He kisses me again, before he says, "Evie, what I have to tell you is very important." Then, he averts his eyes from me so that he can't see my body lying beneath his.

"What I have to show you is more important," I counter, trying to get him to look at me again.

"It's about Brennus and Russell," Reed says softly. I still as if he had hit me. I think he sees that I can't form words because those two names, spoken together, are doing painful things to my mind. "Russell is okay. He is with Brownie and they are on the move. We have been in touch with them and they will keep moving from place to place until we can catch up to them. Zephyr has been in almost constant contact with them and is in charge of their evasion," Reed assures me, but I don't feel reassured. I feel cold and sick, like he has just splashed icy water on me.

I think he notices because he gathers me up in his arms, holding me close. "Scouts were sent to pursue the information you provided to the council and the cave was uncovered. They found several corpses and a couple of human survivors, but the Gancanagh weren't there. They are more than likely in pursuit of you and Russell," he says, pausing to stroke my hair. "It is fortunate that the human women didn't see what happened between Russell and the Gancanagh. They didn't talk about Russell, just you. They corroborated what you told the council. It seems you were discussed among the Gancanagh. Brennus' soldiers were excited that you were going to be one of them," he says as his lips turn in a grim line.

I feel a millisecond of relief regarding the information about Russell. Then, what Reed is saying starts to race around in my mind. Brennus is hunting us. He's not going to let us live, not after what we did to them. He will destroy Russell, and then he will torment me for eternity.

Reed continues, "The council wants to speak to you again. They want to know if you heard of any of his other holdings—residences—businesses that they can investigate."

I shake my head. "Do you think he knows where I am?" I ask Reed, feeling numb.

"The Gancanagh have a highly developed sense of smell. He could easily follow your scent, since you were openly bleeding. I don't know if he was able to follow you after you entered the plane and left the area. Would he have known where you were heading?" Reed asks.

I think about it for a few seconds, and then I nod. "Alfred told us that he had turned you in to Dominion and that you were subsequently arrested. I told Brennus how I feel about you. He's very clever; he has existed for a very long time...he can probably put two and two together," I say, closing my eyes as my heart pounds. "If he figures out that we went to Quebec, he would only need to walk into airport security to smell me all over the offices. I was there for at least ten hours and my neck wouldn't stop bleeding. We had to file a flight plan there, so it would tell him exactly where we were heading," I reason. "And, if he can follow me here, then he can follow Russell, too, because he used his fake passport and Brennus knows our names. The real ones and the fake ones," I say as my eyes widen in fear.

Panic is threatening to crush me. "You have to call Russell!" I plead. "You have to warn them—oh my God! What am I going to do? I can't protect Russell from here! We have to go, Reed," I say, scrambling out of his embrace and looking around for the ridiculous outfit I was wearing earlier. I don't see it right away, so I wrap the sheet around myself and run to the small cabinet in the room. But, it doesn't have anything other than sarongs in it.

Reed follows me to the dresser, trying to get me to look at him. "Russell is safe enough. He and Brownie are constantly moving. They are somewhere in Europe right now and they are treating it like it's a sightseeing adventure."

I whirl around to look at Reed. "Oh right, Reed! That's some vacation! Being hunted by demons and hoping that you don't stumble into a fallen angel, or God forbid, a Power who thinks you're a freak!" I go to the closet, searching inside it to see if there is anything I can wear in there.

Sighing heavily, Reed says, "It's less than ideal, but they are doing well. Zephyr is extremely good strategically. He will keep them ahead of the Gancanagh until we can protect them."

I want to believe everything he's saying. But after what I have been through with the Gancanagh, I know that we can't afford to be wrong. Being wrong makes Russell and Brownie very, very dead.

"When can we leave?" I ask, giving up on my search for clothing and sitting on the edge of the bed wrapped in the sheet.

"That is what we have to talk about, Evie," Reed says, sitting next to me. A look of confusion shows on his brow, like he doesn't know how to say the next part of what he needs to say to me.

My panic increases. "Oh, my God! What's wrong, Reed?" I ask, losing color.

He immediately grasps my hand and clasps it tight in his own. "The council ruled that Zephyr and I acted in accordance with all of our laws. They have agreed to release us immediately," he says in a soothing tone as he studies my smaller hand in his.

I exhale in relief. *They're letting him go. He's free,* I think, and then suddenly, the reality of what he is saying to me hits me. *He is free, but he didn't say that I am free, too.*

"When will you leave?" I ask in an even voice that makes me feel a little bit proud of myself because it doesn't break or crack, but I can't look at him.

"That depends on you," he replies in his sexy voice.

My head snaps up as I gaze into his beautiful green eyes. *He wants something from me. He used his sexy voice on me.* I hear the waves hitting against the breaker in the gulf beneath my open balcony doors while I inhale the scent of water and Reed as they mingle together to entice and entrap me.

Reed continues in a soft tone, "Right now, I cannot act in your defense. I have no influence with the war council on how they treat you, or what they do with you." He squeezes my hand tighter in an unconscious way.

"How will they treat me?" I ask as my lips twist in a sad smile. He hesitates as anger enters his eyes. "Please tell me," I whisper.

"They are a war council—they wage war. They have found a new weapon and it makes some of them anxious to test it. Some want to know just how attracted the Fallen are to you," he explains.

I turn white in an instant. *Am I to be an enticing lure? Will they hold me out as bait for all the evil out there?*

"Oh," I say, trying to keep my hand steady in his so that he won't feel it shaking. He has been through enough with me. He doesn't deserve me making him feel guilty for having to go on without me. *What else can he do?*

"You will have to stay here with them and I will have to leave. I'm not a part of Dominion, I will not be allowed to stay," he explains.

"So, how long do we have until we have to say goodbye?" I ask, angry with the war council for their interference in my life. I should have the right to go if they don't believe that I'm evil enough to destroy me.

"I cannot leave you," Reed says.

"You just said they won't let you stay," I state as my eyes search his.

"Yes, but I cannot leave you here," he replies with his jaw tensing.

"But…they won't let me go," I murmur, wondering what I'm missing.

"They might not have a choice in that," he replies with a seductive smile.

"What are you saying? Have you figured out another loophole?" I ask as a glimmer of hope pulses through me like electricity.

"Yes," he purrs in my ear.

A sigh of relief issues from me. "Oh, thank God! You are so brilliant! What is it? Whatever it is, I'm in," I say gratefully, seeing his eyes light up with hope and desire.

"Bind to me and they cannot keep us apart," he says as he nuzzles my neck in a seductive way, making me feel weak and languid.

"What do you mean?" I ask, fascinated by the way he is looking at me—possessive and protective. "Are you saying that we need to get married or something?" I ask, feeling a little foolish because he already told me once that angels don't marry.

"No. Humans marry; it is a sacrament that we do not engage in because it's only for their lifetime on Earth. Binding is older and different—angelic…a little more intense," Reed explains, studying me as his finger traces my collarbone just above my sheet.

"How is it more intense?" I ask in a whisper, trying to focus on what he is saying instead of what he is doing.

"When we swear a binding vow to each other, making us one, then I can act on your behalf with the war council. They will lose their authority over you because your fortune will be tied to mine so whatever fate exists for you, exists for me," he informs me as his finger moves over my shoulder and down my arm, tracing the veins and artery that run down the inside of my arm to my palm. "They will not be able to do to me what they are planning to do to you because I'm not half-human. So if we are one, they have to treat you like they would treat me."

I close my eyes, savoring his touch for a moment. Then, I open them when what he says registers in my mind. "Are you sure that they will treat me like they treat you? Or, will you be treated like they treat me?" I ask, countering what he is saying.

What if it doesn't work out the way he wants and he then is subject to whatever fate I'm given? The thought of that makes me ill. I can take what happens to me, but if he has to suffer because of what I am, it will cause me more pain than I can conceivable endure.

"I'm certain," he says, unwavering, but he is really good at tricking me when it comes to things he's afraid will hurt me.

"So, this vow…what does it mean?" I ask, seeing pleasure growing in his eyes as I probe his plan. It's so strange to see him look like this when we are discussing such a serious subject. He looks happy.

Reed gives me a sublime smile. "It means that you are mine and I am yours and no one will come between us. It means we become one and it's irrevocable."

"So, if you are essentially me, and I am essentially you…what happens when someone decides I'm evil and that I need to be destroyed? I ask in confusion.

"Then I can fight for us," he says, sounding smug and satisfied.

This loophole is sounding frighteningly like he is jumping in the frying pan with me. I bite my lower lip, and then I ask, "But what if there is no way to fight it? What if it's some kind of ruling and they decide to execute me?"

His answer is simple and absolute. "Then, I die too. We will share the same fate."

I shoot to my feet. "*No!* Absolutely no! No way," I say, shaking my head. He is psychotic if he thinks I'm going to let him go down with me.

"Genevieve," he sighs.

"Reed!" I counter.

"What is it that you object to?" he asks me in a solemn tone.

"All of it," I say emphatically, pacing the floor in front of him, wringing my hands together that have become sweaty all of a sudden.

"You don't want to be mine?" he asks in a low tone, and there is something in his eyes…*he's hurt.* "I'm sure that Zephyr will bind with you, if that is your wish, but you might consider Buns for a second," he says with a taut quality to his voice that I hadn't expected at all when I had responded. I stop my pacing to look at him.

"Reed, you can't be serious. I would never consider binding with anyone but you," I say, and his eyes shine as the corners of his lips pull upward. "I just can't let you do something like that for me. I can't do that to you."

"Genevieve, I am already bound to you…I'm not afraid of anything in this world. There is nothing the Fallen could throw at me that I haven't already seen, but I can tell you that when it comes to you…" he says, standing up and catching me in his arms, hugging me to him. "You don't even know our language and you are so young and you don't even expect justice for yourself."

His face is very serious when he says, "I'm sure that Pagan had many friends here that didn't enjoy watching her die. I have encountered a few who, although are not openly hostile to me, may not hold back their hostility with you if I were to leave," he says, and I understand what he is saying. They wouldn't pick a fight with him because he is an elite fighter, but I'm not. "Preben and his men are assigned to protect you now, but I don't trust all of them either. We have made a powerful enemy in Gunnar. I think he has some plans that include you because he is anxious to have me gone, along with Zephyr."

A shiver runs through me. Just because the council have ruled not to kill me openly doesn't mean that it won't happen. If someone here wants me dead, there are ways to accomplish that without much fuss. These Powers may not be the elite caliber of assassin as Reed and Zephyr are, but they are all probably highly effective killers.

"Would you stop being noble?" I ask with a sigh. "I should've done what you asked me to do when we first met. I should've left, like you told me to. I didn't know—I wouldn't listen and now you are trying to protect me, but I know right from wrong and this is wrong. You don't make the person that you love the most a target. If you love someone, then you have to do what's best for him, not what's best for yourself."

"This is best for me. No one can save me but you. I can't walk away from you, so I will have to stay and fight them all to remain with you. If that is what I must do, then I will do it. Do you believe that I lied when I said I love you? I will prove to you that I did not," he says as his lips form a grim line, and there is no doubt in my mind that he is serious.

I turn my face into his chest, shaking it back and forth, picturing him fighting to remain here with me. I wait several agonizing seconds before I turn my face up to look at his. "If I bind with you, then you won't have to fight them all to stay with me?" I ask, because I need to be sure.

"They will be unable to stop me from taking you away because I'm free and we are one. You are not Fallen because you are not stained, like the Fallen are all marked," he says, and he is as still as a statue. "You are also not a Nephilim...you may have a similar parentage, but you have a soul and that means you have redemption."

"So, you will have to love me for eternity or something?" I ask, because I know that I have no concept of the infinite space of time he will be promising to me. Reed, on the other hand, probably knows just how long we are talking about and he doesn't seem phased by it.

"Yes," he says like a meditation, "and then, it will be you and me. You will never be alone in this again because you will have me...always," he breathes.

Every cell in my body responds to what he says and before I can stop myself I say, "Okay, I'm in." I smile, feeling euphoria spreading through me.

I am only allowed a few moments of pure bliss before the image of Russell enters my mind. A part of me feels really guilty and there is another part of me, my soul that wants to resist again because Reed is not Russell; he is not my soul mate. The deep burden of what this will do to Russell enters my mind then, sending a slicing pain straight

through me. Russell begged me to come back and this is the only way
that I can conceivably do that now. If I don't bind with Reed, I will
have to stay here with the Powers because they will not willingly let
me go. It probably won't be long before I annoy one of them with the
simple fact that I'm still breathing air. Russell said that his love for me
is unconditional. We will see if that is true.

"What do I need to do to bind with you?" I ask, looking up at
him. His face changes from grim to one of pure pleasure. Reed lifts
me off my feet and kisses me with a passion that I don't expect. I'm
lightheaded and wobbly when he finally sets me back down. The
shape of his lips still echoes on mine as he goes directly to the balcony. After signaling someone, he steps back in the room. In an instant, Buns and Zephyr are on the balcony with someone else that I
have never met.

"Sweetie, I knew you would say yes!" Buns says, flying at me and
embracing me in a tight hug. "Reed thought we might have to make
you bind to him because of how overprotective you are of all of us,
but I told him that you would see reason," she smiles, ushering me to
the bathroom and closing the door. "But, just in case, we took away
all of your clothes so that you wouldn't go anywhere." She hugs me
again and says, "Thank you—for Zee, I mean. He told me what you
did for them and I—I'm really mad at you—and I'm really grateful,
too. I knew you had moxie, I just didn't know you had that much."

"It wouldn't have worked without your help. Thank you for everything you did to get us here," I say, squeezing her tight. "You were
right about the outfit. They couldn't kill me because of it."

Buns gives me a knowing grin. "I told you. We just had to remind
them of what they were missing, but we have to hurry with this. We
don't have much time because we don't know when the council will
decide they need to see you again," she says, pulling away from me.
She disappears out the door, and an instant later, she is back with a
bag full of things. Buns pulls out a protein bar from her bag, along
with some water and insists that I eat. After I'm done, she shoves me
in the shower. When I finish, she sets to work on my hair, sweeping it
back from my face with a gold clip and letting the length flow down
my back.

Buns frowns. "I'm sorry that you have to wear a borrowed dress
for an occasion like this, but Zee says we can't afford to wait. We have
to leave as soon as possible to catch up with Brownie and Russell,"
she says. She helps me put on the gown; it's a silk chiffon tunic-style
dress with a rounded collar that slips off of my shoulder, baring it on
one side in an innocently daring kind of way. The color of the gown

is a beautiful sage green that has an iridescent quality to it and it's belted at the waist with golden cord that flows the length of the dress as it reaches to just below my mid thigh. When I see my reflection in the mirror, I frown because, although the dress is beautiful, it makes me look fay. Since I don't care for the faeries I have met, I don't like the effect.

"You don't like it," Buns says dejectedly as she reads my expression. "I think you look lovely. I have never seen a more beautiful Seraph," she says, sounding breathless.

I force a small smile. "It's very pretty. Thank you for bringing it," I say quickly to reassure her. I remind myself that none of this matters. What really matters is what I'm about to do. The thought of it is making me panic a little because I know how selfish I'm being in accepting Reed's offer, but now that it's out there, I want it. I want it more than I should. I want him to be bound to me for eternity because I will always want him…need him…love him. He is perfect and I can't give him up. But I also can't give up Russell; he will always be my best friend…always. What is that going to do to Reed?

Buns must be reading the panic on my face because she grasps me by my shoulders and makes me look at her when she says, "You have to do this, Evie. This is the only way we can save you and we can't go on without you. We can't just leave you here to fend for yourself—they might try to use you as bait for the Gancanagh. Zephyr overheard the council discussing it. If they let the Gancanagh capture you, Brennus might be lulled into enough complacency that he wouldn't expect their attack, making him an easier target. They think that what you saw was only the tip of the iceberg, so to speak. They have uncovered some things in a short amount of time that leads them to believe that Brennus has an army of Gancanagh at his disposal," she informs me.

"Then I can't do this! I can't put you up against an army like that," I say, turning white. *They'll be crushed.*

Buns shakes her head and says, "We can amass our own army now. We don't have to keep you a secret anymore. Reed and Zee can be in charge and they have many associates who will be thrilled to be involved. Don't even think about staying here, Evie. These angels don't have your best interests in mind."

"Maybe they won't kill me, you know, maybe I can turn them to my will," I say, throwing out ideas that do not include putting everyone I love at risk again.

"Evie, don't hand yourself over to them. Zee found out that Gunnar was Pagan's lover. He wants to hurt you…bad. He has ordered several of his personal guard to hunt for Fallen and to capture them alive. He wants to bring them back here and put you all in a room together to see how they react to you," she says bluntly, and the fear that goes through me is enough to make my hands shake.

"Oh," I reply, beginning to see the big picture. One way or another, Gunnar will avenge Pagan.

"I'm sorry I told you that. I just need you to see why you have to do this. You have no choice," she says, placing her hand on my cheek and gazing into my eyes.

I nod. She's right. If I want to live I have to do this. There is nowhere I can run. I need protection and the only protection I want is Reed's protection and by some amazing feat of chance, he is offering it to me freely. He will use everything at his disposal to protect me from Dominion and the Gancanagh.

Buns nods back at me, looking extremely relieved when she asks, "Are you ready to do this now?" I nod again, because I'm not sure I can say anything, yet. I have so many levels of fear regarding what I'm about to do, ranging from the fear of inadequacy to the terror that this action may lead to Reed's end. But that is fear. I have to control my fear, because if I don't, I'll be lost, since there is nothing but uncertainty about my life now and for the foreseeable future.

Buns opens the door and walks out first, going to Zephyr's side as he stands back near the balcony. I step out and see Reed standing with the other angel in the room. Reed doesn't say anything, at first, when I come to stand by his side. He just stares at me like I'm prey and he is going to pounce on me at any moment until the angel next to him clears his throat and gets his attention.

"Genevieve," Reed says formally, "this is Phaedrus. He is here to witness our binding oath and bestow upon us God's blessing. He is a Virtue angel."

I smile at Phaedrus who has a different look to him than all of the other angels I have met thus far. He doesn't have the long, sleek, powerful wings of Seraphim, Archangels, or Powers, nor does he have wings like any of the Reapers I have seen, which are more like insects and butterflies. Phaedrus has wings with feathers that look like they have a more downy texture, like the wings of an owl that almost look furry in comparison to mine. The color is also amazing because the primary feathers are a cream color with dark brown spots and the secondary feathers are a mix of caramel and copper that form almost a mantel over the crest of the wings. His hair has the same caramel-color tones in it as his wings do, but the most startling thing about him are his eyes. His sclera and iris are both black. They are wicked looking, and staring at his eyes, I feel a little unnerved by them.

I try to cover my reaction to his eyes by saying, "Thank you for coming, Phaedrus."

"No, thank you," he says, looking me over slowly. "I thought that I had seen everything at least once, but I can see that God continues to be mysterious." He makes a circle around me, taking in all of my attributes. "You are remarkable," he says, like he is stunned and a bit in awe of me, which is such a different reaction from what I usually get that I instantly like him. "Do you see how God blesses me when I least expect it?" he asks with a grin that lights up the planes of his face. He has perfect human features other than his eyes and wings, but I wonder how he blends in with humans because of them.

I can't help the smile that creeps to the corners of my mouth or the blush in my cheeks at his words. I look up at Reed to see him watching me with a smug smile, like a kid who is getting everything he wants for his birthday. "Are you ready?" he asks me.

"Yes," I reply, trying to figure out what is going to happen next.

Phaedrus, approaching us, places one of his hands on each of our heads and speaks in Angel. It feels right to close my eyes while listening to him. His voice is musical, with deep rhythms of sound, but with a humming sort of undertone that I have never heard before now. The vibrations of his voice are permeating through my mind, eliciting a primal sense of peace.

The music Phaedrus makes ends abruptly as he withdraws his hands from our heads, and then Reed gently turns me to look at him. He speaks to me in Angel and it is the most perfect sound from the most perfect voice. I glance over at Zephyr when I hear him grunt in approval to whatever Reed is saying to me. Buns, however, rolls her eyes a little at Reed's words and I make a mental note to ask her later what that is all about.

My focus drifts back to Reed, and when he finishes Phaedrus asks me, "Do you think you can repeat after me?"

"I'll try," I reply with skepticism. I listen hard as he makes sounds that have no meaning to me. I stumble through them, trying really hard to mimic the cadence he utters, but my version lacks the beauty of his tone. When I finish, I glance over at Zee to see him biting his lower lip, trying really hard not to laugh over my butchering of their language.

"Do you know what you just said?" Phaedrus asks, and I shake my head. He glances at Reed and says, "Let's also do her vow in her language so that we make sure that it is accepted and is binding."

Phaedrus looks at me again and says kindly, "Can you repeat after me again?"

"Yes," I reply, because this version should be much easier for me to accomplish.

"I ask God to bind my life to your life so that my mind will be one with your mind," I repeat the words Phaedrus says while I gaze at Reed and hold his hand. "My heart may be one with your heart," I recite it with a small smile on my face, "and my body may be one with your body," I blush a little when I say this part, seeing desire register in Reed's eyes. "From this moment through eternity, so let it be," I repeat Phaedrus, intoning the vow word-for-word. I can't contain the grin that breaks on my face when I finish. It's really a beautiful vow and I'm a little surprised because there is usually a catch to these angel things that I least expect until it's in my face.

No sooner do I have that thought then Zephyr steps up, handing Phaedrus a jeweled dagger. With a perplexed glance at Zephyr, I turn back to Phaedrus who speaks in Angel again as he holds out the dagger so that it resembles a cross. Pausing after a few moments, he then turns to Reed. Then, Phaedrus uses the blade of the knife as he chants something in Angel, scoring a small, downward slice in Reed's skin just over his heart. Phaedrus, turning to me next, holds the dagger above my heart and I know it is my turn to get cut.

I hold as still as possible as Phaedrus pulls the material of my tunic dress aside a little to expose my heart. I try really hard not to flinch when he cuts a downward slice in my skin over my heart. He turns away from me as I bleed to return to Reed. Using the same blade, Phaedrus cuts another slice into Reed, this one horizontal, and it bisected the other slice to form a cross, mixing my blood on the blade with Reed's blood from his wound. When he finishes with Reed, he turns again to me, making a similar slice, mixing Reed's blood with mine. Phaedrus gives the blade back to Zephyr, before putting his hands on our heads, chanting musically.

The cut on my heart is burning in an unusual way while it's slowly healing. It doesn't feel like any cut I have ever had before because of its odd, tingling sensation. Analyzing the cuts, they are not very deep, but my skin doesn't look normal. I want to examine it further and compare it to Reed's, but Phaedrus is still speaking so I have to wait.

When Phaedrus finishes, he pulls his hand from my head. I lift my eyes to see that they are all staring at me with an air of expectation. Confused as to what I am to do now, my eyes shift to Reed's for direction, but he has such a euphoric expression on his face that it captivates me. In a reverent way, Reed's hand rises to my heart. Buns is by our side in an instant, handing Reed a small towel. As he wipes away our blood from my skin, Reed reveals something that I never expected. Where the cut used to be, there is now an almost tattoo-like marking that resembles the coloring and characteristics of Reed's wings. It's no larger than a quarter in diameter, but as I look close, it has all of the same color variations and traits that Reed's wings possess.

My eyes fly to the cut above Reed's heart, seeing his is different, too. I take the towel from his hand and wipe our blood away from his chest to find the perfectly branded image of my crimson wings over his heart.

"Your vow has been accepted by God. May you honor each other and treat this like the blessing that it is," Phaedrus says, but I almost don't hear him because I'm so amazed by what just happened that it's difficult to think of anything else.

Reed turns to Phaedrus and thanks him for his help with the binding ceremony. I thank him, too, making him smile again at me as if I am some amazing creature that he can't believe exists.

Then, I catch Reed staring at me with a smug smile on his face. "This makes us one?" I ask as my fingers trace the shape of my wings on his chest.

"Yes," he says, watching me.

With a smile that shows I have gotten more out of this bargain than him, I lean nearer to Reed. I press my lips against the mark on his chest, kissing him, and then I pull back and gaze into his eyes. "Good," I whisper. "Now, where should we go on our honeymoon?" I ask, because I want nothing other than to be with him for the rest of eternity. Everyone laughs over what I just said, but I'm not joking. Reed picks me up off my feet without effort and returns my kiss with one that proclaims, hands down, that he is the winner in this agreement.

Clearing his throat, Zephyr says, "Reed, we have to meet with the council now. Buns will stay with Evie until we can arrange to leave. It's important we secure her release." Zee walks to the balcony doors, closing them while engaging the lock that might as well not be on the door at all, since any angel can push the door open with ease.

Reed's eyebrows pull together in concern. "Evie, I want you to stay in this room. I don't want you to leave this room. I will come back to get you. Do you understand?" Reed asks. I gauge his expression and I see that he doesn't want to leave me, but he doesn't want to take me with him either. He also doesn't trust me; he is afraid that I will do something unexpected—like leave him again.

"I'll try this once to be orthodox and listen to orders," I promise, hoping to alleviate some of his worry.

"I mean it," he breathes against my ear, gathering me close to him.

"What if the room catches on fire?" I ask, snuggling into his embrace, wanting to see just how adamant he is about me staying here.

"Find a way to put it out, but don't leave the room," he replies.

"Reed," Zephyr says with exasperation. Reed squeezes me tighter, and then he reluctantly lets me go. Zephyr walks with Phaedrus to the door of my room. They are taking Phaedrus with them to validate that the binding has taken place. Reed follows them slowly and when he gets to the door, he turns, looking at me like he wants to memorize my every contour. Our eyes meet, and then he turns and leaves the room, closing the door softly behind him. It's now up to Reed to negotiate for our lives.

CHAPTER 18

Earth and Sky

For the next few hours, Buns and I both pace every inch of my room while we wait for Reed and Zephyr to return from negotiating my release with the war council. "Why did you roll your eyes, Buns?" I ask her suddenly, as the thought pops into my mind while I go over every detail of the binding ceremony in my head. It seems a safe enough subject to pursue in my quest to make small talk and alleviate some of the anxiety that sitting and waiting has wrought on us both.

"When did I roll my eyes?" Buns asks absently, pacing the room a little too fast to look normal.

"During the binding ceremony when Reed was saying his vows to me. Zephyr grunted and when I looked over at you, you rolled your eyes," I explain while I try to sit on the chair near the desk again. I'm finding that it's harder than I expected as I fidget on it with nervous energy, my knee bouncing up and down in agitation.

"Oh, that," she says with a little smile on her face as she stops pacing. "Well, Reed's vow to you was a little more elaborate than your vow to him. You will have to ask him to translate it for you later—when you're alone."

"Can you give me a preview of what to expect?" I ask with curiosity.

"Sweetie, you know that he's a Power, right?" she says. Whenever she begins a statement with that sort of preamble, I know I'm in for an earful.

"Uh huh," I reply.

"Well, he had to tell you what kind of warrior he is. You know… 'I will eviscerate your enemies and sear them in the fires of agony' blah, blah, blah—'if they dare speak your name I will cut out their tongues' blah, blah, blah, and then he essentially swore the same vow that you did," she says, grinning at me.

I shake my head because I should have known it would be some-thing like that. "He is such a romantic, my man," I remark with sar-casm and we both laugh until we almost cry. But when we quiet, anxi-ety comes back and I listen hard to all of the sounds going on outside my door.

We give up all attempts at small talk and speculation after the fourth hour of waiting with no word from Reed or Zephyr. I eat an-other protein bar that Buns hands me while trying to listen for any sounds of their approach. I open my door a couple of times to see if I can see them below, but I only see the angels that have been as-signed to guard my room pacing up and down the interior balcony. There are other guards posted on the exterior balconies, just above and below the French doors, to make sure that I don't leave. Reed really shouldn't be concerned about my going anywhere because this is basically a dungeon in the sky for me.

Just when I am finishing my water, I hear an unusual sound out-side my door that leads to the interior of the Chateau. It sounds like a heavy *thump*, and then nothing for a few seconds. I look at Buns to see if she has heard it, too. She nods in quiet assent to my silent ques-tion. Tiptoeing to the door, I stand just by it, listening. At the same time, Buns retrieves the jeweled dagger from the bag she brought with all of her supplies. The doors to the balcony are closed, so Buns goes to stand near them.

A soft knock sounds against my door. Looking at Buns across the room in silent question, she lifts her shoulders, indicating that she doesn't know what to do. "Yes?" I ask in a soft tone.

"Genevieve?" a familiar voice says. Every hair on my body stands on end at the sound of it. Backing away from the door, I look around with wild eyes for a place to hide. Running to Buns, I grab her wrist, tugging her to the bathroom where she gazes at me with fear in her eyes in response to the fear she is seeing in mine. Pushing her in the shower, I hold my finger to my lips, silently begging her to be quiet. I close the curtain on her, hurrying back out of the bathroom and closing the bathroom door behind me.

"What's the password?" I ask through the door, trying hard to buy time to think. I see the dagger on the floor by the balcony doors so I run to retrieve it.

"Banjax?" the voice says as he pushes the door of my room in without effort. It takes everything that I am, not to cower when I see Faolan, Lachlan, and Declan walk into my room in one of the highest turrets of a fortress swarming with Power angels.

"Wow...you see what I've done here? I crashed the gates of this exclusive club and now they are letting anyone in." I say, watching my hulking Gancanagh bodyguards casually enter my room. "How did you find me?"

Declan sniffs the air around him and looks at me, smiling. "We followed yer blood. 'Tis everywhere. How long did ye bleed before dey decided ta help ye?" he asks. I shrug. "I can smell it on dat knife ye are holding right now. Did ye cut yeself?" he asks. I nod because I'm not about to tell him it was from a binding ceremony.

"Ye see, Genevieve, ye can na trust da *aingeals*. Dey are no good for ye. Ye need a family. Ye need us. We are here ta rescue ye," Declan says offhandedly, approaching me while scanning the room with indifference. "Dis is kind of a crap room dey gave ye. Dey must na know who ye are," he states emphatically, shaking his head in disgust.

"What do you mean? Who am I?" I ask with a wary look, glancing around at their faces, completely baffled.

"Ye are our queen," he replies with absolute seriousness, his pale face registering not a hint of doubt or humor. "We are here ta take ye home," he adds, picking up the bag that Buns had brought with her and asking, "ye need dis or can we leave it for da next poor bastard who has ta stay here?"

"How come I can't smell you and why don't you feel cold to me like you normally do?" I ask Declan, trying to keep fear out of my voice and buy time until I can figure out an evasion plan. Declan doesn't seem to notice my fear as he studies my room with a perplexed frown; he opens the drawers of the desk to see what they contain, looking puzzled by what he finds.

"Caul? Oh, ye know we're faeries…'tis magic," he replies nonchalantly. "We will teach it ta ye when ye become one of us. Are ye ready ta go now?" he asks as he gives up his search for anything that interests him and looks at me with a raised eyebrow. All three of them are standing around me now, waiting for my answer.

"What if I said I would like to stay a little bit longer?" I ask, watching their faces for their reactions.

Declan's frown deepens. "Brennus said ye might na want ta come back. He is afraid he might have hurt ye a wee bit too much when he tried ta change ye," Declan says, almost apologetically, which shocks me until I think that they will probably say anything to get me to agree to go with them.

Then, Lachlan chimes in, "He feels really bad about dat. 'Tis jus dat he is always trying ta create soldiers and he did na really know how he should create a queen."

"And he has never tried ta change an *aingeal* before—jus faeries, so he admits it may have been a wee bit harsh for ye," Faolan adds. "Finn told him dat he would have ta go easier on ye dis time, or ye might end up hating him."

Faolan smiles at me. "He wants ye ta know dat he's na gonna make ye change right away when ye come back. He said he'll let ye decide when ye're ready—if ye do na take too long because he really misses ye." Faolan says, and I'm aware of what he means when he says Brennus misses me. Faolan leans nearer to me and nudges my side, making me flinch as he adds conspiratorially, "He's so obsessed wi' ye dat he was going ta come wi' us today, but Finn talked him outta it." I look at him and he raises his brow, like I should be flattered by being the object of Brennus' obsession instead of being completely freaked out, like I am right now.

"Well, you can tell Brennus for me that he did hurt me, quite a lot actually, so I really don't want to come back. Tell him he should choose a new queen," I reply, putting my hands on my hips and looking at them with a stern expression.

They all grin at me while Lachlan says, "Brennus is so lucky. Do ye have an *aingeal* friend dat ye can introduce me ta, Genevieve? I want one jus like ye."

Declan seems to be getting bored with our conversation when he sighs, "Come now, Genevieve, we have ta leave before our enchantment wears off and we have every bleedin' *aingeal* in da place in here."

"No. I'm not going with you. You should leave before they find you," I retort, backing away a step when Declan takes a step nearer to me. "Don't make me toss you out of here, Declan," I add, trying to sound tough.

"Ach c'mon, Genevieve. Do na be a bleedin' hallion all yer life. Ye know we can na go back wi'out ye. He loves ye. Ye have ta come," Declan says. He is able to grab me when I'm momentarily distracted by an ominous whistling sound that is followed by the entire room shaking violently, like an earthquake has rocked the island. My eyes must be huge because when the fellas look at me they all burst out laughing over my reaction.

Declan squeezes my hand in his. "Do na fret, Genevieve. Dat was jus a wee distraction set off by da fellas so we can get ye outta here wi'out dem harming ye. Brennus was going ta clear da *aingeals* outta dis place and give it ta ye as a present, but den he decided dat he did na like da way dey were treating ye, letting ye bleed like dat for so long. He tought he would jus burn da place down for ye—ye know, as a gift," Declan says, tightening his grip on my hand in his and talking conversationally. "Did Brennus or Finn tell ye dat we deal in arms? It started off as a hobby, but ye know 'tis really quite lucrative. A couple more rockets and ye will never recognize da place," he says with a smile, while leading me to the balcony doors and onto the balcony. My heart is in my throat. Reed is in the other part of the Chateau, the part that they probably hit with their rocket.

"Now we are jus going ta go for a wee bit of a dip. Can ye swim?" Declan asks me, but before I can answer him, he says, "No matter. I'll be holding on ta ye and I…" Before Declan can finish what he is saying, his grip slips from mine as he is plucked from my side on the balcony. My eyes widen as Declan is hurled downward toward the gulf below.

I rush to the railing of the balcony, looking over it just in time to see Declan crashing into the water below. I turn back around as Lachlan rushes toward me. He never makes it near me before his feet leave the ground and his body is sent into the gulf, just like Declan. Looking up, I see charcoal-colored wings beating just out of sight of the doors. Faolan tentatively sticks his head out the door, but he doesn't even see Reed coming as Reed pulls him out by his hair. Faolan does a couple of flips in the air before making it over the balcony railing on his way toward the gulf.

In an instant, I'm in Reed's arms, pressing tight against his chest as he speaks to me in Angel. His heart is thumping hard as his hands slip over me, making sure I'm not injured. Finding nothing out of place, he pulls back from me so he can see my face. I must look scared because he presses me back into his chest just as another rocket hits the building somewhere to the west of us. "Buns!" I exclaim, remembering that I had left her inside in the bathroom.

"She is with Zephyr. The Gancanagh were distracted by you and she was able to slip out of the bathroom and find us." Reed says, holding me back from running back into the Chateau to look for Buns.

"Hold on to me, we are leaving," he says with a grim look as he waits just long enough to make sure I'm ready before he leaps into the air. I see the destruction to the Chateau from our lofty height. Gaping holes mar two of the sides that face the water as massive, billowing black clouds of smoke pour out of them. The side of the Chateau that my room is on is still untouched. Hundreds of super fast boats that look like hydrodynamic, floating torpedoes and wave runners swarm the Chateau. Pale-face fellas that can only be Gancanagh pilot them. Brennus brought some of his army with him to rescue his queen.

Swarms of angels are flying around in the destruction of the Chateau as the rhythm of automatic gunfire rattles off near the water.

I shut my eyes, not wanting to see the fight going on beneath me. *Brennus has been busy.* I think as a surge of terror hits me. *Just how long has it taken him to create all of those soldiers? Is that what he was doing in the mines? There were dozens of cells down there. Do they have an agenda? Have they been finding faeries and bringing them down there for decades to create this army? Did he turn all of them or did he have help?* I had no idea he was this powerful. He told me he was, but I didn't comprehend the scale of power he was talking about.

I'm surprised I'm alive at all. Brennus could have crushed me so easily, but he didn't. By standing up to him, I have won his affection and now he wants me back in one piece, so he can break me again. He had been planning on making me his pet when all this began, but now he wants me for a queen.

In a matter of minutes we are on the airstrip of the island. Zephyr meets us just outside the small hangar that had housed his aircraft. They speak rapidly to one another, and as I look around, I note that the Gancanagh have been here already. They disabled all of the aircraft that were out in the open by puncturing the tires on the landing gear and the large hangar is smoldering as flames lick the sides of it. The hangar Zephyr's jet was in is well on its way to becoming an inferno, too, but Zee had managed to pull the plane out before it had been too late to do anything about it.

Boarding the plane immediately, Zephyr disappears into the cockpit along with Reed. Buns bounces off her seat in a fraction of a second, hurling herself at me.

"I'm sorry I left you there," she says in a frantic tone. "I was afraid they would touch me and I would do whatever they told me to do. I went for help and I ran into Reed and Zee on their way to your room, but—" she says so fast I can hardly understand her, "they think you're their queen!" she says in shock, pulling back from me to scan my face.

"Yeah," I agree, and then I have to make a grab for the chair near me when we lurch forward as the plane moves precipitously.

I sit down in the seat facing the one Buns has fallen into. We both claw at the seatbelts that dangle loose from the seats, pulling them onto our laps as we speed along the ground like a massive cyclone. The jet bounces along the runway, picking up speed rapidly for the ascent into the air. Shooting into the sky, things crash in the kitchen as they slam into each other behind the closed cabinet doors because of the almost vertical ascent we are making.

Glancing over at the seats adjacent to our own, I notice that Phaedrus is also on board. He is in a seat facing mine in the other seating area. *Thank God they got him out of there!* I think, looking him over to see if he is okay. He is calm and undisturbed by our hasty ascent. He is sitting and watching Buns and me with a small smile gracing his perfect mouth. I try to smile back, which seems to please him.

After several minutes of flying straight up, the plane levels off, but it doesn't slow down any as we rocket through the atmosphere to an unknown destination.

"Are you okay, Buns?" I ask as she gazes around in confusion.

"No," she admits, shaking her head. "They just attacked a base filled with Powers and they were winning," Buns whispers, her face pale as she searches my face with her eyes. I nod, not knowing what to say to soothe her. There is nothing to say that will make it better. I think that Buns has been on the winning side so long that she doesn't know what it is to lose. I haven't been given those kind of odds, so I'm beginning to get used to the rollercoaster.

"They were there for you, sweetie," she says, looking horrified and I nod again because they nearly had me. If it weren't for Reed, I would be taking a dip in the St. Lawrence with Declan right now. Or, maybe I would already be reunited with Brennus and that thought makes me feel off kilter and cold inside.

"I know, but they didn't get me because you got away and went for help. Thank you," I say as I unbuckle my belt and join Buns in her seat, hugging her tight as she rests her head on my shoulder. We sit together like that for a long time, each of us numb from fear, listening to Reed and Zephyr talking in Angel from the cockpit of the plane. "Who are they talking to?" I finally murmur to Buns, because I can't understand them, they are both speaking at the same time.

"Zephyr is talking to a few different contacts," Buns replies. "One is Dominion. He told Reed about an hour ago that the Gancanagh have stopped attacking the island. They must have realized that you were on the plane that left, so they pulled out. Dominion is planning a counter offensive to try to head them off, but since the Gancanagh took out all of their vehicles, the angels will have to fly inland for reserves, which will take time so they will likely lose Brennus."

"The Gancanagh are not attacking anymore?" I ask, while relief floods through my system like a sedative. I'm not a big fan of Dominion, but I don't want them destroyed by the Gancanagh, especially when Declan had pointed out that Brennus is doing it as a gift to me.

"No. They are trying to follow us," she says. "Zephyr just told Reed that Dominion wants us to come back. They now understand your potential as a weapon; you are an irresistible lure for evil. No one has attacked the Powers in several millennium, and then you show up and you have already drawn out an army of Gancanagh who have been operating under the radar for a long time now," she explains while she listens to the angels discussing things in the front of the plane.

"So, we have to go back?" I ask, trying to clamp down on the surge of panic I'm feeling at the mere thought of having to go back there after all that has happened.

"Have you lost it?" Buns asks, smiling for the first time since this all happened. "We are not taking you back there. Reed told them 'no way.' He said they are welcome to join our army, but that they will not be given any say in what happens with you."

"He can do that?" I ask as my heart swells with love and admiration for his strength and cunning.

"He can because you gave him that power. He can now show them the door and tell them to hit it," Buns says, beginning to regain some of her swagger. "You kind of gave him an upgrade, sweetie. He has Seraphim wings on his chest—he outranks all of them now."

"Really?" I ask, not understanding any of that because I'm half-human, so how can my wings help him out at all? Buns nods. "Oh, thank God. I thought I was going to have to go back to Dominion and hope for the best." I feel a wave of relief hit me when I realize that we aren't going back.

"I bet Brennus is livid. He brought all those soldiers to get you and you slipped away from him," she says.

I shiver as I think of just how angry that will make him. *I wonder if Declan, Faolan, and Lachlan will survive his rage.* I can almost see the anger in his light green eyes as a quiver of fear shakes me.

Buns doesn't notice as she says, "Reed has been in contact with his agents regarding his holdings. He told Zephyr that several of his properties have been ransacked. The Crestwood house is a mess apparently." She listens some more to the conversation in the cockpit, and then reports, "Reed just told Zephyr that the Gancanagh have been there and they took everything that was in your room, sweetie. They also took everything that you put in storage—the stuff that belongs to you and your uncle."

I cringe. There were pictures in storage of me with my uncle that I want—that I need. Now, Brennus has them. He has all of my personal memories. A deep sense of violation overcomes me in that instant. *He is collecting pieces of me. Freaking stalker!*

Buns is all business now as she says, "Zephyr is also talking to his agents and setting up a stop for us where we can ditch the plane, get new identities and an alternate means of transportation because this jet is too easy to track. I'm going to go up front and see if I can help them. We need to check on Brownie and Russell and get an update on their status. I can work on that angle. Squaring her shoulders, she gets up from the seat we share.

"What can I do?" I ask, wanting to help. I start to rise from my seat to follow her up front, but she stops me with a hand on my arm.

"Sweetie, there is nothing for you to do right now. You can't speak Angel, so just try to relax," she advises, and then she hurries up front to join the fray. I exhale slowly, slumping back in my seat, trying to relax because there is really nothing I can do right now, but sit here and not get in their way.

I sit staring at the cockpit doors, listening to their musical voices. I try not to think about what just happened, but I'm finding that utterly impossible. Brennus won't stop. He feels like he owns me, so in his mind, he is just taking back what's his. I have to make some plans of my own. There has to be a contingency plan in place for the worst-case scenario happening because it nearly did. I'll have to talk to Zephyr about it. I can't involve Reed. Reed's only focus is to protect me, but what if he can't? Will he follow me to his death? I can't talk to Reed about this; it will have to be Zee. I need to get him to promise me that Brennus won't get me back. He will understand that I won't be asking him to protect me, but to end me, if it becomes clear that Brennus will get me. I chew my thumbnail, meditating on what I will say to Zephyr when I approach him with my request. If he won't do it, then I know I can ask Russell, but I would rather Zee do it. Russell wouldn't survive hurting me. It would kill him.

"Would you like a drink?" Phaedrus asks, holding out a beautiful glass to me that smells suspiciously like wine.

"Yes," I say gratefully, taking the glass from his hand and sipping it. "Thank you," I say as the pleasant burn eases my throat. He sits across from me with his own glass in his hand. We quietly regard one another for a few minutes. "You look like you are taking all of this in stride. This doesn't bother you?" I ask, because my hand that holds my glass is still shaking a little, but Phaedrus doesn't seem to be disturbed by our escape from the Gancanagh.

"I am not very bothered by what evil will do. God usually gets me out of the worst of it. I think He has a soft spot for me," Phaedrus says, smiling at me. I instantly feel calmer and it has nothing to do with the wine.

I can't help returning his smile. "I can see why He would have a soft spot for you. You are very kind. Are all Virtues like you?" I ask.

"I like to think I'm an original," Phaedrus says, toying with the glass in his hand.

"Well, you are original to me. I have never met anyone like you. Can I ask you a question?" I ask, trying not to sound like I'm being pushy, but I'm really interested in him and his role here.

"Yes," he says, looking flattered that I want to know about him.

"What do Virtue angels do?" I ask, staring into his black eyes that I have decided are mad cool. I have little insight where he is concerned because no one has mentioned the Virtue angel division to me prior to today.

"Miracles," he states flatly, like it's of no consequence.

My eyes widen. "Miracles! How do you do that?" I ask as my mind races to figure out what he means.

"Now that would depend on what I'm sent to do," Phaedrus replies cryptically. I just stare at him, hoping that he will say more, but he doesn't, he just takes another sip of his drink and stares back at me, looking amused.

"Do you perform miracles for humans?" I ask.

"I go where I'm sent," he answers with a shrug. "Mostly, I assist humans because they are more willing to ask for help than other beings are. They pray a lot," he adds with a wink.

"What do they ask for?" I wonder, and I see him smile again.

Phaedrus shrugs again and says, "Well, they usually ask for everything, but they get what I can give them at the time." I must look puzzled because he grins and says, "Have you ever seen reports of a tornado ripping through a house and miraculously leaving the bathtub filled with a couple of frightened humans behind?" I nod silently. "Well, that's me holding the bathtub down. They are usually very grateful until they see the rest of the house is gone."

I instantly grin at him because I had no idea—I mean I know it's a miracle, but I didn't actually think that an angel is sent to provide it.

"Who sends you?" I ask, because I want to know if he is in direct contact with the angels in Paradise.

"I get pictures—images really of places or people, so I set off to find them," he explains.

"How do you know where to go?" I ask in confusion.

"Have you ever played the game hot and cold?" he asks with a humble sort of a smile.

"You mean the game where you have to look for something and someone tells you if you're hot, meaning you are close to the target, or cold, meaning that you are further from the target?" I ask for clarification.

"Exactly, it's just like that except I actually feel the heat," he admits, smiling.

"That's amazing!" I reply in awe. "Then, what happens when you find your target?" I ask him avidly.

"A solution usually presents itself," he responds vaguely.

"But, don't the humans get suspicious of you hanging around until a solution presents itself?" I ask. I don't want to point out to him that I would've been a little creeped out if I thought that I was still just human and Phaedrus showed up with his black eyes during the time I needed a miracle.

Phaedrus laughs out loud as he says, "Humans can't see me. I'm invisible to them," he says, and I think for a second that he is joking.

"Seriously?" I ask.

"Yes. It makes the fact that you can see me that much more refreshing," he says, beaming at me. "Don't get me wrong, every once in a while I stumble upon a human with a sixth sense who knows I'm there, but to actually see me, that's unusual."

"So, how do you know what they want? The humans?" I ask, confused by how he can discern what they are asking for if he can't speak to them.

"I can hear their thoughts," Phaedrus says, and I know my eyes get bigger after he says that. Taking a sip of my drink, I speak to him in my mind. *Can you hear my thoughts Phaedrus?* I ask him silently.

"Yes. But you were really trying to give me that thought. I can hear humans quite well, but you I cannot hear as clearly. I just get the very powerful thoughts that you have been having, or the ones you direct specifically to me," he says, watching my eyes get bigger. "I can't hear other angels, so that is probably why I don't hear everything you are thinking."

What have you heard? I wonder as I study his fuzzy wings that look so soft.

Phaedrus answers, "You told me with your thoughts that you liked me instantly when we met. You were a little afraid of my eyes, but now you think they are 'mad cool.'" He smiles. "You were very relieved to see that I was on the plane when we took off because you didn't want me to be left behind with the Gancanagh," he continues. Goose bumps rise on my arms because it's like I've been talking to him without knowing that I have been saying a word. "You were very worried that you were making a mistake by accepting Reed's offer to bind with him because you're afraid that he will suffer because of what you are. There is also a Russell that you fear will suffer from your decision as well."

I blush hotly because he has heard my deepest thoughts. "You are very perceptive. I would hate to be someone you *can* read very well. You would never get any rest from all of my thoughts," I admit, trying to smile at him. He has a really gnarly gift that I wish I could borrow from him because it could really come in handy when dealing with all of the different beings I have encountered lately.

"I have been concentrating on you very hard to get that out of you. It is making me lightheaded," he says seriously. "I have to admit to you that it's a little intoxicating being around you," he adds, lowering his chin with guilt as he watches my reaction.

"What do you mean?" I ask in confusion.

"You radiate a different kind of light than an angel or a human does. It is like you are giving love in the form of energy," he says in a serious tone. I squirm a little in my seat, uncomfortable with what he is saying. "You are so concerned about the ones you love, but it extends to others as well. That is probably why you have the Gancanagh after you. They can feel the love you emit indiscriminately. It is so appealing to be near you," he says with a smile.

"You're joking, right?" I ask with my mouth hanging open a little in shock.

"No," he shakes his head. "I can see why they want you. You are a light for them. A being who gives love to the damned, highly intoxicating and as we can see by their reaction to you, highly addictive."

"That's bad. How do I stop doing that?" I ask with frank concern. "I don't want to be a light for evil," I add in all honesty, while I lean forward in my seat, waiting for him to give me the answer so that I can stop all of the craziness from happening again.

Phaedrus shakes his head at me. "It would be like asking me how I can make my eyes a different color. They are black. I could disguise them in some way, but that will not change the fact that they are black," he says, trying to explain it to me. "Some things we cannot control."

"I can't accept that," I say, disappointed with his answer. I have to find the angle that gets me out of being an unwilling demon lover. *Brennus called me the brightest light and the darkest night. Is this what he meant?* I wonder sadly.

"Ah, that is very poetic, maybe Brennus is right. I will have to think about it. You can look at that several different ways," Phaedrus says, having read my thoughts and answered my question. "Instead of asking yourself how you can change that aspect of you, maybe you should be asking yourself why you were created that way. For what purpose do you exist the way that you are?" he says in a gentle tone.

His words are so poignant that they bring tears to my eyes. "I don't know," I reply gravely.

"Maybe it's okay not to know why, today," he says reassuringly. "Maybe it's enough to know that God has a soft spot for you," he adds without a hint of doubt.

"What?" I almost scoff, but I don't because I see that he is being sincere.

"You have been given incredibly hard tasks. Only the elite are given those kind of tasks," he says with earnestness. "You are not alone in this either. Look at the angels that have aided you in your missions. They are the best at what they do. And the tools that you have to accomplish your tasks, they are perfectly matched for the job."

"What tools have I been given?" I ask him, feeling stunned.

"You have too many to name, but I will point out one of the obvious for you," he says rapidly. "Do you find it odd that you are the only being that we know of that does not react to the skin of the Gancanagh, and you were the one to draw them out? You do not believe this to be a coincidence, do you?" he asks.

I blush because it does seem a little more than coincidence to me. "That's a different perspective than I'm accustomed to hearing, Phaedrus," I say, while I think about what he is telling to me.

"Can I say one more thing?" Phaedrus asks, studying his glass.

"Of course," I reply, wondering what he can possibly say that can top what he has already told me as I wait for him to speak.

"I heard your thoughts right before I sat down to speak to you," he admits, looking at me in the eyes and it takes me a second to realize he heard me plotting my contingency plan. I pale a little because I thought that those thoughts had been private.

"Oh. You don't approve?" I ask, feeling a little like a coward for not wanting to get caught by Brennus again. "I'm trying to figure out how to protect my soul, should it become necessary."

"Yes. I see your dilemma. But if you find yourself in that situation, perhaps you should pray for a miracle instead," he says, looking me in the eyes again.

"Maybe I will," I reply, considering what he is saying. "Phaedrus... how are you feeling right now?" I ask casually, but my heartbeat kicks up a notch.

A smile shows at the corners of his lips. "What do you mean?" he asks, but I can see that he already knows what I'm asking him. He probably heard my question before I spoke it.

"Do you feel hot or cold?" I ask, pressing the issue.

"It's a little stuffy in here," he replies evasively. "Let's just say that

I do not normally visit with the angels at Dominion."

"No, I don't suppose that you would," I reply, and I can't distinguish all of the emotions that I'm having in reaction to what he just said. Suddenly, I feel really tired. This is all so immense; it's on a scale of things that is so grand that it makes me feel small. It's like realizing that an orchestra has been playing in the background the entire time that I thought that I was playing a solo piece and now their music is deafening. "What am I suppose to do now, Phaedrus?" I ask, holding his black eyes in my stare. "Because I'm no longer lost, but being found is far more frightening."

"I don't know, but I can't wait to find out what you will do next," he replies.

"Are you hanging around then?" I ask in surprise.

"It would seem you are amassing an army. I could be of some use in that, I have many contacts in my realm," he replies.

"Thank you," I say simply, because I'm so overwhelmed that someone like Phaedrus would want to help me.

"You are welcome. Yes…God is very good to me," he says, taking my empty glass from my hand as he rises. When he goes to the kitchen, I watch the night sky outside and listen to the angels in the front of the plane navigate our escape. The gentle swaying of the jet lulls me to sleep. I awake in the huge bed in the back of the jet as it descends steadily. We touch down on a runway at a small, private airport, by the look of the place that I glimpse out of the window.

Buns, coming through the door, sees me sitting on the end of the bed. "Sweetie, we just landed in Iceland. We are going to stay here until we get our new passports," Buns says, scrutinizing me with her hands on her hips. Dashing into the bathroom, she comes out with a hairbrush and her cosmetic bag. After spending several minutes working on me as we taxi to the hangar, she manages to make me look presentable enough for her high standards. Producing a digital camera, Buns makes me stand against the wall as she takes several shots of me. "For the passport," she informs me. "Now, we are going to be spending a few hours here while we arrange for documents and bank accounts because we all need new ones. We don't know how much Brennus knows about all of us so we are all going to get new identities from Iceland."

"Iceland? Is that where we are now?" I ask, rushing to the window to see just what Iceland looks like, since I have never even imagined coming here. It's dark outside, but I can see lights to a city nearby and mountains on the horizon.

"Yes, you had better do all of your sightseeing quickly because we aren't going to be staying for more than a few hours. We're too close," Buns informs me. She packs up a few things that we might need into a bag. "We're going to stay at a spa here. I'll pack some things for you. Make sure you take everything that you need because we will probably have a different plane when we leave here."

"Where are we going when we get our passports?" I ask, helping her put things into a couple of bags she has already started packing on the bed.

"We have to catch up to Brownie and Russell—they are in the Ukraine, heading for China," Buns replies, scanning the closet.

"China!" I say with surprise. On one hand that sounds like an adventure, but on the other, it's so foreign that I won't even be able to speak the language, or read a street sign. Fear edges through me because I will have to rely on everyone else to help me. It's like that now, but there is always a chance that I can help and play a role in my own survival. *How am I going to do that in China? How is Russell coping with all of this? It's like culture shock on the grandest scale imaginable.*

"Are you ready, sweetie?" Buns asks in a gentle tone. She is reading the panic on my face. I nod because I don't want to be the weak link in this chain anymore than I already am.

Leaving the room, we walk to the front of the jet where the stairs are already let down so that we can debark. As I step out of the plane, I see Reed and Zephyr waiting for us at the bottom of the staircase. Attired in tailored gray trousers and white collared shirts, they have the appearance of high-class international travelers as they stand near an extremely sleek-looking car. Both Reed and Zephyr are on their phones, speaking rapidly in Angel. Reed, however, is watching every step I take down the stairs. Reaching his hand up to me, he helps me down the last couple of steps.

"Where is Phaedrus?" I ask when I look around and don't see him.

Buns answers, "He's going to take care of the passports for us. He has a contact. Phaedrus is an unknown entity in our group, we thought it would be the safest to use his associates," Buns explains, while I get into the back seat of the car after Reed holds the door open for me. Buns sits in the front passenger seat that Zephyr opens for her, and then he goes around to the driver's side while Reed sits in the back with me. Reed's arm wraps around my shoulder, pulling me close to his side while still holding the phone to his ear with the other.

Resting my head against Reed's shoulder, I watch the scenery of Iceland speed by outside of my window. We soon leave the large city behind as we drive over the dark roads to the base of a mountain. "We're here, sweetie!" Buns says with excitement, smiling at me from over her shoulder. "It's called 'The Lake of Earth and Sky' and it's built into the side of a volcano. There is a hot spring that surrounds the back of the spa, containing the best mineral water available." As we pull up to the Nordic glass fronted building, it is literally supported by the volcano's lava rock on one side of it. Thick, rolling clouds of steaming fog shrouds the building in mystery. Taking Reed's hand, I step from the car.

Buns leads us in and takes charge of acquiring our suite of rooms in the VIP section of the spa. The VIP section affords us our own private access to the hot spring lagoon, which is walled from the rest of the clientele by a lava rock privacy enclosure. I gaze at the stunning pictures of the lake in daylight; it is almost sky blue in color with the scintillating iridescence of an opal. Steam rises from the water invitingly and rolls over the black volcanic sand that has a myriad of arching wooden bridges connecting the small inlets throughout the estate.

When we are shown to our suite, I marvel at the uniqueness of it. One wall is comprised of rough, black volcanic lava rock that sparkles with small particles of quartz and silica embedded within it. The opposite wall is entirely comprised of glass that overlooks the lagoon outside. I bet that when the sun shines through it in the morning, the lava wall will shimmer like twinkle lights from the reflection of the quartz. The floors of the main room are polished wood. The furniture is cut in clean lines and boxy shapes that are meant to be calming and soothing, positioned as they are around a freestanding fireplace in the heart of the room.

It's immediately apparent to Buns and me that Reed and Zephyr intend to treat this layover as a work opportunity. Neither of them spare the rooms more than a cursory glance as they both pace around it, negotiating on their phones. Walking to the window, I look out at the patio outside to the dark lagoon beyond it. Buns, managing to get my attention, gives me a devilish grin while she crooks her finger at me, ushering me to one of the bedrooms. "I call shotgun on the room with the waterfall and spa tubs. You and Reed can play in the private lagoon outside."

"Uh huh. How am I going to get the phone away from him long enough to do that?" I ask with skepticism. "He's a Power and he is at war right now trying to raise an army. How am I going to compete with that?" I ask, watching her rummage through her bag.

"He's a Power who has been dreaming about you for months. You will have no problem, trust me. Here, this will help," she says, tossing a tiny, red bikini at me. I blush a little when I see just how much of me it doesn't cover when I have it on. "Play it cool," Buns says, walking to the door of the room in her sexy black bikini. Pushing the door open, she strolls out into the main room saying, "Sweetie, I'm going to check out the spa room. The concierge informed me that it's exclusively for us and it has it's own waterfall. Do you want to come?"

I notice the sly look on her face and quickly catch on to her game. "That sounds like fun Buns…but I want to go look at the lagoon outside first. I want to see if I can see the aurora borealis, and then I thought I would take a dip in the hot spring because it's a little chilly here." I have my back to Reed, so that he can see just how much of me my suit doesn't cover.

"Oh," Buns says in disappointment. I try to hide my smile as I see Zee watching her like she is a rare piece of weaponry that he would like to wield. "I guess I can go alone," she sighs as her lower lip pushes out in a sensual pout. She turns, walking toward the door. When she is through the door, Zephyr follows her in a millisecond. Turning around, I find Reed a hair's breath from me, no longer on the phone.

"Reed!" I gasp, startled because I hadn't heard him move.

Reed wraps his arms around me and holds me to him, rubbing his hands up and down my back soothingly as he asks, "Are you upset?" he murmurs against my hair. "We need to talk about faeries and magic and what happened back at Dominion."

"Not now, we don't need to talk about that now—I don't want to think about them," I reply as a shiver passes through me, making Reed pull me back from him to look into my eyes.

"You didn't know he has an army, did you?" he asks, assessing the dread in my eyes.

"No. He told me he was powerful and I told him that the mere fact that he had to say that means that he's not," I reply, watching as the corners of Reed's lips curve in a small smile that his eyes can not suppress.

He says softly, "There is little wonder why he wants you, and he is very resourceful, so we will not underestimate him again. You told me that he would come for you, didn't you?" he asks. I nod because I don't want him to hear fear in my voice. "I believed you when you told me that he would come…but I did not anticipate that he is willing to risk everything that he has achieved to have you—that means he is vulnerable. We have to find out who his allies are…" Reed trails off when I press my lips to his in a desperate attempt to make him stop talking about Brennus.

"Shh...No more talking about him," I whisper to Reed when I pull back. "I'm here with you now and I'm not going to waste a second of that discussing him. I want to have this moment with you without him in it."

"Are you afraid that we will not have many moments left together?" Reed asks, narrowing in on the core of my terror. His eyes are scanning mine, so I drop my eyes from him because I don't want him to see just how sure I am that that is the case.

"When I was in my cell with the Gancanagh, I began to understand something that I should've made more clear to you. I was not being unrealistic when I spoke to the war council. There are only a couple of ways this can end," I say, clutching Reed's hand. "It's a game to the death: Brennus' or mine. This ends with me as an undead queen or when Brennus ceases to be. He's not going to stop... ever."

"Yes, he is desperate for you, and when he comes, there will be no mercy for him. He will cease to be," Reed says emphatically with absolutely no doubt in his voice. But, there are no feelings of satisfaction in his pronouncement for me, which frightens me even more because I should burn for Brennus' death, like I had burned for Alfred's.

I pull away from Reed, moving toward the glass doors that lead to the lake. Reed catches my hand and pulls me back to him possessively. "Where are you going?" he asks, and his head dips nearer to mine, inhaling the scent of my hair just near my neck. Then, his eyes focus on the mark over my heart and he stills. The image of his wings that graces my skin just above my left breast is making his eyes grow dark, filling them with raw desire.

"Come with me, I'll show you where I'm going," I reply, tugging on his hand, leading him to the balcony doors. The doors exit onto a massive, elevated patio; it's flanked on either side with lava stone steps. The steps travel down to the murky, volcanic beach below. The black sand is shrouded all around by hot, misty fog that dampens our skin before we even make it to the water's edge. In contrast, the sky above is pristine and clear, flaunting every star in the sky like diamonds on fire, not that I can spare much of my attention for the stars with Reed at my side.

Stepping tentatively into the water, I realize that it's deliciously warm. In the dark, the water looks almost sapphire blue, sparkling in the moonlight. The silica that the water contains is lending it an opal fire, which is such a sharp contrast to the black sand. Standing on my tiptoes, I wrap my arms around Reed's neck while pressing my body into his. I brush my lips over his, and then I gently bite his lower lip, tugging on it teasingly, watching as his eyes cloud with a hunger that I know well.

Reed pulls back from me then and whispers, "Evie, we shouldn't... the way I feel...so wild inside...I will hurt you," I know what he is saying. It has been months since we have been together without the blanket of exhaustion to deaden our senses. Now, the butterflies have intensified since then, or maybe it's that we haven't been desensitized to them by being near one another constantly. Whatever the case, there is a churning need inside of me for Reed that is lethal and I feel that if I am denied him now, I will burn forever.

Without looking at him, I wade into the water, letting it swirl around my calves while I reach up and untie the strings that secure my top. I let it fall from me. I unleash my wings with a decisive snap, allowing them to stretch out boldly. When I turn around, I see the way his eyes are touching every part of me almost like a caress. I try to savor the feeling that his heated stare is making me feel, intoxicated and lovely.

"Reed, I know that you think that it's better to wait until I evolve fully, but I don't think I can wait any longer," I murmur. "You are in my blood now and I'm in yours. We are bound to each other in every way possible but one and I...I don't know where I'm going, I don't even know what I've become, but I know that if I'm with you, then I'm free...I'm home. Let me show you what you mean to me. Let me pull you into my world, as you have pulled me into yours."

From the edge of the water, I hear a tear as Reed's shirt falls shredded to the beach. His powerful wings are arching out with vengeance. They are almost black in this light. The fierceness of his expression is heightening my senses as fear and desire mingle to increase my already palatable anticipation. Reed paces the beach. His wings are moving agitatedly, making noises like a sheet hanging on a clothesline, waving in the wind. There is a war going on within Reed. His hands are balled in fists at his sides while he struggles against his desires. Trying not to smile, I wade farther away from him into the comforting heat of the lagoon, waiting to see what he will do next.

I don't have more than a fraction of a second to wait as I am swept up off my feet and carried further out into the water by Reed. When he is waist deep, he slowly lowers me into the water again, allowing my body to slide down his until my feet reach the sand beneath us. I melt against him as he nibbles my ear and tugs on it gently, making my whole body ignite from my core. "I can't fight you," he says effacingly. "I can fight everything but you. Evie…if I begin to hurt you, you must stop me…" he begins to say.

"Shhh…a little pain is nothing compared to the pleasure of being with you," I whisper in his ear as the fog gathers around us, hiding us from the water's edge and I can believe, in this moment, that we are the only two beings that exist in the world.

Slowly, Reed gathers me to him as the heat from his lips press to mine, stirring passion in me that is like an inferno. His lips break from mine as he brings them lower to my neck, and then to the symbol of him branded in my skin. He presses sultry kisses into the image of his wings, making my fingers cling to the muscles of his back. He speaks to me in Angel with his lips still pressed to my skin, making me feel beautiful in a carnal way that I have never felt before.

Raising my head back up, I capture his head in my hands, entwining my fingers in his damp hair. "What did you say?" I whisper in his ear.

Reed's cheek brushes mine as he gently strokes my hair, and then he says, "I was telling you that I have waited for you to come to me for an eternity. You set me free and I would wait for you forever because there is nothing about you that I would change…you are perfect."

The flood of desire his words create almost overwhelms me. Letting my hands drop from his hair, they rest on his shoulders. My fingertips slide slowly down his back under his wings, feeling his skin against mine while I press my body to his. Reed's fingertips trace a line down my neck and over my collarbone.

"You are certain you are ready for this, that this is what you want?" His voice is strained and sexy, making my heart beat faster because he is asking me if it is him that I truly want.

"You are what I want," I reply breathlessly. "It's you that I love. It will always be you," I whisper to him.

"Evie…" Reed says my name softly, before he touches his lips to mine.

ॐ

"I will never be able to stay away from you," I whisper dreamily.

"You say that like it's a bad thing," Reed replies, holding me tight in his arms while he carries me to the water's edge. I can't help the smile that is pulling at my lips after I hear his reply because it's the echo of mine after our first kiss.

He lays me down on the sand as he sinks to the ground next to me and then he immediately pulls me in his arms once again so that I can rest my head on his chest. The cool night air, blowing against my skin, feels wonderful after the heat of the water and the fire that consumed us. Looking up at the night sky, my breath catches in my chest. I see the cascading, emerald and azure colored lights bleeding across the skyline. I had been so wrapped up in Reed that I hadn't noticed it.

"Reed, it's the northern lights!" I say with a hushed tone. Gazing at the serpentine, green shimmer, that almost matches the color of Reed's eyes, it seems like it is dancing in the sky above us.

"Evie…promise me something," Reed says in a serious tone, bringing my hand to his lips.

"Anything," I reply, feeling Reed kiss my hand as I watch the lights above raining color down on us.

"Never disappear from me again," he says softly. My heart contracts in my chest because his voice contains the pain and hurt I had created when I had left him.

I think about his request for a moment, knowing that it may not be within my power to comply with that request, so I say, "I will never willingly leave you again…but if I do disappear, know that I will fight to come back to you."

Reed is above me in a fraction of a second, his intense stare boring into my eyes as he says, "Then, know that I will never stop looking for you because we are one." He presses me back into the sand and makes love to me again with a stormy strength that leaves no doubt in my mind that I am his and he is mine. Earth and Sky.

Glossary

a ghra – beloved
aingeal – angel
fella – Gancanagh soldier
Gancanagh – undead Faerie who possesses toxic skin, which can
enthrall his victim with a simple touch.
máistir – master
mill – a fistfight
muirnin - sweetheart
mo chroí – my heart
mo shíorghrá – my eternal love
na – not
rua – red-haired
sclábhaí – slave
wan – human woman

Acknowledgements

Poe, Edgar Allen. "The Raven." The Complete Tales and Poems of Edgar Allen Poe. New York: Random House, Inc., Vintage Books Edition, 1975. Pg. 945.

COMING SOON

Indebted

THE PREMONITION SERIES
BOOK 3

CHAPTER 1

Jade Dragon Mountain

He can't hide from me. Not that he is ever trying to, but still, it's impossible. I know where he is at all times. I'm attuned to his voice, his scent…the beat of his heart. It's my favorite pastime these days—stalking Reed. It's a game that I play without knowing that I'm playing it half the time. I hunt him…and he lets me.

As I move through the stone-walled courtyard, my bare feet make almost no sound while I traverse the stone bridge that crosses a tranquil, plunge pool in the middle of the Zen garden. A galaxy of stars reflects in the water beneath me, but they can't hold my attention. Reed is ahead of me, in the bedroom of the Naxi-inspired pagoda that we have been sharing. He is poring over maps of the surrounding terrain. Reed studies these maps frequently, learning everything he can about Lijiang and the Jade Dragon Mountain that has been our base of operations since we arrived in China last week. He has been very busy—too busy.

My eyes shift to the banyan trees in the courtyard that nestles just outside the wide doorway of the pagoda. Illuminated red-paper lanterns are strung within its weeping branches. The light from the lanterns turns my pale skin pink as I creep behind the twisted trunk. I scan the slate porch from my leafy position. The doors are open, allowing the breeze to pass freely through the room on either side. Reed hasn't looked up from his seat at the desk, but that doesn't mean that he doesn't know I'm here. I can't tell if he has sensed that

I'm stalking him; he never gives anything away.

I study him for a moment. His dark brown hair has gotten longer than how he had been wearing it in Crestwood. But, I like it; it looks very sexy. His body is curved at sensual angles, making me want to touch him, to feel the raw power beneath his skin. His wings are in, so he looks completely human, well, as human as Reed can look. Since he is absolutely ethereal, I can't see him as anything but angelic now.

When I look up at the arcing, gray tiled roof of the pagoda, I try to see if there is another way in—a sneakier way because I want to take him by surprise—jolt him out of his tactical plotting. He has been singularly focused since our arrival: amassing an angelic army, one strong enough to match Brennus' army.

I shiver at the thought of Brennus. With a little luck, Brennus and his army of Gancanagh are half a world away. Reed is going to great lengths to protect me from Brennus. He has literally gone to the other end of the Earth to accomplish it, bringing me to China, to the secluded base of an enormous snow-capped mountain. Reed and Zephyr have been working on little else other than keeping me safe from the Gancanagh leader who wants to make me his queen…his undead lover. I cannot allow that to happen. If he gets me back and bites me, there is little chance that I will not succumb to his venom and become one of them. Now that I'm reunited with Reed, I'm desperate to remain with him, no matter what.

A deep, primal growl, coming from the room ahead of me, makes me freeze where I am. I glance back toward the room and every hair on my arms rises. Another low, rumbling growl drifts to me on the gentle breeze that stirs wisps of my auburn hair around my face. The sound is terrifying in its intensity and every instinct within me urges me to run from it as my eyes connect with the animal making it. Fierce green irises peer at me from the enormous, sleek cat crouching before me near the doorway to the pagoda. A shiver of pure fear shakes me as I involuntarily take a step back from the massive, black killer.

"Nice kitty…" I whisper to it, taking another shaky step backward and feeling the rough bark of the tree at my back, impeding my retreat. "Reed!" I whisper urgently as I cast a glance into the room, but he is no longer seated at the desk. My eyes fly back to the aggressive animal in front of me that is stalking me like I'm a luscious morsel. The panther's muscles tense, looking as if it will pounce on me at any moment. I look wildly around for an exit strategy while several killing scenarios pulse in my mind, but I would rather try to run than try to engage it.

"Stay!" I command the panther, watching its tail swish as it deepens its crouch. It's not listening to me—it looks like it's enjoying itself immensely, the way its tail is swishing back and forth like it's toying with a mouse or something. *Hide,* I think when the hackles rise on its sleek, black pelt.

"Reed!" I squeak, watching the cat bound up and lunge in my direction. I squeeze my eyes closed, holding my breath and pressing deeper into the tree, waiting to feel its sharp teeth sink into my skin.

"Evie!" Reed says from directly in front of me. I open my eyes to find that Reed is no more than inches from my face, looking at me with panic in his eyes. His powerful, charcoal-gray wings are arcing out around him, shielding us. His hand reaches out, cupping my cheek.

I try to answer him, but I find that my entire body has gone rigid, so much so that I cannot even move my mouth to speak his name. Reed braces his hands on my shoulders, running his hands up and down me as if he cannot see me. "Evie?" he says again, but this time he is leaning into me, inhaling the air near my face. I try again to speak, but I feel stiff.

It takes several seconds for some of the rigidity in my limbs to ease, allowing me to inhale a breath as I look up into the face that I love above all others. "Big cat!" I utter as I attempt to pull away from the tree at my back only to find that I am entangled in vines that are holding me to the trunk. Looking at my arms, they have taken on the rough texture of the mossy bark of the tree. When I raise my hand to my eyes, my fingers appear twig-like as I wave them in fascination and horror. "What the—" I inhale a sharp breath, my eyes move to Reed who is observing me now with a mixture of pleasure and awe on his face.

"You can relax, Evie, it's not permanent," Reed says to reassure me. "You are evolving. It appears, you can change your shape now," he says, smiling and raising one of his brows.

"But—I'm a tree," I whisper to him, feeling appalled by my current shape. I have taken on the mossy exterior of the banyan tree that I'm near.

"Yes, but you are not really a tree—you are more like a chameleon," he says as he leans his face closer to my ear, brushing his cheek to mine. I feel the suppleness of his skin against the course, roughness of my current bark-like exterior, which causes a small measure of my fear to melt away.

"Buns said that when this shapeshifting thing evolved I would be able to turn into butterflies or something like she can." I respond, remembering how Buns had shapeshifted before my eyes into a swarm of butterflies to demonstrate her angelic ability to me. I'm beginning to feel disappointed over my current predicament of looking like some sort of woodland sprite. I was really hoping to be more like my friends, the angels, when I evolve, not less like them. I'm already too different from them, being only half angel and the rest of me human that this is just one more thing that will separate me from being seen as one of them.

"This is so much better than that, don't you see? he asks me, grinning.

"No, from this angle, it kind of sucks, Reed." I reply, stepping forward as my knees become less rigid, enough to bend them as I pull away from the tree that I had become a part of only moments ago. Reed wraps his arms around me, steadying me by pulling me tight against him.

"No, what you can do is so much better. We have to change into something animate, like butterflies or a panther, but you can change your shape to reflect your surroundings…camouflaging yourself. It's a huge asset—" Reed says with excitement until I cut him off.

"That was *you!*" I accuse him as my skin begins to take on its normal hue and I start to change back to my original form. "You changed into a panther!"

A chuckle escapes Reed then as he hugs me tighter. "I thought for sure you knew it was me, but you didn't, did you?" he asks.

"I probably should've known. Your eyes were the exact same color as the cat's eyes. I've always thought that you move just like a cat," I say, gazing up into his perfect face that is mere inches from my own. "Is that the only shape you can take or will I be running from a bear next time?"

"Oh, I can take many, many forms, but I cannot do what you can do—my forms have to be animate. I have to change into an animal, but you—do you think you can do other forms?" he asks with excitement. "Do you think that it has to be just a solid form—can you be liquid…air?"

"I don't know." I reply honestly.

"What were you thinking right before you changed?" he asks. "Were you thinking 'tree?'"

"No…I was thinking 'hide,'" I reply.

"Of course!" Reed exclaims. "I have someone I want you to meet. His name is Wook and he is a Virtue angel, like Phaedrus, who has lived near the Naxi for several centuries. He has studied the Tibetan monks and the Naxi mystics and has seen some of their abilities. Perhaps, he can instruct you to hone your human capabilities. I will not be much help to you in that, as I have little insight into the human side of your nature."

"You think this is a human trait?" I ask Reed with a skeptical look, "Because I can't think of any human that I know of who can change herself into a tree."

Reed's eyebrow arches in a cunning way. "I don't know, maybe it's a hybrid trait. No angel I know of can do what you just did. It is very unique," he says and awe is back in his voice again.

"I don't even know if I can do it again, Reed," I reply, feeling strange about what just happened. *This evolution into a stronger being is really disturbing. It takes the awkwardness of puberty to a whole new level*, I think. "And maybe we shouldn't tell anybody about it."

"Why not?" Reed asks, frowning now while scanning my face.

"Because it's unnatural and…freakish," I reply as casually as I can, but I'm a little too stiff just yet to pull off the casual shrug.

"Evie, you don't understand, this is 'mad cool' to use your words. It makes you even more dangerous!" Reed breathes and I can see he is really charged up about this. Searching his face for signs of disgust, I can find none. He is truly happy that I can now turn into something else. He must be worried that he will not be able to defend me. He must see this as one more evasion technique.

"You think a tree is great? Just wait until I can turn into an avalanche and come pouring down the mountain," I smile as my arms creep around his neck, pulling his face closer to mine.

"Yes…that would be excellent," he exhales near my ear, causing shivers to run through me.

"So you don't think this is sketchy?" I ask, feeling relief that he is not repulsed by me.

"I don't question your existence anymore. I'm just grateful you are here, in any form," he says, picking me up off of my feet and carrying me back into the bedroom.

The bedroom is sparse by the standards of western culture. It just contains a rather large bed and a writing desk. The silk clad bed is centered in the room on a low wooden platform. Folding doors open up the entire room to the outdoors so that the room is exposed to the gardens and courtyard. High stone walls that allow for privacy from the other pagodas cluster around our own to shield the entire pagoda.

"Isn't it your job to question my existence?" I ask him teasingly.

"No, my only job was to annihilate fallen angels and since you are not one of them, you do not fall under my job description," he says, nuzzling my neck and placing me in the middle of the bed. Following me down, he brushes the hair back from my forehead with his strong fingers while gazing into my eyes. "But now that we are bound to one another, I have a new job description."

"You do? What's your new job?" I ask, fascinated by the sensual turn of his mouth. I trace his lips with the tip of my finger that has now returned to normal.

"To love Evie…" Reed says, holding each of my fingers to his lips, kissing them one by one, "to protect my brave girl from any evil that would dare to speak her name…" he continues, tracing a line from the palm of my hand to my wrist. "To make her enemies bow at her feet…" he says before his lips find mine. I recognize his words as those that Buns had translated for me after Reed said his binding vow to me in his Angelic language. He had promised to protect me in the descriptive detail that only a Power angel can convey. It is a little over-whelming to hear the words, even when it may become necessary for him to actually do all of the things he is saying in order to protect me.

"Reed," I whisper against his lips, "that's kind of scary—"

"Thank you," he replies smugly just before deepening the kiss as he completely misinterprets my words as a compliment. At the moment, I'm in no mood to correct the mistake. Kissing him back, I reach my hand up to gently stroke his wing. A soft groan escapes Reed at my touch. *I love that.*

Slowly, Reed's hands move over my body and the feel of his hands on my bare skin, although exquisite, is shocking because I just realize that I'm not wearing anything. I squeak in surprise, causing Reed to pull back a little so that he can look into my eyes again in question.

"My clothes?" I ask.

"Trees don't wear clothes," he replies. "That very pretty little sundress you were wearing is now shredded at the base of the tree outside."

"Oh…and where are your clothes?" I ask as a smile forms in the corners of my mouth, allowing my eyes to rove over his perfect form.

"Panthers don't wear clothes either," he shrugs.

"How…convenient," I sigh, wrapping my arms around his neck again and pulling him back down to me.

Just then, Reed's cell phone rings annoyingly on the desk behind us. I tense, holding Reed tighter to me. "You are absolutely forbidden to answer that phone," I whisper against his lips.

"What phone, love?" he says as his head dips lower, tracing my collarbone with his lips, causing shivers to course through me. I relax as the phone stops ringing and my hands slip to his hair, threading through it and feeling the softness of it.

I trace the line down his neck to the place just above his heart, the place where my wings have been symbolically branded into his skin. I'm still fascinated by the way in which it appeared after the binding ceremony that linked Reed's life to mine was performed. I can't hide the smile of satisfaction that this mark on him makes me feel. It literally screams the word "mine." Reed is mine and no one can take him away from me now. Our fates are connected and I know that I should feel guilty for tying him to me like this. My fate can turn on a dime because most angels, when they first see me, believe that I must be evil, since no angel before me has ever possessed a soul. But in this moment, I can't feel anything but happy that we are here together.

"What are you thinking right now?" Reed asks, searching my face.

"Umm, right now?" I ask, trying to stall because I just got caught reveling in the fact that he's mine. "I was just thinking about how happy I am, about this," I say, feeling myself blush as I trace the shape of my wings that are imprinted on his chest.

"This makes you happy?" he asks and when I nod he speaks to me in Angel as he tenderly kisses the symbol of his wings etched into my skin just above my heart.

"What did you say?" I whisper because I haven't learned to speak his language yet. It still sounds like music to me, like a hypnotic lullaby.

"Me, too," he replies, smiling broadly.

"That sounded a bit more than 'me, too,'" I counter, but Reed's smile only broadens. "And I wasn't just thinking that, I was also wondering what I can call you." At his look of confusion, I go on, "I mean, you're not my 'husband' because you're much, much, more than that..." I trail off, waiting for him to say the word for what we are to each other, now that we both swore a vow to be united for eternity.

He responds immediately in Angel and I smile because I should've known that it wouldn't be English. It sounds like he said *aspire*, but in a way that is so beautiful that it makes tears form in my eyes. My voice is thick when I ask, "Translation?"

Groaning, Reed's brow creases in a frown. He is struggling with the limitations of the human language, so I wait patiently for him to answer me. "It means...'beloved above all others'...'most revered, venerated'...but it's more than that. It means 'essential to me' and 'a part of me.'"

I can't help the tears that slide from my eyes. "*Aspire*," I whisper to him as my hand cups his cheek. His eyes close briefly, savoring the contact.

Feeling Reed tense against me, his eyes snap open as he begins scowling right before he says, "We are busy right now, Zephyr. Come back later." Quickly, Reed covers me with a silk sheet.

"I cannot. This is important," Zephyr replies from somewhere outside of our room. From the distance, it sounds like he is standing near the stone bridge that traverses the jade tiled pool in the courtyard. "You should answer your phone."

"He was kind of in the middle of something, Zee. He still is—how important is it?" I ask, trying to hide the irritation in my voice.

"Very," Zephyr replies and at the sternness of his voice, dread seeps through my senses. It causes my arms to tighten on Reed, pulling him nearer to me.

"What's wrong?" I ask, hearing panic in my own voice.

A growl comes from Reed then as he leans his forehead to mine. "Evie, it's okay, whatever it is, I'll take care of it," Reed says soothingly, trying to calm me down. But I have seen too much lately to be reassured by his words.

"Is it Dominion?" I ask Zephyr with my heartbeat drumming rapidly in my chest. I look over at Reed, seeing that he is already dressed. Startled by the fact that I hadn't even seen him move, I sit up in the large bed, pulling the sheet up with me and wrapping it securely around me. Zephyr steps into our room then, keeping his eyes averted from me as he speaks directly to Reed, but he is using their Angelic language that I can't understand. My panic increases. Zephyr never does that. He never speaks in anything but English when I'm around because he knows I can't understand them. Something is wrong— something big—something he doesn't want me to know about.

"What's going on, Zee? What's happening?" I ask them, looking between their two faces as they debate something important. If it has to do with Dominion, it can't be good for me.

The next thought has all of the blood draining out of my face as I whisper, "Brennus—"

"No, it is not Dominion or the Gancanagh," Zephyr says rapidly, trying to reassure me, but still, his face looks grim.

There is only one other thing that can be severe enough to warrant a look like that from Zephyr and my brain can't even move past the name that it keeps repeating over and over like a prayer. *Russell.* Something inside my heart recoils painfully.

"Where are Brownie and Russell?" I ask them, watching their faces closely. They both have blank expressions like they are deliberately trying to hide something from me.

"They are still in the Ukraine," Zephyr replies in a calm, sooth-ing voice. "They are being very cautious and they are moving slowly. Many, many kingdoms have risen and fallen in that part of the world. Many beings still like to call it home," Zephyr explains with patience.

I exhale a breath that I didn't know I was holding as his words register with me. I know I won't be able to completely relax until they are both safely with us. I still have no idea yet what I will tell Russell about Reed and me. I made Buns and Zephyr promise that they wouldn't breathe a word of the binding vows to either Brownie or Russell. I have to be the one to tell Russell and it has to be face to face. No matter what I say to him, he's going to have a hard time understanding why his soul mate has chosen to bind her life to some-one else, after all of the lifetimes we have shared together. I don't think I'm going to be able to explain it to him, my need for Reed. I don't even understand it. All I know is I tried to live without Reed and it was impossible. I was dying inside everyday.

"Maybe we should go to them. We can pick them up and bring them back here," I say because I'm extremely worried about them. Brownie is a Reaper angel, and although she's immensely stronger than a human, she does not possess the brute strength of a Power angel. Russell is part Seraphim angel and part human, like me. His strength will soon rival that of Reed and Zephyr, and all other Power angels, but he has not fully evolved yet, so he is at a disadvantage should he run into a fallen angel...or Brennus.

"Zee and Buns are going to go to the Ukraine. They are leaving within the hour," Reed says softly and I bounce out of the big bed and head to the bathroom wrapped in a sheet. After I retrieve some clothing on the way, it only takes me seconds to change before I am back in the room, searching for a bag to pack some of my clothes in.

When I look up, I see Zephyr and Reed studying me. "How long will it take us to get there?" I ask, trying to gauge what I will need to take for the trip. Buns has done some shopping for us, but Zephyr has been attempting to lock her down. He has been trying to explain to her that she is a target for the Gancanagh, too, since she is my friend, but she doesn't want to listen to him. She has never really had to take any of this into consideration before because she is a divine Reaper angel. Since her job is to negotiate for human souls, she has essentially been immune to the fighting taking place between divine Power angels and the Fallen. As for other beings, they too, leave her alone because of her divine status. But the Gancanagh have vowed to get me back. They have even gone so far as to attack Dominion's compound while I was there to "rescue me." It would be nothing to them to use Buns to get to me and I can't have that.

"You are safer here, for now, love," Reed says and he uses his sexy voice when he says it.

Narrowing my eyes to him because I'm on to his attempts to soothe me, I say, "I want to go, too. I can help, if there's trouble."

"No, you cannot, not right now, Evie," Zephyr replies in a low tone, like he is talking to a child. "You are too emotional right now."

"I can handle whatever comes, Zee, I promise. I'll be fine, trust me." I reply, not looking at him and continuing to pack my clothes into the bag.

"Evie, listen to me," Zephyr insists as he moves nearer to me in order to make me look at him. "I can see that you believe that, but I can prove to you, right now, that you are unable to separate yourself from your emotions."

"Zee, I'm fine—really. Let's go," I insist, crossing my arms in front of me in defiance.

"Brennus has Russell," Zephyr says quietly.

Panic hits me and I struggle to take the next breath. My heart twists and pounds in my chest as my hands shoot out to grasp Zephyr's forearm so I won't fall down. Flashes of Russell's smile, his face, the way he looks at me when I enter the room come to my mind in an instant. "How?" I breathe, searching his face. "We have to go now! I have to talk to Brennus—he will listen to me—"

"Shh…Evie, it's okay. The Gancanagh don't have Russell," Zephyr says with a soft tone, putting his warm hand over mine to comfort me. "I said that to emphasize my point. Right now, you will do anything, agree to anything, in order to keep the ones you love safe. *We* can't have *that*."

"That was mean, Zee," I accuse him with a grimace as my hand trembles underneath his. Reed hovers near me and I can tell by the look on his face that he wants to jump in and comfort me, but he is trying really hard to hold himself back from doing it.

"I am sorry you think so," Zephyr replies with an even tone; his amazing blue eyes reflect his regret. "I have decided that I need to take a different approach with you from now on."

"Oh yeah, have you decided on the scare-me-half-to-death approach?" I ask with a salty tone in my voice as I look at him.

"No. My approach will be to emphasize what is best for you. I will be your mentor and the first thing that you will learn is that we will protect you from now on, not the other way around," Zephyr says. "The word is out about you, Evie, and it is trickling down like rain to even the lowest level of demons. Many will come for you and they will die. We are organized and well equipped to deal with them, but you must listen to us and believe that we have your best interests in mind.

"I already know that, Zee," I reply rapidly. "But, you have to understand that I have *your* best interest in mind as well."

Some of the sternness leaves his face then as he glances over at Reed and then he looks back to me again. "Evie, you are a Seraph and it is in your nature to guard and protect, but we are ancient warriors while you are still very young and have had little training. You have been born on the frontline of a battle that you are still ill prepared to fight. I will train you so that, one day, you may fight at my side. I promise that I will teach you all that I know so you will become very powerful, like me."

Hearing the sheer arrogance of his last words makes a small smile curl in the corners of my mouth. I move forward and put my arms around his waist, hugging him tight. "It's hard for me to remember you're scary old, Zee, because you look as young as me."

"I *am* scary old and you will listen to me from now on," Zephyr replies as he picks me up off of my feet and gives me a bone-crushing hug.

"I'll hang on your every word if you let me come with you to get Brownie and Russell," I whisper to him because it's hard to talk when all of the air is being squeezed from of me. "You can explain all of the strategy that you have planned to protect me."

"Nice try," Zephyr replies, setting me back on my feet, "but there is little chance that I will take you to the Ukraine with us. You are staying here with Reed. I am sure you will find something to do while we are gone."

"How come Buns gets to go and I don't?" I ask Zephyr as I pull away from him.

"Reed will have his hands full watching one wild card. He does not need another unpredictable female to pin down," Zephyr replies.

"Are you sure that's the reason, Zee, or is it that you can't be away from Buns?" I ask, watching him close.

"Is it my fault that neither of you respects authority?" Zephyr counters gruffly, but I can see that he is worried about Buns and unwilling to let her out of his sight for too long. Since we have been here, it is rare to find one without the other. Zephyr guards Buns close. Several plots take shape in my mind as I consider ways to make Zephyr take me with him to get Russell.

Seeming to read my mind, Zephyr says, "Reed is staying here alone. What if he needs your help?"

"Zee!" I exhale as if he drenched me in icy water. He knows me well enough to know that I can't seem to tear myself away from Reed for very long. I'm constantly monitoring him at all times. A part of my brain is always tracking him. Reed explained that it's instinctual for Seraphim to protect what they consider theirs. I don't think that I can stop doing it, even if I wanted to. I reach out involuntarily to Reed, hugging him to me. His arms immediately wrap around me, encompassing me in a feeling of security.

Zephyr grunts in satisfaction. He knows he has just outmaneuvered me and so do I. "We are leaving soon, Reed. I want to go over some things with you before we go."

"I will meet you in your rooms in a minute," Reed says to Zephyr over my shoulder, snuggling me closer to him. Zephyr nods and is gone in a fraction of a second.

"It's going to be okay," Reed whispers against my hair.

I'm quiet because I know better. My dreams have made it horrifyingly clear to me that something big is coming. It's so big and terrifying that I have trouble remembering what I dream when I awake. My conscious mind keeps trying to blot it out, denying what the future holds in store for me. A word keeps filtering through my mind: *kazic...kazic...mer.* "Do you know the word 'kazic?'" I ask Reed as my cheek leans against his shoulder.

Reed stiffens and replies, "It means 'to destroy.' Where did you hear that word?" he asks me quietly.

I ignore his question. "What does 'mer' mean?"

"It means, 'the great,'" Reed responds instantly. "What is this about?"

"I don't know," I reply, giving him a smile as he pulls back to look at me. His eyes narrow, telling me he is not buying my attempt to cover the fact that his answers have freaked me out.

"Again, where did you hear those words?" Reed asks with persistence. He wants to interrogate me about it and I really don't have many answers for him.

"I think I may have dreamt them," I reply, resting my cheek back on his shoulder.

"What else did you dream?" Reed asks in a low tone, his hands running up and down my back gently.

"I can't remember," I say.

"Try," Reed replies, brushing his lips against my hair.

I tip my face up to meet his. "I will, I promise," I breathe against his lips as I kiss him. Reed's phone rings again on the desk.

Leaning his forehead to mine, Reed gazes into my eyes, "That is

Zee. Let me speak to him and I will be right back, and then it will be just you and me...alone."

The thought of being alone with Reed without the potential of being interrupted is a delicious one. "Okay," I agree in an instant, causing a grin to appear on Reed's face. He kisses me one more time and then he is gone from sight.

Left alone in the room, I look around for something to do. There is a television in the next room, but Chinese T.V. is really weird and I can't understand much of it because I can't speak their language either. The commercials are bizarre, too. There is always some sort of huge, stuffed animal mascot bouncing around on the screen holding the product and looking jovial. It reminds me of Yo Gabba Gabba!

Spotting Reed's new laptop on the desk, I open it up and log on to the Internet. I love this computer; it's uber fast. Surfing the Internet for a while, I check the Facebook website under Leander Duncan. Russell has been using his site that I had set up for him to correspond with his family and me. He has posted pictures of Brownie and him as they have been traveling through Europe in the last week. He has written about what he has seen. I especially like the picture of them traveling through the rural vineyards in France. He looks stoked.

I post a note on his wall, telling him that I miss him and I'll see him soon. I do miss him. He is my best friend, but I don't know how he will feel about me after I tell him what I've done. I try not to think about it and move on to other websites. I really want to talk to some-one about how I should tell Russell about what happened between Reed and me while I was at Dominion's chateau. I need some advice. I wish that I could ask Uncle Jim what I should do. The thought of my uncle sends waves of sorrow through me because I miss him, too. There has to be someone I can talk to about this.

Molly, I think as my adolescent friend pops into my mind. Summer is almost over and she will be going back to Notre Dame soon for her sophomore year. I haven't spoken to her since I left Crestwood with Russell. I was afraid to contact her, because if I let her know where I was going, Reed could have persuaded her into revealing it to him. His uncanny ability to use his voice to persuade humans would've rendered Molly unable to refuse to answer any question that he asked her. If she had any clue where I was all summer, he could've found out instantly and been there to take me back to his home.

I know that Molly has probably emailed me a zillion messages, but I haven't checked them because I had been afraid that Reed could have been able to find me if I logged onto my email. Now, with all of Brennus' resources and the fact that he has ransacked both Reed's house and my storage unit to collect all of my possessions, I think it's pretty safe to assume he is monitoring things like my email. *Creepy vampire*, I think as Brennus' face looms in my mind.

He may be monitoring my email, but that doesn't mean I can't send Molly one from a different account. With that in mind, I create a new account under a fake name and write her a quick message, telling her that I'm alive and that I need to talk to her. Sending the message, I contemplate what I can tell her when she writes me back. Maybe I can say that I had an opportunity to travel that was just too good to turn down. While thinking about different excuses, an email alert window pops up on my screen. *Molly must be online*, I think excitedly. I look at the message line, it reads: "I miss you."

Quickly, I open up the message, but it's blank. It has an attachment to it so I click on the attachment and I wait briefly while a video feed sets up. Curious, I watch as a dark, hazy room comes into focus. Loud, bangin' music is playing in the background of the video as the camera pans past several colorful looking individuals. It looks like this is some kind of nightclub filled with scensters. The camera is moving down a dreary, graffiti enshrined hallway. Panning around, there are several emos standing near the wall watching a band that is in the back of the club on the stage. The camera moves again to the bar where people are milling around trying to get the attention of the bartender.

Slipping in and out of focus several times, the cameraperson uses the lens to scan the crowd near the band that has just started playing a whiny cover song. The thumping of the amps and flashes from a strobe light make the video chaotic as I try to see what this is all about. The camera is slowly coming back into focus and is zeroing in on one particular individual who is milling around with a group of friends. I recognize Molly immediately. She is sipping her drink coyly, holding it close to her as she laughs at something someone leaning near to her is saying. I can't see her companion well because he has his back to the camera.

I reach out and my hand trembles as I touch the screen where Molly's image appears. She looks exactly the same, like nothing has changed with her. Seeing her smile again at whatever the person next to her says, she doesn't even move when the tall man reaches over and gently touches her cheek, caressing his fingers down it. The look on Molly's face slowly changes; her flirty smile seems to sag. My throat tightens and I find it hard to take the next breath.

The man turns then, looking at the camera behind him. Walking toward it with the stealthy grace of a supernatural predator, his eyes never waver from it. His face is exactly the same as the image I have of him in my mind. His eyes have an iridescent shine in their watery-green depths, piercing with intensity. His ebony hair is artfully falling over his arching eyebrows and the planes of his face are just as beautiful as they ever were—as exquisite and youthful as they had been on the day that Aodh, his Gancanagh sire, had changed him from a Faerie into a parasitic creature. Nearing the camera, he poises before the lens, like he is looking directly at me. "*Mo chroí...*" Brennus breathes. Hearing Brennus call me "my heart," I instantly feel the burning infection of his venom within my blood flare up in response to his voice.

About the Author

I live in Michigan with my husband and our two sons. My family is very supportive of my writing. When I'm writing, they often bring me the take-out menu so that I can call and order them dinner. They listen patiently when I talk about my characters like they're real. They rarely roll their eyes when I tell them I'll only be a second while I finish writing a chapter…and then they take off their coats. They ask me how the story is going when I surface after living for hours in a world of my own making. They have learned to accept my "writing uniform" consisting of a slightly unflattering pink fleece jacket, t-shirt, and black yoga pants. And they smile at my nerdy bookishness whenever I try to explain urban fantasy to them. In short, they get me, so they are perfect and I am blessed. Please visit me at my website: www.amyabartol.weebly.com